"A wi . . . and heart-breakingly plausible scenarios that move at a fast clip, with a heart-pounding finale." —*Publishers Weekly*

"Solid storytelling, sharp dialogue, and genuine, sympathetic characters . . . An . . . enjoyable and very entertaining read."
—*RT Book Reviews*

"A wonderful debut novel." —*Bookpushers Reviews*

"Purchase this book ASAP!" —*Dark Faerie Tales*

"Tracy Solheim will have you laughing and cheering and crying as her football hero butts up against the one woman who doesn't find the Devil of the NFL to be irresistible hot stuff. If you're missing Susan Elizabeth Phillips's *Chicago Stars*, then it's time to meet Shane Devlin." —*Rendezvous Books*

"Refreshing contemporary . . . A surprisingly deep romance."
—*Bookaholics*

"*Game On* is a novel that has a lot going for it." —*Book Binge*

"Five stars for *Foolish Games*! A recommended read!"
—*Harlequin Junkies*

"*Foolish Games* is a very touching and beautiful story of forgiveness, trust, and love." —*HEA's Are Us*

"Betrayal, babies, and blazing hot passion—*Foolish Games* has it all! Tracy Solheim has delivered an engaging sports romance with her second Out of Bounds novel." —*Wit and Sin*

continued . . .

Berkley Sensation titles by Tracy Solheim

GAME ON
FOOLISH GAMES
RISKY GAME

Risky Game

TRACY SOLHEIM

BERKLEY SENSATION, NEW YORK

THE BERKLEY PUBLISHING GROUP
Published by the Penguin Group
Penguin Group (USA) LLC
375 Hudson Street, New York, New York 10014

USA • Canada • UK • Ireland • Australia • New Zealand • India • South Africa • China

penguin.com

A Penguin Random House Company

RISKY GAME

A Berkley Sensation Book / published by arrangement with Sun Home Productions, LLC.

Berkley Sensation Books are published by The Berkley Publishing Group.
BERKLEY SENSATION® is a registered trademark of Penguin Group (USA) LLC.
The "B" design is a trademark of Penguin Group (USA) LLC.

For information, address: The Berkley Publishing Group,
a division of Penguin Group (USA) LLC,
375 Hudson Street, New York, New York 10014.

ISBN: 978-0-425-26665-6

PUBLISHING HISTORY
Berkley Sensation mass-market edition / May 2014

PRINTED IN THE UNITED STATES OF AMERICA

10 9 8 7 6 5 4 3 2 1

Cover art by Claudio Marinesco.
Cover design by Rita Frangie.

This one is dedicated to the next generation of girl power:
Meredith, Kirsten, Jillian, Casey, and Catherine.
Don't just follow your dreams, OWN them.

ACKNOWLEDGMENTS

Thanks, as always, to Cindy Hwang and the wonderful staff at Berkley who guide me through the writing process.

To my agent, Melissa Jeglinski, thanks for always having my back.

Also, I couldn't do this without a dedicated group of beta readers—Melanie, Chris, Mary, Allison, and Kathy. Thanks ladies.

Thanks to my fellow authors at Women Unplugged, Romancing the Jock, and Georgia Romance Writers for always answering my pleas for help.

To Kim and the staff at Read It Again, a huge thank you for your support.

Thanks to the women of Talking Volumes Book Club, the gym rats, the barn moms, the band moms, and my Epiphany People, for understanding when I needed backup—and that was often this year!

It goes without saying that I couldn't do this without the love and support of my family, particularly my husband, Greg, and our two works-in-progress, Austin and Meredith. Love you guys.

Finally, and most importantly, a heartfelt thank-you to all the readers. You are what this is all about and I am truly humbled by your enthusiastic support of my books. You rock!

Prologue

THE GIRLFRIENDS' GUIDE TO THE NFL

It's that time again, girlfriends! Kickoff weekend in the NFL. Men in tight pants fighting over a ball. Yum. And while those macho talking heads on cable are breaking down the plays, we'll be giving you all the stats you really want to know: the inside scoop on your fantasy players. Ladies, forget about the games, because we all know the real scoring takes place *off* the field. So let's get right to it.

Rumor has it Miami running back Al Stephens and his estranged wife are reuniting—in court that is. According to sources, Stephens will spend his day off next Tuesday in a Dade County courtroom answering to his wife's claims of infidelity. Prepare yourselves, ladies, because it's about to get nastier than an episode of the *Real Housewives*. My spies tell me Stephens's wife, Jackie, will be naming the girlfriend of one of his Miami teammates as the *other woman*.

Wouldn't you just *looove* to be in that locker room next week?

Speaking of *other women*, a little bear told me that Chicago head coach Ray Clooney has not one, but two new ladies in his life—besides his wife, of course. Clooney is apparently the secret father of a daughter with a certain Chicago-area restaurant hostess. No word on Clooney's wife's reaction, but I think it's a safe bet he'll be dining out for the foreseeable future.

Finally, the return of the pigskin brings back the fine tight end of Baltimore's Brody Janik, every girlfriend's favorite fantasy player. Brody and his sexy baby blues have been lying low this off-season. Apparently, he's lost interest in a certain flavor of Candi. One has to wonder how—and with whom—he's been spending his free time.

Got some football fantasies to share? Maybe a photo of our favorite guys of the gridiron doing something naughty? Send it to us at TGFGTNFL@twitter.

One

Shannon "Shay" Everett had been in some compromising positions in her life. Many of them even of her own doing. Growing up in a small town in Texas as the daughter of a down-and-out rodeo rider and a beauty salon owner, the rebellious tomboy had gotten into more embarrassing scrapes than she could reckon. That being said, she never envisioned herself stuffed into a cubby inside an NFL locker room late at night. A locker room that was supposed to be empty. Only it wasn't.

Hell's bells.

Shay would have kicked her own butt for this little escapade if it wouldn't call attention to her presence. The guilt she felt over her task had already swayed her to abort the whole thing the minute she'd entered the players' domain. Not to mention that she was risking her internship with the team and her scholarship along with it. She'd just have to keep riding her bike to work and the bus downtown to campus because the money to replace her car's muffler wouldn't be coming from some mystery Internet blogger who paid handsomely for personal information on professional football players. Shay was ashamed for even attempting it, but desperate times called for desperate measures.

Now she just needed to quickly extricate herself from her perch huddled in a dark corner of the Baltimore Blaze's state-of-the-art locker room. Unfortunately, her punishment was to endure painful pins and needles in her legs and feet as she waited out the room's other two occupants; both of whom seemingly had all the time in the world. Not that any woman would complain given the view. Standing twenty feet in front of Shay was Blaze tight end and all-American heartthrob Brody Janik.

A deliciously naked Brody Janik.

Shay willed her stomach not to growl at the sight before her, but Brody was a spectacular example of grade-A prime athlete in all his physical glory. Her mouth watered as she took in six feet three inches, two hundred ten pounds of perfectly sculpted muscle standing beneath a single shaft of light, the scene reminiscent of a statue of a Greek god on display in a museum somewhere. All that was missing was the pedestal for him to stand on.

Not that she hadn't seen nearly this much of his perfect body before. The whole world had. As the spokesman for an international designer's line of men's underwear, pictures of Brody wearing nothing but his sparkling blue eyes and his skivvies had been plastered all over billboards and buses for months now. Except tonight, his BVDs were noticeably absent.

She licked her lips as he scrubbed his neatly trimmed brown hair with a towel, the muscles in his broad back rippling. Her eyes drifted lower to the two fine dimples on his backside—one that saw a lot of sun based on the lack of a discernible tan line. She slammed her eyelids shut as he turned to reach for something out of his locker. Surely this was an invasion of his privacy and she ought not to be looking. Except when would she get another chance like this one?

She blinked one eye open. *Dang!* He'd already pulled on a pair of skintight gray boxers, a noticeably abundant bulge hidden beneath the Egyptian cotton.

"It's going to be hard to keep this under wraps," a heavily

accented male voice said from the shadows, a few lockers over.

Ain't that the truth, Shay thought. She mentally shook herself in an effort to refocus her attention from the sexy scene in front of her and tried to make sense of the conversation. The other voice in the room wasn't hard to recognize; the distinct accent belonged to Mr. Pomegranate Smoothie with Extra Flaxseed, Brody's personal trainer, whose last name was something Scandinavian and unpronounceable. Shay only knew him by what he ordered in the Blaze commissary each time he visited.

"It won't be that hard, Erik." Brody tugged on a pair of jeans over his well-defined, long legs as Shay stifled a sigh. He sat down on the folding chair in front of his locker and pulled on his socks and sneakers. "The Piss Man only checks for banned substances. He's not checking my blood sugar."

Pardon? She tore her eyes away from Brody's still nude torso to concentrate on the words coming out of his wicked mouth. She'd heard the phrase *Piss Man* before; it was the players' nickname for the league representative who tested their urine for illegal steroid use. It was the second part of Brody's sentence that sent Shay's brain scrambling. *Was something up with his blood sugar?*

"That's not the point." The fair-haired Dane moved out from the shadows to stand beside Brody's chair. "What if you get disoriented on the field again and miss a route or a pass? It was only practice today, but it could happen during a game if you can't keep your sugar regulated."

Brody stood up from the chair, his chiseled body elegant and assured as he peered down at the stocky trainer. Good looks, superior athleticism, and an affluent upbringing gave him the confidence to believe he could beat anything. Even, apparently, a problem with his blood sugar.

"Not gonna happen." He pulled a black Lacoste polo over his head.

"You can't beat it by mainlining Pop-Tarts like you did before your training camp physical," his trainer persisted. "That ended with you nearly comatose two hours later."

Shay worried her bottom lip as she considered the implications of Brody's predicament. As a PhD candidate in nutrition, she knew full well how the tight end's fluctuating blood sugar could spell doom for his career. She also didn't want to contemplate the scenario of him trying to regulate it by himself.

Brody shoved his sweaty clothes into his mesh bag. "You worry too much. I'll take precautions before and during games. Whatever I need, I can have on the sidelines or in the locker room during halftime. My plan worked fine during the opening game last week."

His friend shook his head. "I'd feel better if you told the training staff. That way, someone could keep an eye on you during the game. You aren't always aware that your sugar's dropping until it's too late."

"No. Nobody knows. Not even my family." The vehemence in Brody's voice echoed throughout the empty locker room. "I'm in the last year of my contract and my mom is a diabetic. If the team finds out my blood sugar is a little schizophrenic, the negotiations for a new deal will spin out of control. Besides, Nate the Narcissist is a pain in the ass. The guy's got a real Napoleon complex. He'd lord it over me and take over my life. No thank you, dude." Brody shuddered as he tossed the bag into the equipment manager's cage.

Shay sucked in a breath. Nate, the team's head trainer, was her boss and she had to agree with Brody's assessment of him. As her mama would say, Nate was "all hat and no cattle." It was a relief to know she wasn't the only one who suffered under the man's delusions of grandeur.

When she'd accepted the internship, Shay was told she'd be working with the training staff on the day-to-day nutritional coaching for the players. The information she obtained would be useful in the compilation of her dissertation, an examination of carbohydrates used during peak athletic performance. Instead, Nate had banished her to the team's cafeteria, telling her the caterer needed extra hands during training camp. Now, the season was in its second week and he showed no intention of allowing her to move up from food service. By the time Shay realized she wouldn't get the experience she wanted, all the other internships had been taken. She needed the credits to fulfill a requirement to receive her degree at the end of the semester. Worse still, she wasn't even getting paid for the work she did.

"I don't like the risk you're taking, Brody."

"It's not a risk. I'll be fine as long as I make sure to eat a balanced diet every day. I wasn't diligent during the off-season and I'm paying for it now, that's all."

His trainer let out a harrumph of displeasure.

Brody's whole body tensed, his cover-boy jaw firm as he spoke. "I assume this is something we can keep between us. Or do I have to specifically invoke client-trainer confidentiality?"

The trainer bristled at Brody's tone. Normally laid-back and carefree, Brody was all business now, forcing his trainer to take a step back.

"Whoa." He held his hands up. "I'm on your side, Brody. Of course this stays between us. But you pay me to train and advise you. I'm just giving you my opinion, that's all."

Brody's face was cool and calculated for a brief moment before relaxing into the boyish charm he was famous for. "Duly noted, Erik." He slapped the trainer on the back, leading him toward the exit. "Tell you what. You can *advise* me on what to order for dinner tonight to keep my blood sugar from taking a nosedive."

"Are you buying?"

Brody's laugh was hollow, almost as if he was resigned to picking up the tab. "Aren't I always?"

The room went dark and Shay waited a few minutes before letting out a pained breath as she eased her numb legs out from under her. She sat still for another moment, allowing her eyes to adjust to the darkness and her mind to adjust to everything she'd heard. Her heart skipped a beat when her cell phone buzzed in her pocket, its noise loud in the now ghostly locker room.

"Holy shitake!" she whispered, nearly jumping out of her skin. "Good thing that didn't go off five minutes ago." She hadn't thought to silence her cell phone, innocently assuming the locker room would be empty. Her hand shook as she checked the bright screen to scan her text message. It was from Ken Daly, the manager of Celtic Charm, one of Baltimore's newest nightclubs.

I need a bartender tomorrow night. R U interested?

Shay exhaled a slow, cleansing breath. She'd entered the locker room earlier to do something nefarious, only to have her conscience remind her that the ends don't justify the means. Now, the answer to her financial woes had just landed in her lap—or on her cell phone to be precise: Her mama would call it providence. Shay just called it dumb luck. Whatever it was, she needed to get out of there before someone else wandered in and spotted her where she shouldn't be.

She stood up slowly, her legs still tingling. Using the flashlight app on her cell phone, she carefully traversed the dark room toward the exit, happy that she didn't have to betray any of the team's players. The Blaze organization was known around the league for its professionalism and values. Aside from Nate, everyone Shay came in contact with at the training facility was friendly and she actually enjoyed the work—even if it wasn't what she'd expected.

Of course, the author of the blog *The Girlfriends' Guide to the NFL* would probably pay big money for Brody Janik's secret. But a Friday night tending bar at the hugely popular Celtic Charm could bring in several hundred dollars in tips—more if she dressed in a tight blouse and the kilt the waitresses wore. That kind of money would buy a new muffler and a month's worth of cell phone service, if she was careful. She didn't need to sell anyone's secrets.

Shay made it to the door and listened carefully to make sure no one was lingering in the hallway. The building was supposed to be empty, but Brody and his trainer friend could still be wandering around. Leaning against the doorjamb, she thought about the Blaze tight end.

Brody Janik was the epitome of a superstar jock: talented, rich, and gorgeous. Men wanted to *be* him and women wanted to be *with* him. Even more appealing, arrogance hadn't tainted his persona. Brody used his slow, wicked smile to charm everyone he met. He doled that smile out to everyone like it was candy. Everyone except her. Instead, he treated Shay with his innate politeness. Almost as if he didn't put her in the same category as other women. And that stung. *A lot.*

Just like every other female between the age of two and one hundred and two, Shay had a big-time crush on Brody. Of course, she knew it would never amount to anything. After all, she was the tall, awkward brainiac with frizzy hair and a wide mouth who was used to being the last one chosen to dance. At twenty-four, she'd had a lifetime of experience being ignored by men like Brody as they scoured the room for the attractive, self-assured catch.

A more callous woman, bent on revenge, might sell Brody's story. But Shay Everett wasn't that woman. Brody was just like every other man who'd looked through her at one point in her life. She really couldn't single him out for it. It wouldn't be fair to all the rest of the men who'd ignored her.

Slipping out the door into the deserted hallway, Shay resolved to forget everything she'd heard while hiding in the locker room. Brody Janik wasn't her problem. It's not like they'd exchanged more than a please and thank-you in the cafeteria as she slopped his meal on a plate each day. And she *wouldn't* worry about his blood sugar, either. At least that's what she kept telling herself as she crept out of the Blaze training facility.

Grabbing her bike, she donned her reflective vest and headed out on the ten-minute trek to her apartment, her conscience clear. She'd do some research for an hour or so before grabbing some sleep. She had swim practice to coach in the morning before arriving at the training facility at eight thirty. If she happened across information on hypoglycemia while she was scanning articles for her dissertation, so be it. As she pedaled along, she told herself it was professional interest making her curious. *Not* anything special about Brody Janik.

Two

The bar swelled with throngs of Charm City's beautiful people as they mingled and preened. The bass of the music throbbed through the floor of the warehouse-turned-nightclub, the DJ spinning a Pitbull track. Lasers flashed along to the beat, jarring Brody Janik's nerves. He sat inconspicuously in a corner just off the dance floor trying in vain to hear what his friend was saying. A parade of women sauntered past his table, invitation in their eyes and the sway of their hips.

"I can't believe you've never been here!" Robbie had to shout to be heard.

Ignoring the come-hither looks from the women vying for his attention, Brody leaned closer to his best friend from childhood. "It opened this spring while I was away. But, I've been wanting to check it out," he lied.

Sure, he'd heard of the meat-market mega-bar from his teammates and other Baltimore celebrities, but he never intended on actually walking in the place. A few years ago, a club like this might have been his scene, but Brody's tastes had mellowed after five seasons in the league. At twenty-seven, he was at the top of his game athletically. By virtue of his good looks and talent, he was practically a household name. He should be out reaping the benefits of his celebrity. But a melancholy had settled over Brody like a blanket of fog rolling over his vacation home on Cape Cod and he couldn't seem to find his way out of it.

He was tired of everyone wanting to be with him because of *what* he was and not *who* he was. And he was scared shitless that when the game was gone, Brody himself might not know who he was. A college buddy had busted up a vertebra in his neck playing football last season, an injury that was felt throughout the NFL. While other players shoved the incident into the recesses of their minds in order to keep up the nerve to play every week, Brody had trouble shaking the image. It didn't help that he had a time bomb ticking inside him that could end his career at any moment.

A waitress dressed in a pleated thigh-length kilt and a blouse two sizes too tight placed a tray of beers onto their table. Her bare thigh not-so-casually brushed against Brody's forearm as she leaned over.

"Compliments of the ladies at the bar," she said brightly, gesturing toward a trio of women seated at the far end of the room, their perfect white smiles making them look innocent. *If someone bothered to check their IDs, they'd probably all be fake*, Brody thought to himself.

"Wow, man, you've got the life." Robbie's tone was reverent as he plucked a fresh beer off the table. "I don't think I've ever had a hot woman buy me a drink."

Brody was ashamed of himself as he wondered if Robbie, too, only wanted to be seen with him because he was a big-time jock. Reaching for his glass of mineral water, he reminded himself that this was one of his oldest friends. Sure, their lives had been on different paths the past ten years, but Robbie knew the real Brody. *Didn't he?* It was hard to tell over the noise in this place. Brody would have preferred he and Robbie catch up in one of the small neighborhood restaurant bars in Fell's Point, but his buddy was visiting town and wanted to experience Celtic Charm, Baltimore's newest place to see and be seen.

Robbie was also enticed by the opportunity to party with some of Brody's teammates.

"Shoot, man, check out that girl in the white skirt! Oooowee, she can sure shake that thang." Running back DeShawn Wilson flicked his dreads over a shoulder as he crooked a finger at the woman in white. "Com'ere, baby!"

The object of DeShawn's desire either didn't like what he was offering or she was playing hard to get. After throwing him a disdainful look over her shoulder, she sauntered off toward a table of women on the other side of the dance floor. DeShawn's fellow members of the Blaze receiving corps nearly busted a gut laughing.

"Oh, no she didn't!" Righteously indignant, DeShawn grabbed his drink as he rose from the table to follow her. Judging by the slowness of her sashay and the way she was peeking over her shoulder to see if he was following, Brody figured the wide receiver would be rewarded for his efforts before the night was over.

His place at the table was immediately taken by Shane Devlin, the Blaze quarterback, who, after ten years in the league, was happily assured of a place in NFL history and a life after football. The old man was also well situated in his personal life with a new wife and a baby on the way. Hell, the guy even had a dog that shagged passes on the run.

Jamal Hollis, the rookie among the Blaze receivers, quickly dashed to the bar to get the quarterback a drink. In a quirky NFL tradition, Devlin wined and dined his offensive linemen each week, while the ball handlers—namely the receivers—paid for their quarterback's drinks whenever he was out with the team. Rookies, like Hollis, thought the effort might result in seeing more passes thrown their way. Veterans like Brody knew better.

"So, this is what all the fuss is about. It looks like half of Baltimore is shoved inside this nightclub." Devlin leaned back in his chair, crossing his legs at the ankles and surveying the dance floor like the field general he was. "Who's your friend?" he asked, eying Robbie. After a few bad dustups with the tabloids, Devlin guarded his privacy tenaciously, preferring not to mingle with strangers.

"Robbie Henshaw, meet last year's Super Bowl MVP, Shane Devlin. Robbie and I grew up next door to each other," Brody explained.

"It's Rob," Robbie said as he reached across to shake Devlin's hand. Brody watched his oldest friend try to contain the face-splitting grin threatening to erupt, as he wondered when Robbie had changed his name. "It's a thrill to meet you. You played amazing in the Super Bowl."

Pausing before taking a sip from the bottle of beer Hollis had brought him, Devlin grinned at Brody. "See, even your friend thinks my MVP was deserved."

Brody grunted as he chewed on a piece of ice from his empty glass. Shane Devlin had been awarded the Super Bowl MVP after completing all but one of his twenty-seven passes, four of them for touchdowns. Two of those touchdowns and eleven of the passes were caught by Brody. In the locker room after the game, it was revealed that the MVP balloting had been close between the two men, which led to a lot of good-natured ribbing by their Blaze teammates.

But Brody didn't begrudge his quarterback the title. Without his leadership, the Blaze might not have made it to the Super Bowl. Besides, at the time, Brody figured he'd get another shot at the elite award. Now, he wasn't so sure.

Ricky Gerrard, the Blaze receiver who caught one of those other Super Bowl touchdown passes, laughed from his seat beside Shane. "Yeah, Devlin, tell Brody's buddy who your favorite receiver is," he challenged.

It was a familiar refrain among the ball handlers; one that Devlin never bit at.

"The one who doesn't drop the ball," Devlin answered, his eyes fixed on Brody as the rest of the table laughed. Brody kept his posture nonchalant and his own gaze steady on the quarterback, not giving an inch. Those two drops in practice the other day were a blip in his performance. His hands were as reliable as his grandpa Gus's daily constitutional each morning. And Devlin better damn well know it, because if his quarterback doubted his ability, it was going to be a long black-and-blue season blocking for the other guys.

"So, Rob, what brings you to Baltimore?" Shane asked.

"Actually, I've been in DC all week trying to get some federal funding for a project our company is doing overseas," Robbie answered.

"Oh yeah?" Devlin took another pull of his beer. "What type of project?"

The quarterback's attention was rapt as Robbie explained his work as a mechanical engineer in his father's company and their efforts to harness sufficient drinking water in West Africa. Surprisingly, Devlin asked pointed questions about the project and its funding. Having heard of Robbie's work before, Brody tuned out, instead wondering when his boyhood friend had gotten a grown-up job to go with his grown-up name. Robbie—Rob, was out doing something good for society while Brody was making millions playing a game.

"I'm headed back to Boston tomorrow morning," Robbie was saying. "My fiancée is meeting me there. It's the big meet-the-parents weekend. We met each other while we were in Africa this past year. Faith was in the Peace Corps."

Of course she was, Brody thought, bewildered at the disgust he felt.

"So you'll be up there for our game Sunday," Devlin said. "Tell me something, has this bum given you tickets?"

Robbie laughed. "I'm sure everyone wants tickets from Brody, seeing as Boston is his hometown. Our firm has a box, so I don't have to rely on his comp seats. Between all of his sisters and their families, he needs all his tickets and then some. Besides, I should probably sit with my folks and Faith's family just in case I need to run interference."

"It sounds like you might need an extra ticket just to watch the game," Brody joked.

Devlin took another swallow of his beer. "When's the wedding?"

"We haven't gotten that far in the planning," Robbie said

sheepishly. "But I'm sure the mothers will work it all out this weekend."

"Can I give you some advice?" Devlin asked, continuing on before Robbie could answer. "Just go with the flow, unless something feels too ridiculous. Your game plan should be to just 'Yes, dear' it all the way to the altar. Aside from that, being married is great." A rare, wistful smile actually appeared on the Devil of the NFL's face, forcing Brody to his feet.

"If you two are going to discuss china patterns now, I'm headed over to the bar for a refill."

"Hey, if you sit here long enough, the waitress will bring you another freebie," Robbie said.

Brody didn't want a freebie. In fact, he didn't want any alcohol. What he wanted was another glass of mineral water and a slice of lime to disguise it. "I'll be back," he called over his shoulder as, empty glass in hand, he negotiated his way around the dance floor, trying not to make eye contact with any of the patrons who wanted his attention.

He made his way up to an empty spot at the end of the bar next to the double doors leading to the kitchen, hoping he could hide for a moment in the darkened hallway. Scrubbing a hand down his face, Brody wondered what the hell was wrong with him. His best friend had a great career and a woman to spend his life with, he should be happy for him. Instead, he was insanely jealous. *Him. Brody Janik. A man who was supposed to have the world by the tail.*

DeShawn's contagious laughter snapped Brody out of his contemplation. The tailback stood with a few Blaze players huddled at the other end of the bar, the female bartender entertaining them with a trick of some sort. In no hurry for his refill, Brody let his eyes drink in the tall woman chatting up his teammates. Like the rest of the servers, she wore a white blouse—hers tied at a knot at her waist, the sleeveless arms exposing toned muscle. Her kilt was a little shorter in the back, giving Brody a tantalizing view of long lean legs as she bent to scoop ice out of the ice maker. His body suddenly perked up at the mental image of those legs wrapped around him.

Maybe that's the problem. He'd gone too long without sex. But he'd been caught in the vicious cycle of getting involved with women who were too attached to being Brody Janik's girlfriend. The rise in his popularity had spiked a surge in kiss-and-tell tweets and posts on social media by the women he'd been with. It was impossible for him to enjoy a night of uncommitted sex. And, deep down, Brody didn't think he really wanted that anymore.

He caught a glimpse of the bartender's elegant, nimble fingers as she twirled a drink straw before putting it in DeShawn's glass. Brody shifted his hip against the bar. His body was screaming at him to make the moves on the bartender. Maybe he could take just one more chance.

"It's like that scene out of *Flashdance*," a voice said behind him, startling Brody.

He turned to find Nate Dumas, the Blaze trainer, standing beside him, his shorn head barely reaching Brody's shoulder.

"Nate," Brody tried not to groan. He'd meant it the other night when he'd said the man was a pain in the ass. The two didn't see eye-to-eye on anything—literally and figuratively. Not that Brody had an issue with people who were shorter than him, most people were. But Nate wore his vertical challenge as if it were a disability, taking it out on those around him, and that pissed Brody off.

"You know, the movie where the guy in the bar is fascinated with one of the dancers, and his buddy not only gives him her phone number but her Social Security number as well," Nate babbled on.

Clearly he and Nate had vastly different taste in movies because Brody had no clue what the jerk was talking about. He shot the trainer a baffled look. "I'm not fascinated with anybody."

"Bull," Nat said smugly. "You can't take your eyes off her. Of course, you don't need her phone number. You can just stop by the commissary at the training center and flirt with her. Too bad she doesn't dress like that every day, huh?"

Brody's head snapped back around toward the bar, taking in the woman's tall frame and her kinky auburn hair, recognition suddenly dawning on him. "Is that Hairnet Lady?" He hadn't meant to ask the question out loud.

Nate laughed. "Hey, Shannon, how's about you concentrate on some of your other customers!"

The bartender turned just in time to see Brody gesturing to his hair. Her whiskey eyes widened infinitesimally at the sight of Nate before narrowing as she took in Brody's mimic of a hairnet. It was her eyes that always did him in. From the first moment she'd leveled them in his direction, those whiskey eyes had unmanned him. Brody couldn't figure out what it was about them, but he was lost every time he looked into their depths. He'd made a point to keep his distance until he had his reaction under control. Based on how his body was responding tonight, he had a long way to go to gain that kind of restraint.

Her face was all angles; her wild hair forming a messy halo while her wide mouth, fixed in a polite smile that could almost be a smirk, greeted Nate.

"What can I get you?" Her smoky Texas drawl seemed out of place with her gawky body, but it was doing crazy things to Brody's.

Nate went into full narcissist mode. "We're thirsty. I'd figure you PhD candidates would possess a little more powers of observation than the average Joe."

Huh? She was a grad student? That explained her constantly cowering in the corner with a computer each day. It didn't explain what she was doing with the Blaze, though.

"I see that. What can I get you?" she patiently repeated.

"I'll have a Michelob in a bottle. No glass necessary. How's about you, Brody?"

There was no way in hell he was letting Nate know he wasn't drinking. "I'm good."

"No way, man, let me buy you a drink. Our lovely *Hairnet Lady* is pouring."

The bartender—Shannon, Nate had said her name was—didn't flinch at the little prick's words or his tone. Points to her for having a backbone. *A very sexy backbone.* Reaching into the cooler beneath the bar, she pulled out a bottle of

Michelob, opened it with flick of her wrist, and handed it to Nate.

"Come on, Brody, order up. Pick something complicated and let's see if we can fluster her."

"You can't fluster Sha-nay-nay," DeShawn said as he joined them, offering the bartender a wide smile. "She's a pro at this. Learned at her grandaddy's knee."

Her mouth twitched as her eyes met Brody's. Before he knew what she was doing, she'd taken the empty glass from his hand. She dumped it in the slop sink as she pulled a fresh one from the shelf. DeShawn and Nate were busy checking the baseball scores on Nate's phone. Brody watched as she filled the glass with ice and covertly poured a Perrier on top. Tossing in a slice of lime, she brought the drink over to him.

"This should do the trick," she said softly.

Brody stood still. He'd ordered his earlier drink from the bartender downstairs. How had she known what he was drinking—or not drinking? She offered up a lopsided smile before taking off down the bar to wait on other customers. Brody desperately wanted her to come back. Except he didn't. He was afraid those whiskey eyes could see right down to his soul.

Three

No doubt about it, Nate Dumas was a narcissist.
A textbook one at that. Shay didn't have to go back to her
undergraduate psychology class notes for the diagnosis; she
had real-life examples to back up her findings. Starting with
the previous night at Celtic Charm. He'd taken great delight
in strolling up and informing Shay she'd be joining the team
for the game in Boston. She would have been ecstatic for
the opportunity provided she'd been given some sort of
notice. Her gut told her Nate had only decided to include
her after he'd seen her tending bar. Judging from the challenge she'd seen in his eyes, he knew he had her over a
barrel. If she said no, he'd leave her in the commissary,
serving meals for the rest of the season. If she said yes, she'd
be scurrying when her shift ended at three A.M. to make the
team's noon flight.

What Nate didn't know was that this wasn't Shay's first
rodeo. She'd grown up in a house with a game-playing narcissist. While her physique may be tall and gangly, Shay
didn't break easily. It had actually been humorous to see

Nate flinch slightly when she'd told him she'd be on the shuttle to the airport at ten thirty.

That was twenty hours ago.

Right now, Shay was dead on her feet and regretting her decision to rise to the trainer's bait. After a brief nap, she'd woken early this morning to throw a change of clothes in an overnight bag, drop her car off at the repair shop, and reschedule the swim lessons she'd planned to teach that weekend. She'd made the charter bus with minutes to spare. Once they'd arrived at the Boston hotel, Shay was furious to learn that she was again relegated to serving food to the players.

The Blaze commandeered one of the large ballrooms, using it for meetings and to run through plays. Off to the side was a separate dining room where the team, staff, and guests could enjoy a buffet dinner or a snack. It was eight o'clock in the evening and most of the players were taking advantage of their downtime by either giving interviews to the media or relaxing in their rooms before a mandatory team meeting at nine. Trying to keep her body awake, Shay occupied herself by clearing some of the tables in the room.

A teenage girl, one of the coach's daughters, sat alone at a table, her head in her hand as she stared forlornly at a textbook in front of her.

"Chemistry," Shay said wistfully as she glanced over the girl's shoulder. "One of my favorite subjects."

The girl's crystalline blue eyes went round as she gazed up at Shay in disbelief. "Are you kidding? You actually understand this stuff?"

"Sure. It's all just math."

The girl let out a melodramatic groan, before doing a face-plant right into the open textbook. "Shoot me now, because I might hate math more than chemistry," she mumbled against the pages.

Shay had to smile at her antics, but science and math were her bedrocks and she hated when teenage girls felt threatened by the two subjects. Sitting down in the chair beside the teen, Shay tapped the tube of lip gloss next to the girl's pencil. "Did you know that cosmetics companies employ teams of specialized chemists to develop and test each new line of makeup, perfume, lotion, or soap?"

The girl blinked a wary eye at Shay.

"I'm serious," Shay went on. "There are thousands of career opportunities for a girl with a solid background in math and science."

"No offense, but you're a cafeteria lady. Did you study math and science for that job?"

Ouch.

Shay belatedly remembered her ever-present hairnet, whipping it off her head.

"Actually," she scrubbed at her frizzy hair in a futile attempt to fluff it out. "I'm about to get my PhD in nutrition from Johns Hopkins. I'm only doing an internship with the Blaze for college credit."

"You're getting college credit for serving food?"

"No . . . er, yes, I guess. I'm supposed to be working with the trainers, but Nate keeps me on soup kitchen duty."

The girl wrinkled up her nose. "Nate, ick!"

Shay laughed. "My thoughts exactly."

"So what will you do with a PhD in nutrition?"

"I hope to work with world-class swimmers to train them how to properly fuel their bodies with food for peak performance." Of course, what she hoped to do with her degree and what she was being forced to do with it were two different things.

"Like with Michael Phelps? That actually sounds cool," the girl said before fingering her textbook with a sigh. "But we've been in school nearly two weeks and I can't understand anything Mr. Wu has taught so far. And we have our first quiz on Monday."

"Maybe I can help?" Shay pulled the textbook closer. "I used to tutor high school math and science when I was an undergraduate."

"You did?"

Shay nodded.

A hopeful grin spread over the girl's face. "I'm Emma," she said sheepishly.

Shay reached out a hand. "Shannon. But my friends call me Shay."

The next hour flew by as Shay helped Emma with her homework, her exhaustion and anger forgotten as she let her mind exercise its way through chemistry problems and higher math, two things that had always been her escape.

Reality came crashing in as the players began to straggle back toward the ballroom.

"Shannon!" Nate called in his drill sergeant's voice. "You need to make sure the snack trays are ready. These guys need carbs before they go to bed tonight."

Shay shoved her hair into her hairnet with a grimace. "Back to the grind. Hey, if a miracle doesn't happen next week and I'm still in the commissary, stop by and tell me how the quiz went, okay?"

Emma nodded, her bright smile dimming to a look of horror as DeShawn Wilson burst into the room, spewing obscenities and ransacking chairs.

"Hey!" Emma's father, Blaze head coach Matt Richardson, charged after DeShawn.

"That bitch wrote about me in her blog!" DeShawn yelled. "Personal stuff! Things only someone in our locker room would know about." He threw another chair for good measure.

"What are you talking about?" Donovan Carter, chief of security for the Blaze, tried to subdue DeShawn.

"That bitch who writes *The Girlfriends' Guide to the NFL.*"

"Hey!" Coach yelled again, gesturing toward his daughter.

Shay helped Emma gather up her books and motioned her out of the ballroom as DeShawn mumbled an apology.

No sooner had Emma cleared the door, he started his rant again. "Someone on this team sold me out to her. One of you told her things about me that now everyone can read in her damn blog! That's betrayal man! You betrayed this team's trust."

"All right, all right." Coach held his hands up to calm the

crowd of players in the room. "That's exactly what this woman wants. To turn us against ourselves right before a big game. Whoever is behind this is just trying to get in our heads."

DeShawn wasn't about to be pacified. "That damn woman read through my devotional book I keep in my locker and found the appointment card for when I got my teeth whitened. Man, I've got a six-figure endorsement deal with a toothpaste company. You think they won't drop me when they find out?"

"Who says it's a woman?" The words were out of Shay's mouth before she realized it. Sixty pairs of testosterone-charged eyes turned to her in stunned silence, including Brody Janik's. She was a fool to speak up. After all, she'd been in that locker room looking for gossip to sell to the same blogger. Apparently someone else had been in there, too. Someone who could have just as easily been in there the other night and heard Brody's secret. And that was a piece of gossip that could derail a career.

Brody's deep blue eyes studied hers, searching for something. The familiar heat surged to the surface of her skin as he gazed at her. Could he somehow know she'd been in the locker room the other night? That she knew his deepest secret? That she'd take it to her grave?

"Is there something you'd like to share with us, miss?" Donovan Carter asked, rousing Shay back to the present. *Hell's bells, I've stepped in it now.* Her mama always warned her about her mouth being faster than her brain. The blogger's identity could be easily uncovered with a little effort and deductive reasoning, but she couldn't say more without giving herself away. Jerking up her chin, she decided the best course of action was to play the female card.

"Just defending my gender," she said before parading past a seething Nate to take her place in the galley.

Four

"Tell Mom to stop hassling me, Gwen. I'm not bringing an inappropriate date to Tricia's wedding because I won't be bringing a date at all. Problem solved," Brody snapped at his sister.

It was Monday evening and he was testy after the Blaze were narrowly defeated by the Patriots the night before; the loss resulting from a controversial play with seconds left in the game. The winning touchdown should have been his, had it not been for a defensive player's hand glued to Brody's back, knocking him off his route. A hand that was apparently invisible to the referee because interference hadn't been called. Adding salt to the wound, the Blaze players watched in disgust as the scene was replayed on the jumbotron, the infraction glaringly obvious, as the Patriots trotted off the field in victory.

"Do you think going dateless is such a smart idea?" The humor in Gwen's voice traveled through the cell phone mounted in the dash of Brody's Range Rover. "You'd be fair game for every woman there. I think Mom just wants to make sure you don't detract attention from the bride. Like when one of the Kennedy kids tried to bring Taylor Swift to his cousin's wedding. She's worried you'll bring Candi the porn star or someone equally scene-stealing."

Brody gritted his teeth. "For the one millionth time, Candi is an *adult-film actress*."

"There's a difference?" his sister teased.

Braking at a red light, Brody massaged his left shin where another player's cleat had left a painful bruise. He'd spent the last couple of hours with several of his teammates at the practice facility letting the training staff administer to his various aches and pains. "Do you have anything work related to discuss? Because, if not, I'm gonna hang up now."

Gwen laughed. "You are such a poor loser."

"Bye-bye." He reached out a hand to disconnect the call.

"Wait! I do have some decisions I need your okay on. I'll be nice, I promise."

Twelve years and three sisters separated him from his oldest sibling. But Brody felt closer to Gwen than he did to his parents; probably because while he was growing up, she'd been the one to intervene when his other sisters insisted on using him as their own personal plaything. The mother of two school-age children herself, Gwen was responsible for handling Brody's personal correspondence and other publicity issues. It was a job she could do from her home in Boston, which suited them both perfectly. Brody loved his four older sisters. He just loved them more when they were eight hours away.

"Get to the point," he said as he punched on the gas, merging with the cars on Central Avenue. "I'm on my way home to watch *Monday Night Football*."

"I know tomorrow's your day off, but please go over the proposal for the charity auction. You have a meeting with the board next week and they'll want your agreement."

"More like they want my money," he grumbled. Brody didn't mind sharing his wealth with those in need, but lately he was beginning to feel like a blank check, autonomous in the whole operation of his own charity.

His sister ignored his comment. "*Menswear* magazine

wanted you to do a resort spread on your bye weekend, but
I had to nix that since Tricia's wedding is the same day. They
won't give up. They were wondering if you'd do a shoot for
their holiday issue, but it would have to be before the end
of this month. And they'd need you in New York. Should I
tell them they'll have to come to Baltimore if they want you?"

Brody scrubbed a hand down his face. One of his other
sisters, Ashley, was a buyer for Nordstrom. She'd been dressing Brody his entire life. Fortunately for him, he'd outgrown
her doll clothes by the time he was eighteen months old.
Ash was talented, though, and thanks to her critical eye, he
knew he always looked his best, unintentionally finding his
way onto many best-dressed lists. But he was getting tired
of being known as just another pretty face.

"No." Time to draw the line on the turf. "Tell them I'm not
interested in doing any more photo shoots. I'm done
modeling."

"Crikey, Brody, you are grouchy today."

He remained silent, easing up on the gas as he entered a
school zone.

Gwen blew out a breath. "Okay, as you wish. I'll tell them
the holiday spread is a no, but I'm not closing the door on
future shoots in case you're less hormonal tomorrow and you
change your mind. Now, about this personal chef person you
want; are you serious? It's not like you to be so pretentious as
to want someone to cook your meals for you. Did I misun-
derstand your text? I already order all your groceries for you
every week. Is there a problem with the delivery service?"

"No, Gwen, you're the perfect mommy. I just want someone to actually prepare the food you have sent in."

"Well, jeez, Brody, if you're that lazy, I'll tell the company to deliver the food already prepared. They can do that,
you know. It just gets a little pricey, but, hey, if that's what
you want."

It wasn't what he wanted. Because then he'd have to tell
his sister about his blood sugar issues. If his coven of moth-
erly sisters found out, he'd be toast. And that was before

they'd rat him out to their mother. Just the thought gave him the willies.

"No, I want someone to cook the meals fresh. Someone who understands nutrition. I'm trying to eat a more balanced diet to keep my body at its peak." As lies went, his was easily sustainable.

His sister let out a snort, which Brody ignored.

"Just figure out how I hire such a person, Gwen."

The laughter was back in her voice. "Are there any other specifications you have? Blond? Brunette? Maybe a redhead? Ooh la la, should she be French?"

"Hanging up now." Brody punched the disconnect button, silencing his sister's laughter.

All the talk of food made his stomach growl. He'd ventured into the commissary at the practice facility earlier to grab a snack, telling himself he wasn't looking for a certain whiskey-eyed, leggy woman in a hairnet. But when he didn't see her there, he'd left without eating anything. Now he wanted a sandwich. A meaty concoction from Santoni's deli.

It was dinnertime in suburbia and the parking lot of the gourmet market-deli was full. Navigating his SUV into a spot, Brody tried to stroll inconspicuously into the store, but a buzz went up immediately as he was recognized by the shoppers.

"Tough game last night."

"Damn refs. They're all blind."

Brody acknowledged the comments of the Blaze faithful with a head bob and a slight smile as he made a beeline for the deli counter.

"Hey, hey, number eighty, where you been?" Tito, the deli manager, greeted Brody with a booming voice. "Those freakin' refs were all a bunch of homers last night. They need binoculars, for sure. You want your usual?" He was already slicing the bread before he'd finished his question. Despite the fact he liked celebrities in his store, Tito knew Brody didn't want to stand around and field questions from fans after a loss.

Trying to look busy, Brody was scanning his cell phone

screen when a pair of familiar legs, decked out in formfitting yoga shorts, passed through his peripheral vision. His heart rate sped up as he followed her with his eyes. Unfortunately, his weren't the only ones trailing the cafeteria lady–bartender. He watched as three college-age twerps tailed her down an aisle, their body language shouting they were up to something.

"Be right back," he said to Tito as he rounded the corner of the endcap stacked with Goldfish crackers.

"Aww, come on," one of the frat boys was saying. "I know you were into us the other night at the bar. Why don't you come by our place tonight and hang with us. We can do some shots and watch some football."

Brody could only imagine what the three idiots wanted to do to her once they'd gotten her drunk. Whiskey Eyes—he thought he remembered Nate calling her Shannon—was tougher than she looked, though; something he'd already figured out about her. Sporting a "Don't Mess with Texas" T-shirt, she kept her stance casual even as the three boxed her in.

"Sorry, fellas. I have class tomorrow. But thanks." Her sexy drawl lulled two of the boys into dazed adoration.

Frat boy number three wasn't taking no for an answer, though. Belligerently shifting closer, he reached out and grabbed her elbow. Before she could yank her arm free, Brody was heading down the aisle. He grabbed a random box from the shelf and stepped around to her other side.

"Babe," he said as he slipped the box—a brownie mix—into the handbasket she was carrying. "Do we have any eggs? I thought we could make these tonight." Placing his palm on her lower back, he pulled her closer toward him, the gesture a universal signal of possession among males.

Brody wasn't sure who was more startled, the bartender or the three guys hounding her. Her eyes dilated briefly before her long lashes blinked closed. When she opened them again, she seemed to recover a bit of her equilibrium.

"Umm . . ." Her tongue darted over her lower lip, and Brody's whole body went on alert. "No. No, we, um, we need eggs."

Giving her back a reassuring rub, he took her basket and guided her away from the three, treating them to the cat-ate-the-canary grin he gave defensive players when he'd beaten them to the football. Once they'd rounded the corner, she blew out a breath, stepping away from his hand at her back.

"Whoa there, Texas." Brody wrapped his arm across her shoulders. "Keep playing along until they leave," he said quietly as they made their way toward the dairy section. She kept her eyes down, avoiding the rest of the shoppers who'd begun to take notice of him again.

"That's Brody Janik," college boy number three yelled out to his friends. "No way he's tapping someone like her! Not when he's got hot models and porn stars to choose from."

He felt her cringe beneath his arm.

"Ah, hell. Now I'm gonna have to hit that guy," Brody muttered, his body teeming with anger.

She turned on him, those whiskey eyes filled with alarm. "No! You're not going to fight over me," she cried as her hands clenched on to his shirt, the tips of her fingers brushing his chest. Heat surged through him.

"Fine, we'll do this the pacifist's way," he said, just before he dropped the basket and pulled her in for a kiss.

His timing was impeccable, the pests rounded the corner just as Brody took a hold of her toned ass. Not that he was paying attention to the three stooges anymore. He was too busy enjoying the soft mouth of the pliant female in his arms. She was tall enough that he didn't have to bend himself like a pretzel to kiss her, his body parts meeting up nicely with hers. Her lips parted easily and Brody took advantage, exploring her wide, sweet mouth. A soft moan escaped the back of her throat and her fingers gripped his shirt a little tighter, but she didn't engage in the kiss. Too bad, because Brody could have kissed her all night. Her skin was warm beneath his touch and he realized she was flushed with embarrassment. Jesus, he was mauling a stranger in a grocery store. Reluctantly, he broke contact, resting his forehead against hers as he tried to get his breathing—and his body parts—under control.

"That ought to do it," he whispered.

"If you say so."

Her eyes remained closed—probably from shame—and he was disappointed that the sexual attraction was so obviously one-sided.

Brody Janik was kissing her, exploring her mouth with a delicacy and tenderness that belied the power of his muscled body. Shay was so stunned by the events of the previous five minutes, that all she could do was stand there. *Stand there and enjoy it.* Truth be told, she was enjoying his kiss right down to the tips of her toes, not to mention everywhere else south of the border. Her fingers, furled in his shirt, itched to feel the sculpted chest she knew lay beneath the soft cotton, but she couldn't summon the strength to move them. The masterful stroke of his tongue against hers held her entire body transfixed.

And then, just as suddenly as the kiss began, it ended. Shay kept her eyes closed in an effort to retrieve her scattered wits. The murmur of the shoppers surrounding them began to penetrate her senses, but it was Brody's words that brought her crashing back to reality.

That ought to do it, he'd murmured.

Shay's eyelids snapped open to see Brody's trademark baby blues inches from her own face, his forehead resting against hers. His pupils were bright with mischief and that's when it hit her: Brody Janik wasn't kissing her to *kiss* her. He'd kissed her as part of some sort of male-posturing ego trip; the big steer in the herd asserting his dominance. The flush stinging her cheeks, originally brought on by potent desire, was now fueled by embarrassment. And anger.

Closing her eyes again in order to calm the bitter sting of reality, she uttered something. What words she spoke, she wasn't sure, but her tone was enough for Brody to break the contact between their foreheads. When she pried her eyelids open once again, his own eyes had dimmed and his body was rigid. Shay forced her fingers to release their death grip on his shirt.

"Don't blow it with a knee to my groin, Texas," he murmured. "I think they've bought it and they'll leave without any more nonsense."

Her gaze locked with his. "Does that mean your hand can leave my person now?"

The warm caress of his palm on her left butt cheek relaxed and Shay felt a little bereft as he slowly lifted it away. Her glute muscle twinged in protest.

"Sorry." His apology stung further, but she still couldn't seem to walk away, to put some distance between their two bodies. They stood in the crowded market, inches apart. She could feel the heat radiating from his body, smell the sweet scent of freshly showered skin, and taste the mint left from his tongue. Which meant he could probably smell and taste the chlorine on her. *Argh!* Shay took a giant step back, just then noticing the eyes of the shoppers who didn't bother hiding their interest in Brody's activities. Her face felt like it was on fire now.

One of the deli workers slipped a sandwich wrapped in white butcher paper into the handbasket Brody had retrieved from the floor. Her handbasket!

"Enjoy your dinner, Brody." The man grinned, wagging a bushy eyebrow at her before he slipped back behind the counter.

The three men who'd tried to pick her up were no longer within sight. Shay reached over to take her handbasket back, but Brody tightened his grip; his other hand taking a firm hold of her elbow.

"We need eggs, remember," he said as he steered her toward the dairy section.

Shay tried to pull out of his grip, but it was no use. "Why are you doing this?"

"Because someone needed to help you back there."

Planting her feet firmly, she watched Brody's face war with whether to make a scene by pulling her along or to stop and answer her.

"I could have handled them." She jerked her chin up in victory when he finally ceased pulling.

A lazy smile spread across Brody's face, igniting a firestorm in Shay's belly.

"Yeah, Texas, you could have," he admitted after a speculative pause. "One of them. Maybe even two. But not all three. That third guy was after a lot more than just a few beers and an episode of *The Hills* on MTV. He was all set to take advantage of you."

"Recognize something of yourself in him?"

Brody pulled back as if she'd slapped him, his grip tightening on her elbow.

It was a cruel thing to say and he didn't deserve it. Shay wasn't sure why she'd even said it, except that she'd enjoyed his kiss and the knowledge that he'd only done it as a lark hurt.

She opened her mouth to apologize, but she was interrupted by one of the seniors from the water aerobics classes she taught.

"Oh my, Shay," Mrs. Goldberg was saying, her silver curls bobbing with excitement as she stepped in their path. "No wonder you left the pool in such a hurry today. What a nice hunk of beefcake you have for yourself."

"Stella!" Mrs. Benvenuto, a retired school teacher who was forever trying to keep her outspoken friend in line, parked her shopping cart next to Shay. "You're embarrassing the poor girl. Look how red she is." Still, the woman managed to smile coyly at Brody.

Shay didn't need her geriatric clients to tell her that her skin was flaming, her entire body felt like she was about to self-combust. The firm grip Brody had on her arm wasn't helping matters.

Mrs. Benvenuto tapped Shay's free arm. "You've been holding out on us, honey." Her gravely pack-a-day voice was laced with awe before she fixed her attention on Brody. "You may be some hotshot football player, but if you break our girl's heart, you'll have to answer to us and the rest of her aqua clients. We may look frail, but thanks to our Shay, we're tough."

Shay didn't know whether to laugh out loud at Mrs. Benvenuto's misperception—did anyone really think Brody Janik would look twice at her—or to shed a few tears at the loyalty of a group of arthritic angels she worked out in the pool three times a week. She wasn't given the chance to do either, though, as Brody wasted no time unleashing another one of his devastating smiles, its impact nearly vaporizing both grandmothers into puffs of the Shalimar perfume they wore.

"Have no fear, ladies," he said, the effortless laid-back charm oozing out of his pores practically steaming up Mrs. Goldberg's glasses. "I have no intention of breaking any hearts tonight. Just cracking some eggs. We're making brownies." He lifted up the handbasket for their inspection. "If you'll excuse us, we need to grab a dozen so we can get these in the oven. It was a pleasure seeing you both."

Mrs. Goldberg sighed lustfully as Brody tugged Shay around the two ladies.

"Brownies from a box? Doesn't he know the woman is practically a gourmet cook," Mrs. Benvenuto said to Mrs. Goldberg. But Brody wasn't paying attention and, judging from the tense grip he still had on her elbow, he was apparently as eager to get out of the store as Shay was.

"Bye-bye, Shay!" Mrs. Goldberg called. "We want to hear all about those *brownies* in class tomorrow!"

Laughter from the two ladies echoed through the small store as Brody and Shay finally reached the dairy aisle. Releasing her elbow, he grabbed a dozen eggs and gingerly tossed the carton into the basket. Shay rolled her eyes.

"You need to make sure none of them are cracked." She opened the carton and inspected the eggs, gently fingering each one.

Brody stared as she carefully closed the carton.

"Is there anything you don't do?" he asked. His voice held a bit of reverence, the tone making Shay's knees a little wobbly.

She held his gaze, letting the moment stretch. There were quite a few things she didn't do, but she didn't think he needed to know about them.

Mistaking her silence for misunderstanding, Brody continued. "If I'm to believe everything everyone says about you, you're a grad student, a food worker for the team, a bartender"—he gestured toward Mrs. Goldberg and Mrs. Benvenuto— "and a water aerobics instructor. Where do you find the time for all of that?"

Lack of time wasn't her problem, lack of money was, but Shay doubted Brody would ever be able to relate to that. He was financially independent, his future secure while Shay was still trying to claw out from under her family's fiscal crisis. Not that Brody needed to know her life's history.

"Some of us are just more industrious than others, I guess." It was the second time she'd hit him with a stinger and Shay felt a little guilty, but she needed to maintain some distance, some sense of control here because if Brody turned his magic on and kissed her again, she wasn't sure she'd be able to keep from throwing herself at him.

He dragged his fingers through his hair. "I'm not even sure I know your name." His soft voice sounded as perplexed as Shay felt.

The words left her body on a breath, almost as if he were pulling them out of her. "Shannon. Shannon Everett. But my friends call me Shay."

And then he smiled; that slow easy grin she'd been dreaming he'd direct her way. And suddenly Shay couldn't recollect why she needed to maintain a safe distance at all.

Five

Man, she was a prickly one. Most women liked
when a guy paid for everything, but Shannon—Brody wasn't
sure he was elevated to friend status and could call her
Shay—wouldn't have anything to do with him buying her
groceries. Instead, she insisted on tallying up the cost of the
items in the basket that were hers—two bananas, three containers of yogurt, and a carton of soy milk—and digging
deep into her purse to count out the exact change. The eggs
and the brownie mix were apparently on his dime.

Dusk was falling as they left the store. An engine revved
in the parking lot and Brody caught sight of the three guys
who'd been pestering Shannon earlier. They were sitting in
a souped-up Camry two rows away from the entrance, Emi-
nem blaring from the stereo.

"Where's your car?" Brody asked.

Shannon hesitated at the curb, her eyes drifting to a
dilapidated bicycle chained to a pole. Despite the fact he
already knew what was coming, Brody swore under his
breath in annoyance. If there was one thing he should have
learned from all those dopey Disney princess movies his

sisters made him watch when he was a kid, rescuing the damsel in distress usually took longer than a five-minute commitment.

"I rode my bike."

She bent over to unchain the bike, giving him a perfect view of what his hands had been fondling ten minutes ago. Brody stifled a groan. He wouldn't mind the disruption of his evening if she was as into him as he was to her. But she wasn't. She'd made that abundantly clear.

"You're not riding a bike in the dark." Brody wasn't sure why he cared anymore, but he did. Somehow she'd become his responsibility and he wasn't driving away until she was home safely. Even if he did sound like his father right now.

Pulling out a reflective vest from her purse, she turned toward Brody, her eyes and her stance mulish. "You're not the boss of me."

In his entire life, Brody had never met a woman who wasn't susceptible to his charm; one who wouldn't immediately acquiesce to his wishes. Over the years, he'd watched, amused, as his friends and teammates went "caveman" with their girlfriends and wives in order to get their way, never imagining he'd need to do the same to get a woman to do his bidding. *Until right now.*

Grabbing the plastic bag containing their groceries in one hand, he stalked over to where Shannon held her bike, scooped it up by the crossbar, and carried it over to his Range Rover. With a push of a button on his key fob, the liftgate opened. Brody tossed the bike and the groceries into the back. If the eggs ended up cracked, tough. He was done being nice to this woman.

Apparently, Little Miss Texas wasn't used to being told what to do, because she was protesting loudly, her once-sexy drawl now an annoying twang.

"How dare you! I'm perfectly capable of getting home without being run over. It's only a five-minute ride."

"Good," he said closing the liftgate. "Then it'll only be *two* minutes by car."

Brody turned to find her standing inches from him, those

whiskey eyes still mulish. *Damn*. He needed to leave her
here. To go home, change clothes, and hit some bar where
the women would be a lot more accommodating.

"Give me my bike back."

He actually considered it. It would be so easy. This whole
rescuing thing was starting to feel too much like work. But
the Camry's engine revved a second time and those caveman
instincts he never knew he had took over once again.

"We can do this the easy way or the hard way." He
stepped closer, bringing them nearly nose-to-nose. "Easy
way, you get in the car and we're home in two minutes. Hard
way, we have a little instant replay from inside so those three
jerks get the hell out of here. What's it gonna be?"

Surprisingly, he found himself pulling for her to choose
the hard way. Despite her lack of response to their earlier kiss,
he'd enjoyed it, and he wouldn't mind a second attempt at
coaxing a reaction out of her. Her eyes darted over her shoulder at the frat boys in the Camry. He watched her slowly
swallow as she seemed to consider her options. The moment
stretched on and Brody's body began to tense up as the muscles in her graceful neck worked. Just when he thought he'd
kiss her anyway, she shook her head and headed toward the
passenger side of the Range Rover. He wasn't sure, but he
thought she'd mumbled something sounding like "Hell's
bells" as she slid into the front seat. The Camry squealed out
of the parking lot just as Brody climbed in on his side.

As he predicted, the apartment complex she directed him
to was barely three minutes' drive from Santoni's. Shannon
didn't want him to see where she lived, that much was obvious by the terse directions she gave and the rigid way she
held her body. Brody thought her reaction had to do with
her desire to get some distance from him, but when he
caught a glimpse of the former motel that was supposed to
pass for an apartment complex, he realized the stiffness in
her chin might be brought on by something more: shame,
most likely. He was a little ashamed himself for letting
things get this far, but he couldn't have left her alone in the
parking lot. He'd been raised better than that.

The place was neat and clean, but it lacked any of the amenities a woman in her twenties would want. Like security, for starters. He pulled his SUV into one of the parking spaces and killed the engine. "If you're a graduate student, why don't you live in the dorm?" Brody realized the question was equal parts absurd and insensitive as soon as the words left his mouth.

Shannon released a little huff as she let herself out of the car. "Dorms cost money."

Brody was getting a little sick and tired of her maligning him. "Really? And here I thought they were free," he quipped as he met her at the rear of the Range Rover and opened the liftgate.

"They're free to athletes and the beautiful people," she said as she pulled out the bag of groceries, taking a moment to inspect the eggs for damage. "The rest of us poor slobs have to pay. And this place costs less than half of what the university would charge me."

As he lifted her bike out of the cargo area, Brody contemplated her situation. He'd gone to Notre Dame for free, courtesy of a football scholarship. But there had never been any doubt he wouldn't go to a top-notch school because his parents could afford to send him. A college education—and all that went with it—was assumed in the Janik household. He knew other students didn't have it so easy, but Shannon had gotten as far as graduate school, so she'd obviously worked it out. *Work* being the operative word since she had three jobs.

"I've got it," she said, reaching for her bike.

"For Pete's sake, Shannon! Let me carry this bike to your apartment. When we get there, you can slam the door in my face, as long as you're safely on the other side of it. Can you just do that for me, huh?"

She stood there in the parking lot, gingerly cradling the bag of eggs and other groceries, studying him quietly. "Okay," she said finally, with the same breathless voice she'd used to tell him her name.

Brody felt it all the way to his groin.

Turning on her heel, Shannon made her way up the concrete steps to the second floor. As they rounded the corner, a burly man with an unkempt mullet stepped in their path.

"Shay," the man said. "My mail key's gone missing again. I need a replacement."

"I can take care of that, but it'll be thirty-five dollars to replace, Mr. Metz."

"Thirty-five bucks!" the guy bellowed.

"It's the third time I've had to ask the landlord to replace it for you. They're specialty keys and he has to send out for them. He likes to get paid up front to ensure he gets the money."

Mr. Metz growled something unintelligible, but Shannon held her ground. Brody suspected she'd stand firm against the man who outweighed her by at least a hundred and fifty pounds even if she didn't have a professional athlete at her back. The guy slunk back into his apartment, slamming the door.

Shannon walked to the end of the balcony, stopping at a locked box mounted to the wall. She jiggled the lock to check if it was secure before pulling out her own key and unlocking her door.

"You've gotta be kidding. Don't tell me you're the super here, too?"

She looked over her shoulder at him. "Fine. I won't tell you."

Carrying the bike into her apartment, he shook his head in exasperation. Clearly, this woman worked harder than anyone he'd ever met. He glanced around her home. The small living area was furnished with a hodgepodge of secondhand furniture, but somehow she'd made shabby chic work with an eclectic mix of bright pillows and funky accessories. It looked like a room where Brody would love to kick back and relax with friends. Or a sassy Texan.

Emerging from the small kitchenette, Shannon handed him the bag with his sandwich, the brownie mix, and the eggs.

"Thank you," she said softly.

He stood gazing into her eyes like a dumbass, unsure whether to make his escape or beg her to let him stay, those whiskey eyes casting a spell on him yet again.

"Keep the eggs and the brownie mix." He tried to hand the bag back to her. "You can make yourself some brownies for later."

She put up her hands to say no, but they were both startled by a small voice coming from a door behind Brody.

"You gonna make brownies, Shay?"

A young, caramel-skinned boy dressed in Redskins pajamas stood in the doorway, his big, puddle-brown eyes wide with excitement. They narrowed quickly when they landed on Brody.

"Hey! We got rules about bringing strange men home, Shay. Remember?"

Brody looked between the boy and Shannon, a twinge of jealousy flashing through his gut as he envisioned her bringing other men home to her kitschy apartment. The jealously was quickly replaced by bewilderment as he wondered what the hell she was doing with a little boy.

"Maddox, you should be in bed. It's a school night." Shay tried to maneuver Brody toward the door, but he stood firmly transfixed, his large body seeming to take up all the air in her tiny apartment. Or maybe it was her nerves sucking the breath out of her. Not two feet from where he stood, the card table that doubled as a dining area and desk was littered with articles on hypoglycemia. She needed to get Sir Galahad out of there before he spied them scattered among her textbooks.

"It's only seven-forty. I still got twenty more minutes." At seven years old, Maddox had not only mastered telling time, but the argumentative skills of a top litigator. "Hey, you're Brody Janik."

Oh snap. Shay had hoped to get Brody out of there before anyone recognized him.

Brody gave Maddox a smile; not one of the bone-melting

ones he used on women, but his patronizing "aw shucks, I'm a celebrity" grin she'd seen him use on fans.

"That's me. And you are?"

"I'm Maddox." The boy tilted his head, studying Brody. "You look a lot tougher on Madden."

"You're wearing Redskins pajamas and you're talking smack?"

Shay pulled Maddox against her body, throwing Brody a warning look over the boy's head. Brody shrugged his shoulders as if to say, *He started it.*

"Is your sister asleep?" she asked.

Maddox nodded, never taking his eyes off Brody. "Mrs. Elder fell asleep watching *Wheel* again, so I gave Anya her bottle."

"Good boy." Shay gently rubbed his back. "Now why don't you go brush your teeth?"

Without another word, Maddox slipped through the adjoining door to the apartment he shared with his mother and baby sister.

"So, do we add nanny to the list?"

Shay rolled her eyes. "Just neighbors helping neighbors."

"Does his mother often leave him alone to take care of his baby sister like that? Because I'm pretty sure that's against the law."

Shay took exception to Brody's tone. "You know, not everyone lives in the bubble of affluence like you do, Brody. Some of us have to do whatever we can to survive. Jackie is a labor and delivery nurse. It's part of her job to work nights. Her husband is in Afghanistan and childcare is expensive. We—Mrs. Elder and I—pull together to help out."

In her exasperation, she'd unwittingly come to stand inches from him again. She could feel the censure and tension radiating off his body. Bafflement shone in his blue eyes, too. And something else. Something she couldn't quite define.

"You are a conundrum, Shannon Everett." He spoke softly, but his tone sent shivers through her body. "And I'm fascinated by conundrums."

Shay sank her teeth into her bottom lip, and Brody's

nostrils flared. Her breath caught as she realized he might kiss her again. Only this time, she wasn't sure she could keep her own response in check. He leaned toward her, but the slap of Maddox's bare feet against the parquet floor roused Shay out of her trance and she stepped back.

"I got a Baltimore Blaze poster, Mr. Janik. Will you sign it?" Maddox burst back into her apartment, the poster dragging on the floor behind him.

Obviously the moment hadn't affected Brody as much as it had her because he had no trouble slipping back into celebrity mode.

"That depends. Are you gonna keep wearing those Redskins PJs?" A teasing glint shone in Brody's eyes.

"My daddy grew up in Anacostia. That's in DC," Maddox said, puffing out his chest with belligerent pride. "We're Redskins fans first and Blaze fans second."

Brody rubbed the top of the boy's head. "Atta boy. Show your pride for your home team. Don't be that kid who says what he thinks people want to hear." They both crouched down on the floor, spreading the poster out before them. Brody signed his name and then poised the marker over Shane Devlin's face. "Should we put some devil horns on him?"

Maddox giggled and Shay found herself smiling with them both. Brody's effortless boyish charm always had that effect on her. She ached to live the life of carefree exuberance that he did. He lifted his gaze to her, his lazy smile causing her knees to nearly buckle.

"Shay, can I have one of those brownies in my lunchbox tomorrow?" Maddox asked. He looked at Brody, his face earnest. "Shay makes the best brownies."

Brody rose from his haunches, rolling up the poster, his grin a bit more predatory now. "Does she now?"

The skin on her cheeks burned. "Not tonight, Maddox. I have to finish up an outline for my thesis counselor. But maybe when I get back from campus tomorrow. You can help me after school." She needed to get Brody out of her place. Not only was he taking up all the air, but he was sucking up her composure, too. "Why don't you go pick out a book and we can read it together before you go to bed."

Maddox hesitated, but his good manners finally won out. "Thanks for signing my poster, Mr. Janik."

"Sure thing." Brody gave the boy's head another rub before Maddox slowly shuffled off to his bedroom.

"So what does a guy have to do to get one of those brownies?" Brody asked as he ambled toward her. Everything about his demeanor said he wanted more than just dessert. Shay wasn't accustomed to men looking at her the way Brody was right now. The desire in his eyes was doing strange things to her brain.

Like cutting off all rational thought.

"You can't have brownies, Brody. It'll mess up your blood sugar." The words were out of her mouth before she could think. It was the story of Shay's life.

The desire faded from his eyes, replaced by astonishment—and a trace of fear before he quickly reined that in. His carefree smile disappeared, leaving behind a tight grimace. He closed the distance between them as Shay pressed her back up against the wall.

"What did you say?" His words were like a whip cracking through the air.

Shay stared at him, wide-eyed, her normally fast-acting brain unable to come up with a response.

Brody grabbed her upper arms, pulling her to within inches of his face. "Who told you?" he demanded, giving her a little shake.

"No one," she answered, the words barely a whisper. Her body should have been gripped in fear, but instinct told her Brody wouldn't physically harm her. The shame consuming her was another matter, though. "I . . . I, um . . . I overheard you talking with your trainer about it."

She watched Brody's face as his mind worked through the logic of her answer.

"The only place you could have overheard us was in the locker room." His eyes went wide as he realized the implication. "You're the snitch! The one who told that damn blogger about DeShawn. You know, he's losing his endorsement money because of you!" He gave her another shake.

"No," she cried. "I didn't tell the blogger anything. I couldn't go through with it!"

Brody released his grip, pushing her away in disgust. "Oh yeah? I'm supposed to believe a woman who'll do anything for a buck?" He went over to the table and picked up one of the articles she had sitting out. "Reading up on the condition before you try to blackmail me?" he accused, waving the paper in her face.

"No! I'm studying nutrition. Working for the team is my internship this fall. I was looking for ways to help you." Her excuse sounded pathetic even to her own ears.

"Give me a break, Texas. I might not be a PhD candidate, but I did graduate from college. You're nothing but a gold digger like the rest of them. But you're not going to be able to use your hairnet to get any more information on my teammates. Not when I'm through with you." Tossing the paper to the floor, he headed for the door.

Panic seized in Shay's chest. "What are you going to do?"

"Rat you out to management, for starters."

"You can't." Once again, Shay's mouth was operating faster than her brain could keep pace. "If you get me fired, I'll tell them about you. About your blood sugar." Shay felt nauseous as she made the threat. It wasn't in her nature to bully other people, not after she'd spent her own life being bullied. But she needed the credits the internship provided. Time was running out. She only had this semester to finish her work. Her mama was counting on her.

Brody paused with one hand on the doorknob; his normally carefree posture rigid with fury. Obviously, he hadn't considered the consequences of his plan. He turned slowly and leaned his back against the door, crossing his arms over his chest as he tucked his hands beneath his armpits. She felt the heat of his anger radiating clear across the room.

"It seems we've reached an impasse." His tone was lethal,

with a hint of resignation. Not surprisingly, it galled him not to get his way. Shay took no pleasure in her small victory.

"Please, you have to trust me. I swear I won't say anything to anyone."

Brody contemplated her for a moment, his eyes hard, before he slowly crossed the room. Shay had to work to keep her knees from buckling, but she held her ground. He stopped before her, leaving a few scant inches between them.

"I don't trust you, Texas." He reached up, gently tracing a finger along her cheek. The breath hitched in her chest. "Like I said before, you're a conundrum. Only not so fascinating anymore. Just threatening."

Shay swallowed as her heart plummeted to the soles of her feet. *Survival of the fittest*, she told herself. Still, despite years of being the lesser choice, the U-turn of his opinion smarted.

"Are you gonna kiss her?" Maddox's question caused them both to jump apart again.

He stood in the doorway, a well-read copy of *Harry the Dirty Dog* in one hand and a stuffed elephant in the other. Brody looked over at the boy and then back at Shay, his face giving away nothing. "No," Brody said, the single word a punch to her gut.

He paused on his way out of the door. "We'll resolve this tomorrow. One way or another." He gave Maddox a terse nod. "Sleep tight, buddy."

Shay figured Maddox might be the only one of them who would be sleeping that night.

THE GIRLFRIENDS' GUIDE TO THE NFL

Well, girlfriends, it seems our favorite fantasy football player has indeed satisfied his sweet tooth and sworn off Candi. The game's finest tight end—and it *is* fine—was caught in a serious lip lock with a new lady last night. Check out this cell phone video. Number eighty and a mystery woman were steaming up the windows of the deli counter, if you know what I mean. But the story just gets better. According to my sources, Brody was playing kissy face with one of the team's interns, a graduate student named Shannon Everett. Ms. Everett is the not-so-identical twin sister of Dallas Cowboys cheerleader Teryn Everett, seen here shaking her, um, pom-poms. It just begs the question: Brody, did you know which sister you were kissing? Or, could this Blaze player be consorting with the enemy?

Six

The woman is diabolical, Brody thought to himself as he stormed through the halls of the practice facility Wednesday morning. Not only had Shannon made herself scarce the entire day before, but she'd managed to feed that blogger a cockamamie story about the two of them being involved. Sure, he'd initiated their kiss, but he'd obviously played right into her plans. He'd look like a fool if he tried to get her fired now. Little Miss Texas might think she had the upper hand, but she was about to find out that Brody had a brain, too.

"Dang, Sha-nay-nay," DeShawn was saying as Brody entered the commissary. "You've been holding out on us. You've got a twin sister? And she's a Dallas Cowboys cheerleader?" He whistled and the rest of the players and staff congregated around Shannon laughed.

Shannon stood tall amid their teasing; the ever-present ugly hairnet perched on her head as she doled out protein shakes to the players for their midmorning snack. She made each shake individually according to the player's tastes and nutritional needs and they'd become something of a daily institution among his teammates. Brody doubted the other guys knew she had a nutrition background; they just liked the effort she put into making them taste great.

"We don't even play the Cowboys this year, Shay," Jamal Hollis whined. "But you gotta find a way for me to meet her."

"Does she have a boyfriend?" another player asked.

"What does that matter? She hasn't met *me* yet," Jamal said. The other players laughed at his rookie exuberance.

"Finally, you develop some taste in women," a voice at Brody's shoulder said.

Biting back his denial, Brody didn't bother turning to acknowledge Blaze defensive captain Will "William the Conqueror" Connelly, instead keeping his focus on Shannon. It was better not to make eye contact with the cerebral linebacker who had a way of knowing the truth just by looking at a guy. Except of course when the truth had bit Connelly on his behemoth ass a few months ago.

"I'd say the same about you, but then you wouldn't still be married to your beautiful wife if I hadn't talked some sense into you."

Connelly scoffed. "As if." He was quiet for a moment. "She's not your usual fare, Brody. A woman like that can get hurt easily."

"Whatever you're trying to say, Connelly, just spit it out." Unfortunately, Brody knew exactly what the linebacker was saying. It burned a little to know his friend bought into the premise that Brody was a love-'em-and-leave-'em kind of guy. He couldn't very well tell Connelly there was no relationship, though. Brody had decided to live by the adage, keep your friends close and your enemies closer. As long as Shannon knew his secret, he needed to keep a strict eye on her. Her little lie to the blogger provided the perfect opportunity to do just that.

"Just be gentle with her heart, that's all. She's a nice girl trying to make something of herself."

Brody didn't have to wonder why Connelly empathized with Shannon. From what he could discern, the two had similar backgrounds.

Nate Dumas joined in among the players surrounding

Shannon. "And that asshole doesn't help matters," Connelly muttered.

"One sister is a hot Dallas Cowboys cheerleader and the other is . . . not," Nate bellowed to the crowd. "It's kind of like Gisele Bündchen and her twin sister. One of them got all the good looks and the other just got the brains, I guess."

"Tell me he didn't just say that," Connelly growled.

Brody didn't stick around to answer him, instead making a beeline to where Shannon stood, her face expressionless. It was one thing for Brody to want to chew her up one side and down the other, but Nate Dumas was not going to get the satisfaction of dissing her.

"Are you saying Sha-nay-nay isn't pretty, Dumas?" DeShawn asked, going toe-to-toe with the trainer.

Brody had a newfound respect for the running back for sticking up for her, but he'd rather fight his own battles. He stepped between DeShawn and Nate, giving the trainer a measured glance before turning to Shannon. Despite a pinched look about her mouth, she showed no outward reaction to anything being said about her. Undoubtedly, she'd heard it all before—many times judging by the extent of her composure. But Brody didn't have time to contemplate her mental toughness. He had a score to settle with Shannon, and for that, he needed privacy.

Donning his best Janik charm, he slipped into the role of devoted boyfriend. "Hey guys, can I borrow Shannon for a minute?" His teammates let out a few snickers and knowing grins as Brody reached for her hand. A wild jolt shot up his arm the instant his fingers slid between hers, totally catching him off guard. The only reaction from her was a quick intake of breath.

"Whoa," Nate called from behind them. "See, this is why I have a problem with romance in the workplace."

"You have a problem with romance, period," DeShawn mumbled.

"You two can't just go trotting off for a little nooky while she's on the clock," Nate continued.

Brody wasn't aware he'd turned around until Shannon

squeezed his hand—hard—halting his progress toward the loudmouthed trainer.

"For crying out loud, Dumas, she's an intern. She's not on the clock." Connelly crossed his arms over his massive chest, treating Nate to his patented menacing stare.

Nate shrugged. "Hey, I'm not the one writing the checks, but I do sign off on her school credit hours."

Shannon's whole body stiffened next to Brody's.

"Go. Take your five minutes, you two. Just try to keep it G-rated for the video cameras in the storage room." Nate laughed as he slithered out of the commissary, leaving behind a group of players shaking their heads at him.

Before Brody knew what was happening, Shannon pulled her hand from his grip and marched over to the storeroom behind the kitchen. By the time he crossed the threshold, she was searching the four corners of the small space.

"What are you doing?" he asked.

"I wouldn't put it past that vermin to have video cameras in here," she said from behind a steel shelf.

Brody closed the door, leaning up against it. "Wouldn't that be convenient? Then you could sell that blogger audio *and* video."

"I told you I didn't sell anything to that blogger."

Brody crossed his arms over his chest. "Really? Because yesterday's story was certainly conveniently timed."

Shannon looked up from her inspection. "You think *I* sold that information? For pity's sake, Brody, there were at least ten customers in that store with their cell phone cameras out. All of them ready to auction your story to the highest bidder. Believe me, it isn't me that blogger was interested in. I'm just as much the victim here, you know. Now everyone thinks I'm involved with a football player." The last two words were uttered with disgust.

It bothered Brody that fans were so eager to sell him out for cash; worse, that some mystery blogger was exploiting his celebrity and that of his friends. But the second part of Shannon's denial bothered him even more.

"Have you got a problem with football players? That would make you the first woman I've met who does."

Shannon rolled her eyes, mimicking him by crossing her arms under her breasts drawing his attention to them like a laser. They may be small, but they were perky and the sight was doing a number on his body.

"Then give me a medal, Brody. I grew up in Texas. You can't fling a cat there without hitting a football player. I'm immune." She took a step closer. "Let's move on to something else. How dare you stalk me at my home yesterday, annoying my neighbors."

Brody had to mentally shake himself to catch up. "I told you the other night we'd discuss our situation yesterday. But you had a great time dodging me."

"Well, golly, Brody, did you expect me to sit around all day and wait for you to just drop by when it was convenient for you? I know you'll find this hard to believe, but I actually had work to do yesterday. Not everyone jumps when you say so."

She was beginning to royally piss him off. "Oh, we all know how industrious you are, Shannon. And for the record, I wasn't annoying your neighbors. They actually like football players."

Again with the eye roll.

"Maddox is seven and his father is deployed five-thousand miles away. Of course he likes you. Especially when you show up with all kinds of Blaze gear. But you bullied poor Mrs. Elder to no end."

"That woman?" Brody hadn't bullied anyone, least of all the little old lady. He'd merely pointed out the need for some safety and security measures if she were going to watch children in her apartment. She'd told him in no uncertain terms that the only safety and security measures she needed was her cane. That was before she'd nearly taken out a lamp and some china figurines demonstrating her stealth with the stupid thing. "She shouldn't be babysitting those kids. She's one cat short of being a crazy cat lady!"

Shannon opened her mouth, presumably to defend her

batty neighbor, but no sound emerged. Somehow they were standing inches apart again, her warm palms flat on his chest, his hands kneading her shoulders, their breathing fractured. She smelled like berries and vanilla, the ingredients from her protein shakes, and Brody wanted nothing more than to lap her up. Cameras or not, he began calculating the best way to lay her down on the storeroom floor and show her a thing or two about football players. He reached up to trace his finger along her jaw. His gut clenched when he caught sight of her damp eyes.

"You have to believe me," she whispered. "I didn't tell the blogger anything. I couldn't. I wouldn't." She swallowed. "I swear I won't tell anyone your secret, Brody. I'm very trustworthy. Please. I need the internship credits. There aren't any other slots left. Believe me, I tried yesterday."

Once again, those whiskey eyes were nearly his undoing. His body wanted desperately to believe her, but his head was telling him not to trust her. Not to trust anyone. She was definitely a conundrum. But right now, she was his conundrum.

He touched his forehead to hers and sighed. "We might be able to work something out."

"I'm not going to sleep with you, Brody."

Well, he hadn't heard that too many times in his life. Brody pulled back. "That wasn't what I had in mind," he lied. "Sorry to disappoint you, but I'm just not into women in hairnets."

Shay took a giant step back, whipping the stupid hairnet off her head, trying to smash down her wild hair. Of course he wasn't attracted to her. He was just toying with her, to get her to do . . . what exactly? Certainly not sleep with her. Although she'd lied when she said she wouldn't sleep with him. Worse, he knew it. Because, honestly, what women wouldn't sleep with Brody Janik? She really, really needed to master thinking before speaking.

Brody leaned a shoulder against the metal shelf, his lazy smile making her uneasy. She was cloistered in a storeroom with *People* magazine's Sexiest Man Alive and she needed to get out of there before she said—or did—something else foolish.

"Can we just get this breakup over with here?" She crushed the hairnet in her fist.

He arched an eyebrow at her, but said nothing.

Shay heaved a sigh. "Look, we can't very well deny we were kissing—it's all over the Internet. I have no problem with you telling everyone you were drunk or confused and didn't know what you were doing. As long as I'm left alone to finish out my internship."

Brody's expression remained bland. "No."

"No?" Shay was exasperated now. "Fine. I'll dump you. I'll tell everyone you were a dud, proving my point about all football players."

He bristled at that. "Not gonna happen, either."

"Oh, this is ridiculous, Brody. We're arguing over something that isn't even true. Just tell everyone the whole thing was a joke or something and let it go at that." She made for the door, but he grabbed hold of her wrist.

"We're not breaking up," he said evenly.

"There's nothing to break up! We're not a couple."

"No, but we're going to use this little farce as a cover."

A shiver passed through her body. She wasn't sure if it was caused by fear or something else. "A cover? For what?"

"You know something that I don't want other people to know. I don't trust you with that secret. As it happens, I'm in need of a personal chef with experience in nutrition. Someone who can help me control my blood sugar." He nodded at her. "It's really a win-win situation. For me at least."

Shay tried to process what he was saying. He'd keep her secret about being in the locker room if she'd keep his. In return, she had to prepare his meals for him. It seemed like a straightforward plan. Except for the part about being around him. That might not be so straightforward given how her body reacted every time he was near.

"You won't trust that I'll keep your secret, but you will trust me in your home? A place where I'll have access to lots of your other secrets?"

"One step ahead of you, Texas." He pulled an envelope from his pocket. "I took the liberty of having my agent draw up an agreement. One that holds you libel if any personal information about me is leaked to the press. If you squeal, I'll ruin you."

Shay doubted that. She and her family were pretty close to ruination already. He unfolded the document, laying it on the shelf in front of her. As she scanned the page, her lungs seized.

"The Platinum Palace?" she whispered. "How did you know about Mama's salon?"

"Thank your blogger friend. All it took was a few keystrokes for my agent to find what he needed. The Internet is a powerful tool, even for us football players."

Mama had dedicated her whole life to the Platinum Palace. At first doing hair was just a side job—her daily dose of gossip and gab—while she raised Shay and her twin, Teryn. But then Daddy got kicked in the head by a cutting horse that just didn't want to be broke. The blow left him with the mental faculties of a senile old man. It left Mama with a mountain of medical bills and other debts her daddy had run up and no income. She'd mortgaged the Palace to the hilt, working full-time to turn it into a steady income stream. Thanks to urban sprawl, the ladies of Dallas found her salon and made it profitable. Thanks to the recent economic downturn, those profits had been eaten up quicker than Texas wintergrass in a wildfire.

Mama's only option to make the balloon payment due at the beginning of the year was to refinance, but she needed more income to qualify. Shay's income. Courtesy of a "friend" of her meddling paternal grandmother, Meemaw, a well-paying government job awaited her—provided she received her degree in December, as planned. No one ever asked if it was a job Shay wanted. It didn't matter.

But Brody's agent had apparently strong-armed someone at the bank, who spilled the beans about her mama's financial woes. Now Brody could scuttle the whole dang thing with a few choice words to her academic advisor. In a moment of madness, Shay wanted to tell Brody he could take his personal chef's job and shove it. If the Platinum Palace were gone, she'd be free to do what she wanted. But it was a fact of life that Shay would never be free to do what she wanted.

She looked from the ugly paper in front of her to his blue eyes. There was nothing charming about them now. Instead, they were shrewd and calculating. Shay doubted many people saw this side of Brody Janik and she rather wished she wasn't seeing it, either. But as her daddy would say, Brody had her between a rock and a hard place. The only thing to do was to figure out a way to work it to her advantage. Having access to a professional athlete and his diet would definitely provide her with the information she needed for her thesis. It meant she wouldn't have to get up with the roosters to meet with the high school swim team every morning to collect data.

Shay scanned the document again. "The deal is I cook for you. Nothing else."

"We've already covered that there'll be nothing else."

She tried not cringe at his words. "You have to eat what I prepare, when I tell you to."

Brody narrowed his eyes. "Within reason."

"No. This is nonnegotiable. If you want to properly manage your blood sugar so it doesn't affect your game, you have to do it my way."

Shay could tell from his body language that she was testing his patience. Part of her hoped he'd back off from this loony plan—but only a small part. The rest of her was excited to put some of her skills to use. After all, it might be the only opportunity she had to use her education as she'd intended.

"I'm not eating anything crazy," he argued. "Like tofu or funny vegetables."

"What constitutes a funny vegetable?"

"Anything that isn't green beans or corn."

She rolled her eyes as her brain geared up for the challenge. "Corn is like pure sugar, a simple carbohydrate, actually, and something you need to avoid."

Brody sighed in annoyance. "We'll take it one step at a time. Just e-mail my assistant with a list of the groceries you need and she'll have them delivered." He handed her a business card for a Gwen Olsen. "Now, give me your phone."

"Why?"

"So I can call you when I get hungry." He snatched the phone from her hand, presumably entering his number on her keypad. The phone in his pants pocket rang and he handed hers back to her. "The contract prohibits you from distributing my number also, in case you get any ideas." He handed her a pen. "Do we have a deal?"

"Do I have a choice?"

A flicker of something passed over his face, but it was gone before Shay could identify it. "No. Neither one of us does."

Shay took the pen and signed the form with less reluctance than she should have felt.

"You can start tonight, so tell your neighbor you're not available to babysit."

Maddox's mother, Jackie, worked weekends mostly, when her mother-in-law could come up to watch her kids. Shay and Mrs. Elder were only backups, but he didn't need to know that. "I don't get finished here until two thirty. Then I have my seniors for water aerobics at three thirty. That doesn't leave me time to get a grocery list to your assistant and have the food delivered."

"Excuses already?" But he pulled his wallet out of his pocket and handed her a fifty. "Is that enough to get you started?"

Shay nodded.

"I'll have a taxi pick you up because you are *not* riding your bike the ten miles to my house."

"I have a car." She tried not to grin at the look of surprise on his face.

"Fine. I put the address in your phone. The guard at the gate will be expecting you."

Taking the contract back, he folded it up, before gesturing for her to precede him out the door. Shay hesitated, her hand on the doorknob, as she looked over her shoulder at Brody.

"You can trust me, Brody. But can I trust you not to sabotage my degree? Or my mama's livelihood?"

He looked truly affronted by her question. "This is just insurance. To keep you from spilling my secrets. As long as you don't go shooting your mouth off, you'll be okay."

Which meant she had to find the team snitch before he or she *did* spill more of Brody's secrets.

Shay left the storeroom, Brody on her heels, both of them nearly colliding with the Blaze head coach who was leaning, nonchalantly, against the doorframe.

"Hello, kids," Matt Richardson said, a knowing grin on his face.

She felt Brody inhale sharply behind her before he stepped out to stand next to her.

"There's quite a lot of chatter going on back there about you two." The coach eyed Brody.

"It's none of their business." Brody's body was rigid with tension beside her, but his face sported that aw-shucks smile he used as a shield.

Shay's stomach did a flip-flop. The contract she'd just signed wouldn't matter if the team dismissed her. *Hell's bells.* All her work may have been for nothing.

"Normally, this is when I give the speech about not wanting my players to be distracted by anything or anyone. But right now, this lady"—he nodded toward Shay—"is more important to the team."

If Shay wasn't so mortified by the coach's incorrect assumption of what they were doing in the storeroom, she might have laughed at the complete look of bafflement on Brody's face. As she'd already discovered, he wasn't used to not being the center of the universe.

Coach Richardson's gaze softened as he shifted it to Shay. "I'd have a mutiny on my hands if the players didn't get those shakes you make every day. And my daughter would kill me, too. She got an A-minus on her chemistry quiz and is demanding I hire you as a tutor."

A proud smile broke out on Shay's face. "I'd love to. She's a sweet girl. Smart, too."

Brody draped an arm over her shoulders. "Well, Coach, Shannon's a pretty busy girl, what with studying and her work here. Did you know she also teaches water aerobics? I'm not sure she has an extra minute in her day for anything else."

Shay knew exactly what Brody was up to; he wanted her to be available anytime he hollered. But, by eliminating the need to collect data from the swimmers, he'd inadvertently just given her back an hour and a half to her day. She'd have plenty of free time to tutor Emma.

"Don't be silly. I can work with her here in the commissary one or two days a week. Or, I can come to your home on the weekends. Just let me know."

Relief spread over the coach's face. "Great. My wife will bring her by tomorrow after school. Just let her know how much you charge." He glanced back at Brody. "Practice is in ten minutes, Janik. And remember, don't do a thing to make this woman unhappy or you'll answer to me."

Brody turned to her, his eyes smoldering—with what, she wasn't exactly sure. "Oh, that shouldn't be a problem, Coach," he said, the smile on his face as fake as the pearls her mama wore to Junior League. Before she knew what he was up to, he leaned over to place an openmouthed kiss on the sensitive skin just below her ear. His breath was warm as he lingered a moment before whispering just loud enough for the coach to overhear, "I'll see you tonight."

Shay didn't bother answering. She couldn't. After that kiss, she was too busy reaching a hand out for the wall, trying to keep her body from melting into a puddle on the floor.

Seven

Shay shouldn't have been shocked by Brody's house, but she was. It wasn't at all what she'd imagined. Not that she was expecting a stripper pole in the living room, but she wasn't prepared for the bachelor athlete's house to be so—homey. Comfortable oversized furniture took up most of the great room. Books and magazines—surprisingly suitable for both men and women—were spread out on the oak coffee table next to a well-used backgammon set. Most startling of all was the basket of toys in the corner of the room.

"Somehow, I figured there'd be more TVs and gaming systems decorating your place, as well as . . . other things." Embarrassed by the path her thoughts were taking, she turned away, opening the wide double doors of the Sub-Zero refrigerator in the roomy kitchen.

Casually dressed in a pair of well-fitting jeans and a designer T-shirt, Brody leaned a hip against the granite counter, watching intently as she inspected the contents of the vegetable bin. "Sorry to disappoint, but my mom isn't a big fan of all that crap. There's a TV downstairs in the man cave if there's something you just have to watch."

Shay jerked her gaze back to Brody. "You didn't tell me you live with your mother?"

He had the audacity to laugh. "I don't. But she and the rest of my family visit often."

"How often?"

"I don't know. One of them is here at least once a week. Does it matter?" His lips curved into that dangerous smile. "I'm more curious about the other things you pictured in my house. What were you thinking of, Texas?"

She let out an exasperated sigh, ignoring his second question. "It does matter, Brody, if you eat what they're eating. I'm putting you on a strict diet here; one you can't veer off of if you want to keep your blood sugar level."

Brody scoffed at her. "My mom's a diabetic. I can have what she has."

"Oh and that's been really successful so far." She rolled her eyes in exasperation. "Look, Brody, just because your mama has diabetes doesn't mean you're going to get it. Even if you do, you burn twice, maybe three times as much glucose as she does just by virtue of the fact you're a professional athlete. You can't control your blood sugar the way she does. But your low blood sugar may be caused by something else. Didn't your doctor mention a thing called reactive hypoglycemia?"

His smile long gone, he remained silent, which Shay took as a no.

"You *have* been to a doctor for this?" She was a little afraid of what his answer might be.

"Of course," he replied, his tone indignant. "My cousin keeps an eye on my blood sugar."

"And your cousin is a medical doctor, right?"

Brody crossed his arms over his chest. "Funny. He graduated first in his class at Tufts."

"So your family knows about your blood sugar issues."

"Just Jerry, but he's not talking."

Shay pulled a bag of arugula out of her shopping bag and began searching the well-stocked cabinets for a colander. "You either paid him off with Super Bowl tickets or your Machiavellian agent has something on the good doctor."

The corner of his mouth twitched, but he didn't answer.

"Are you sure your agent isn't the leader of a Mexican drug cartel?" She mumbled as she rinsed the lettuce in the sink.

"I'm sure. Now, tell me what I need to know about this reactive hypoglycemia."

"It's pretty simple, actually. Hypoglycemia occurs when your body uses up more blood glucose than your food intake supplies. Ninety percent of blood glucose in the body is used and disposed of by the skeletal muscles. Athletes have a greater percentage of lean skeletal muscle to body mass, so it makes sense that they'd use more blood glucose."

"So are you saying that my teammates may have the same thing?"

"Not exactly. There's a bit more science that goes into it, involving your glucose transporters. Normally, a rapid decrease of blood glucose is offset when your hormones stimulate your liver to shoot more glucose into your system, but in the case of some extreme athletes, that doesn't happen."

Brody ran his fingers through his hair. "Well I need it to happen."

Shay reached out and placed a hand on his shoulder. "Brody, reactive hypoglycemia is almost always controlled by regulating your diet. What and when you eat. That's what you have me for. You're going to be fine."

He glanced at her hand on his shoulder before looking at her face, a hint of uncertainty briefly flickering in his eyes. "Are you always this confident about everything you do?"

Ha! If he only knew. "My daddy likes to say I'm tough as a boot."

They stood there for a moment, the silence profound, until a slow grin spread over Brody's face. "Your father sounds like a smart man."

Shay wondered what Brody's reaction would be if he knew her daddy wore adult diapers.

"So your sister is a Dallas Cowboys cheerleader, huh?"

Reluctantly pulling her hand off his shoulder, she went back to preparing his dinner. She'd wondered when he'd get to the subject of her iconic sister. Most of the time, it didn't take a man five minutes before he asked about Teryn. Brody must have had infinite self-control because Shay knew he was not slow. Either that or he'd already experienced his share of Dallas Cowboys cheerleaders.

"Yep. For three years now." Shay pulled the salmon out of its wrapper, slapped it on a cutting board, and doused each side with olive oil, before spreading a mixture of chopped parsley, fresh chives, and some zest of lemon over top.

"Does she like it?" Brody's gaze was intense, almost as if he sensed that she was uncomfortable discussing her sister and he wanted to get a reaction out of Shay by asking ridiculous questions.

What girl wouldn't want to be a Dallas Cowboys cheerleader? Except for Shay, of course, but she'd been different from the start, something her Meemaw never failed to point out. For Teryn, the position was a dream come true. Her sister had craved being the center of attention all her life. She was gorgeous and she knew it. Now, she was an international sex symbol. The beautiful Everett daughter was doing exactly what she was bred to do. Shay didn't feel like elaborating on her sister's perfect life, so she just shrugged her shoulders in answer.

"You don't know?" Brody asked. "I thought twins were supposed to be close."

"Obviously we're not identical twins so we don't have that kind of bond. But we are sisters." She shrugged again when an explanation wouldn't come. "Even though we're pretty different, I guess we're close. We shared everything growing up."

Brody let out a little snort. "I have four older sisters. Growing up, the one thing they hated to do was share."

He'd hit the nail on the head with that statement. Teryn hated sharing. She'd wanted to exist in her own orbit, leaving Shay rusticating at its far corners. Far enough away so as not to remind their family that one of them was less than perfect.

"Is she as industrious as you are?" Somehow he'd made the word *industrious* sound sexy and Shay wasn't sure whether the heat she felt was from the open oven or Brody's stare.

Teryn was industrious, mostly when it came to having the best-looking man on her arm. She was happiest when a man was buying her things and treating her like the princess their Meemaw brought her up to be. The problem was, Teryn had a habit of hitching her wagon to the wrong stud. Her last boyfriend had promised to finance her training as a dental hygienist, only to leave her halfway through school. As a result, Teryn had a barnful of student loans and was no help with their mama's financial crisis.

It was ironic how Shay was actually having a conversation with a hot guy and her sister was still able to butt in from nearly fourteen hundred miles away. It was the story of Shay's life. She needed to take the bull by the horns and steer their conversation to a different course.

"Last week, when you were in the locker room talking with your trainer, did you notice anyone else around?"

If Brody realized she was changing the subject, he didn't comment on it. He gave her a speculative look. "I didn't even see you there."

"I was hiding in the back."

"You must have had a pretty good view."

"Not really. I didn't see anything." Her feverish skin undoubtedly gave her away.

Brody leaned in close to her flushed cheek. "Liar. You couldn't have heard what you did without being close enough to get a good look. Did you like what you saw, Texas?"

Shay needed to put a stop to his flirtation because they both knew he wasn't going to follow through. Once again, her mouth took the lead, forcing her brain to play catch up. "I'm going to find the snitch, Brody."

The quiet certainty in Shannon's voice startled Brody. The sight of her in his kitchen, all legs in a pair of black jeans tucked into hand-tooled cowboy boots, was doing strange things to his body. Again. Instead of smelling like a swimming pool as she had after her water aerobics class earlier in the week, she smelled fresh, like baby powder and sunshine. She'd tamed her unruly hair into a braid at the side of her face that threatened to come undone at the first shake of her head. Her pale blue sweater made the flecks of gold in her eyes sparkle. Unfortunately, those eyes held a little bit of crazy in them, too.

"What?" Surely he hadn't heard her correctly.

"I said I'm going to find the snitch." She squeezed some lemon juice over the lettuce concoction.

"Shannon, we both know who the snitch is and I'm looking at her." The feeling swirling around in his gut was probably hunger because there was no way it was doubt.

She poured olive oil into the bowl and sighed. "No, Brody, as I keep telling you, I'm not. But when something else is reported on that stupid blog, I'll have no way to prove it wasn't me. So I have to find the person who's been leaking information about Blaze players just so I can exonerate myself." She spooned some capers in with the lettuce mixture.

"You're not going after any snitch and I'm not eating anything with capers in it." His inner caveman had taken over his personality again and Brody realized he just didn't care anymore.

Shannon gave him a look of disgust. "Oh for glory sakes, Brody, how old are you? Just pick the capers out. And you *will* eat all the vegetables because you need the vitamin K to help regulate your glucose production." She tossed the green stuff together with the capers. "And don't for one minute think you can keep me from going after the snitch."

Brody stood, his hands firmly on his hips so he wouldn't strangle her, wondering exactly when he'd lost control of the situation. His plan had been simple enough: keep a close eye on her by having her prepare his meals to keep his blood sugar in check. He should have known by now, however, that with Shannon nothing was simple. She didn't operate like other women he knew.

"When you're ready to eat, put the fish in the oven for nine to ten minutes. The salad goes on the side. There's a loaf of five-grain bread here, too, but you can only have the amount I've cut for you. That's a big piece of fish, so if you only eat two thirds of it, you'll have enough protein to last until later." She pointed to a spreadsheet she'd attached to the door of his stainless steel fridge. "Here's a list of the snacks you need to eat over the next six hours and again when you wake up in the morning. The first snack of the day is really important, so don't forget."

"You're not staying for dinner?" Growing up in a big family, Brody hated eating alone. It'd been two years since he'd had roommates living here, but he still hadn't gotten used to the quiet house around him.

"Nothing in our deal specifies that I have to actually *feed* you your dinner." Her eyes narrowed. "Or clean it up, in case that's what you're really after."

He groaned in exasperation. "A housekeeper comes in the mornings to clean."

"Sheesh, Brody, how many of those extortion contracts has your agent executed for you?"

Her mouth twitched slightly at the corners and Brody realized he desperately wanted to see what she looked like when she smiled. Hell, he wanted to know everything about her.

"You said yourself the piece of fish is larger than I need. Don't you want to make sure I eat it all? Or do you have other plans for the evening?" Even as he asked the question, he didn't want to know if the answer was yes. Jealousy clawed at his belly, there was no mistaking that for hunger. Unless it was his hunger for her.

She crossed her arms over her chest. "You can't handle not getting your way, can you, Brody?"

"Is that a yes or a no?" he ground out.

"I really should get home. I have lots of data analysis to finish tonight."

Triumph surged through his veins. She wasn't meeting

another guy for dinner. "Fish is brain food. Stay and eat a quick dinner first."

She shot him a measuring glance before turning and placing the salmon in the oven. He wasn't sure, but he thought he heard her mumbling something about him being spoiled as he grabbed two plates out of the cabinet.

"So what type of data are you analyzing?" he asked.

Carrying the lackluster salad to the table, she studied him carefully, as if to assess whether or not he could understand what she was researching. It galled him that she apparently thought he was nothing more than a dumb jock.

"Actually, I'm studying the effects certain foods have on the body's athletic performance," she said, evidently deciding he could grasp the basics. "That's how I was familiar with reactive hypoglycemia. I've been using a group of high school swimmers to gather my data, but now I can use you instead. And, since I'll be able to really regulate what you eat, my data will be more precise."

Brody wasn't sure he liked the idea of being her human guinea pig, but he had been the one to force the contract. She'd just found a way to use it to her advantage. As he pulled a bottle of pinot grigio from the fridge, he reminded himself again that Shannon was a force to be reckoned with and he couldn't manipulate her the way he would any other woman.

He poured the wine into a glass.

"You can't have that!"

He turned to find her staring in horror at the wineglass, the basket of bread in her hand, nearly a casualty.

"Give me a break. I'm not that stupid, Shannon. The wine's for you." He took the basket from her hand before she dumped it on the floor, putting it and the wineglass next to their plates.

Shannon had the grace to blush. "Oh, well you shouldn't have bothered. I don't drink wine. It makes me silly."

Brody laughed. "All the more reason you should have some. You're the most serious person I know."

Her face dimmed and he felt like a heel. "Shannon, come sit down and tell me about your research while the fish cooks," he pleaded.

She looked as if she wanted to be anywhere but in his kitchen as she reluctantly slid into the chair at the wide breakfast bar. Her mind seemed to be warring with itself as she scrunched up her brow and contemplated the wineglass in front of her before finally taking a sip.

"It's pretty boring, Brody. Are you sure you want to hear about it?" she asked shyly.

Brody would listen to her explain the theory of relativity if she kept looking at him like she was just now. He nodded his encouragement.

"It's complicated, so keep up."

So much for her vulnerability.

The next half hour flew by as she explained carbohydrate burn and ketones and how his body processed glucose. He ate his dinner—capers included—in rapt fascination of her knowledge and exuberance about the science of nutrition. Despite her earlier warning about the subject being complicated, she took her time to explain the concepts in a way he could relate and easily understand. She would make a wonderful teacher.

When she'd finished, their plates were clean and her wineglass was empty, leaving a soft glow on her cheeks. He wasn't sure if it was the wine or her excitement for the subject matter, but he did know he liked this relaxed Shannon. Somehow he didn't think she let herself enjoy this state too often.

"No wonder Nate is so nasty to you," he said in all sincerity. "He's afraid of you. You're brilliant, Shannon."

Her face flushed deeper and he felt a measure of satisfaction at making her happy.

"Why did you pick nutrition?" he asked as he cleared both their plates to the sink.

"I was the cook in the family. Mama always worked in the evenings and Meemaw fried everything until it was unrecognizable as anything other than a shoe." She actually laughed and Brody was transfixed. "It was a matter of self-preservation, I guess. Then I discovered that if I ate properly, I would swim faster and what was once a chore became part of my training regimen."

"You swim?"

"Since I was seven. It's how I was able to go to college. I swam backstroke for the Longhorns for four years."

He wasn't sure why he was so surprised, she had the build of a sleek backstroker.

Shannon twirled her fingers around the stem of her wineglass. "It was nice to have something I was good at."

"Did your sister swim?" He sat back down next to her, his own fingers itching to reach out and stroke her the same way she was touching the glass.

"Yeah, every morning until we were twelve. Meemaw made her stop because the chlorine was too damaging on her hair. Teryn could have argued that it didn't matter, she wore a wig for pageants, but truth be told, she hated getting up at five thirty every morning."

"Your grandmother didn't care about your hair?" Brody wasn't sure why, but he felt defensive of Shannon.

She gave a self deprecating laugh. "No, my hair didn't matter. I wasn't the pretty one."

An ugly burn settled in his stomach.

"So tell me your secrets, Brody. For instance, why does a grown man in his late twenties have a basket full of Tonka trucks in his great room?"

Brody relaxed in the chair again, ready to divulge anything she asked of him. "I'll give you three reasons: Adam, Chandler, and Rachel, my nephews and niece."

Her eyes danced. "Do they come over to play with you often?"

"Like I said, my family is in and out of here a lot. One of my sisters is working on a big class action case with a law firm here in Baltimore, so she's in every other week. My oldest sister Gwen, mother to Adam and Rachel, is my assistant, so she tries to visit a couple of times a month. The sister closest to me in age, Tricia, is getting married in a few weeks, so she hasn't been down lately. Chandler's mom, my sister Ashley, is my stylist so she comes down to go through my clothes once a month."

"Pardon?" she asked. "Did you say your sister is your *stylist*?"

Okay, maybe he should have been a little more circumspect with the types of things he shared with her. "She's in the fashion business and she figures it's a reflection on her if I look bad in public."

Shannon's smile was wide now. "And what exactly does she do?"

"I don't know." He was growing a little more defensive. "She coordinates my clothes so everything looks like it goes together."

"Does she leave you a list or something?"

"No. She organizes them in my closet." Yep, he'd definitely gone too far if the twinkle in her eyes was any indication.

"Like Garanimals?" She sprung from the chair. "Oh, Brody, this I have to see."

Shannon was out of the kitchen before he could stop her, those long legs eating up the distance to the center staircase. The house's lighting system was operated by sensors, the hallway lights illuminating her path up the stairs with each step toward the master bedroom.

"Shannon, wait!" But it was no use, her rich laughter taunted him from the just inside the door to his bedroom. It stopped suddenly as Brody crossed the threshold. Shannon stood still, her eyes glued to the king-sized bed in the center of the room, the pillows mussed from where he'd laid down earlier, a pair of his nylon running shorts lying on the floor beside the big bed.

He leaned up against the doorframe, crossing his arms over his chest. "If you wanted to check out my bed, Shannon, all you had to do was ask." He'd meant it to be flirtatious, but when she turned around, her face was a contortion of desire and embarrassment. Once again, he was reminded she was a conundrum.

"Next time you come over, Texas," he warned softly, "you should probably wear a hairnet."

Her face aghast, Shannon bolted from his bedroom and his house.

Eight

Shay's palms had begun to sweat. She tried not to squirm in her chair under the shrewd gaze of Donovan Carter, the director of security for the Blaze. He studied her carefully from his perch on the corner of general manager Hank Osbourne's desk. Fortunately, Mr. Osbourne's eyes held more amusement. Once again, she'd acted on impulse, seeking out management before coming up with a plan. She blamed her rashness on lack of sleep brought on by studying and working long hours. It was either that or acknowledge a deep character flaw.

"Not really, Mr. Carter," she said. "I just know whoever is writing the blog can't be everywhere at once. Someone is feeding him or her information. And for some of the more personal stuff, it has to be someone with access inside the organization."

"She has a valid point, Carter," Mr. Osbourne said, peering at Shay through his steepled fingers. "The league is pursuing the blogger, but maybe there's something we can do to step up security so nothing else gets out about Blaze players."

Mr. Carter bristled at the affront on his current security measures. From what Shay had seen, he was a man who took his job seriously. "There's not much else to step up. Ever since the abduction of Carly and Troy Devlin and the coach's daughter last season, we keep a pretty tight watch on who comes and goes into this facility, our hotels, and any stadium we play in."

"Begging your pardon, sir, but it might be someone who's already in the organization. Perhaps an employee who needs money?"

Both men stared at her. "Is this just supposition, Miss Everett?" Mr. Carter asked. "Or do you have some actual knowledge?"

Shay was walking a fine line here. If she shared too much, she risked implicating herself. She unfolded the piece of paper in her lap, its edges frayed where she'd been gripping it in her damp hands. "This was inside my cubby last week." She handed the paper to the director of security. "I saw them in all the kitchen staff cubbies. The housekeeping cubbies, too."

Mr. Carter scanned the sheet, swiping a hand over his bald head in exasperation before handing it to Mr. Osbourne. The silence stretched in the room as the GM read the text. He heaved a sigh. "So, she's offering money—a lot more than I presumed—for the stuff she reports. And she's soliciting the low-income staff on the teams to obtain it. She's aggressively diabolical, I'll give her that. But it still begs the question, what's her bigger purpose? And who's bankrolling the whole thing?"

"We still aren't even sure it's a she."

Both men's eyebrows shot up at Shay's statement, but as a scientist, Shay knew it was foolish to rule out half the population without proof.

Mr. Carter picked up the paper that Mr. Osbourne had flipped onto his desk in disgust. "I'll call around to the other teams to alert them to be on the lookout for one of these.

Can I keep this?" The question was obviously a formality because he quickly stood, his body poised for action.

Shay waved a hand. "I don't want it."

The director of security contemplated her. "Thanks for bringing it to our attention." If he wondered why it had taken her a week, he didn't ask.

Shay stood, too, ready to make her escape.

"Miss Everett?" The amusement was back in Mr. Osbourne's tone. "My sincerest apologies if this incident has upset you personally in anyway."

"Pardon?" She wasn't sure where the GM was going with his apology.

"Your . . . *relationship* . . . with Brody Janik. I'm sure a woman like you couldn't be too happy to see it spread all over the Internet."

Oh, snap. She'd left the door wide open for him to weigh in on her relationship with Brody. What if the GM wasn't as tolerant as the coach and he dismissed her right on the spot? She'd lose her internship for sure. All because she didn't want Brody to think she was the snitch. What was her mama always telling her? *Pride goeth before the fall.*

Shay was embarrassed that the GM thought she and Brody were involved. No doubt the man believed she was incredibly unprofessional, a starry-eyed student who looked at the job with the team as an opportunity to score. Heat stained her cheeks at the thought. She stammered, hoping something intelligent would come out of her mouth.

Before it could, she caught sight of Brody sliding to a halt in front of the open door of the GM's office. His eyes went wide as he spied her looking very much like a chastised schoolgirl standing in front of Hank Osbourne's desk. He was obviously dressed for practice, in gray knit shorts and a white Blaze T-shirt stretched over well-defined muscles. Shay was confused as to why he'd be in this part of the building.

"There you are." Brody stepped into the office, his normally cool composure seeming a bit frayed.

He came to stand beside her, thankfully not touching. Her

own nerves were still fraught from the night before when she'd been in his bedroom. Her skin burned more furiously at the thought. She'd been so forward, charging up to his room. How many women had he brought to that mammoth bed? All of them more beautiful than her. How he must have laughed at her when she charged out of his house.

"Everything okay here, Hank?"

A bemused smile spread over the GM's face. "Yes, Brody, everything's fine. Isn't that right, Miss Everett?"

Shay nodded, hoping that was her cue to head for the door.

"Cool." Brody gestured for her to precede him out of the office.

"By the way, Miss Everett," Mr. Osbourne called after her, halting her progress. "Thank you for helping out with food services. I know it wasn't the intern experience you expected, but with the catering liaison out unexpectedly with a serious illness, Nate has had to fill in to coordinate the nutritional aspect of training. He tells me you've been a big help. I just wanted you to know how much the team appreciates it."

Shay was so stunned she could barely manage a thank-you. *Nate was singing her praises to management? What could he possibly want from her?*

"I believe practice is about to begin, Brody," the GM warned.

"On my way," Brody said as he herded her out of the office.

Shay pulled on her hairnet and quickly made her way toward the stairs leading down to the commissary. She needed to get the protein shakes ready before practice began. Apparently whatever had Brody in the management side of the building was forgotten because he was shadowing her stride for stride.

"What the hell were you doing?" he hissed.

"What I said I was going to do." She bounded down the stairs, trying to distance herself from him, but the attempt was futile. "I'm trying to catch the snitch."

"Jeez Louise, you're one bull-headed woman. Will you give it up already about this supposed snitch?"

Shay had to catch herself to keep from stumbling at the base of the stairs, she was so angry with his refusal to believe her. Brody quickly grabbed her elbow to steady her. Unable to bear the reaction her body had to his touch, she tried to yank her arm free.

"Go away, Brody. I can take care of myself."

"That's debatable." He opened one of the training room doors, tugging her inside before closing and locking it behind him.

Shay was too angry to panic about being alone in a room with him again. "You're going to be late for practice."

"Yeah and it's your fault. I had to track you down all over this building to make sure you didn't do something stupid."

So he'd been looking for her. She tamped down the flutter of excitement in her chest. "What's it to you?"

"Shannon, if they find out it was you in that locker room, they'll fire you. Isn't that what we're trying to avoid here?"

And there it was. _We._ "Oh, for pity's sake, Brody. You're not worried about me. You're worried about you. As usual. If I get fired, you lose your leverage over me and you won't have anyone to fix your meals."

His lips formed a grim line. "Not quite all my leverage, Texas."

That part was true, but it was against Shay's nature to concede defeat. "What's done is done. Now can you let me out of here so I can go do my job?"

Brody blocked the door, his muscled arms belligerently crossed against his chest, his feet spread wide. He muttered something beneath his breath. "Do you give all your boyfriends this much trouble?" he asked as he took two steps toward her.

"You're not my boyfriend, Brody." It was a credit to her acting abilities that she could hide the disappointment in her voice.

Somehow he'd managed to move to within striking distance. He narrowed those cobalt eyes at her and suddenly there wasn't a breath of air left in the room.

"So then I shouldn't do this."

Ever so gently, he cupped her face in his hands. Shay was too stunned to react as his lips descended toward hers. *He definitely shouldn't be doing this*, she thought to herself. But she did nothing to stop him. She couldn't. Even more embarrassing, she wasn't able to stifle the soft moan of pleasure that escaped from the back of her throat as his lips made contact with hers. The sound was all the encouragement Brody needed.

He opened her mouth with his and she welcomed the invasion, his tongue sliding along her own. Heat pooled in her belly as Brody groaned, her embarrassment quickly replaced by satisfaction. Her hands had somehow found their way into his hair and she threaded her fingers through the soft strands, the movement bringing their bodies closer. Brody lifted his hands from her face to explore the contours of her body, leaving a warm flush to her skin everywhere he touched. She sighed in protest as his lips left hers. But when they moved to caress the sensitive spot beneath her ear, her knees nearly buckled from the pleasure.

"I should have never let you leave my bedroom last night."

The sensual haze was surely playing tricks on her hearing because men like Brody didn't say those kinds of things to women like Shay. If she were dreaming, she didn't want this interlude to end. Turning her head, she sought out his lips again. He didn't disappoint, claiming her mouth in a full, searching kiss. Shay arched her body into his as his hands cupped her bottom. Her own hands had somehow managed to slip underneath his T-shirt, her fingertips trailing over the smooth skin of his muscled abdomen.

Brody suddenly flinched, his breath catching in a hiss. Shay came to her senses with a start, breaking the kiss and taking a giant step back. She glanced up at his bewildered face. His hair was mussed from where her fingers had been and he was breathing as if he'd just run the length of a football field.

It was a moment before he broke the charged silence. "Sorry. I got a stinger in practice yesterday, that's all." He lifted up his T-shirt to show her his bruised stomach. "See, nothing serious."

Shay wasn't paying attention to his babbling, however. Shame washed over her as she caught sight of his very lusty arousal. She'd been two minutes from shedding her drawers in the building where she interned. With a man who'd most likely done this thing a hundred times before; maybe in this very room. Worse, she'd wanted it as much as he did. *Probably more*.

"Shannon?" His tone was gentle as he took a step forward.

Shay put her hands up to stop him, unable to find her own voice. She needed to get out of there. Making a halfhearted attempt to right her appearance, she spied her hairnet lying on the floor next to his sneakered feet. But she didn't dare retrieve it. Not if it meant getting close to him again. Instead, she scrambled out of the room as quickly as she could, a strangled sob escaping her throat. Brody swore as she sped out, but thankfully, his current condition forced him to stay put.

Two days later, Brody was still edgy from his close encounter with Shannon. She'd made herself scarce again, prepackaging his dinners and snacks while he was at practice and leaving them in his fridge with detailed cooking instructions. He'd been wrong when he said Nate would be a prick about his diet. Shannon Everett was worse. *Way worse*. She strictly regimented his day by what he ate and when. But he couldn't complain because his head was finally as clear as it had been before his symptoms started five months ago. As maddening as he found her routine, it was working. Now all he needed to do was to make the other parts of his body happy.

"Yo, Brody! Where's your girlfriend?" DeShawn called across the ballroom of the Baltimore hotel the Blaze stayed at the night before every home game. The team was reassembling for the coach's nine p.m. motivational pep talk before they dispersed to their rooms to catch the recap of the day's college football games and get some shut-eye. The same local restaurant catered the pregame meals for all the home games, so Shannon had the night off. Of course, that hadn't stopped her from organizing Brody's meals. How she'd managed it with the caterer he didn't know, but he was beginning to suspect that nothing stopped Little Miss Texas when she put her mind to it.

He gave his teammate a shrug. "She has the night off."

"Man, you need to be more careful with your lady," the tailback said. "You shouldn't let her tend bar without us there to keep the riffraff away."

"She isn't tending bar tonight, either." At least he hoped not. He'd spent five hours the previous evening nursing mineral water at Celtic Charm, keeping watch on Shannon as she mixed drinks. The three slugs from Santoni's had wandered through the bar area, along with the rest of the frat house, but they didn't linger. Most of the men vying for Shannon's attention had been his teammates, allowing Brody to relax a little. But only a little.

Thanks to the charade he was perpetrating with Shannon, he couldn't very well have hooked up with any of the women who'd been hitting on him last night. That little miscalculation was wreaking havoc with his body, with no relief in sight. Making matters worse, he wanted Shannon. God only knew the reason why. She wasn't going to grace the cover of the *Sports Illustrated* swimsuit edition anytime soon. Not to mention Little Miss Texas was ornery as a mule. A man didn't stand a chance controlling a girl like that. Especially one with an IQ in the *Big Bang Theory* range. Hell, given the choice, he'd take a high-maintenance woman any day; she'd be less work than Shannon Everett.

The problem was, Brody couldn't stop thinking about kissing her. He'd known that if he got that second chance, he could coax a response out of her. What he hadn't been prepared for was the intensity of her response. She was equal parts innocence and sex kitten, a conundrum even when she kissed. He'd been so overwhelmed by the way her body came alive beneath his hands and his lips that he'd nearly taken her right there in the training room. Even more astounding, he didn't think she'd put up any resistance if he'd tried. His body grew hard just thinking about it, making him squirm on the already uncomfortable banquet chair.

"You got ants in your pants, Janik?"

Brody stifled a groan as Shane Devlin slid into the chair next to him.

"More likely he's missing his new pretty girlfriend," Will Connelly said as he folded his big body into the seat on Brody's other side.

Devlin waved a bag of nacho cheese corn chips in front of Brody's face. "Chip?"

Brody shook his head and the quarterback reached across to offer the bag to Connelly.

"What's up with you, Janik?" Connelly asked, taking a handful. "You normally eat like you've got a tapeworm." The damn linebacker was way too observant.

"Just being careful about what I fuel my body with before a game. All the better to optimize my performance."

Devlin laughed as he crunched on a mouthful of chips.

Connelly eyed him shrewdly for a moment. "What did I tell you about trying to navigate the Internet on your own? Don't get sucked into one of those crazy diet plans," he teased.

"Piss off," Brody said, and the two laughed harder.

Great. Not only was he jonesing for a certain whiskey-eyed bartender, but he had the bad luck to be sandwiched between the team's two most happily married men; one of whom was waving a tempting snack food in front of his face.

Coach Richardson took the podium and Devlin whispered to Brody. "I've got two words for what ails you, Janik. *Phone sex.*"

Connelly snorted beside him as Brody whipped his head around to stare at the quarterback.

Devlin kept his eyes fixed toward the front of the room. "No diet's gonna fix what's eating you tonight, Brody. You need to call your girlfriend before you go to bed."

Brody turned to his right where the linebacker smirked in his chair. "Don't knock it until you've tried it."

"TMI." Brody shook his head in bewilderment as both men chuckled beside him. The image of the two men engaging in phone sex with their wives creeped him out. Unfortunately, thinking about talking dirty with Shannon was punishing his body further. *Hell*. It was going to be a long night.

Nine

The midmorning sun felt good on Brody's shoulders as he jogged the perimeter of the painted football field. Kickoff wasn't until one o'clock, but it was his habit to take the earlier of the two team buses headed for the stadium. The gates wouldn't open for another half hour, allowing him to rehearse his routes without the distraction of the crowd.

As he suspected, he'd had a restless night of sleep, but the exactitude of his game day routine enabled him to relax into his playing zone. As he did every home game, Brody walked from the hotel to seven thirty mass at St. Leo the Great. He sat in the back with Sister Agnes, a nun who'd become a local celebrity for her weekly football picks on sports talk radio.

"Make sure you keep an eye on their corner, Chris Bailey. He had some speedy moves against Chicago last week," she'd whispered during the homily. "He's faster to the right, so keep him on your inside when you can."

Talking football with a sixty-two-year-old nun always made Brody smile. Best of all, Sister Agnes knew the game and asked more astute questions than most of the media that hounded him in the locker room after the game. Brody had the benefit of game films to pick up that detail about Bailey, one a normal viewer might miss. He wasn't convinced that Sister Agnes didn't bring some divine intervention to her analysis of the game.

But mass had been three hours ago and he was starting to get antsy again. His cell phone buzzed inside the pocket of his shorts. Normally, he'd have turned it off by now, not wanting the distraction of family and friends calling, but he'd texted Shannon with a trumped-up excuse of needing one of her shakes before the game. He figured if she were in the stadium watching, he'd be able to concentrate better on his play. As usual, though, she drove a hard bargain.

She'd texted him back that she'd need two tickets. Brody hadn't counted on her bringing a date. Instead of his plan helping to mitigate his desire, he'd managed to add jealousy to the catalog of feelings he had for Shannon.

We're at the VIP entrance. Where should we meet you?

Fans were starting to head to their seats, letting loose cheers and catcalls in Brody's general direction. The rest of the team would soon be on the field along with their opponent. He needed to head to the locker room, but first he'd face down another opponent—her date. Texting Shannon, he trotted toward the tunnel into the stadium.

When he finally rounded the corner to the VIP entrance, his body fired up at the sight of Shannon. She looked cool and relaxed in a pair of skinny jeans and a black Blaze V-neck T-shirt. Best of all, standing next to her, his face painted red and black, was her young neighbor Maddox.

"Mr. Janik! Lookee what I got done to my face!" A ball of boundless energy, the boy launched himself at Brody. "Shay said I can have a hot dog and maybe some nachos. And we're gonna stay for the whole game."

Brody rubbed the top of the boy's head. "Whoa there, little dude. First of all, you can call me Brody. My dad is Mr. Janik."

Maddox laughed.

"That's some pretty fine artwork on your face."

"The tailgaters were going a little bit crazy out there," Shannon explained. "Jackie will probably kill me when she sees him."

"I'm not washing my face. I'm going to school with this on tomorrow."

Shannon groaned. "We'll see what your mama has to say about that."

"Well look who's here on her day off." Nate Dumas materialized from the locker room. "Only coaches, players, and *working* Blaze personnel are allowed in this area of the stadium before a game, Shay. Of course, when you're dating one of the players, you can play fast and loose with the rules. Just keep the kid from getting underfoot."

"Don't worry, we're not staying," Shannon bit out, her mouth a grim line.

"That's too bad. I might have let you observe some game day training techniques," Dumas taunted before he slithered off toward the training area.

Shannon shook her head as Brody tried to convince himself not to go after the trainer and squeeze his throat until his head popped off.

"Can we go out there?" Maddox asked, pointing toward the tunnel leading to the field.

"Not today." Shannon wrapped an arm around the boy.

"I don't see why not," Brody said at the same time. He was so glad she'd brought Maddox and not someone else that he'd promise the kid anything. "Hey, Troy!" He flagged down Shane Devlin's half brother, one of the team's ball boys. "Can you take my buddy Maddox out to the field? And maybe grab him a ball so he can get it signed?"

"Sure thing, Brody." Troy shoved his wire glasses up on his nose. "Come with me."

"Make sure you stay with Troy, Maddox," Shannon called after the two boys as they sprinted down toward the sunshine at the end of the tunnel.

Brody needed to get to the locker room to suit up for pregame warm-ups. The problem was his body still hummed with pent-up desire remaining from their interlude in the training room the other day. If he could just talk things out with her, maybe he'd be able to get his head back in the game.

"Shannon, you came." They were interrupted by one of the coach's daughters. "I thought you had to study?"

"Hi, Emma. I did," Shannon said and Brody felt a twinge of guilt for dragging her to the game under false pretenses. "But it was a beautiful day and I brought my little neighbor I was telling you about. He just disappeared out onto the field with one of the ball boys."

He could hear the worry in her voice. She hadn't wanted to be separated from the boy, but Brody just wanted a few minutes alone with Shannon. The arrival of the coach's daughter provided the perfect opportunity. "Hey, would you mind keeping an eye on Maddox while he's out there so Shannon and I can talk for a minute?"

A knowing smile—eerily similar to her old man's—spread over the girl's face. "I'd be happy to." She crooked an eyebrow at Shannon just before skipping through the tunnel.

Concern clouded Shannon's eyes. "Are you feeling that poorly, Brody?" She reached into an insulated bag and began to pull out the shake.

"Not here." He gestured to one of the empty offices the coaches used during halftime to revise the game plan.

"Let me see your latest reading," she said as she deposited the shake and her bag onto the desk. "How low is it?"

This was the tricky part. "Lower than it should be." He grabbed the shake, now more like a slushie, and took a pull from the straw.

Shannon's eyes narrowed. "Exactly what does that mean?"

He didn't answer, instead taking another drink of the fruity concoction.

"Dang it, Brody. There's nothing wrong with your blood sugar this morning, is there?"

"No," he admitted sheepishly. "But that doesn't mean it couldn't drop during the game. And then where would I be with you at home, your nose buried in a book."

"Oh, for pity's sake!" She stomped around the desk. "You are such a big baby, Brody. You can't stand having to do anything for yourself. Well, I'm not one of your sisters who is going to jump when you bellow. I really don't know what you want from me."

"I just want you!"

His admission stopped Shannon in her tracks. Her breathing hitched briefly as she stared into his eyes.

"You don't want me, Brody," she said softly.

"The hell I don't!"

"No, you only think you want me because you can't have me. You're not used to being told no. If I'd been willing and easy, I wouldn't be so interesting. Admit it." Her voice wavered a bit and her shoulders slumped slightly.

If she'd been willing and easy, he'd have already had her in the training room and he wouldn't be so damn restless right now. Someone had really done a number on her self-esteem. They'd given her a real inferiority complex. Brody suspected it might have been her twin, the Dallas Cowboys cheerleader. He wanted to tell Shannon how wrong she was; that for such a brainy woman, she really misunderstood the facts. But before he could, she went in for the kill.

"You don't even trust me, Brody. I'd never sleep with a man who didn't trust me."

The silence in the room was profound. Brody couldn't dispute her argument. He'd been celibate the past several months because he couldn't trust the women he was involved with to keep his private life private. That didn't even count the women who made up crap about him. His mother had been devastated two summers ago when a story was leaked that Brody was marrying his pregnant girlfriend. A woman his family had never met who was definitely not pregnant and certainly not his girlfriend. Shannon was no different than the rest of her gender. She'd already proven herself untrustworthy the night she snuck into the locker room.

"I need to go find Maddox," she said, gathering up her things. "Finish that shake and remember to check your sugar at halftime. If you need it, eat the protein bar I left for you."

She paused in front of him, her whiskey eyes sad. "Text me if you need me, but you shouldn't. You're a big boy,

Brody. You can handle this. Now go catch a few touchdown passes."

Brody waited a few minutes after she slipped out the door to unleash a string of curse words. The fact that she was right didn't make his body feel any better. His only recourse was to go unleash his frustrations on the football field. And do as she said: catch a few touchdown passes.

He nearly tackled Nate as he left the office.

"Trouble in paradise?" the trainer asked. The guy was really starting to piss Brody off. Couldn't he mind his own damn business?

"No, dude," Brody lied as he stalked into the locker room. "Everything is freakin' wonderful."

"Here's your new mail key, Mr. Metz." Shay dropped the key into her neighbor's beefy hand. "Try to keep an eye on it," she teased. Mr. Metz was a bit of a curmudgeon, but he was quiet and he did his part to keep the place neat by mowing the lawn each week. Technically speaking, cutting the grass was Shay's job, but he'd taken over one afternoon when she'd nearly wrenched her arm out of the socket trying to get the mower started. In exchange, Shay baked him brownies or cookies.

Mr. Metz murmured his thanks and Shay made her way up the stairs. A familiar giggle rang out as she rounded the corner. Maddox was sitting outside his apartment door with a book in his hands, a familiar pair of long legs decked out in yellow running shoes spread out beside him.

Maddox looked up from the book; the red and black face paint had faded, but the blaze was still noticeable. After a convincing victory over San Francisco the day before, including a touchdown reception by Brody, Jackie had relented and let Maddox keep his "tattoo" for show-and-tell.

"Hi, Shay! We're reading."

Shay smiled at the boy. "I see that. What are you doing here, Brody?"

"Phonics." He accompanied his smart-aleck answer with that slow easy smile that never failed to make her stomach dip.

Carefully stepping over his muscled legs and trying not to look at how nicely they were displayed in a pair of khaki shorts, Shay unlocked her apartment door. Brody rose to his feet behind her as if to follow her in.

"What do you want, Brody?" she snapped.

She hadn't meant to sound so peevish, but she was tired from a late night of studying for her early morning statistics test. That was followed by two hours in her un-air-conditioned Corolla staking out Brody's house until after he'd left for the practice facility so she could prepare his dinner and leave it neatly packaged in his fridge without him tormenting her. After that, she'd taught her water aerobics class.

But mostly, she was tired of fighting off her body's reaction every time he came near her.

"I'm hungry." His breath was warm on the back of her neck and before she realized it, he was standing in her apartment.

They both knew his excuse was a bald-faced lie, but Shay didn't have the strength to tell him to leave.

"I got Skittles." Maddox pulled a snack-sized bag of the brightly colored candy out of his pocket and offered them to Brody.

Shay snatched the bag out of the child's hand before Brody could take them. "He can't have that. And neither can you, Maddox. You'll spoil your dinner."

"Mom said we could have pizza for dinner." Maddox rubbed his belly. "Umm. Hey, maybe you could eat with us, Brody? Pizza'll fill you up."

"Brody can't have pizza, either," Shay said.

"Dang, Brody. Did you forget to leave the seat down or something? How come you can't have candy or pizza?" Maddox asked earnestly.

The corner of Brody's mouth twitched.

"Brody has a perfectly good dinner at home, Maddox."

Maddox's shoulders slumped forward and his voice went

soft. "That's what Danny's mom always says when I invite him over for dinner."

And just like that, Shannon had turned into her Meemaw, nasty as the Wicked Witch of the West. Brody stared at her, hands on his hips. His mouth was a grim line, but his eyes twinkled at her as though he knew the battle she was fighting within her own head.

"Maddox, go tell your mother I'm buying," he said.

With a high-pitched whoop, Maddox raced next door.

Shay shook her head in defeat. "You're going to mess everything up."

He tossed his OneTouch onto the table. "My blood sugar has been stable for a week now. Go ahead. Check and see."

She'd been talking about more than his blood sugar, but if he understood what she meant, he ignored her.

"I can handle a couple of slices of pizza and a beer."

"Beer?" Shay nearly choked. "Who said anything about beer?"

Brody winked at her. "You can't have pizza without beer. It's sacrilege."

"Are we gonna have beer, too?" Maddox practically shrieked as he ran back in.

"Root beer for you, little dude. Go ask Mrs. Elder what she wants on her pizza."

"Okay. But don't give her any beer. It makes her burp somethin' awful." Maddox scooted back outside.

Apparently, Brody was inviting the entire complex to his impromptu pizza party.

"I fixed you a perfectly healthy meal. It's in your refrigerator."

In two strides he was standing within arm's length. "Yeah. But while I'm eating my nutritious meal, what would you be eating?"

Shay refused to get sucked into his baby blues. "Probably a bowl of Cap'n Crunch."

Brody groaned, closing his eyes. "You're killing me here, Shannon. God, I miss Cap'n Crunch." His eyelids snapped open and his smile was wicked. "But I'll have to sacrifice with pizza and beer. Just for you, I'll make sure the beer is that low-carb crap."

"Fine. You go enjoy yourself. I need a shower and to study."

His nostrils flared at the mention of the shower. Shay sucked in a breath when he gently traced a finger beneath one of her eyes. "You're exhausted. But you need to eat. Take your shower and I'll bring the pizza back here. I promise I'll have them out of here in an hour so you can study."

It was no wonder people never refused the man. The combination of his blue eyes and infectious smile did her in. "Sure. Whatever. Just make mine extra cheese."

It wasn't until halfway through her shower that she realized Brody hadn't said *he'd* be out of her apartment in an hour.

An hour later, Brody and Maddox were karate-chopping the pizza boxes into the recycling bin. Mrs. Elder had taken the baby, Anya, next door to get her ready for bed.

"I can see why my son loves him," Jackie said. "Brody is like a big kid."

Shay took another sip from the bottle of beer she'd been nursing. True to his word, Brody had bought a low-carb version, but he'd also only consumed half of his bottle. Despite his little fall off the diet wagon, he was still cautious about what he put into his body.

She smiled at Jackie, who was watching their antics from the sofa while Shay sat in the chair next to her. "Yeah, but unlike Brody, your son will actually grow up one day."

"Oh, now, I don't know, Shay," Jackie said as she stood. "That boyfriend of yours may be a bit playful at times, but he's a pretty sharp cookie. Not as smart as you, but most people aren't. He does have a big heart. Mmm. And a mighty fine body, too," she whispered with a wink.

Shay coughed, nearly choking on her beer. It hadn't occurred to her that Jackie would see the blog post. Surely, she didn't think Brody was actually her boyfriend? Before she could correct her neighbor, Jackie was corralling Maddox for a bath.

"Let's go, son."

"Aww, five more minutes?"

Brody scooped Maddox up off the floor. "No way, dude. You need to get that paint off your face before it becomes permanent." He tickled Maddox's belly and the boy shrieked with laughter. "Do what your Mom says or there'll be no more football games for you."

Maddox squirmed out of Brody's arms and headed for the adjoining door to his apartment. "No way! I'm taking a bath right now 'cause Troy said I could be a ball boy."

Jackie laughed. "Thank you, Brody. For everything." Somehow, Shay didn't think her neighbor was just talking about getting her son in the bathtub. "Tony and the rest of his unit appreciate that you're thinking of them. Heck, I appreciate it." She kissed Brody's cheek before turning back to Shay and giving her another wink. "Night, Shay," she practically sang as she pulled the door closed behind her.

Brody flopped down on the sofa, his long legs dangling off the end.

"What was that about?"

He draped an arm over his eyes. "Nothing."

Shay wasn't sure what peeved her more: his lack of response or the fact that he seemed disinclined to vacate the premises.

"Clearly, it isn't *nothing* or Jackie wouldn't have mentioned it." Jackie's husband, Tony, was deployed in Afghanistan. Obviously, Brody had done something for the Army specialist. But the only information she could get out of Brody was a noncommittal grunt. After a few minutes, it seemed as though he'd fallen asleep.

Too bad he tempted her even in slumber. She was sure she wouldn't be able to study with him there. He was too much of a distraction to her already flustered body. Stretching out her bare foot, she nudged him on the shoulder. "Brody?"

Lightening fast, his hand grabbed her ankle almost as if he were snaring a football out of the air. Her leg tingled where his fingers met her skin. Shay gasped, trying to yank her foot free, but it was no use.

His blue eyes were open and they held that wicked glint again. "Give it up, Shannon. Once I catch a pass, I rarely drop it."

Her overly large foot seemed small in his long-fingered hand. Without taking his eyes from her face, he sensuously grazed the pad of his thumb along her arch. Shay gnawed on her bottom lip as heat swarmed to her lower extremities. Everything south of the border was beginning to throb as he stroked her foot more firmly.

"You have beautiful feet," he murmured.

His words were so nonsensical that Shay thought she laughed. At least she tried to cover her moan of pleasure with what sounded like a laugh. Closing her eyes, she leaned back against the chair, her body aching. If it felt this good having Brody Janik rubbing one foot, what would it feel like to have his hands on the rest of her body? An uncontrollable shiver racked her whole being at the thought.

"Give me your other foot, Shannon."

If she gave him her other foot, she was as good as giving him all of her. Quickly, she snatched her ankle back from his now relaxed grip and tucked both her feet under her bottom in the chair.

"We already covered this yesterday," she managed to croak out around the rapid pulse beating in her throat.

He flung himself back on the sofa, slamming his arm back over his eyes. "You started it."

"You can't stay here all night, Brody. I have to study."

"Give me a minute to digest my pizza."

Shay couldn't figure out what annoyed her more: his frustrating behavior or her maddening desire for the man-child. Jumping to her feet, she stomped over to the small end table she used as a desk for her laptop. Brody showed no signs of leaving. There was no way she could concentrate with potent sex appeal soaking up all the air in her apartment. And, no way was she going to let him fall asleep on her sofa.

"I have a plan to catch the snitch."

It worked like a charm. Brody opened his eyes. "Shannon, I told you to leave this to security. Donovan Carter used to be with NCIS. He knows what he's doing."

"But he's not going about it the right way."

With a heavy sigh, Brody raised himself to a seated position. Now she was getting somewhere.

"I'm serious, Brody. Tracking down the IP address is useless. Whoever this blogger is, he or she isn't stupid enough to leave a trace. If they were, the NFL would have found him or her already. We need to catch the person feeding the blogger info about the Blaze."

He stood up. Shay could tell by his body language he was exasperated. "And just how do you think you're going to do that, Texas?"

"Well, maybe we could plant something in your locker. Something so inflammatory that the snitch won't be able to resist." Shay was actually getting into the idea as she paced her small apartment.

"Like what?" His tone indicated he was well past annoyed.

Shannon gnawed on her lower lip as Brody contemplated her, hands on his hips. His eyes were mere slits in his gorgeous face.

"I haven't figured that out yet. But it has to be something really good." She paced another lap before stopping short in front of him, a gem of an idea popping into her head. "Do you have any sex toys?"

The look on Brody's face could almost be construed as comical. "What? Hell no!" He stammered. "I don't need any toys." His jaw was like granite as he waved a finger in her face. "And believe me, the women I've been with don't need toys either."

Shannon rolled her eyes. She should have known he'd start stomping around like a gelded stallion on her. Heck, it wasn't like she was questioning Brody's ability to perform— on or off the field. But her plan had merit and it just might work. All she had to do was narrow down who has access to the locker room and eliminate suspects.

"I guess I could order one online," she said, thinking through her strategy out loud.

"Like hell you will," Brody blustered. "It's a stupid plan and it won't work. Not to mention it's totally embarrassing to have something like . . . that in my locker."

"That would be the point, Brody. We need something pretty dramatic."

Brody narrowed his eyes at her. "Forget about it, Shannon. I'm not going to do it."

She contemplated him with a measuring glance. "Fine. I'll do it."

"I said no!" Gone was the playful man-child. Brody had transformed into full alpha male on her in two minutes flat.

"Look," Shannon said. "The snitch needs to be caught. We can rule out players and coaches or anyone within the organization who doesn't need money. But it has to be someone with easy access to the locker room, so it's definitely a person associated with the team. Do you want to catch this person or not?"

Brody scrubbed a hand down his face. "Yeah, I want the snitch caught."

"So you'll do it?"

"Damn it, Shannon. Can't you leave the detective work to the professionals?"

"No. And admit it, my logic is correct. Whoever is doing this is doing it for the money."

"Which brings us right back to you, as the prime suspect."

Shay felt the wind leave her sails. Was this man never going to believe her? But she wasn't giving up that easily. Not when she had her innocence to prove.

Crossing her arms over her chest, she went toe-to-toe with Brody. "I don't need your help with this. I can do this on my own."

He grabbed her by the shoulders, gently shaking her. "Damn it, Shannon, don't you ever do what anyone tells you to do?"

She jerked her chin higher. Brody's blue eyes glared at

her as his fingers massaged her shoulders. As her limbs started relaxing beneath his hold, she felt her eyelids drifting shut.

"No chasing after the snitch," he demanded softly. "No sex toys. No phone sex."

Shay's lids snapped open. "Phone sex? Who said anything about phone sex?" The mere words sent titillating spikes of heat to her girl parts.

Brody released her with a jerk, his face a picture of bewilderment and embarrassment. "Jesus," he muttered as he took a big step back. "Forget it. That's not what I meant. You just had me all fired up, that's all." He shoved his fingers through his hair.

"Maybe you should call a nine hundred number or something." Shay tried not to sound too disappointed at the possibility of him chatting up another woman about sex.

He snatched his sweatshirt off the sofa. "I don't need a nine hundred number. What I need is a full-service girlfriend."

"Fine," Shay said, wrapping her arms around her body to keep it from trembling. "End our agreement and go out and get yourself one."

He stood stone-faced, staring at her, and Shay realized that even though he'd blackmailed her into it, she'd be disappointed if their arrangement ended. She tried to tell herself it was because of her research, but she knew that was a lie. The sexy man filling the space of her small apartment excited her and she reveled in being needed by such a man, even if it was just for food.

Brody finally broke the charged silence. "No. This whole thing was my idea. It's working out—most of it anyway. This is the last year in my contract and I need to put up stellar numbers. For that, I need my blood sugar staying level. So our little agreement stands. We just need to set a few more ground rules."

Shay arched an eyebrow at him.

"No more touching and no more sex talk."

Dropping her hands to her side in exasperation, Shay

opened her mouth to remind him that he was the one who'd been initiating their kisses.

"Whoa there, Texas. You started it tonight. Both times," he said as if he'd read her thoughts.

She slammed her mouth closed in embarrassment.

"I came by to tell you that I'll be in Boston all day tomorrow. I have the meal plan you left for me. If I have to deviate, I'll text you with what's available so you can advise me." He headed for the door. "And Shannon, no more playing Nancy Drew. Leave the investigating to the professionals. I'll touch base when I get back. Until then, behave."

He was out the door before she could get out a retort about his heavy-handedness. Brody Janik may be blackmailing her into doing his bidding but he was most definitely not the boss of her. Still, when he'd been giving his reasons why he wouldn't break the arrangement, he hadn't mentioned anything about not trusting her any longer. A little bloom of happiness started to unfurl in Shay's belly. She allowed herself to enjoy the glow for a moment. Reality would set in soon enough.

THE GIRLFRIENDS' GUIDE TO THE NFL

The season is heating up, ladies. And so are your favorite men of the gridiron. Several Miami players were caught sizzling after dark with a trio of exotic dancers early this morning. According to sources, the guys were working on their "footwork." No word on whether this extra training was sanctioned by their position coaches or not.

In Denver, a few wide receivers are not only tearing it up on the field, but they're tearing up speeding tickets as well. Rumor has it that Denver's Finest will look the other way in exchange for a few choice seats to a home game. Too bad all police don't operate on the barter system.

Things are noticeably quiet with the WAGs (wives and girlfriends) in the league. Even our favorite Blaze tight end has managed to keep his romantic escapades from reaching our ears. Of course, that's probably because his current piece of arm candy isn't very tasty. But we're hearing some whispers of big news coming out of Minnesota concerning one player's love interest. Keep watching this space for details.

Ten

"**I worry about you, sweetie.**" Her mama's voice sounded pensive on the other end of the phone. "You work so hard. You must be exhausted. Are you takin' care of yourself?"

"I'm fine, Mama." Shay stirred some honey into her tea. "And I'm not working any harder than you do."

It was a sad state of affairs that most of her conversations with Mama took place during the *Late Show with David Letterman*. Both mother and daughter typically burned the candle at both ends.

June Dowling Everett hadn't been prepared for life as a struggling businesswoman. The former beauty pageant contestant had grown up the pampered daughter of the mayor of Lake Hamilton, Texas, and a former first runner-up for Miss Texas. Shay's paternal grandmother, Meemaw, used to say that with those bloodlines, it was a wonder that only one of her granddaughters had a lick of beauty.

When June's parents were killed in a tragic boat accident, the eighteen-year-old dropped out of college and quickly married the small town's favorite son, rodeo rider Dusty

Everett. The two led a charmed life for nearly twelve years. They enjoyed minor celebrity status in Lake Hamilton, as the small town morphed into a sleepy east Dallas suburb. Dusty traveled the rodeo circuit eight months out of the year while his pretty wife and twin daughters held down the home front.

The fairy tale ended when Shay and her sister were ten and their daddy suffered a debilitating brain trauma resulting from the strike of a horse's hoof to his head. Dusty's injury not only brought with it major medical expenses, but a few secrets as well. One of them an eighteen-month-old son he'd been hiding in Oklahoma.

Instead of crumbling beneath the shame of her husband's infidelity and an onslaught of debt—including child support for her husband's son—the thirty-year-old June took the bull by the horns and faced the situation head on. She'd figured out a way to make the money she needed to provide for her daughters, care for her husband and honor his debts by building up her hair salon business from the sunporch of their home to a three-thousand-square-foot facility that housed twelve stylists. Shay was proud of her mama and how she'd taken on such responsibility. It was June's work ethic that she emulated.

"I just wish you didn't have to accept that job." The regret in her mama's voice was palpable. "I know you're doing it to help me, but your Meemaw is unforgivable in her meddling."

Shay knew Mama's greatest regret in the whole unfortunate situation with her father was that she'd been forced to move her mother-in-law into their house to care for her husband and daughters. *Meddling* wasn't strong enough of a word to describe Shay's narcissistic grandmother.

"It's a federal job, with great pay and benefits. In this economy, I'm lucky to find a job at all." If she kept repeating it, maybe she'd believe it. "Besides, we agreed the only way to secure the loan to make the rest of the childcare payments is with my income."

"You'll be running a kitchen in a prison!" Mama's voice was tinged with despondency.

Shay tried not to cringe at the thought. "Yeah, I know, but it's only for a year and I'll be at home. It's been so long since I've lived with you and Daddy. How is he?" she asked softly. The subject of her father was still a tender one fourteen years later.

"The same," her mama said with resignation. The state had deemed Daddy fit to live at home as long as someone watched him every day. Meemaw cared for him just as she'd done when he was a little boy, dressing him, feeding him, and changing his diaper. Daddy wasn't bedridden, just unresponsive. Mostly he just sat and watched television or stared out the window. It didn't seem fair that Mama had to be burdened with him, but a private facility was out of the question both because it was too expensive and Meemaw wouldn't allow it. "Teryn was by last weekend and that always perks him up."

Shay wasn't surprised. Her daddy had always favored her sister. A weak smile never failed to touch his eyes when he gazed at Teryn. If he recognized Shay when he looked at her, he never let on.

"She was very curious about your new boyfriend."

"You didn't tell her anything, did you?" Shay had told her mama about her arrangement with Brody, leaving out the part about him blackmailing her, however. Her mama didn't need to worry any more than she already was about securing the loan.

"No way," Mama laughed. "It was nice to see the girl have her comeuppance, finally. Let her think you have a hot stud for a boyfriend. Meemaw allowed her to live in the limelight for too long. It's your turn, now."

Shay swallowed around the lump in her throat. Teryn may share their mama's killer good looks, but Shay knew she and Mama shared a lot more, including a more realistic outlook on life.

"Thanks, Mama, but the relationship's not real. I'm just doing a job."

"Well, if that boy doesn't see how much you have to offer, then he's a dang fool."

"I don't think either of us should get our hopes up," she said as she fingered the sex toy catalog she'd picked up at a store near campus. Just reading the descriptions of some of the "toys" in the catalog made her sweaty. *And agitated.* No wonder Brody said he would be embarrassed to have the glossy pages in his locker. He'd claimed he didn't need any of these things to make a woman happy. Shay quivered just thinking what exactly Brody could do to make *her* happy.

"You okay there, Shay?" Her mama's question pulled Shay out of the sensual fantasy with a start. She shoved the catalog into the folder with her paperwork accepting the job at the prison so she wouldn't have to look at either.

"I'm here, just woolgathering. You get some sleep, Mama. I'll talk to you tomorrow, okay?"

"G'night, Shay. Don't stay up too late studying, ya hear? Love you, baby girl."

"Love you too, Mama."

Shay disconnected and stared at her cell phone. As it had for nearly a week now, her mind wandered to the subject of phone sex. What exactly constituted phone sex? Brody had been emphatic that there would be no phone sex between them, so she wasn't likely to find out. Trouble was, Shay suddenly wanted to know a whole lot more about it.

Brody's father eyed him carefully over a plate of chicken wings. "You're looking a little pale there, Brody. You okay?"

No, he wasn't okay. It had been unusually warm on the field for late September, and the heat had drained him. His blood sugar tanked at halftime, but Shannon had anticipated the weather, leaving him extra oranges and a protein shake in the training room. The woman was a veritable Mary Poppins. *A very sexy Mary Poppins.*

"Just a little dehydrated, Dad." Brody took a pull of his water, making sure to avoid his dad's clinical gaze. "I didn't take enough fluid during the game."

"You wouldn't have known by the way you played today,

Brody. Twelve receptions with two of them for touchdowns. My fantasy football team might have a chance this week with that performance." His brother-in-law, Mark, saluted him with his bottle of beer.

"I can't believe Garrett had to miss the game," Skip, his sister Gwen's husband, said. "I still don't get why the poor schmo had to be there for the shower."

Brody, his father, and his two brothers-in-law were having dinner on the patio of a local bar after the Blaze had soundly defeated the New York Jets a few hours earlier. The males of the Janik family jumped at the excuse of a football game to escape Boston in order to avoid his sister's bridal shower.

"It ought to be a crime to make a guy go to his fiancée's shower," Skip said.

"Speaking of fiancées, Rob Henshaw and his girlfriend set a date for their wedding. It's next spring some time." His father was obviously on a mission of some kind because he'd sooner know when Robbie was getting married as he'd know his wife's shoe size. "First Tricia and then Robbie. Your mother and Joyce Henshaw will be looking for another wedding to plan."

"Jeez, Dad, I hope you're more subtle when you're giving your patients a root canal." Brody chewed on a chicken wing.

His father had the grace to laugh. "Okay, I promised your mother I'd mention it. You boys are my witnesses." He glanced at Skip and Mark. "Sybil will just have to wait a few more years for another wedding."

"Mom does know she still has another unmarried child, right? Even better, Bridgett is a girl. Mom would have free rein to plan the entire thing."

Mark coughed to cover his laugh while Skip openly snickered. Brody's father sighed heavily. "It's going to take a special man to put up with your sister."

"What your dad is trying to say as kindly as only a father can is that Bridgett is a ball buster. She's brilliant and gorgeous and sometimes that isn't the best combination in a woman, if you know what I mean," Skip said.

Brody waited for his dad to argue with Skip, to defend Bridgett, but his father just shrugged as he reached for another chicken wing. *Was this how Shannon's family felt about her?* In Brody's opinion, his sister wasn't any prettier than Shannon. Bridgett just had a bit more fashion sense and a lot more disposable income. Both women were uncannily bright—Bridgett graduated fourth in her class from Harvard Law—and determined to be successful. *And stubborn.* He recalled a time when his sister refused to dissect a frog in biology, claiming it was inhumane. Brody had been the only one in a family full of dentists to side with Bridgett back then. He smiled at the memory, thinking that Shannon would easily relate with the same mulish determination.

"Anything else Mom needs to know?" Brody asked.

The trio of men went silent for a moment. He let his gaze circle the table from his brothers-in-law to his dad.

"Well, your mother is a little upset that you're not bringing your new girlfriend to Tricia's wedding," his dad said sheepishly.

Brody tossed his finished chicken wing into the bone bowl. "It's a little early in the relationship for that. Everyone knows you don't bring a woman to a family wedding unless it's serious."

"So this is just a casual thing then?" Obviously, his father was given strict instructions from the coven of Janik women to somehow quantify his relationship with Shannon. Brody declined to comment, crunching on a celery stick instead.

"Those are the best kind," Skip said. "Especially when she's pulling double duty as his own personal chef."

Brody made a mental note to speak with Gwen about how much of his private life she shared with the rest of the family. He also didn't like the way Skip trivialized his relationship with Shannon.

Disappointment flickered in his dad's eyes. "You're not using that girl, are you Brody?"

Mark chimed in before Brody could answer. "Dan, it's what they call a mutually beneficial relationship." He grinned and it was all Brody could do to keep his dinner down as his brother-in-law added: "I'm sure the woman is very happy to oblige."

His dad slumped back in his chair, disheartened, and suddenly Brody was angry. Mark and Skip made him sound like a jerk celebrity jock who used women and Brody was getting tired of being portrayed as that guy. He was more than that. Problem was he just hadn't figured out exactly what he was yet. He did know one thing: the last thing he wanted to do was hurt Shannon. Or let down his parents.

Shay was late. Nate had insisted she stay thirty minutes longer to help in the kitchen because the league brass was visiting the Blaze offices and, on the off chance they might want coffee from the commissary, he'd made her stick around while he headed off to practice. The team practiced most of Wednesday afternoon each week before breaking out into various classrooms to study film and review that week's game plan. The sessions normally lasted well into the evening.

But Shay was glad she'd been forced to hold down the fort. As she was rushing to her car to hightail it to her seniors water aerobics, she'd overheard Donovan Carter speaking with one of the league security people. The Blaze and several other teams were implementing tight restrictions on access to their locker rooms as a result of the blogger's latest post. For their road trip this weekend, the Blaze would only be allowing players, coaches, trainers, and team officials in the locker room area. If she wanted to plant a morsel for the snitch, this would be the perfect time to do it in order to narrow down the suspects. Now all she needed to do was convince Brody to go along with her plan.

Stopping at Santoni's after her swim class, she'd picked up the ingredients for stir-fry. She and Brody had been avoiding one another since the night in her apartment more than a week ago. Shay usually fixed his dinners and snacks at her place, leaving them in his fridge while he was at afternoon practice. So far, their arrangement was working well. But tonight, she needed to speak to him in person, to persuade him to plant something in his locker, and that meant cooking at his house.

Struggling with a bag of groceries and her book bag, Shay punched the code to Brody's door. The sound of a whistling teakettle greeted her as she rounded the corner from the mudroom to the kitchen. She stopped in her tracks at the sight of an elegant woman standing in front of the stove as if she belonged there.

"Hello." Flawless makeup and beautifully styled long blond hair made pinpointing the woman's age difficult. If Shay were gambling on it, she'd guess late twenties, early thirties. The woman's business suit was designer and it fit her petite frame to perfection. She'd shed her shoes some- where else in the house, standing in Brody's kitchen in her stocking feet as if it was her right.

The mystery woman was everything Shay wanted to be when she grew up. But as evidenced by her own chlorinated hair and her shabby sweats, she still had a long way to go.

"Um, hi," Shay managed.

Brody had said something about his family visiting often. Could this be one of his sisters? He usually warned her when one of the Janiks was in town, though. Suddenly, Shay was hit with another uncomfortable realization: maybe this woman was a former girlfriend? Or worse, a current one?

"I'm Bridgett." Mystery woman poured water into a mug she had no trouble locating.

"I'm Shannon. But everybody calls me Shay." Neither woman offered up a handshake. She glanced at the bag of groceries in Shay's hands.

"I'm Brody's personal chef." Shay thought before the woman made her out to be a vagrant, she best explain her presence in Brody's kitchen.

The woman's eyes were calculating as they studied her over the rim of her mug.

"But not his girlfriend?"

"No, um, I mean, yeah, I'm that, too." Shay sounded horribly unconvincing. She knew Brody wanted to stick to the girlfriend ruse, but what if this woman *was* a jilted lover and had come to exact some sort of revenge? Suddenly she started to feel a little shaky.

The woman gave her a shrewd smile. "Interesting."

Before Shay had time to calculate ways to defend herself, Brody's voice came booming through the garage. "Bridgett!"

The soles of his sneakers squealed on the hardwood floor as he screeched to a halt in the doorway. Judging by the expression on his face, he didn't expect to see either woman in his kitchen.

"Hey, Shannon."

Shay gave him curt nod before turning to the counter to unpack the groceries.

"I thought you were flying out tonight," he asked Bridgett.

"Fog in Boston." Bridgett blew on her tea. "It's supposed to clear in a few hours. I should get out by nine."

Brody fisted his hands on his hips as he contemplated both women.

"So, you two have met."

Shay nodded, not bothering to mention she only knew the woman's name, but not who she was.

Bridgett perched herself on one of the barstools. "We've established that she's your personal chef and maybe your girlfriend."

Brody mumbled something. "Ignore my sister's third degree, Shannon. She's an overachieving lawyer who likes to harass people."

Letting out a breath of relief that Bridgett was his sister, Shay began to slice up the vegetables for stir-fry.

Bridgett laughed. "I thought maybe we could grab some dinner, but I can see you've already got plans."

"I bought enough for two," Shay said before realizing her mistake.

Brody narrowed his eyes at her.

"Interesting," Bridgett repeated. "You're not eating with him?"

"Um, no, not tonight." She looked anxiously at Brody for rescue, but he was no help. "I have a class to teach at the pool," she lied.

Bridgett studied them both before deliberately placing her mug on the bar. "All right out with it. Tell me he's at least paying you to cook for him, Shay?"

"Uhh . . ." Shay stammered.

"None of your business," Brody growled at his sister.

"And please, don't tell me the commodity he's offering is sex, because, ick, he's my little brother and the thought of that just disgusts me." She shuddered. "What's more, you're not his usual type. I suspect there's actually more than a bubble between your ears. So what's he got on you?"

"Dammit, Bridgett, leave her alone! Keep your nose out of my business."

Bridgett ignored her brother, peppering Shay instead. "My brother is Tom Sawyer incarnate. He can persuade people to do whatever he wants just by batting his eyelashes. But I know you're not his girlfriend. So what are you doing in his kitchen cooking his meals? And what the heck do you need a personal chef for anyway, Brody? You never cared how nutritious your food was before. What gives?"

"She is too my girlfriend!"

Shay's heart was beating out of her chest at the vehemence of Brody's declaration. Heck, she almost believed him. But she knew he wanted to distract his sister from her other line of questioning: the one about his diet.

"No way, Brody. You've been in this kitchen five minutes and you've both been dancing around the room as if you're afraid of being in the same space together. Furthermore, you call her Shannon when"—she did a passable imitation of Shay—"everyone calls her Shay. Isn't that right, Shay?"

"Sorry, Nancy Grace, you're not right this time." Charging across the room at Shay, he pinned her against the fridge. "Play along," he said before his mouth took hers in a savage kiss.

Shay had no time to react. Brody was kissing her so deeply it was almost if he wanted to lay claim to every part of her. Trapped between his hard hot body and the cool stainless steel of the refrigerator, her own body had no trouble *playing along*. Trailing her hands over his pecs, she swiped her tongue against his. He groaned deep in his throat as his arousal pressed against her lower belly. Shay's own sensitive parts throbbed and she brought her hips closer to his. Her fingers were on his scalp now, a piece of her own wild hair catching in the stubble of his five o'clock shadow as their kiss became more urgent.

"Okay! That's enough. You're grossing me out here." Bridgett's voice permeated their passionate fog. "Please don't make me spray you two down with the kitchen faucet hose."

Brody broke the kiss, but he didn't move away, which Shay was thankful for. She wasn't sure she could stand if he released her. Touching his forehead to hers, they both took a moment to regulate their breathing. She couldn't read his eyes—they were contemplating the floor at the moment— but she had a nice view of his full lips wearing a satisfied smile. His fingertips had found their way beneath her sweatshirt and they were drawing lazy circles on her skin just above her hips. Shay knew it was all an act but she couldn't help dreaming of what might happen if his sister wasn't standing five feet away.

"You've only proved that the two of you are hot for each other like a pair of rabbits, but I'm not sticking around for any more evidence."

Bridgett had apparently found her shoes because she was tapping across the floor toward the door.

"But Brody, my purpose for getting together tonight was to warn you about the litany of single women awaiting you at Tricia's wedding."

Brody groaned, moving his head off Shay's to bang it on the refrigerator door. The move gave Shay's lips access to his neck and she had to bite the inside of her check to keep from kissing him there. Or possibly licking him.

"There's a list of at least eight eligible bachelorettes although I've warned them about keeping Megan Riley on it because she's only seventeen and that would leave you vulnerable for all things statutory in nature. Consider yourself warned." The garage door opened. "It was nice to meet you, Shay. Please don't be a fool and lose your heart over this idiot."

Eleven

Brody heard his sister slam out of the kitchen, but he couldn't seem to take his hands off Shannon. Her breath was warm against his neck and he wanted nothing more than to seal his mouth over hers and finish what they'd both started. He didn't even care if they made it to the bedroom; the kitchen floor would work just fine.

"She's gone now." Her raspy voice caressed his ear. She squirmed against him and Brody couldn't keep the hiss from escaping as his hard-on got unbelievably harder.

He turned his head so his lips rested just beneath the shell of her ear, her pulse beating steadily against his mouth. "Hold still before you frickin' kill me," he groaned, breathing in the wildflower scent of her skin.

"We're not having sex, Brody." Too bad she didn't sound as sure of herself as she had the first time she'd said that to him.

His hand slid up over the bare skin beneath her sweatshirt. She shivered as his thumb grazed her pebbled nipple. "Parts of you are saying otherwise."

She let out a lusty sigh that was nearly his undoing. "Those parts don't get a vote."

Apparently her brain was doing a better job ignoring the rest of her body than his was.

Her voice trembled. "I'm not sleeping with a man who's blackmailing me. One who doesn't trust me."

And there was the crux of their problem. No matter how great the sexual attraction was, neither trusted the other. Brody had already slept with too many women happy to sell out intimate details to the highest bidder. Shannon knew his most damaging secret. Taking her to bed would just give her more reason to share his secrets when he broke up with her.

"You're right. I don't trust you." He felt dejected as he said it.

Again, he banged his head against the refrigerator. Slowly slipping his hands out from under her clothing, he patted her sweatshirt down. Shannon ceased kneading his lower back, one-by-one slapping her palms against the stainless steel door. Her breathing was still a bit shallow as he stepped away, avoiding all eye contact. Staggering to the sink, Brody sloshed his face with cold water. Definitely not the part of him that needed it, but he'd have to make do under the circumstances.

When he turned back toward Shannon, she was chopping vegetables again, her hand on the knife trembling slightly. Brody felt like an ass for revving her up like that, but he'd needed to get Bridgett off his case. His sister was way too intelligent. Once she got hold of something, she was like a terrier, not letting go until she discovered what's inside. A lot like the woman standing in front of him.

Shannon chewed on her bottom lip. "If we caught the snitch, we wouldn't have trust issues anymore."

Yep, definitely like Bridgett.

Brody grimaced. "Not this again," he said, leaning a hip against the countertop.

She looked over her shoulder at him, trepidation in her whiskey eyes. "I'm serious, Brody. This would be the perfect weekend to try it. I heard Mr. Carter talking with the staff from the league office. All the teams are restricting access to their locker rooms until the blog site is identified. With an away game, that means we could narrow down the suspect pool significantly."

"*If* the snitch takes the bait."

Apparently, that was all the go-ahead she needed. She grabbed a manila envelope out of her book bag. "There's a store right near campus. All we have to do is pick something out of this catalog . . ."

"Jesus, Mary, and Joseph!" Brody roared as she waved a color catalog of sex toys in his face like a red flag in front of a charging bull. "I was this close"—he held up his thumb and forefinger scant millimeters apart—"to jumping your bones a minute ago and now you shove this thing at me. Just what are those two people doing on the cover, anyway?" Forget the cold shower; now he needed a long swim in an icy pond.

Shannon tried to cram the catalog back into the envelope, but Brody grabbed it out of her hands. "This stuff is disgusting," he said thumbing through the slick pages featuring cock rings, vibrators, and various restraints. His jockey shorts were getting tighter with each page he eyed. He looked up into her mulish face. "Tell me you didn't go into a store that sells this . . . smut?" he demanded.

"And if I did?"

Her answer angered him and excited him at the same time. "I told you already, I'm not displaying a *sex toy* in my locker for some snitch and all my *teammates* to see!"

"For pity's sake, Brody. If you're that chicken, just put the catalog in your locker. You obviously find it arousing." She glanced down at his shorts. "Maybe the snitch will, too."

Brody felt the muscles in the back of his neck squeezing off the oxygen to his brain. "No." He tried to cram the catalog back into the envelope, but there were other papers inside of it. Shannon's face went white as he pulled them out. "What the hell is this?"

A tussle ensued as Shannon tried to retrieve the document. She was all Texas wildcat, but Brody was stronger and she ended up pinned against the refrigerator again. Only this time, he was the only one turned on. The passion reflected in her eyes was definitely anger, and if he was reading her right, a little bit of embarrassment. She tried to wiggle free, but he held her fast as he scanned the pages in his hand.

"Holy shit," he whispered. All the fight left her body and she went limp against him. "This says you're going to work at a prison." Brody couldn't believe the words coming out of his mouth. "I don't understand."

"What's to understand," she said crisply. "Prisoners have got to eat, too."

He shifted his weight, pushing her into the stainless steel door while summoning his caveman. "You can't work in prison."

"Ooooof!" Shannon yelled, jabbing her nails into his chest to shove him off her. Tears were leaking from her eyes. "Says the man who has everything. Who's never had to work for a thing in his *life*!" She jerked the papers from his fingers and waved them in his face. "This, *this job*, will ensure my mama gets to keep her livelihood. A situation you or your family has never faced. And you never will face with your gobs of money!" She stabbed a finger into his shoulder. "The rest of the world wasn't born with your gifts"—she practically spat the word out at him—"of good looks, affluence, and athletic ability. The rest of us have to carve out whatever we want." She shoved the papers back into her book bag. "Some of us are so desperate for money that we'll do things we know we shouldn't. Yes, I was in that locker room that night, but I couldn't go through with it. I don't care if you believe me anymore, Brody." She swiped a tear off her cheek. "The terms of your blackmail only require me to make sure you eat a nutritiously balanced diet. But you have no say-so in what I do with the rest of my life!"

She turned back to the cutting board and began to furiously chop up the remaining vegetables. Brody dragged his hands through his hair. He didn't dare move a muscle near her, fearful of what she'd do with the knife.

Shannon was right, he didn't understand what drove her. The perfect bubble he lived his life in insulated him from the type of drama she persevered through every day. Not for the first time, Brody wondered what his life would have been like if he'd grown up more like her. What type of man would he have become outside of football?

She moved to slicing the chicken, her breath coming in deep gulps. "You know what the sad part is, Brody?" she mumbled. "I would have considered the phone sex thing if you'd agreed to help me."

He had to smile at her tenacity. *And her willingness to fool around.* This woman never gave up on the things she believed in. Her family. Her neighbors. Hard work. And the truth. Brody desperately wanted her to believe in him, too. And, in a moment of pure clarity, he knew what he had to do.

Still wary of the knife, he carefully stepped behind her, bracketing his hands on the counter on either side of her and rested his head on her shoulder. "We're not having phone sex."

Her whole body slumped in dejection.

Brody smiled against the delicate skin on her neck. "You're not that woman who trades sexual favors in exchange for something else, Shannon. And phone sex, if it's done well, is definitely a sexual favor."

Shannon's breath became more fractured.

"I'll tell you what I am going to do," he murmured against her ear. "I'll agree to plant something in the locker room this weekend to catch the snitch."

She let out a squeal and Brody grabbed the knife before she could accidently impale him.

"On one condition," he continued and her shoulders slumped again. Her reaction nearly made him laugh as he nuzzled her jaw. "If I have to embarrass myself in front of my teammates, you have to be my date to my sister's wedding."

She spun around in his arms, the close contact of her body making him groan again.

"You want me to go to your sister's wedding with you? As your date?"

"Well, more like as my human shield."

"I'm guessing this isn't being held at the VFW?"

"No, it's at some prissy four-star inn in Vermont. Does it matter?"

She shoved him again and Brody took a step back. Embarrassment flooded her whiskey eyes. "I can't do it, Brody. I don't have the clothes. Judging by your sister's outfit, I could never afford the clothes your family would expect of your date."

"Why are you women always so concerned with what you have to wear?"

"Says the man whose sister lays out his clothes for him each day so he looks good."

He sighed in resignation as he rubbed the back of his neck. "No problem. I happen to have a good friend who loves playing fairy godmother to Cinderella."

Shannon opened her mouth to protest, but Brody laid a finger across her lips.

"And I'm paying. For everything. Buy whatever you need and keep them as payment for being my date."

"That sounds more like *Pretty Woman* than *Cinderella*," she said around his finger.

Brody couldn't respond, he was so aroused by her lips brushing against his fingertip.

She stepped back farther, crossing her arms over her chest. "And you promise you'll put the catalog in your locker?"

"Oh, I didn't say my locker, Texas." He rocked back on his heels as her eyes narrowed to slits. "I'll be putting it in another player's locker."

"Whose?" she demanded.

"If I tell you, we won't be eliminating you as a suspect." He pulled her in closer. "And I really want to eliminate you as the snitch."

Her eyes shone with relief and a little bit of hunger. Suddenly, he wanted nothing more than to prove her innocence. It wouldn't solve the bigger problem of her knowing about his illness, but he'd deal with one thing at a time.

"I need to go take a shower. A long cold one."

She gnawed on her lower lip and nodded.

"Leave me the catalog, Shannon. And take some of that home to eat." He brushed a damp spot from beneath her eye.

"I'm sorry I'm such a conundrum, Brody," she whispered.

Brody kissed the tip of her nose. "I already told you, Shannon, I like conundrums."

The scene that greeted Brody when he arrived the following evening at Will Connelly's loft apartment was one of such pure domestic bliss he had to stifle his gag reflex. Two of the league's most ruthless players had been reduced to lovesick puppies. William the Conqueror Connelly was frolicking on the floor with his six-month-old son, belly-farting the baby, who shrieked with laughter in response. The Devil of the NFL, Shane Devlin, was cramped on the end of the sofa, massaging his pregnant wife's feet.

"Wow, if this is a hot night in Married Land, count me out."

Connelly lifted his son off the floor and tossed him in the air. "Julianne, didn't I tell you to take away Brody's key?"

"I did take his key away," Connelly's wife said as she carried a tray of desserts to a table beside the sofa.

"Then how'd he get in?"

Julianne's amber eyes sparkled as she stretched up on her tiptoes to kiss Brody on the cheek. "I let him in," she said with a smile. "Now, stop throwing Owen like that before he throws up on you." She steered Brody toward a chair. "Help yourself to a cannoli, Brody. I just made them."

His mouth watered at the sight of the cream-filled dessert. Julianne was as much a genius in the kitchen as she was a fashion designer, but tomorrow was Friday, a heavy practice day, and he couldn't afford to tamper with his blood sugar.

"Brody's on a diet," Devlin said, saving him from an awkward moment with Julianne, who took it personally if anyone refused her offering of food.

Carly Devlin looked up from her throne of pillows on the sofa. "A diet?" She patted her baby bump. "Great. The man with the perfect body is on a diet while I grow to be as big as a house."

Her husband placed his hand over hers on her belly. "Carly, you're beautiful. You're just tired. Especially if you think his body is more perfect than mine."

Connelly laughed.

Carly beamed at her husband. "You're right, I'm definitely confused. But I'll need to do some more research later."

The couple stared at one another, silently communicating their thoughts and affection. The intimate byplay made Brody squirm with discomfort.

"Brody's new girlfriend has him on a special diet," Connelly teased. "Its purpose, apparently, is to enhance his performance."

Both women arched an eyebrow at the sexual innuendo as their husbands laughed. Owen rocked on his hands and knees, trying unsuccessfully to crawl to Brody's shoelace. Scooping the baby onto his lap, Brody let him gum the string on his hoodie.

"Laugh all you want, but my reception rating is the best in the league right now." The two men could rib him all night, but Brody's play on field spoke for itself. His game was at its peak thanks to Shannon's nutritional assistance.

Devlin nodded in acquiescence before taking a swallow from his coffee mug. "Of course, you're just standing there catching the ball."

"All right, you two, leave Brody alone." Julianne made herself comfortable on the floor, leaning her back against her husband's wide chest. Connelly's arms closed around her as his lips found her mahogany hair. "What's wrong, Brody? When you called, you said it was important," she asked.

This was the tricky part. Julianne would happily help Shannon pick out clothes, in fact, she'd revel in it. But executing the second part of his plan was more delicate and Julianne's help was crucial for it to work.

"Actually, I was wondering if I could speak with you alone a minute."

All four pairs of eyes homed in on him. Julianne's and

Carly's were intrigued. Devlin's, not so much. And Connelly's—the master of the caveman persona—were wary.

"I thought we were through with you having private conversations with my wife!"

Julianne patted her husband on the chest. "Down boy." She got to her feet, lifting Owen off Brody's lap. "Come on, Brody. We can discuss your girl problems upstairs while I get this little one in his pajamas."

He stood to follow her, wondering when he'd become so easy to read. He hadn't mentioned Shannon or any other woman when he'd called.

"I warned you to be nice to Shay, Brody." Connelly narrowed his eyes at him.

"The team took a vote," Devlin teased. "If you two break up, it's you who has to leave. How's she at running a fade route?"

Brody flipped them both off as he climbed the narrow stairs leading up to the loft's bedroom. Julianne laid Owen down on the changing table and began to undress the squirming baby. "Tell me what this is all about, Brody, before Will comes charging up here." She smiled smugly to herself. "Not that I mind when he throws around the testosterone."

Jeez Louise. This entire night was chock-full of TMI. Brody sat on the corner of the king-sized bed his teammate undoubtedly used to *throw his testosterone around* in before springing back to his feet to pace the room.

"You know my sister is getting married next weekend," he began.

"Of course I do, Brody. I designed her gown, remember?" She eyed him quizzically from over her son's naked belly. "Will and I are guests, too. The inn is supposed to be gorgeous." She kissed Owen's feet. "And this little guy is going to stay with Grandma and Hank."

Damn. How did he not know that? Probably because he didn't give a crap who his sister invited to her wedding. Except all the single women queued up to dance with him.

As if the weekend wouldn't be awkward enough. He and Shannon would not only have his family to convince they were dating, but his über-observant teammate as well.

Brody shoved a hand through his hair. "Perfect. Listen, I was wondering if you could help out my date."

Julianne's hands stilled, half the snaps of the baby's onesie undone. "Your mom said you weren't bringing a date."

He stopped his pacing, dumbfounded that his mother was discussing this with more people than just his sisters. "Well I am bringing a date," he said a little too defensively.

Julianne tsked at him, resuming her task. "You need to let your mother know. There's a lot that goes into planning a wedding, Brody. Last-minute surprises won't be appreciated."

Brody processed her reprimand, making a mental note to text his mother later that night. "Got it. Now, will you help me?"

Handing him the now fussy baby, she disappeared into the bathroom to dispose of the diaper and wash her hands. "Of course I will, Brody. But who's the lucky girl?"

"Her name is Shannon. She's a grad student who works for the team."

Julianne's face registered her surprise as she came out of the bathroom drying her hands on a towel. "So the girl from the cafeteria really *is* your girlfriend?"

He sank back down on the corner of the bed, cradling Owen who gummed the ear of a stuffed bunny. "We're involved." It wasn't exactly a lie. Still, he kept his eyes on the baby rather than meet Julianne's shrewd ones.

"I thought you gave up on casual flings? You said you wanted to find a girl who *gets* you?"

Brody wasn't sure if it was the sweet smell of a sleepy baby in his arms or the unabashed happiness and desire he'd witnessed between his friends, but he suddenly felt as if he were suffocating. He wanted something except he didn't know what that something was. "It's gonna be hard to find a woman who gets me if I don't even get myself," he blurted out.

"Oh, Brody," Julianne whispered.

The concern in her eyes frustrated him even more. He

jiggled the whimpering baby. "Look can you just help me, please? For some reason she's hung up on what to wear to the wedding. Can you help her out? Take her shopping."

Understanding dawned on Julianne's face. "Of course I can. We can go to the local discount shops and find something perfect that will fit into her budget."

"No." Brody shook his head. "Not discount. I want her to have the best. I'm paying. Deck her out in whatever she'll need for the weekend. Head to toe."

Julianne's mouth gaped open.

"I want her to be comfortable, Julianne. To not feel . . . ashamed of anything."

A rapturous smile lit up her face and Brody felt like a hypocrite. Yeah, he was blackmailing Shannon into going with him to his sister's wedding, but he did want her to feel good about herself. He wanted to see those whiskey eyes relaxed and shining with happiness.

Julianne patted him on the head. "Brody Janik, you are a sweet, sweet man."

"Well, keep that in mind because I have a second favor to ask and it's a lot more delicate."

Taking the baby from his arms, she pressed a pacifier into Owen's mouth. "Well, you've just given me carte blanche with your credit cards. I guess I can handle one more favor."

Twelve

Shay sat with Emma Richardson in the nearly deserted commissary of the practice facility, the girl's chemistry homework spread out on the table. The rest of the building was a beehive of activity as the players and staff prepared to board the buses that would take them to the team's charter flight to Cleveland later that morning.

"Are you going to the game, too?" Emma asked.

Shay shook her head. "I think my trip to Boston was a one-time thing."

She didn't realize Nate was standing behind her until he spoke. "You got that right. That trip was before I knew about you and Janik being an item. You're benched now, Shannon. I can't risk you fraternizing with one of the star players in the hotel. He needs to be focused on the game."

"Why don't you worry about your own job and stop harassing Shannon about hers, Dumas."

All three of them jumped as Brody and Shane Devlin stood behind the trainer, both men with their game faces on.

"I'm not harassing her, Brody. I'm just doing my job as her supervisor to ensure she sticks to her assigned duties.

As far as I know, sleeping with the players isn't in an intern's job description."

Shane Devlin's legendary reflexes weren't underrated. His arm was out and restraining Brody before Shay could bat an eye.

"If you want to leave this room with all your teeth in your head, Dumas," the quarterback said, his tone brokering no argument, "go find the rest of your staff to supervise. I'm pretty sure this is Shay's day off."

Nate smirked at the two players. "Unlike you players who only have yourselves to look after, I have a staff of twenty to supervise and to keep out of any hanky-panky. It's a lot harder than it looks. I don't tell you how to do your job, Devlin. Don't tell me how to do mine."

Brody mumbled something profane as he took another step toward the trainer. Nate put his hands up. "Save the testosterone for the field, fellas. I'm out."

Shane didn't remove his forearm from Brody's chest until Nate was clear of the commissary.

"That prick's really starting to piss me off," Brody said.

"Yeah, too bad he's the best trainer in the league or none of us would be able to put up with him." Shane walked over and kissed his niece, Emma, on the top of her head.

"He's a turd, Uncle Shane," Emma giggled.

"I'll second that," Brody said, oozing his wicked charm at the teenager. "Emma, can I borrow your tutor a moment?"

Emma nodded, her face spellbound by the impact of Brody's smile.

The power of Brody's charm on people never ceased to amaze Shay. As they made their way out of earshot, she felt her own heart speed up. The Blaze dress code required that players travel in their Sunday best and Brody cut a fine picture dressed in a charcoal designer suit and silk tie. His blue dress shirt made his eyes more vibrant. If clothes made the man, Brody would be ruling the world in his current state of dress.

The charming grin faded as he turned to speak with her. His eyes were weary and Shay couldn't help but express concern. "Brody, is everything okay? Your blood sugar isn't crazy again, is it?"

He shook his head. "No, I'm just annoyed at that . . . turd." Laugh lines fanned out from his eyes and his mouth relaxed. "At least he'll be with us, where he can't bully you."

Relieved, Shay stepped closer so as not to be overheard. "Don't worry about me. Just make sure you stick to the schedule, eating what I wrote down for you every couple of hours, and you'll be fine."

The corners of his mouth turned up as his hands spanned her hips, pulling her closer. "Just in case, you'd better keep your phone with you at all times."

Shay studied the perfect Windsor knot of his tie, her fingers resting on the soft wool of his suit jacket. Their bodies had once again unconsciously ended up only inches apart. "As long as you hold up your end of the bargain."

He sighed. "You'd just better hope it works, because I'm not doing this a second time."

His fingertips slipped inside the waistband of her jeans and she released her own breathy sigh as he gently traced them along her skin.

Need coursed through Shay; the need to find the snitch so she could prove her innocence. Then she'd be able address her other pressing need, the one constantly pulling her into Brody's arms. She didn't want to consider her plan not working. Just as she didn't want to consider that Brody's attentiveness was just an act. It felt way too real, not to mention way too good.

"It has to work," she whispered. Looking up, she studied his face, the desire she saw reflected there nearly made her weep with frustration. Her attention focused on a movement over Brody's shoulder as Nate made another pass through the commissary, obviously hoping to catch her alone. "Maybe if we're lucky, Nate will be the snitch."

Brody chuckled. "That would be too easy. Besides, as irritating as his attitude is, Devlin is right, he is the best in the business."

"Well, he's back for round two." Irritated, Shay tried to step out of Brody's arms, but he held her firm.

"Then we should give him what he expects," he said before he captured her lips in a slow, searching kiss.

Shay didn't bother resisting. She'd been desperate for him to kiss her again since the other night. But this kiss wasn't like the hungry exchanges they'd had before. This time, Brody kissed her as if he had all the time in the world. Heat simmered through her as he slowly explored the inside of her mouth with his tongue. His palm seared the skin on her back where he held her to him.

The scent of his woodsy cologne teased her nostrils as she tugged on his lapels in an effort to shift her body closer. She whimpered deep in her throat as the edge of his arousal nudged against her. Breaking the kiss, Brody gently caressed her cheek.

"Whoa there, Texas."

Shay's chest hurt, her pulse was beating so erratically. Embarrassment and frustration flooded her and her eyes couldn't seem to focus. She tried to break contact with his body, but his fingers dug into her back.

"Shh," he whispered, sounding a lot like her father did years ago when he needed to gentle one of his horses. "It's okay."

Except it wasn't okay and Shay couldn't seem to quiet the maelstrom in her belly and everywhere else below her waistline. Brody put two fingers beneath her chin and lifted her gaze to meet his. She sucked in breath at his anguished expression.

"Aww, Shannon," he groaned before wrapping his hand behind her neck and pulling her mouth in for another kiss.

This time he brought the heat. Pleasure shot through her as she molded her body to his, her fingers searching for skin beneath the soft cotton of his dress shirt. All recollection that they were standing in the corner of the Blaze commissary fled her mind until a female voice behind Brody sifted through her fog of passion.

"Oh my."

Brody swore as he broke the kiss. His hands steadying her shaking body, Shay stepped back to put some distance between them. With a ragged breath, she yanked down her sweater, trying in vain to hide the flush she was sure covered her entire body.

"Umm, Brody, you should probably come up for air. The buses are getting ready to go soon. You don't want to get fined." The stylishly dressed woman standing beside Brody was having a difficult time suppressing a grin of amusement.

"Shit." Brody's voice sounded like Shay felt: wrung out. He turned to the woman and she gave him a smug smile. "Shannon, this is your fairy godmother, Julianne Connelly, better known as JV Designs. Jules, this is Shannon."

Julianne extended her hand, her amber eyes dancing.

"Everyone calls me Shay," she managed to eke out as she shook Julianne's hand.

Julianne contemplated her a moment before nodding. "Shay it is. And can I say that I am thrilled you and your sister are not identical twins. Dressing a trophy isn't much of a challenge. Did anyone ever tell you that you have the body of a classic runway model?"

The only one who'd ever commented on her body had been her Meemaw and that was to tell her she looked like a gangly boy.

"We're going to have lots of fun with those legs of yours." Julianne winked at Brody and he groaned.

"Just remember, Julianne, that you're on my team and not my mother's."

Julianne linked her arm through Shay's. "No, Brody. I'm on Shay's team."

Shay had no idea what the two of them were talking about, but it was reassuring to know that for once in her life she had a team.

"Shoo, Brody. Go catch your bus." Julianne waved him toward the door.

He hesitated a moment, stepping toward Shay as if he was going to kiss her again, before thinking better of it. With a swift nod, Brody hurried out of the commissary.

"Yay, can we go shopping now?" Another teenager had joined Emma at the table. Dressed in animal-print pants and a daring white sweater, the older girl also had a dramatic slash of blue through her blond hair.

"It seems I've recruited two assistants," Julianne explained. "I've been dressing Emma since she was three, and her fashion sense is impeccable. Sophie is my sister-in-law, and don't let her blue hair fool you, she has an exquisite eye for the artistic touches we're going to need to make you shine."

"Hey there," Sophie said with a wave.

Sophie helped Emma pack up her books as Shay studied the woman next to her. Julianne was married to Blaze line-backer Will Connelly, a most unlikely combination if she ever saw one. According to what she'd read on Internet celebrity blogs, the two had conceived a son together and married quickly after the baby was born. Most predicted the marriage wouldn't last, but the few times Shay had seen the couple, they looked very much in love. She wasn't sure why the famous designer had agreed to help Brody, but Shay was grateful nonetheless.

"Thank you for helping me. And Brody. I hope it's not too much of an imposition."

Julianne gave her another one of those I've-got-a-secret smiles, her eyes once again assessing Shay from head to toe.

"It's not an imposition," she finally said. "I'd do anything for Brody."

So would I.

It wasn't until Shay saw the other woman's arched eyebrow and beaming face that she realized she'd said it aloud.

The winds off Lake Erie were icy as the rain pummeled Cleveland's FirstEnergy stadium. It was only the first week of October, but winter had already come calling in the Great Lakes region. The sloppy field made for an even sloppier game. It was the end of the third quarter and the Blaze were up nine to three. For an offensive player, there was nothing worse than having the game decided by the defense and the kickers.

Brody sat on the heated metal bench, a heavy poncho draped over his shoulders during the five-minute television time-out between quarters. A hiss of steam rose up off the bench as Will Connelly sat down next to him, his uniform drenched in mud, sweat, and rain. He shook his head, showering Brody in the process.

"Dude," Brody complained. "Ever heard of a towel?"

Connelly shot him one of his menacing looks before grabbing a warm towel from a bag hauled around by one of the equipment boys who marched up and down behind the bench. "You're such a pretty boy, Brody," he said as he scrubbed at his face. "And I told you not to speak to me again."

Brody scoffed. "Jeez, dude, you'd think I asked you to cut something off. As favors go, mine was pretty painless."

"Painless?" Will glared at him. "Because of your stupid favor, I did have something cut off: sex with my wife. And that was a dirty move involving Julianne in your little scheme."

"Would you have put the catalog in your locker if I hadn't?"

"Hell no! But thanks to you convincing my wife to hold out on me until I put that stupid thing out there, now I've got to listen to a bunch of shit from my teammates."

Brody shrugged. Of all the players on the Blaze, he knew Connelly could easily take a little heat within the locker room. The linebacker had been through much worse just a few months before. Besides, no one on the team would challenge Will Connelly on his toughness. It was his sense of fair play that Brody was counting on.

Connelly chugged down a cup of Gatorade. "What I don't understand is why this whole blogger thing has got your jockstrap all tangled. Your love life has been played out in the media for years and it never seemed to bother you."

Shows what you know, Mr. Ivy League, Brody thought. But he kept his thoughts to himself.

"It's the girl, isn't it," Connelly probed. "This is about Shay."

Brody kept his eyes on the game clock above the opposite sideline. Sixty seconds left in the time-out.

"Hell, Brody, I told you not to hurt that girl."

"What do you think I'm trying to avoid here," Brody snarled, aware too late that he'd given Will the information he wanted.

Forty-five seconds left. Connelly nodded finally. "Good, see that she stays that way."

"Go play in the mud and try to keep them from scoring."

Connelly hefted his helmet back on his head before slapping Brody on the back. "Stay dry, pretty boy. I did your favor and now I'm going to win this game. After that, I'm going home to my warm, welcoming wife."

Brody grimaced.

"You can take your catalog home as a consolation prize," he called as he trotted back onto the field.

Thirteen

Shay felt as though she were having a total out-of-body experience. Standing in the large parlor of the quaint New England inn surrounded by Brody's family and their closest friends, she felt like an imposter. Julianne had had her plucked, waxed, and dyed until she hardly recognized the attractive woman staring back at her from the antique beveled mirror hanging above the roaring fire in the stone fireplace.

Carefully clutching her wineglass so that none of the rich cabernet spilled on the winter-white silk pants Julianne had picked out for her, Shay tried to listen to the boisterous conversation between Brody's sisters. The four women hadn't let her out of their sight since she'd arrived in Vermont earlier in the day.

"So what other stories can we tell you about our darling little brother?" Bridgett linked her arm through Shay's, her smile mischievous. She wasn't sure if the lawyer totally bought into the charade that she and Brody were actually a couple, but his sister was being a good sport and playing along anyway.

"Bridge," Tricia, the bride-to-be, said. "Maybe we should lay off the tales for a while, before poor Shay runs screaming into the woods. Besides, this weekend is supposed to be about me, remember? Brody gets his time in the limelight every other weekend." The twinkle in her blue eyes belied her fake pout and it was easy to see that, despite their unrelenting teasing, the Janik sisters were truly smitten with their younger brother. *The problem was, they weren't the only ones.*

Ever since their heated exchange in the Blaze commissary the previous Saturday, Shay had played least in sight, leaving his meals at his house while he was at practice, thus avoiding Brody all week. They'd exchanged a few text messages about the logistics of the weekend, with Brody flying up separately yesterday so he could work out with his personal trainer and Shay traveling with Julianne and Will Connelly this afternoon, arriving just in time for the rehearsal dinner. Shay wasn't sure, but she thought Julianne had orchestrated their late arrival to achieve some sort of dramatic reveal of her total transformation to Brody. But the fashion designer was unaware that it didn't matter what Shay looked like, nothing was going to happen between her and Brody.

Because her plan had failed.

A fresh wave of disappointment squeezed her stomach at the thought. She'd been so sure the blogger would bite. Only they hadn't. And she and Brody were no further along on their trust issues than they had been a week ago.

Julianne had come clean at the salon the day before, telling Shay her husband had placed the catalog in full view of the locker room in Cleveland. Without her confession, Shay never would have agreed to have her hair highlighted and straightened. But knowing Brody had gone through with his end of the bargain, there was nothing left to do but honor her part—even if it killed her to be so close to him all weekend.

The intense desire that seemed to overtake her whenever she laid eyes on Brody mystified her. Even more surprising: he seemed to feel the same way. Shay wasn't delusional enough to think Brody Janik wanted her in the same way he wanted other women. She still believed his interest was based on the fact she hadn't stripped naked the minute he looked her way. The problem was she didn't care anymore.

After this semester, her life wouldn't be her own; not for a while, anyway. Girls like Shay didn't get chances with guys like Brody. She needed to take hers while she could. If only the blogger had exonerated her by reporting on the sex toys.

Julianne was talking animatedly about Tricia's wedding gown when the skin at the back of Shay's neck began to tingle. She looked toward the doorway to see Brody standing among a throng of men—presumably the groomsmen— who'd been out golfing on the Indian summer afternoon. The caress of his gaze brought a flush to her cheeks. Dressed in black slacks, a tweed sports jacket, and a crisp white shirt open at the neck, he was a devastating sight. He slowly made his way across the room, stopping to greet everyone in his path. It was all she could do not to reach up and run her fingers through his damp hair as he stopped beside her. The smile he greeted her with was warm, if not a little chagrined, and the churning in her belly twisted into a painful ache.

Introductions were made as the rest of the wedding guests joined their circle, but Shay had difficulty concentrating. Her senses drank in not only the sight of Brody, but his clean woodsy scent as well. Feeling a little lightheaded in the now crowded parlor, she released a soft breath. Brody's hand was on her elbow immediately, but his touch caused her to sway on her feet. Tossing one of his most charming smiles over his shoulder, he quickly culled her from the herd, steering toward the butler's pantry that joined the parlor with one of the large dining rooms in the inn.

Shay set her glass down on the counter and ran her fingers through her hair. The silky, straight locks confused her, making her feel more out of place, and she felt tears pooling in her eyes.

"Deep breath," Brody whispered. "You can do this."

"Not if you keep touching me."

His hands had made their way beneath her cashmere sweater and he was slowly massaging her hips. Surprise registered on his face, almost as if his fingers had sought out her bare skin subconsciously. Pulling his hands out, he reached for her wineglass and guzzled its contents. Shay couldn't summon the strength to admonish him.

"I'm sorry your plan didn't work. I really wanted it to." He placed the empty wineglass back on the counter.

That makes two of us.

"Thank you for coming anyway."

Shay shrugged one shoulder. "Julianne went to a lot of effort. And my mama didn't raise me to break a promise."

His lips curved up into a soft smile. Not his usual show-stopper, but one much more intimate. Her breath caught in her chest.

"You look amazing."

"What can I say? Julianne is truly a fairy godmother. Of course, it all wears off at midnight."

"That's okay," he said softly. "I'm pretty fond of the real Shannon."

A lump the size of a boulder formed in her throat, and her body ached with something more than desire now.

"Which means I'll get to see her later tonight."

Shay blinked in confusion.

"Try not to react too ferociously because my lawyer sister has her laser eyes trained on us," he murmured. "But we're sharing that room upstairs."

Hell's bells, how did that part slip by? The gorgeous room she'd been shown to earlier had its own fireplace, a claw-foot tub, and a comfortable divan chair tucked beneath a window dormer. But only one bed. A fluffy four-poster queen-sized model. It seemed she'd be tortured even in her sleep. If she was able to get any, that was.

"My mom pulled a fast one on me and switched us from two double beds. I couldn't make a scene without blowing our cover."

She nodded. "It's a big room with lots of floor space."

"You might have left me some room in the drawers." His teasing roused her out of her panic. "And Julianne should have bought you some lingerie, at least. Those panties of yours look like ones my grandmother might wear."

Shay knew what he was doing and she was grateful. Brody couldn't soothe her with his touch, but he could turn his charm on her. And it was actually working. She could feel her nerves settling beneath the warmth of his playful gaze.

"What I wear beneath my clothes wasn't part of the deal." She crossed her arms over her chest and joined in with his banter.

Brody scoffed. "My bad. It should have been."

She acted as if she hadn't heard him. "It's pretty disgusting to think you actually know what kind of panties your grandmother wears."

He laughed then. "Atta girl. We'll work out the sleeping arrangements later. For now, I just want you to relax and enjoy yourself. You deserve some time off. Oh, and ignore my sisters. They all go on these crazy starvation diets trying to fit into their dresses before a big event and it makes them a little psychotic." He waved his fingers at his head in disgust.

It was Shay's turn to laugh. "Your sisters—your whole family, in fact—are delightful."

"My family is a pain in the ass," he said, his tone lacking any real conviction. "What about your family, Shannon? Surely they're not as overbearing as mine."

Shay considered him a moment. The differences between their two families couldn't have been more pronounced. The Janik family was large, warm, and exuberant in the security only affluence brings. They were the type of happy family most people dreamed of being a part of. Her own family consisted of just the five of them: Mama, Daddy, Teryn, Shay, and Meemaw. No other grandparents, aunts, uncles, or cousins to share the joys—and heartaches—of life. Meemaw was awful, Teryn self-absorbed, her daddy locked in his own world, and her mama surviving the only way she could. They might not have been perfect, but they were all Shay had, and in the end, she answered him the only way she could.

"My family's delightful, too."

Brody's eyes shone. "I couldn't picture you with a family that was anything less."

The lump in her throat was nearly choking her now, but she didn't have time to think about her lie as they were joined by an elderly gray-haired gentleman with bushy black eyebrows shielding twinkling blue eyes, clearly identifying him as a Janik.

"Leave it to my grandson to keep all the pretty girls in a corner to himself." Brody's grandfather reached out a large sun-spotted hand to Shay. A big man who smelled of Altoids and fresh air, it wasn't hard to see where Brody had inherited his charm from. "This boy has too many women falling at his feet. Make a widower's evening and sit next to me at dinner, darlin'." He placed her hand on his sleeve before she even knew what had happened.

Brody shook his head. "Shannon, this is my grandpa, Gus. Gramps, this is Shannon."

Gus was already leading them toward the large dining room. "So, pretty lady, are you a model or an actress?"

"She's a PhD student, Gramps," Brody said from behind them. "She's studying nutrition."

"Pfft," Gus said. "You're too pretty to be a scientist."

Shay laughed in delight as Gus held out a chair for her. Basking in the glow of someone actually noticing her looks before her brains, she thought to herself that she might enjoy this weekend after all.

Dinner was a circus. Brody's nephews and niece took turns scrambling in and out of his lap while he tried to figure out what he should and shouldn't eat. Shannon was no help. If grandpa Gus wasn't chatting her up, one of his evil sisters was monopolizing her attention.

At least she'd begun to relax. He'd been eaten up with guilt—not to mention sexual frustration—all week at having forced her into this situation. Worse, her little plan hadn't worked and they were both back to square one: roommates without benefits. Not that his trust issues were looming that large anymore. The more he got to know her, the more he believed Shannon was incapable of selling him out. He just didn't know where that left them exactly.

Grandpa Gus reclined back in his chair, patting his lean stomach. "Now that was an amazing meal," he said to no one in particular. "My compliments to the chef."

"Yeah, a meal like that makes you want your *own* personal chef," Brody's brother-in-law Skip called out from a table across the room. "Too bad you're not Brody, Gus, or you'd have one."

Shannon fidgeted in the chair next to him.

"Don't tell me you cook like that every night for Brody?" Grandpa Gus's eyes lit up and Brody could tell he was formulating a plan to spend the entire season in Baltimore.

"I'm not that kind of chef," Shannon said demurely. "My meals aren't gourmet, just well-balanced."

There was snickering from some of the other tables as the room quieted to focus on what Shannon was saying. Clearly, his family and friends doubted Shannon and Brody were together because of her cooking skills.

"I've been trying to get Brody to eat nutritiously for twenty-seven years now," his mother chimed in. She raised her water glass in salute to Shannon. "I'm delighted to know that someone succeeded where I couldn't."

He could have kissed his mother for her attempt at trying to diffuse what was becoming an awkward conversation, but her little course correction didn't take.

"No offense, Sybil," Skip said. "But I'm pretty sure Shay has other means of getting Brody to eat nutritiously."

"Skip!" Gwen hissed at her husband. His brother-in-law had obviously had a few too many during the afternoon's golf outing, but that didn't excuse him in Brody's eyes. He was used to the rest of the world thinking he was a philandering jock, but it pissed him off that even his own family had begun buying into the image. Not to mention the embarrassment Shannon had to feel at Skip's pointed comments.

He glared at Skip while directing his comment to his mother. "I'm sure it's just that my tastes in food have grown as I've grown, Mom." He reached under the table and squeezed Shannon's hand in an effort to offer reassurance. "Besides, she does amazing things with vegetables."

Somehow, the words didn't come out exactly how Brody intended them. Judging by the way Shannon yanked her hand back and the accompanying groans from Bridgett and Julianne, he wasn't the only one who thought so. Skip was laughing openly now and no amount of Gwen's shushing was going to shut him up. Connelly shook his head in disgust.

"Dessert!" His mother sprang to her feet to help the waiter serve the warm apple pie, and Brody thought he heard a mumbled "thank God" from his father. Waving off the piece of pie the waiter set in front of him, he breathed a sigh of relief when the pastry distracted the attention of the guests. He glanced at Shannon, but her face was impassive. Once again, he found himself wondering what she'd had to endure growing up to develop such a thick skin.

Thirty minutes later, the rehearsal dinner mercifully ended. Gwen dragged Skip upstairs under the guise of helping put their two kids down to sleep, but everyone knew he was being sent to bed as well. Ashley and Mark had taken their son up long before dessert. Brody's parents and their friends gravitated to the parlor, where a makeshift bar had been set up, while the rest of the wedding party headed out to a pub in town. Julianne and Will made their excuses and wandered upstairs hand in hand, leaving Brody sitting in the dining room with Shannon, Bridgett, Robbie, and his fiancée, Faith.

"If y'all will excuse me," Shannon said. "I've got some studying to do."

Brody was relieved, standing to make his exit, too. He needed to apologize to her for the remark earlier and clarify the sleeping arrangements for the night. The last thing he wanted to do tonight was to hear about Robbie—Rob's—perfect wedding and his perfect life. Shannon's hand on his arm stopped him, though.

"No, Brody. You stay and catch up with your family and friends."

He wanted to shout, *The hell with my family and friends*, but her eyes told him she needed some space and once again his guilty conscience niggled.

"Sure," he said, sliding back into his chair reluctantly. "I'll be up in a little bit."

"Oh, don't worry about me. Take your time. I've got lots of reading to do."

As brush-offs go, Shannon's couldn't have been clearer if she'd kicked him in the nuts.

She slipped away amid a chorus of "see you in the morning," and Brody was left to face down Bridgett's scowl.

"You sure fumbled that pass, little brother."

Brody flipped her off as Robbie-now-known-as-Rob laughed. "You'd better hope she doesn't have any sharp vegetables in her suitcase," his friend joked.

"Funny," Brody said. He turned to Faith to initiate the one conversation that would send his sister to speeding to her own room. "So, how are the wedding plans coming?"

Sure enough, Bridgett was on her feet in ten seconds flat. "I'm out. I think grandpa Gus wanted to play gin tonight."

Fortunately, he was saved by the arrival of Rob's father. "Brody, I need your advice on my fantasy football roster. Step up the bar and help an old man out."

Brody managed to escape his father's cronies an hour later. The main inn building had twenty guestrooms and as he wandered the long upstairs hall to the room he was sharing with Shannon, he hoped she'd already gone to sleep. His body rebelled at the thought of bunking down on the hard floor, but sharing a bed with her would be even more punishing. If he had to endure any pillow talk, the night would progress to torturous.

Too bad he hadn't packed his body armor because the scene greeting him inside the bedroom was more intimate than he imagined. This wasn't the first time Brody had walked into a hotel room where a woman waited for him. But on those occasions, his guest would be wearing nothing but a G-string and stilettos. Tonight, the sight of Shannon innocently seated on the bed, wearing purple flannel pajamas, her face scrubbed clean, and her hair twisted up on her head with—he did a double take—a number two pencil stuck in the knot aroused him more than any other hotel tryst. Instead of mood lighting and silk sheets, a laptop rested on her crossed legs and she'd spread out papers containing her data around her on the comforter.

"Hey," she said quietly.

Closing the door behind him, Brody leaned a shoulder against the mantel as the fire crackled inside the grate. He swirled his Scotch—now diluted with melted ice—in the glass in his hand. "You weren't fibbing about having to work. I thought you were just saying that to escape."

She piled her papers into a neat stack before slipping them into her book bag. "Sorry to abandon you down there, but the weekends are when I get most of my schoolwork done. I need to get ahead if we're going to be spending all day tomorrow at the wedding."

"Still think my family's *delightful*?"

"I think you could have left the remark about the vegetables in the locker room where it belonged."

He pushed away from the fireplace, charging toward the bed. "Ah, come on, you know that didn't come out the way I meant it. Besides, it would have sounded innocent if they weren't all thinking you're some kind of bimbo."

She chuckled softly. "Actually, that's a first for me, so I was kind of enjoying it."

Brody stared down at her as she closed her laptop and placed it on the trunk that doubled as an end table. Maybe he'd mistaken the desire in her eyes earlier because she was cool and composed now, reclining against the pillows as if sharing a room with him wouldn't affect her at all. She'd arranged a row of throw pillows along the length of the bed, forming a bulkhead of sorts to separate the two halves.

Sighing heavily, Brody flopped down on the mattress, crossing his wingtips at the ankles, the Scotch sloshing in the glass as he rested it on his stomach. "Glad we can provide you with some cheap thrills. But my family should at least take you seriously, even if they can't do the same for me."

Shannon gazed at him speculatively. "Your family adores you, Brody."

"Sure they do. They treat me like the overindulged puppy that never grew into his feet."

She laughed merrily, the sound stirring something inside him. He looked over at her long feet, her slender toes painted a sexy bright red. Stifling a groan, he forced his eyes up to study the crown molding.

"I'm serious. I just spent the last hour with my father, my uncles, and their friends, and all they ever want to talk to me about is football, my stats, or their fantasy teams. Almost as if I'm not capable of conversing in any other subject."

"Doesn't that kind of come with the territory?"

"Even you do it. You did it the other day when you were explaining your research to me."

He saw from the corner of his eye that she had the grace to cringe before she rolled on her side to face him, tucking her hands beneath her cheek. "I did. I'm sorry. I shouldn't have made assumptions. But don't you like being a professional football player, Brody? You're one of the best in the game."

"Not one of the best. I am the best." He took a swallow of the Scotch, its bitterness burning his throat, before turning his head on the pillow to glare at her. "I'm the best tight end in the league. And I don't like being a football player. *I love it*. I love being on the field, outmaneuvering the defense and making the catches no one else can."

A slow smile spread over her face as she took the glass from his hand. "But?"

And there was the million-dollar question. Brody had been struggling with the "but" issue for months now. The problem was, he couldn't articulate why he was so unhappy. "I just wonder if it's enough, you know. I know it sounds selfish to you. I get paid millions to play a game. Little boys—and big boys, too—dream about having that opportunity all their lives." Sighing, he shook his head, unable to come up with anything else.

He reached for the glass back, but Shannon got up, walked to the bathroom, and poured the contents into the sink. When she came back to the bedroom, she stopped at the minibar and pulled out an apple she'd cut up and a small tub of peanut butter. She crawled on the bed, sitting Indian style as she placed the tub of peanut butter on one of the barrier pillows.

"Did you always want to be a jock?" she asked as she handed him the bag of apple pieces.

Brody sat up against the headboard. "Didn't every boy?"

"No, some want to be firemen or astronauts or forest rangers." She took an apple from the bag and dipped in the peanut butter.

He scoffed. "First, they want to be pro ballplayers. All those other occupations are second choice."

"So you're one of the lucky ones who got their first choice," she said matter-of-factly, making his life sound so simple.

Her tongue darted out to lick a piece of peanut butter off her lip and Brody's cock jumped. In his current circumstances, he didn't consider himself lucky at all. He was sharing a bed with a woman he shouldn't find sexy, but he did, with nothing but a retaining wall of throw pillows separating their two bodies.

"I told you it didn't make sense." He crunched on his own apple in aggravation.

"Actually, it makes perfect sense. You're trying to figure out who Brody Janik is without football. You don't want to be defined by the game you play. I get it."

A bit of apple got lodged in his throat at her words and he coughed. "Yeah, something like that," he said when he finally found his voice.

"Nothing is going to happen to your career, Brody. You're controlling your blood sugar and you'll get your contract extension. You have years to worry about who Brody is post-football." She spoke the words with such conviction, he almost believed her.

"Finish your snack so your sugar stays stable," she said as she got up to brush her teeth.

"I'll take the floor. You sleep in the bed."

She poked her head out of the bathroom. "I'm pretty sure we can share the bed comfortably." She gestured to her great wall of pillows.

"I haven't slept in bed with a female since I was five and Tricia and I shared a hotel trundle."

This was greeted with an arched eyebrow.

"When I'm in bed with a woman, Shannon, there's generally not a lot of sleeping going on." It was mean of him to tease her, but her pink cheeks told him she wasn't as immune to him as she appeared.

He patted one of the pillows. "I guess these will do. Unless you're one of those people who thrashes around in the bed. You aren't, are you, Shannon?"

He'd taken his teasing a bit too far, though. Now, he couldn't stop imagining her naked, thrashing beneath him while he made her scream. He pulled one of the pillows over his lap.

Marching over to the bed, she pulled the pencil from her hair and crawled under the comforter with her back to him. "Just to be safe, I won't sleep under the sheet. Good night, Brody."

She lay perfectly still beside him and it was all he could do not to cover her with his own body. He knew she was susceptible to his touch and arousing her wouldn't be difficult. But the issue of trust still lingered in the room like an uninvited guest. So Brody shoved the last apple slice into his mouth and headed to the bathroom for another cold shower.

Fourteen

"I've been thinking about your plan to catch the snitch," Julianne said as she put the finishing touches on Shay's makeup.

The two women were in the corner of the large suite Tricia and her bridesmaids were using to get ready for the wedding. Shay looked around to see if any of the others had heard Julianne, but the rest of the women were busy getting themselves dressed.

"Actually, I've given up on that plan," Shay lied. "It wasn't very well thought-out. It's probably best to leave it to the professionals." The last thing she needed was to have too many other people involved.

"Look up," Julianne demanded. "What were you two doing all night? You've got bags under your eyes. Never mind." Julianne misinterpreted the blush spreading over Shay's cheeks. "I know exactly what you two were doing all night," she said with a conspiratorial smile.

Once again, Brody's friend was way off base—except the part about not getting any sleep. If anyone was a thrasher in bed, it was Brody. Shay had spent the night wide awake, huddled at the edge of the mattress while Brody tossed and turned. He finally settled down just before dawn, but only after he'd snaked a long arm over the pillows and around her waist. The intimacy of his warm hand on her belly should have startled her, but it had the opposite effect, lulling her into a deep sleep. She woke up several hours later with Brody's fingers wrapped around her breast. Shay quickly shoved his hand away and he rolled over with a groan, apparently still asleep.

Escaping to the bathroom, she showered and dressed. Brody was still comatose when she left their room in search of coffee. When she returned an hour later, he was gone, along with his morning snack and his tuxedo.

"This place is very romantic," Julianne was saying as she brushed some powder on Shay's face. "But Brody will have to bring you down to North Carolina to the Tide Me Over Inn. A friend of mine owns it and it's fabulous, too. The beds are also quite cozy, I can assure you."

Shay just nodded, a twinge of regret tightening her stomach. Her plan to exonerate herself hadn't worked and Brody still didn't trust her. The only bed she'd ever be sharing with him would be the one upstairs, separated by a line of pillows.

"And I think it's very sweet of you to want to catch the snitch. Whoever it is shouldn't be selling out members of the team or their families. Trust me, I can relate to the media—even social media—being relentless about invading our privacy. Sadly, it comes with the territory of being involved with a celebrity jock. And with Brody being who he is, things escalate. Still, that blogger has no right to say the things she said about you just because you're dating Brody."

If Julianne knew the truth, she'd hate her. Shay could just have easily been the snitch selling information about Will and his family. Her quest to find whoever was doing it wasn't sweet, it was based on self-preservation. Once again, she felt like an imposter and she slumped in the chair.

"Oh, honey, don't worry." Julianne once again misinterpreted her reaction. "We'll catch whoever it is, you'll see."

"Who are we trying to catch?" Bridgett asked.

Shay nearly jumped out of the chair.

"Shay! I'm not done." Julianne put her fingers beneath Shay's chin and turned her face. "We're trying to catch whoever is leaking information about Blaze players to that blogger who writes *The Girlfriends' Guide to the NFL*. Shay had a great plan, but it didn't work."

Panic gripped Shay. She was pretty sure Brody would be furious if his sister found out about the sex toy catalog. Bridgett was also far too intuitive, already suspecting something was amiss with Shay and Brody's relationship.

"Julianne, I can finish my makeup myself. I think Tricia is getting ready to put on her gown."

Julianne had been very overprotective about the wedding gown she'd designed for Brody's sister and Shay counted on her possessiveness as a diversion.

"Here, let me help you, Tricia," Julianne called as she handed Shay the makeup brush before speeding across the room.

Bridgett gave Shay a wry smile. "That was a beautifully executed play. You and my brother are perfect for one another."

Unsure how to respond, Shay proceeded to pack Julianne's makeup case.

"Most of the women who get involved with Brody enjoy the media attention. But not you. Why?"

Shay shrugged. "I'm not most women."

Bridgett eyed her with a measuring gaze. "No, you're not. Which makes me think you might be hiding something. Are you? Are you hiding something that could hurt Brody?"

She was hiding something, but not from Brody. Wouldn't Bridgett be surprised if she knew her little brother was hiding something as well? Of course, her role here was to protect Brody, so it was better to have his sister cross-examining Shay's life and not looking into his.

"No," she answered, knowing the lawyer wouldn't be satisfied. But if her answer kept Bridgett's attention focused on Shay, then she'd done her job.

Fortunately, the activity in the room reached a fevered pitch and there was no time to finish their conversation before the wedding party was hustled out of the suite for pictures. Julianne trailed behind them like a mother hen who'd just had one of her chicks snatched by a fox, while Shay stayed behind to catch her breath. Unsure of what she was supposed to do next, she killed time by straightening up the mess the women left behind when a familiar tingling at the base of her neck alerted her. She looked up to find Brody leaning against the doorjamb, looking like he was headed for Hollywood in his custom tuxedo.

"Having fun?" he asked.

"I wasn't sure where I should be, so I thought I'd just help out."

"Do you ever relax?"

It was hard to relax as his simmering gaze raked over her from head to toe. "The wedding is going to start soon. We should head down to the pavilion." She looked for her clutch purse among the mess Julianne had left.

The ceremony was being held on the inn's grounds, under a massive wooden pavilion with the Green Mountains in the background, the fall foliage at its peak.

"They're still taking family pictures. My mom wanted you to join us."

A fresh round of panic gripped Shay. "I-I'm not doing that, Brody."

Brody held his hands up as he strolled toward her. "Whoa. I told her no way. But I wouldn't mind having one of you. You look amazing," he said reverently.

The dress Julianne picked out for her was a vibrant teal jersey knit that wrapped around her body like a second skin. Sophie had paired it with a clunky necklace of fall earth tones and Emma had insisted she wear strappy copper heels. The look was casual enough for the rustic wedding, but chic enough to hold her own with Brody dressed in a tuxedo.

He was standing inches from her again, the heat from his body evident through the thin material of her dress, the smell of his cologne taunting her senses.

"You're a good sport, Shannon Everett. I'm sorry I forced you into this, but, truthfully, I'm not sorry you're here with me. I like being with you." He lowered his voice to a whisper, leaning his mouth toward hers. "Even if you put a bunch of silly pillows between us."

"Brody, please . . ."

He was going to kiss her and that would destroy the tenuous truce they'd established. Still, she was powerless to stop him.

"Please what, Shannon? Please no? Or please yes?"

The only thing she could get through her throat was a sigh.

"That's what I thought," he said before his fingers cupped the back of her neck, drawing her lips in to meet his.

Brody's kiss stole her breath and all of her rational thought. Even worse, it stole her inhibitions. Without thinking, she urged her body closer, dragging her fingers through his hair. Her nipples ached as they rubbed against his tuxedo jacket, her body becoming flushed with need. He slid his tongue along hers and she felt like she might fall. Fortunately, his hand was roving over her backside, supporting her. She couldn't prevent the keening moan of need coming from deep down her throat.

He broke the kiss with a harsh breath. "You should have said please no, Shannon, because once I start, I can't seem to stop kissing you."

His kiss was more savage this time as he hungrily explored her mouth while his long fingers easily found their way into the front of her dress and caressed her breast, his thumb kneading the nipple. Shay's breathing was fractured now, her body trembling with a need for release.

"Brody! Get your hands of her," Julianne cried. "You're eating off her makeup!"

Julianne smacked him on the shoulder and Brody reluctantly released her, his blue eyes looking so despondent, Shay's stomach nearly dropped to her knees. He shook his head briefly and licked his lips.

"I mean it. I'm sorry about all of this," he whispered before stepping away.

"Oh, you crushed your boutonniere," Julianne moaned as she repinned the flower to his lapel. "Now go. The groomsmen are gathering at the pavilion. You're gonna be late."

Brody paused in the doorway as if he wanted to say more, and Shay sucked in a breath as a fresh wave of need washed over her.

"Shoo!" Julianne admonished him with a wave of her hand. "I'll make sure she gets where she's supposed to be."

Then he was gone, his athletic tread echoing down the long hardwood staircase.

"Oh, honey," Julianne said, dragging Shay's thoughts from the man who'd just kissed her senseless back to the present. "Whatever you do, don't give that man your heart before you know he's capable of giving you his."

Tears stung the back of her eyes, but Shay refused to let them fall. She nodded in agreement with Julianne because no words could pass through the lump in her throat.

The wedding seemed to take an eternity. As Brody stood with the other groomsmen, he tried his best to avoid Shannon's stare, but it was no use. The longing he saw within her eyes ate at him. Especially since he felt the same urgent sense of want within his own body. There was no way they could share a bed tonight without something happening. Not after the kiss they'd shared earlier.

He watched as his sister Tricia kissed her groom with both passion and the promise of a lifetime of love. The guests cheered and Brody felt lightheaded. He tried to remember when the last time he'd eaten was, but he knew the issue wasn't his blood sugar; the problem stemmed from another part of his body entirely.

As the ceremony ended and the guests wandered to the cocktail hour, Brody contemplated his dilemma. He was pretty sure Shannon wasn't the snitch, but she still held a pretty powerful secret over him. The contract she'd signed gave him leverage over her, but could he trust that was even enough?

It all boiled down to that one word: *trust*.

Glancing around the room, he watched as Rob kissed his fiancée, blissfully unconcerned whether or not Faith would sell his secrets to the media. Tricia stared all moony-eyed at Garrett, her trust in her new husband practically radiating from her pores. His gaze finally landed on Will and Julianne Connelly. Their relationship had begun on a basis of lies and mistrust, yet here they stood today, rock solid, their hands intertwined as they swayed to the pianist's music. If those two could make it work with all the hurdles they'd had to jump over, surely he and Shannon could enjoy one night of sex without his entire world crumbling around him.

Weaving his way through the crowd of guests, he found Shannon laughing over something with grandpa Gus. Just hearing the sound made his body harden. He wanted to make her laugh. Hell, he wanted to make her scream.

Her eyes were a little skittish when they met his. Brody wanted to reach for one of her hands, but she was white-knuckling a champagne glass in one and a small purse in the other. Instead, he slid his palm down her back to reassure her. She trembled slightly at his touch and his hand slid to cup her ass. The wild-eyed look she flung at him made his body even harder.

"Gramps, can I borrow Shannon for a sec?"

Grandpa Gus gave Brody a knowing smile. "She's all yours, sonny." He headed off toward the bar area.

Shannon spun on her heel, brushing his hand away. "Brody, you have to stop this," she hissed. "I can't take all the touching. Please—no!"

Her eyes shimmered with unshed tears as Brody backed her into the now familiar butler's pantry.

Depositing her glass on the counter, she held a hand up to push him away. "I'm serious, Brody. I—"

"I trust you." He practically shouted, thankful that the noise from the party behind them drowned him out.

Confusion swept over her face. "What?"

"I said I trust you." He took it as a good sign that the hand she'd held up to stop him now lay over his heart.

Her eyelids fluttered shut and she took a deep breath.

"I trust you not to sell me out, Shannon," he said, not liking the desperation that was creeping into his voice. But frankly, he thought she'd be a little more excited.

"Are you just saying that because you want to sleep with me, Brody?" A tear leaked from beneath her closed lid.

Brody gently wiped it away. "Technically, Shannon, we've already slept together. I just want to eliminate the chastity belt of pillows tonight."

Her whiskey eyes were damp as she finally looked at him. "Why?"

His gut clenched. "What do you mean why?"

"Why do you suddenly trust me?" she insisted. "And why do you want to sleep with *me*?"

That damn insecurity was really starting to annoy Brody. If he ever got hold of her sister, he'd strangle her. He traced his fingers along the side of her breast, wrapped so neatly in the pretty dress. Shannon shivered beneath his touch.

"I've told you before, Shannon. You're a conundrum. And I like conundrums."

Fifteen

Shay had only been to a few weddings in her life—none as elegant as Tricia Janik's. But still, she couldn't help but feel the afternoon and evening went on too long. Brody rarely left her side, the proximity of his body taking a toll on her, making it difficult to enjoy the event. Common sense told her to flee with the daylight; Brody only wanted her because she was a novelty, the one woman who had refused him. But she couldn't deny her own body's attraction to him and she knew she'd never get another chance like tonight.

Anxiety kept her on edge and she barely made it through dinner and dancing. She was surprised she could keep her nerves from showing as she danced with Brody's father and his grandfather Gus, as well as his brother-in-law Skip, who spent the entire time apologizing profusely for his behavior the night before. Shay didn't care if he meant it or not, she just wanted to get the evening over with.

At long last, the newlyweds were headed to the honeymoon suite in a hotel in Burlington. The rest of the guests found their way to the various parlors while others meandered toward their guestrooms. The excuses he made to his family were greeted with knowing grins and winks, as Brody practically tugged her up the stairs. A fire was glowing in the grate, its light illuminating the otherwise dark room. Shrugging out of his tuxedo jacket, he closed and locked the door. Suddenly, Shay's knees were wobbly. Her breathing sounded loud in the small space. His hands spanned her waist as he pulled her closer.

"Do you need a minute, or do I rip those granny panties off you right here?"

Her fingers shook as they tugged on his bow tie. "Um, I'm not wearing granny panties. In fact, I'm not wearing panties at all. Just a thong. This dress is too clingy."

Brody's nostrils flared and his eyes dilated slightly. "Jeez, Shannon. It's a good thing you didn't tell me that earlier or we would have never made it to the cutting of the cake."

She smiled to herself, his raspy voice steadying her hands as she pulled out the studs in his shirt. He wanted her. Even if it was only for one night. The power in that thought was fortifying.

"Let me see," he commanded.

Placing the studs on the mantel, Shay took a step back, reaching behind her back to lower the dress's zipper. The sides of fabric fell away, revealing her nude push-up bra and a matching thong. His wicked grin bolstered her even further as she let the dress drop to the floor. Brody hooked his fingers into the strings of her thong, drawing her hips flush with his. Shay heaved a sigh, her own fingers tightly gripping his shoulders as his arousal nudged up against the cleft in her thighs.

Brody leaned forward and kissed the sensitive spot on her neck. "Oh yeah, Shannon, just like that," he breathed in her ear as she shifted her pelvis against him. His fingers made quick work of her bra, drawing it down her arms to give his mouth better access. Bending her over his arm, he toyed with her nipple using his tongue. Her heart pounded in her ears when he took the nipple in his mouth, the heat of his kiss spreading across her chest. A slow fever began to burn low in her belly as he sucked and kissed her as if he couldn't get enough. Want took over and her fingers tugged his shirt out of the waistband of his pants. Shay was desperate to feel his hot skin against hers, to spread her hands over the hard wall of muscle pressed up against her.

"Brody," she moaned as she pushed him back, pulling the shirt from his shoulders. His breathing became ragged as her hands explored the smooth sculpted skin on his chest. Leaning into the warmth of his body, she nuzzled his jaw and Brody let out a low growl, before finally taking her mouth in a ravenous kiss. Feverish now, she arched her naked breasts even closer. He groaned, angling his head as both of them nipped at each other's lips hungrily. Somehow, Brody managed to maneuver their tangled bodies over to the bed. The backs of Shay's legs brushed up against the comforter and he gently eased her torso down onto the silky quilt, leaving her legs dangling over the side. Shay whimpered as he broke their kiss. Kneeling between her legs, his mouth slowly explored the terrain of her body as her fingers fisted in his hair.

"Shh." She felt his smile against her skin. "We've got all night, Shannon. There's no reason to rush this."

Restless desire hummed through her, making Shay impatient. They might have all night, but if it was going to be her only night with Brody, she wanted to make every moment count. His tongue found her navel and her body shuddered with anticipation. He hooked his fingers into the thong and began dragging it down her legs, his lips trailing hot kisses behind it.

"God, you're beautiful," he murmured. "I've been dreaming about these long legs wrapped around me for weeks now."

Satisfaction hummed through her along with a little unease, as she began to worry whether she'd measure up to his expectations. He flung the slip of lace onto the floor, hooking her leg over his shoulder as he licked his way back up. All of her anxieties were forgotten as he inserted a finger into the valley between her thighs and slowly stroked. Her eyelids drifted shut on a moan when his mouth joined his thrusting finger.

Shay had never known such pleasure. Her fingers dug into his shoulders as she dragged her other leg over the bare skin of his back. He licked her to oblivion, until bright lights formed behind her eyelids and she released a breathy scream of utter satisfaction, her body convulsing beneath his mouth.

A flush heated her skin, as much from fulfillment as embarrassment at her unabashed outburst. Brody grinned that wicked smile as he slowly crawled up her body. He was still wearing his pants and Shay's fingers began tugging at the waistband.

"God, Shannon, you're amazing. I've never been so turned on watching a woman come like that." His words were raspy as he nibbled on her shoulder. "It was almost as if that were your first time."

"It was," she breathed, her body and mind still in the euphoria of her climax. "That was amazing."

Brody's mouth stilled and he pushed up onto straight arms to look down at her, his eyes quizzical. "First time that way or . . ." He left the question hanging in the air as the fire crackled behind him and the moment of truth crackled between them.

Coherent thought still hadn't penetrated her sated state because, as usual, the words were out of her mouth before she could stop them. "First time for all of it. I've never had any kind of sex before."

Brody's breath seized in his lungs. He felt like he'd been tackled on the goal line, the ball knocked from his hands. *During a blizzard.* The look in Shannon's glazed eyes was hard to discern. The passion was still there, along with a good dose of uncertainty and maybe some alarm, he wasn't sure. He was getting a little panicked at his own body's reaction to her pronouncement.

"Never?" he asked, sounding a lot like he'd taken a kick to the head.

She chewed on her bottom lip, swollen from where his own mouth had nibbled on it. A tear leaked out of her eye as she shook her head slowly from side to side. Her fingers, still tucked just inside the waistband of his pants, weren't as warm as they had been a moment before.

"I need a minute." The roaring in his ears was deafening as he rolled off her and onto his back. Shannon snatched her hands back in an effort to cover herself. He wanted to cover her with his own body, but he couldn't move. Even worse, he had no idea why he was reacting this way. It wasn't as if he hadn't ever been with a virgin before. Sure, it had been way back in high school and maybe college, but, hell, Shannon certainly wasn't acting like she had any reservations. Still, he asked anyway.

"Are you sure you want to do this?"

With a gulping sob, she was off the bed and headed to the bathroom. Brody was momentarily distracted by the sight of her nicely rounded ass before the door slammed shut and both Shannon and her booty were locked in the bathroom. He swore, punctuating it with a fist to the mattress. Two minutes earlier he was hot and hard for a woman he'd been lusting after for weeks. Now, his body was practically limp, a novel situation for Brody.

The sobbing from the bathroom roused him off the bed. He jiggled the door handle, even though he knew it was locked. "Shannon, it's okay. I just needed a minute." Which was a lie judging by the inattentiveness in his groin.

"A minute for what, Brody? To decide I wasn't what you expected?" She cried through the door. "What you wanted!"

"No! Hell, no." He told himself that wasn't a lie. "I just needed a minute for you to decide if this is was what *you* really want."

"What part of me being buck naked gave you the clue I was undecided?" Her accent became more pronounced the angrier she got.

Brody plowed his fingers through his hair in exasperation. "I just meant that it's a big step. You've obviously waited this long—"

"Oh. My. Stars! Do you think I *wanted* to wait this long? Did you think I was holding out for *you*?" Judging by her tone, she'd reached a stage of near hysteria, the scorn in her words causing him to flinch. "I seriously should have given it all to that frat boy after the Texas-Oklahoma game."

And just like that, certain parts of his anatomy were engaged again.

"He was too drunk to care whether or not I was experienced," she sputtered. "I could have gotten it over with and he would have passed out none the wiser."

"Like hell you would have!" he roared through the door. Suddenly, the thought of another man laying his hands—and any other part of his body—on Shannon made him insane. Taking a calming breath, Brody jiggled the doorknob again. "Shannon, come out here, so we can discuss this. We can still do this if you want. The night's still young. We'll take it nice and slow. I'll do whatever you want." His body was revving up at the thought. "Please."

The sound that traveled through the door was either a manic laugh or a sob, Brody couldn't be sure. "No. You've had your chance. I'll just have to find some willing prison guard or, better yet, a convict to perform the deed. I'm sure they won't be repulsed by my inexperience."

The doorjamb splintered as Brody stormed into the bathroom. He'd never felt such rage in his life. "No fucking way!"

Shannon cowered in the corner, one of the inn's big fluffy towels wrapped around her. Eyes round with fear, the makeup Julianne had so artfully applied streaked down her face. For the first time, his Texas Amazon looked fragile, the pain in her eyes searing him to his soul. She'd always been so tough. It was one of the many things he admired about her: her strength and her work ethic. That she had chinks in her armor didn't surprise him, but he wanted to strangle whoever had put them there. Hell, he wanted to kick his own ass for bringing her to this point tonight. Most of all, he wanted to hold her in his arms. Kiss her, sure. Make love to her, definitely. But he also wanted to wrap himself around her and shield her from any and all pain.

"Shannon," he croaked, taking a tentative step toward her.

"Go away, Brody," she cried, wielding a flatiron she'd

grabbed from the vanity. "This was a mistake. All of it. I never should have come here pretending to be what I'm not. What I'll never be. Get out or I'll tell your whole family about your stupid blood sugar. I don't care what you can do to Mama. She wouldn't want me to go through this."

Brody looked from her wild eyes to the busted door. He swore again and Shannon hissed. Putting his hands up, he backed out of the bathroom. "I don't want to leave you here alone, Shannon. Not like this."

"Go!"

He snatched his shirt off the floor and pulled it on. Shoving his arms into his tuxedo jacket, he almost laughed at the fact he'd been so focused on getting her into bed, he still had his shoes on. Hesitating at the door, he glanced back over his shoulder. Shannon hadn't moved. "You're sure you'll be okay?" he asked.

She nodded fiercely, pointing the flatiron at the door. He quietly slipped out of the room, sheer willpower keeping him from slamming the door instead. Thankfully, the hallway was empty. Taking in a deep breath, he leaned up against the wall and wondered if the better question was whether he was going to be okay.

Brody made his way to one of the unpopulated common rooms of the inn. Gravitating to a dark corner, he slid into a chair by the fire, hoping no one would wander out of the music room where his parent's friends were engaged in a noisy sing-along. With an explosive sigh, he dropped his head into his hands.

"Wow, Brody, is that the sound of a crash and burn I hear?"

Bridgett's voice was like fingers on a chalkboard. Brody sprung from his chair, realizing only too late that he had nowhere to escape to.

Slumping back down, he spied his sister sitting serenely behind him in a large wing chair, her stocking feet tucked beside her, an e-reader in her lap, and a glass of Baileys Irish Cream on the end table.

"What? Are you a vampire now, hanging out in the dark

waiting for your next victim?" he asked, not bothering to filter the anger from his voice.

"Interesting." She closed her tablet, leaning forward to study Brody. "By the way you two skipped out of here a while ago, I'd have thought we wouldn't see you for days. Yet here you are looking very . . . unsatisfied. What gives?"

"Damn it, Bridgett, go find someone else to cross-examine. It's none of your business."

"I'm still going with the theory that there's more to you two than what you want us to think. I've said it before, she's not your usual type. She's naturally pretty, even though she does her best to downplay it. And crazy smart, which most people would think might intimidate you, but I happen to know you're pretty smart, too. Not to mention that when you two look at one another, the heat is enough to melt the wax off the floor. But, something's not right. I know one or both of you are hiding something. I just haven't figured out which one. Yet."

There was a reason his sister was the youngest partner ever in her law firm, but Brody really didn't feel like dealing with Bridgett's inquisitive badgering tonight. "Give it a rest, okay, Bridgett."

She had the nerve to smile. "Hitting too close to home, am I?"

Brody charged out of the chair toward the fireplace, resting his hands on the mantel. "Since when do you care who I date, Bridgett?"

"Since *you* started caring who you dated, Brody."

He glanced sharply over his shoulder at his sister. *Damn her for being so intuitive.* Rationalizing that it was better not to give her any more ammunition in her quest, he kept his mouth shut, turning back to stare at the flames in the hearth.

Bridgett sighed. "You'll eventually tell me."

Brody scoffed.

"Because I'm your favorite sister."

He couldn't help but laugh, especially at her smug tone.

"Admit it. I am. I'm the only one in this family who doesn't treat you like a prince and you like that."

"Nope, I love being a prince." Of course, his sister was

right. Of all the women in his family, Bridgett was the one he gravitated to the most. Like him, she was driven, more goal oriented and independent than their other siblings. Growing up, Bridgett was the sister he ran to when he needed guidance or when he was in trouble. She was solid in a crisis and relentless as a bulldog when she wanted the truth. He needed to steer the conversation into more nebulous waters.

Resting his shoulder against the mantel, he studied his sister. She was beautiful, with the elegance of a 1950s movie star. And yet, at thirty-three she was sitting alone in a romantic inn with only her e-reader as a companion.

"Are you happy, Bridgett?"

His question seemed to catch his sister off guard. "Are *you* happy, Brody?"

"Damn it, stop being a litigator and answer the freakin' question!"

Unease unfurled in his belly at the look of despondency that quickly passed over her face before she hid it behind her mask of elegance. Was his sister covering up some deep pain or trauma? Had she ever been reduced to cowering in the corner of a bathroom as a man stripped her of her dignity, her pride, her courage? What had it cost her to rise so quickly in her career? Suddenly, Brody felt like a dick for asking the question at all. Apparently, his insensitivity with women had no bounds tonight.

As usual, Bridgett was careful assembling her answer. "Well, I have a career where people respect me. I'm financially independent, which translates to a fabulous wardrobe. I'm in great health. I have a solid, if not annoying, family. And, I'm not married to someone like Skip. So yes, I'd say I'm pretty happy."

Brody grinned at his sister's response, but he was still troubled by the brief glimpse of pain he'd seen on her face.

"Now your turn, Brody. Are you happy?"

He resorted to his own comfortable mask. "I play professional football for lots of money. I drive fast cars. Women throw themselves at me. What's not to be happy about?"

"God, we sound plastic," she said and they both laughed.

"Did you ever want to do something else with your life?"

"Not if it means marrying someone like Skip." She evaded his question with a quip before taking a sip of her Baileys. "Don't tell me you pine for some life other than a superstar athlete, Brody?"

He was silent for a moment, realizing how silly his doubts were, even in the quiet darkness of the room. "I don't know. I think I'm just tired of people's expectations, you know?"

"They expect too much?"

Brody shook his head. "No, that I can handle. It's the people who expect too little."

"Interesting," his sister said in her most lawyerly voice. "You're finally tired of being the pretty boy."

He shrugged, thinking it was a lot more than that, but he still couldn't put it into words.

"Brody, you're twenty-seven years old. Fortunately, you have a few dollars in your pocket, so you can take your time figuring out what you want to be when you grow up. But you will figure it out. Give it time. You've still got football."

Yeah, but for how long? He wanted to scream.

She stretched her long legs and stood. "In the meantime, I'm going to leave you to brood alone. If you're going to sleep on the sofa, make sure you close the door so Mom doesn't see you and cause a scene."

She stepped closer to the fire and Brody glimpsed something he couldn't pin down on her face. Concern nipped at his belly again.

"Bridgett, you'd tell me if something was wrong. If someone treated you badly?" he asked.

"Of course. Right after you tell me what's going on between you and Shay."

Brody rolled his eyes.

"I thought not," she said, stretching up on her toes to kiss his cheek. "If I were Gwen or Ashley, I'd be telling you to run up there and make up with her. But I'm not. And sometimes it's better to keep a safe distance. She's not the type of girl you use, Brody. But I think you already know that. Good night, little brother."

The inn had quieted down substantially an hour later when Brody crept up the stairs to the room he shared with Shannon. He was grateful she hadn't locked him out because the sofa in the lounge was too cramped and too lumpy to double as a bed. Of course, he had no idea what awaited him inside, he only hoped Shannon had calmed down enough that they could both sleep without bloodshed.

The rhythm of her soft even breathing greeted him, but he didn't see her on the bed. Following the sound, he spied her silhouette curled up on the divan beneath the dormer window. With her long legs, she couldn't have been comfortable. He wanted to lift her over to the mattress, but he didn't dare wake her. Her emotional outburst earlier had cost her and, frankly, he was glad one of them would sleep tonight.

Still showing deference even in her anger, she'd left him the bed and a pillow, only taking the warm comforter for herself. Brody pulled an itchy wool blanket from the closet, figuring it was his punishment. Most women would have tossed his ass out of the inn, but not Shannon. She was still a conundrum.

Not bothering to risk the noise he might make undressing, he laid down quietly on the bed, his eyes drawn in the darkness to the shadow of the bathroom door he'd destroyed. There was going to be hell to pay tomorrow. In more ways than one. For now, he let Shannon's gentle breaths lull him to sleep.

THE GIRLFRIENDS' GUIDE TO THE NFL

Oh my! It seems some guys just don't know how to behave when they're not on the gridiron. Brody Janik—number eighty in your program, but number one in our hearts—blazed his way through his three-day bye weekend enjoying a little too much of his sister's wedding in Vermont. According to our sources, the tight end, who was traveling with the less desirable Everett twin, destroyed the suite the two were staying in. Now, some are saying the couple got into a Texas-sized knockdown drag-out. Miss Everett is reported to have left early the next morning with Brody's teammate, Will Connelly. Unfortunately for Miss Everett, Connelly's wife was also spied in the car. Or would that be unfortunately for William the Conqueror?

Our theory? It's just another example of our favorite tight end's wild sexual exploits. According to his previous companions, Brody does like to "experiment" in the bedroom. Perhaps Miss Everett couldn't handle the *blaze* that burns within Brody. Whichever story you want to go with, Brody is going to need all his strength as he and his teammates face the meat of their schedule these next three weeks.

Sixteen

Nate was hovering again. Ever since the story appeared on the Internet three days ago, he'd been shadowing her, keeping the players and other staffers at arm's length. If Shay hadn't been so danged tired, she might think it was funny. But she was in zombie mode, moving through her daily tasks on autopilot. Nate's concern and attentiveness just didn't compute.

It was Thursday afternoon. The team had just completed drills on the indoor practice field. Several of the players filtered through the commissary to pick up a protein bar or a shake before making their way to their breakout rooms, where they'd study films of this week's opponent and become familiar with the game plan. Will Connelly glared at Nate, making the trainer take two steps back.

"How are you holding up?" Will stirred his shake with his straw as he spoke quietly to Shay.

The smile she pasted on her face felt brittle. "I'm fine."

The big linebacker shook his head. "I'm breaking all kinds of rules of gentlemanly conduct by commenting on your looks, but, honestly Shay, you don't look fine. You look dead on your feet. You can't let this blogger get to you." He took a step closer, blocking her from the other players in the room. "Look, Sophie is having dinner with Julianne tonight at our place. I know they want you to join them. Go. Have dinner. Just forget about all this crap for one night."

If only it were that easy. Everywhere she turned, that blogger's words showed up. Her thesis advisor had been uncharacteristically brusque the other day, rubber-stamping her latest analysis and hurrying her out of his office. Clearly, her seniors at water aerobics didn't know what to think of her. Mrs. Benvenuto had unabashedly inspected her for bruises or signs of any altercation while the young lifeguards had leered at her from their chairs. Even her neighbor Jackie had looked unconvinced when Shay told her the whole story was nothing but crap. Adding insult to injury, Jackie had seemed more disappointed in Brody.

But no one was more upset than Mama. Shay had originally gone along with Brody's cockamamie scheme to help her mama keep her salon. Except in the end, she may have hurt her. Meemaw's friend was threatening to withdraw his support of Shay for the job at the prison because of Shay's "soiled reputation." The man's rant had provided her the only comic relief of the week. *Were they truly worried about who worked with prisoners?* Mama reassured her that it would all work out, but Shay could hear the doubt in her voice. She'd inadvertently brought more shame on Mama and that embarrassed her. Not as much as everything that had—or hadn't—happened with Brody embarrassed Shay, though.

Fortunately, Brody had given her a wide berth this week, avoiding the commissary altogether. His only contact had come through his agent, Roscoe Mathis, who called to assure her that Brody was issuing a statement denying all the blogger's claims. Mr. Mathis had hired a private investigator to interview everyone at the inn in hopes of finding the blogger. And Brody planned to sue for damages on her behalf. All things considered, it was quite an about-face for Brody, who before would have considered Shay suspect number one.

"So, should I call home and tell them you're coming?" Will's question interrupted her musing.

"Thanks, but I have to pass. I'm tutoring Emma this afternoon and then I have some serious studying to do on my own." The part about Emma was true anyway.

Will studied her, looking for a moment as if he was going to say more. Instead he leaned forward and brushed a kiss on her forehead. "That ought to give the snitch something to talk about," he said with a wink. "Don't study too hard. You'll wear yourself out." He gave Nate a hard look before wandering out of the commissary.

Nate scoffed behind her. "Really, Shannon, you shouldn't be so taken in by these guys. They're all full of themselves. They treat their jockstraps better than their women."

Shay tried not to bristle at the trainer's comments. She knew for a fact Will Connelly was devoted to his wife. "I'm a big girl, Nate. And I'm done for the day." Pulling off her hairnet, she headed for the table where Emma had just deposited her books. "And trust me, I've learned my lesson where jocks are concerned." She stopped to pat Nate on the shoulder. "But thanks." It was actually nice having Nate on her side for once, despite his misguided remarks about the players.

The trainer puffed out his chest and headed for the training rooms as Shay sat down next to Emma. "How was the unit test last week?"

"Um . . . it was hard, but I got a B-plus." Emma eyed her warily.

"That's wonderful! So why do you look like I'm going to bite your head off?"

Emma toyed with her mechanical pencil. "It's not that . . ."

Shay cringed in embarrassment. It didn't come as a surprise that the coach's daughter knew about the blog article. "But you want to know about the hooey that blogger said about me, right?"

"Well . . ." Emma's voice dropped to a whisper. "It isn't true, is it?" The look of consternation in her eyes nearly did Shay in.

"Not one word of it."

Relief spread over the girl's face as her mouth curved into a bashful grin. "Oh that's good. I mean, like, I never thought it was true and all. Because you and Brody, you're not like . . . that."

Shay patted the girl's arm. "No, we're not. And it's never okay to be in a relationship like that. Do you understand?"

"Oh my gosh, yes! My mom already talked to me about it. I'm just glad none of it is true, because I like you. And Brody, too. Daddy was threatening to tear him limb from limb. That would have been awful." Her face flushed pink. "I mean, I don't like Brody like that, you know. Because he's your boyfriend and all. Besides, he's too old for me. And you guys are sooooo cute together."

Emma's babbling didn't offer Shay the chance to refute the boyfriend part, which was a good thing, because Shay wasn't sure how she'd explain.

"Hi, Roscoe," Emma beamed at a man who'd come to stand beside their table. Dressed in a suit and tie, he looked out of place in the relaxed atmosphere of the practice facility. Of average height and average build, he clearly wasn't here to play. "Hey there, Emma. Whatcha studying?"

"Chemistry," Emma practically wailed. "But Shay's tutoring me and I'm rocking the class."

Roscoe smiled, his hazel eyes twinkling behind his wire-rimmed glasses. "It's always good to know someone who can walk you through chemistry. I take it you're Shannon Everett?"

Shay nodded, wondering what Brody's agent was doing in Baltimore and why he seemed to be seeking her out.

"Everybody calls her Shay," Emma clarified. "Shay this is Roscoe Mathis. He's my Uncle Shane's agent. And Will Connelly's, too, right?" She looked at the agent for confirmation.

"And Brody's," Roscoe nodded. "Listen, Emma, can I interrupt your study session here for a minute. I just have something I need to speak with Shan—Shay about."

Emma glanced from Roscoe to Shay. "Um . . . sure. I'll just get myself some fro-yo so you can have some privacy."

She made a beeline for the frozen yogurt dispenser as Roscoe slid into her seat. He laid a manila envelope on the table.

"I'm guessing you're not here to tell me they've caught the blogger?"

Roscoe shook his head. "I'm sorry, no. Whoever it is knows how to cover their trail. I'm pretty sure Homeland Security are the only ones who can identify this person. Although, even then it might take them some doing."

Shay's stomach fell. It had been silly, getting her hopes up, but she had anyway.

He slid the envelope across the table. "Brody wanted this returned to you in person."

She raised her eyebrows in question, before peeking inside the envelope.

"It's the . . . agreement you entered into with Brody," he explained.

Shay's breath caught in her throat. Under the terms of the contract, if anything else negative was reported about Brody, he could go after Mama. "He's going to execute it?" she gasped.

Understanding dawned on Roscoe's face and he reached across the table and patted her hand. "No. He's invalidating it. I was just going to tear it up, but he wanted it returned to you to do the honors. Your arrangement with Brody is null and void. The PI did a thorough investigation this week and everything indicates that you're not the individual feeding information to this blogger."

Her heart sank. "He had me checked out?" Had everything he'd said in Vermont been a lie?

"No, he didn't. But I did." The agent's tone was fierce. "It's my job to protect my clients from themselves. It wouldn't have been the first time a woman sold Brody out."

Shay struggled to keep up. Brody's agent had suspected her, but Brody no longer did. She should be overjoyed; after all, she'd wanted no part of Brody's blackmail. Except that she had. Not only because it gave her critical data for her dissertation, but it allowed her to be close to him.

"But what about his . . ." She looked around the commissary to ensure no one was listening. ". . . problem."

Roscoe sighed. "I think I've secured someone who'll supervise his diet and can keep quiet. I'm interviewing her this afternoon."

"No!" Shay said before her brain was even engaged. The fact that Roscoe had mentioned it was a female had nothing to do with it. At least that's what Shay told herself. "I'm in the middle of collecting data for my thesis and I can't change data sources now."

"Come again?" Roscoe seemed genuinely perplexed.

Shay had to force herself not to roll her eyes. "You didn't think Brody was the only one getting something out of this deal, did you? I needed another subject, one whose diet I could control. It's the perfect situation and I really don't see why it can't continue. I order his food for him and prepare it in my apartment. I collect his data electronically online through his Fitbit. The food is left in his house when he's not home. He never has to see me again. But I have four more weeks of data I need to collect and he's not getting out of it now."

Roscoe leaned back in his chair, a slow grin spreading on his face. "Well, I'll be damned. Another one of my clients has found a woman who isn't afraid to stand up to him."

"I'm not Brody's *woman*. But I am going to be his nutritionist. At least for the next four weeks."

"And after the four weeks?"

"I'll collect my dissertation and go away."

"That's too bad," he said as he stood. "I'll let Brody know about the arrangements. It was nice to meet you, Shay. I really hope we meet again someday. See ya, Emma," he called as he left the commissary.

It was a warm Sunday night in the Arizona desert and the roof of University of Phoenix Stadium was open, allowing the dry breeze to ripple the flags, but not interfere with the football while it was in flight. Not that it mattered to Brody. He couldn't seem to catch the ball even if it were coated with Stickum.

"Damn it, Brody," Shane Devlin roared as he stormed off the field toward the sideline. "That one was . . . Right. On. The. Numbers! What the hell's your problem tonight?" Devlin tossed his helmet toward the bench. The Blaze were down by thirteen to the Arizona Cardinals and there was still three minutes and fifteen seconds left in the half. Brody made his way to the end of the bench, better known as no-man's-land. It was the area of the sideline a player gravitates to when he's muffed a play. Brody hadn't seen this piece of real estate since his rookie season, but tonight he'd practically set up camp there.

Purposely trying to avoid the lens of the television cameras, Brody watched with relief as the Blaze's placekicker put the ball right through the uprights for three points. At least his team had come away with something. He guzzled a cup of water, turning to toss it to one of the ball boys, only to see Coach bearing down on him. Not a good sign.

"Are you still on East Coast time or something, Janik?" The bill of Matt Richardson's ball cap brushed against Brody's forehead. Coach wasn't normally an in-your-face kind of guy, but apparently Brody's piss-poor performance brought it out in him tonight.

"No, sir."

"Good," Coach said. "Because I need you to move when the ball is hiked and I need you to catch the ball when it's thrown to you! You're being moved to the third check-down for the rest of this game. If the other two receivers aren't open, Devlin might throw the ball to you. In the meantime, you'd better get your body on that line and block. You hear me?"

"Yes, sir."

It wasn't unusual for a tight end to be called upon to block. In fact, the majority of players at that position spend the bulk of their career doing that. But Brody had made a name for himself as a receiver—the Blaze's primary receiver. The demotion was definitely intended as a punishment.

The Blaze defense held and the half ended with them

only trailing by ten. Once in the locker room, players made their way toward the urinals or to grab a drink before they broke into groups based on positions and went over changes to the game plan for the second half. Brody discreetly pricked his finger to check his blood. As he suspected, the reading was in the normal range. Despite the stressful week, he'd been strictly adhering to Shannon's nutritional plan.

When food continued to show up in his refrigerator, complete with a daily schedule posted on the door, Brody had been surprised—until he remembered the stupid contract he'd made Shannon sign. He'd insisted Roscoe return the document to her in person, letting her off the hook. Roscoe had shocked the hell out of him when he'd told him Shannon demanded she continue to plan his menu so she could collect data for her research project. Brody should have known she was using him as a human guinea pig for her dissertation. He'd actually laughed for the first time all week when he found out. Still, Roscoe warned Brody to hire a food taster, just in case.

"Yo, Janik. You gonna join us or are you daydreaming about destroying hotel rooms over there?" the receiver's coach yelled out. The rest of the locker room snickered, except for Shane Devlin, who just eyeballed Brody as he took his place with the rest of the ball handlers.

The second half went a lot better than the first. DeShawn turned it up a notch, charging across the goal line twice to put the Blaze ahead. The Cardinals pulled within one with an early fourth-quarter field goal. Brody managed to pull down his one and only catch in the closing minutes of the game, but it was for only three yards and his team needed four for a first down. Arizona charged down the field with seconds left, scoring a field goal as time ran out.

The red-eye back to Baltimore was subdued. Brody easily found a secluded spot on the plane since most of his teammates were giving him space. It wasn't unusual for a player to have an off game. It was just unusual for Brody to have one. Most of his teammates didn't know how to handle it. Neither did Brody, frankly.

Midway through the flight, a chorus of snores permeating

the cabin, Devlin slipped into the empty seat beside him. Stifling a groan, Brody turned to stare at the lights on the plane's wings through the small window.

"I never can sleep on a plane. I don't know how these big lugs can even get comfortable in the seat." The quarterback gestured to the offensive lineman slumbering across the aisle.

Brody didn't bother responding, hoping Devlin would give up and go away. It was no use, though. After a few moments of silent reflection, he said something Brody never expected to hear.

"Quit pouting, Brody. Every player has an off game. The great players put it in the past and move on. You're the best tight end in the game and the first guy I want catching a pass I've thrown, so get over it."

Taken aback by the rare show of praise from his quarterback, Brody just gave a noncommittal grunt.

"It's not like you to get worked up over tabloid or, in this case, Internet, trash," Devlin continued. "You gotta let it just roll off you and keep your head in the game. Nobody believes that bullshit anyway."

Brody's curiosity got the better of him. "So that's how you handled all those tabloid firestorms throughout your career? By just ignoring the lies they print about you?"

Devlin settled back into his seat with a melancholy grin. "Actually, I considered each and every one of those sensational stories a badge of honor. Remember, I was in the business of blackening my pedigree, destroying my old man's good name." He closed his eyes for a moment before going on. "I didn't care about the collateral damage, because I honestly didn't think there'd be any. I was a one-man show."

He turned to look Brody in the eye. "In my case, ninety-nine percent of it was bullshit anyway. That had better be the case here, or I'll throw you out the exit door."

Brody flipped him off.

Devlin laughed. "Anyway, Shay seems pretty tough. If you two are going to make a go of it, she'll need a pretty thick skin."

Brody looked back out into the dark night. Shannon was

tough, all right. And there was a connection there—at least there had been before the incident at the inn. But right now, he wasn't sure of his own future, much less one with Shannon. The only thing he did know was he couldn't have another game like today. Everything he'd done these past months to keep his blood sugar under control would be for nothing if he couldn't keep his mind where it was supposed to be: in the game. Shannon didn't need him to fight her battles. She didn't want him to, either; she'd made that perfectly clear. He was better off forgetting about her, the blogger, and the whole mess. Instead, he would just concentrate on his current goal of a contract extension.

Devlin had thankfully buried his nose in a Dean Koontz novel when Brody turned his head from the window. Unfortunately, the quarterback was proficient at multitasking because he spoke without taking his eyes off the page.

"Just to be on the safe side, you and I are going to take a few extra reps every day this week. Starting tomorrow. Be at the facility by one."

Seeing as it was already tomorrow, Brody figured he'd better get some sleep before they landed.

Seventeen

Shay noticed everyone in the Blaze facility seemed a little more on edge after the trip to Phoenix. The team's second defeat had been another nail-biter and the competitive athletes didn't take it too well. Fortunately, the loss took a lot of attention off the poisonous blog about Brody, especially now that the blogger was spewing her venom at the Minnesota Vikings and a supposed homosexual player.

"If her intent is to rattle all the players in the league, she's going about it the right way," Julianne remarked that Wednesday afternoon. She and Carly Devlin had stopped by the aquatic center where Shay taught, joining in her water aerobics class. "Brody was like a deer in the headlights out in Arizona."

Carly reclined in the resin lounge chair, resting a bottled water on her pregnant belly. "The poor boy's been shagging more balls than our dog, Beckett, this week. It's a wonder Shane's arm can take all the added reps."

Shay eyed the clock. While she was flattered the two women had sought her out, she needed to get Brody's dinner made and into his kitchen before he got home from practice at seven. It was already five. Besides, she knew Julianne's real purpose in dropping by the pool wasn't just to sign her and her son up for mommy-and-me swim lessons; the woman wanted to know the status of Shay's relationship with Brody. Which meant Brody wasn't talking, either, because he and Julianne seemed to have a special bond. Obviously, the woman had no clue that Brody and Shay's relationship was a cover.

"We're going to brunch before Sunday's game, Shay. Why don't you join us?" Julianne asked.

Shay had hoped to avoid this weekend's home game, but Maddox couldn't stop talking about being a ball boy with Troy Devlin. Brunch with Brody's friends was too much of a risk, though.

"Actually, I'm tending bar on Saturday night, so I'll probably want to get as much sleep as I can that morning." While it wasn't as much fun working on a night the players couldn't come and act as a buffer—especially after the provocative blog—Shay couldn't forgo the money she earned at Celtic Charm. In fact, her recent notoriety had resulted in a spike in tips.

"Oh, that's right! You work at that mega bar on the Inner Harbor. Shane and I are pretty much homebodies, but I've been dying to see what it's like. Maybe we should have a ladies' night there on Saturday night. We'll get a bunch of the Blaze wives," she looked at Shay, "and girlfriends. We'll have a little party there. That way Shay can still be a part of it. What do you think, Jules?"

Julianne smiled conspiratorially at her childhood friend. "That sounds perfect, Carly."

And just like that, the two women had boxed her in. It seemed Shay would be playing the part of Brody's girlfriend a little longer. After arranging to meet at the bar on Saturday night, she was finally able to make her escape.

An hour later, Brody's vegetable lasagna ready for the oven, she entered his kitchen only to find Bridgett seated at the breakfast bar. *Dang it!* When would she learn to pull her car around to the parking pad in back of the house to avoid such surprises?

"Still dutifully making his dinner, I see," his sister said. "Obviously, he's not paying you with sex, which moves you up in my esteem."

"I'll certainly sleep better tonight knowing that."

Bridgett laughed. "Seriously. I like you, Shay. There aren't too many women I say that about."

Shay placed the lasagna in the fridge along with the fixings for salad to go with it.

"So, what are you getting out of this? Is this really your job?"

Brody's sister was fishing. She was sharp as her daddy's spurs and she already suspected something was up with her brother. A little bit of the truth might just keep her satisfied enough that she'd leave Brody alone.

Shay leaned against the countertop. "I really am a PhD student in nutrition. Brody is one of the subjects I'm using for data to confirm my thesis. He eats a certain amount of carbohydrates at specific intervals and I analyze his vital statistics when he's playing at his peak level."

"Interesting," his sister said. "And what enticed him to participate in your study?"

This was the part that required a little slight of hand. Shay shrugged. "Free food that he didn't have to prepare? Or maybe the novelty of being included in a PhD study? Who knows?"

"Both are likely." Bridgett got up to retrieve the whistling kettle off the stove and Shay nearly sank to the floor with relief that his sister had bought it.

"And what will you do once you have your PhD, Shay?"

"I'd like to keep working to optimize athletes' performance. But initially I'm going to be working in a state prison near my home in Texas. I'll be supervising the overall nutrition of the prison population." Unfortunately, the job didn't sound any cooler the more times she explained it.

Bridgett looked at her wide-eyed, her hand stilled in the process of replacing the kettle on the stove. "Did you say a *prison*?"

Shay smiled at the look of complete wonder on Bridgett's face. "I need to help my mama out for a year or so and pay back my student loans. After that, I'll be able to do what I want."

Coming to stand in front of Shay, Bridgett blew on her tea. "I take that back about liking you, Shay. Like doesn't cover it. I truly admire your determination. It's not easy to sacrifice what you want for someone else." A wistful look passed over her face. "Trust me, I know."

Shay felt uncomfortable under Bridgett's lawyerly gaze. "Well, there's plenty of lasagna if you're staying for dinner. The cooking instructions are on the top of the container."

"So you really don't stay and eat with him?"

Not since the time I embarrassed myself in his bedroom. "No, the whole couple thing is just a ruse to throw off his teammates."

"Not all of it," Bridgett challenged.

"Pardon?"

Brody's sister gestured toward the Sub-Zero. "Whatever you two were doing against the fridge that night was real. And I've seen the way you both look at each other. Some of it is definitely real."

Tears stung the back of her eyes and Shay had difficulty speaking around the lump in her throat. "Sorry to disappoint you, Bridgett, but you're mistaken. I'm not Brody's type. Nice to see you again." Her hand was on the door handle when Bridgett spoke.

"Interesting."

Shay turned to stare at her. Brody's sister had a smug smile on her face as she spoke. "Most women would have saved face and claimed Brody wasn't *their* type."

The monsignor's homily was droning on. Brody fidgeted on the wooden pew while Sister Agnes sat still as a statue. The Blaze were playing the Tennessee Titans at home this afternoon. The mild fall weather had given way to a blustery cold wind off the Atlantic, and Brody felt like the air around him: as if he were in the middle of a squall.

Bridgett had become the houseguest who wouldn't leave, saying she was sick of staying in the hotel her firm had booked her in for the duration of her trial prep. Worse, she'd seemed to develop a fast friendship with Julianne and the other Blaze wives, ending up at a party at Celtic Charm last night. Not that Brody believed any of it was a coincidence. Julianne was up to something and she wouldn't stop until she decided everyone is happy. Which of course meant Shannon's happiness. Unfortunately none of the women seemed to understand Shannon was happier without him.

He sucked in a deep breath, reminding himself that he and Shannon weren't anything more than science fair partners at this point. Clearly, she wanted nothing to do with him other than to use him as a lab rat for her thesis. It was time to move on. Once he got his mojo back on the field, Brody was going to get his mojo back in the bedroom with the first willing woman he could find. It had been way too long.

Squeezing his eyes shut, he tried to block his wayward thoughts out and just listen to the mass. He needed to focus on the game this afternoon. He and Devlin had worked on every pass play this week, and Brody hadn't dropped the ball one frickin' time. Last Sunday's game would seem like a figment of everyone's imagination once he took the field today.

Sister Agnes waited until the end of the homily to get her two cents in. "Was someone else wearing your uniform last week, Brody?"

"Nope. No one to blame but myself."

She shook her head. "It was a horrible loss."

"What are you upset about? We got beat by the Cardinals. At least you nuns should be happy." Brody was the only one laughing at his own joke.

The sister sported a grim look and Brody felt like he was back in the fourth grade.

"And that awful story on the Internet? Was that you, too, Brody?"

"Hell, no—ow!"

Sister Agnes rapped his thigh with her rosary beads.

"No!" Brody whispered hoarsely. "None of that was me. None of that was even true." *Except for the destruction of a two-hundred-year-old door at an estimated one thousand dollars in damages.* Brody's mother had been mortified, the rest of the wedding guests looking at him like he had 'roid rage. He'd made up a story about the bathroom door somehow locking itself with Shannon trapped inside. Shannon had disappeared early that morning with Will and Julianne before anyone else became aware of the situation, so there was no one to dispute him.

The sense of shame he felt angered him, though. His family, his teammates, and the Blaze organization disregarded the blogger's article as untrue. But the average person, like Sister Agnes, would always doubt him.

"It didn't happen the way that blogger wrote it," he reiterated, hating the disillusionment he saw in the nun's eyes.

She nodded. "I never pictured you as an abuser of women. I don't always approve of the women you go out with, though, Brody. You should be more serious in your relationships."

Shit. There was nothing like censure from a nun to discourage him from going out and finding a willing woman to help him rediscover his mojo.

"No time for women anymore. I have to concentrate on my game." Which was the truth. The goal was to get a contract extension. He'd just put Shannon and all women out of his mind until he had that sewn up.

Sister Agnes actually snorted, startling Brody into nearly laughing before he remembered they were in church.

"Hmm. I don't know if I believe that," she said. "But we can discuss that next week. Today, you'd best be concentrating on the Titans."

"Yes, ma'am." Not bothering to tell her he was only agreeing to the second part of her statement. Because there was no way he was discussing his love life—or lack of one—with the nun.

Four hours later, Brody was standing midfield in his sweats as the wind swirled around him.

"It's like a damn wind tunnel in here today," Devlin moaned as he tossed a few blades of turf in the air to see how they'd float. "We're gonna have to keep this game on the ground."

"Does that mean you're not gonna be throwing Brody any passes, Mr. Devlin?"

The quarterback rubbed Maddox's head. The kid seemed to have grown an inch since Brody'd seen him last, three weeks ago.

"Nah, it just means Brody's gonna have to work a lot harder to catch 'em," Devlin told the boy as he pierced Brody with his drop-it-and-I'll-kill-you glare. "Come on, boys. Let's get you out of the wind before you both get ear infections."

Maddox laughed.

"Don't laugh at the butthead, Maddox," Troy said as they trudged toward the tunnel leading back inside. "Ever since Carly got pregnant, he's become like a grandma with his overprotectiveness."

Devlin playfully cuffed his half brother on the back of the head, which only made Maddox laugh more. A crowd was gathered outside the locker room. Connelly was rocking a fussy Owen, while Julianne dug in her oversized bag for a bottle. Carly waddled over to her husband, who proceeded to stroke his hand over her belly.

"I am so not looking forward to that," Troy whined as Maddox plugged his ears.

"My sister cries like that all the time," Maddox said before both boys disappeared into the locker room.

DeShawn laughed loudly, focusing Brody's attention on the woman he was joking with: Shannon. She stood behind the tailback, her long legs decked out in a pair of skinny jeans tucked into her cowboy boots with a sleek, puffy down jacket keeping the rest of her warm. Brody was hard just looking at her legs.

"There you are, Brody," DeShawn was saying. "Shay was going to sneak off, but I kept her here so you could get a proper good-luck kiss. We're not taking any chances today."

Shannon's smile dimmed and her face became even paler,

if that were possible. Those ever-present dark circles were beneath her eyes, the telltale sign she was working herself to death, as usual.

"Don't pin my bad game on Shannon," Brody growled.

"You gotta admit, Brody, you've got some bad karma hanging around you. You need to do whatever you can to shake it off, man," DeShawn pleaded.

Shannon muttered something beneath her breath before closing the distance between her and Brody. Something in Brody's chest squeezed as this proud, strong Texas wildcat raised her chin before gently placing a chaste kiss on his lips.

"Good luck," she whispered, her eyes avoiding his.

"Dang, Shay, is that the best you can do? The dude played like crap last week," DeShawn was saying.

It had been exactly two weeks since she'd crept out of their room at the inn. Two weeks when Brody ached to make things right with her, only he didn't know how to. Still, she'd been in his house during that time, breathing the same air as he did and he'd taken solace eating the food she'd prepared. He'd caught glimpses of her at the practice facility, tamping down on the longing in his body in an effort to give her space. But right now, he was done giving her space.

Before DeShawn finished his sentence, Brody had tangled his fingers in Shannon's hair pulling her in for a deep, searching kiss. The sweet taste of her on his tongue and the feel of her body against his were intoxicating. Instantly, the storm that had been brewing inside his head calmed and he sank in farther to enjoy the warmth of her welcoming mouth. Her response was immediate; fisting her hands in his sweatshirt, she angled her head to allow him better access. Desire, dark and thick, lapped at both of them before Shannon suddenly tensed in his arms. Pulling away abruptly, this time her eyes did meet his; they were bright and damp.

Brody reached out to pull her off to the side, where he could speak privately to her, to somehow make peace with her, but she slipped free of his grasp and hurried down the long hallway to the stadium concourse as a sob escaped her throat. He opened his mouth to call after her, before thinking better of it. Apparently, he'd already given the crowd congregating at the locker room door enough to talk about.

"Damn, Brody, I told you to kiss the woman, not make her cry." DeShawn glared at him before stalking into the locker room.

Juggling a still-fussy Owen and her big diaper bag, Julianne chased after Shannon, but not before leveling a fierce scowl at Brody. Carly trotted behind her, cursing him as she went. He felt like he was in the middle of a really bad dream when his sister Bridgett emerged from the shadows, a pitying look on her face. Shaking her head, she trailed after the other women.

"Shake it off, Janik. I mean it. Kickoff is in an hour," Devlin demanded as he and Connelly entered the locker room.

But Brody couldn't shake it off. He ran his routes perfectly, but somehow the ball wouldn't stay in his hands. Making matters worse, DeShawn went down with a thigh injury midway through the first half, thereby eliminating any sort of running game. For the first time in Brody's career, the boo-birds chorused as he made his way to the locker room after a second consecutive Blaze loss, this one not close at all.

The locker room was quiet, the players keeping to themselves while they shed their pads and dirty uniforms. A few of the receivers whispered hushed comments, peeking over their shoulders at him, but Brody ignored them. The media would be coming in a few minutes and he wanted to make sure he was long gone by then, avoiding the painful locker-front interviews. Normally, only the coach and the quarterback addressed the postgame press conference, so he wasn't obligated to stay.

"Janik," Devlin called across the locker room as Brody headed for the safety of the shower. "Be here at ten o'clock tomorrow morning."

A few snickers escaped from the offensive line, but the rest of the team was silent as Brody nodded, making his way to the showers in disgrace. As he let the warm spray pummel his body, he knew that no amount of playing fetch with his quarterback was going to fix what was bothering him. It was ironic that the one woman who managed to keep his blood sugar under control had managed to mess up every other part of his body. The conundrum that was Shannon Everett had taken hold of him—and his mojo—and wouldn't let go.

THE GIRLFRIENDS' GUIDE TO THE NFL

Number *ochenta* is definitely down on his luck. Some might even say cursed. After his reckless weekend in Vermont, every girl's favorite tight end seems to be having trouble keeping his eye on the ball. Probably because his eyes are too busy mooning over his very off-again girlfriend, PhD student Shannon Everett. Miss Everett, need we remind you, is the not-so-better-looking twin sister of Dallas Cowboys cheerleader Teryn Everett. Apparently brains don't make up for beauty, because according to sources within the Blaze organization, this Everett sister has left our Brody high and dry, taking his game-day confidence with her.

Eighteen

"Damn it, Hank! I want whoever is writing this bullshit found. And when you do, I'm going to rip their teeth out with my bare hands!"

"Whoa, Brody, calm down." The Blaze GM motioned for Brody to sit in one of the chairs in front of his desk. Brody had been feeling twitchy ever since that blogger's ugly words appeared on the Internet earlier that morning. His knee banged the side of Hank's desk as he tried to sit still.

"I can't calm down, Hank. It'd be different if this was just embarrassing me, but it's not. She's after the whole team and Shannon as well. I can't stand by and let whoever this is get away with it."

Hank sighed. "Brody, right now Donovan, the league, and every other club all have people looking for this blogger. Unfortunately, even if she is found, it's going to be hard to shut her down. The crux of the matter is everything she's reported has been factual."

Brody sprung from his chair. "I didn't tear up a hotel room playing some kinky sex game or fighting with Shannon!"

Hank held a hand up to quiet him down. "But you did damage that room, Brody, didn't you?"

Damn. Brody slumped back into his chair.

"And you have had a little trouble on the field these past two weeks." The GM ignored Brody's scowl and continued. "While I think it's admirable that you want to protect Shay from all this, she needs to know some of this comes with the territory of dating a superstar. You can't always control how you are portrayed in the media. She's a smart woman and I think she knows how these things work. On the flip side, Brody, you're getting paid a lot of money to keep all of this off the field. Let us worry about shoring up the leaks within our clubhouse and you worry about catching the football. That's your only job right now."

Feeling chastised, Brody headed for the door.

"Brody," Hank's voice stopped him. "Are you sure that's all that's bothering you? You usually don't rattle so easily."

There were a lot of things bothering Brody right now, one of them a time bomb that—if it were revealed—wouldn't leave Hank looking so calm. Obviously, he needed to play things a lot cooler or the GM would sniff the real reason Brody was feeling so twitchy. Hank was right; getting his game back in synch was the most important thing right now. "It's all good."

"I hope so," Hank said as Brody stepped out into the hallway.

Me, too, Brody thought. *Me, too.*

An hour later, after three unanswered calls to Shannon, Brody stood near the goalpost of the Blaze practice field. The rain peppering the roof of the bubble matched his demeanor. He'd just finished a lengthy conversation with his manager, Roscoe, who kept hinting about bringing on a sports shrink. Brody didn't need a shrink. He just needed a few minutes—or a few days—alone with Shannon to work things out, only she'd gone into hiding. Bridgett was suspiciously missing from his house, too, making Brody think his sister was responsible for Shannon's disappearance.

A football suddenly whizzed by his head, missing his left ear by mere centimeters. Brody jumped, looking over his shoulder to see Matt Richardson standing thirty yards downfield, palming another football. Despite being fifteen years out of the game, the coach could still throw it. The second ball ricocheted off the crossbar of the goalpost, nearly clocking Brody in the head.

Brody shuffled to the sideline, retrieving one of the balls.

"Hey there, Coach. Where's Devlin?" The quarterback had texted him earlier, saying he was going to be late but he didn't mention their coach joining them.

"Home. Resting his arm. The last thing I need is him wearing himself out trying to get you out of your love funk."

Another bullet. Brody had to react fast to catch it in the bread basket.

"You're stuck with me." Coach didn't bother to disguise the menacing glee in his voice. He loved nothing more than to air out his own arm in practice once in a while. Somehow, Brody didn't think today was going to be one of those fun catch-and-release workout sessions.

"I told you what would happen if you made that girl cry." Coach launched the ball like a laser, this one nearly catching him in the family jewels, and Brody cursed. That particular part of his body was suffering enough already.

He had no trouble figuring out who *that girl* was that Coach was talking about. The skeleton crew and players who ventured into the practice facility on Mondays had all wasted no time giving him the cold shoulder. Brody didn't have to wonder whose camp they were all firmly in. But he did take exception to the fact that everyone assumed Shannon was the only miserable one here.

"Run a post route and then glance in," Coach called out.

Christ, he was going to make Brody run. He sprinted thirty-five yards before breaking to the inside in front of the goalpost. Coach threw it a little high, but Brody extended his hands and caught the pass as if it were thrown perfectly. The thrill of catching a ball on the run still gave him a quick high. He trotted back over to the coach.

"Nice catch." Coach flipped another ball between his hands. "Too bad you couldn't manage to do that when it was third and long yesterday."

"You threw the ball better than Devlin." Brody figured it couldn't hurt to do some sucking up.

"Cut the shit, Janik." But Brody noticed the coach stood a little taller at the compliment. "Let's try Rebel Reverse with a right slant."

Thirty minutes later, Brody was dogging it while the coach looked like he could throw all morning. The guy would probably need ultrasound and an hour in the whirlpool by the time they finished. Thankfully, Coach's cell phone rang. He took the call while Brody guzzled some water.

"I've gotta go talk to the trainers about yesterday's injuries," Coach said pocketing his cell phone. "Obviously, your problem isn't anything physical, Brody. So that means you need to get your head back where it belongs, in the game."

Easier said than done. "Yes, Coach," Brody said anyway.

"And whatever is wrong with you and Shay, work it out. Either you're together or you're not, but I don't want it to be a distraction on the field, in the locker room, or in my damn house any longer, got it?"

Clenching his teeth, Brody nodded. *Again, easier said than done.* In order to work things out with Shannon, he'd have to find her first.

Shay managed to avoid Brody for three full days. It had taken her that long to recover from the kiss they'd shared at the stadium. After vowing she'd never allow him to touch her again, she'd let him kiss her as if he were going off to be executed. Worse, she'd kissed him back, like a woman drowning. Even though she knew better than to get involved with a player like Brody, the man had managed to get under her skin. Fortunately, Bridgett had become an unlikely ally, taking her to the hotel suite her firm leased for her use. Shay spent three days reinforcing her heart in five-star luxury. She didn't feel an ounce of guilt about skipping her Tuesday session with her academic advisor and her swim classes with her seniors later that afternoon.

"Brody's been staked out here all day," Jackie told her on Tuesday. "I'm not sure who was more excited when the school bus dropped Maddox off, my son or Brody."

He'd gone to the aquatic center looking for her, too. According to the substitute who'd taught Shay's class, the geriatric crowd had given Brody so much unsolicited advice on his athletic abilities and his love life that she was sure he wouldn't come back the next day.

But it was Bridgett's words that brought Shay out of her seclusion. Brody's sister had been delivering his meals each day, believing she was only helping Shay with her dissertation. If Bridgett knew she was covering up her brother's condition, she might not have been so willing. Shay had played hooky from the practice facility, too, claiming she was sick, so she eagerly soaked up any information about all things Brody.

"Brody's manager wants him to see a sports psychologist," she told Shay over dinner the previous evening.

"Brody's problem isn't in his head," Shay said.

"At least not that head," his sister joked.

Shame and embarrassment washed through Shay. If she hadn't have reacted the way she did in Vermont, none of this would have happened. She should never have gone to the wedding in the first place, but she'd gotten carried away with her own infatuation with Brody, believing he would be interested in an innocent like her.

But Brody's issues on the football field had nothing to do with her. His problem was that he'd been spoiled all his life, with everything coming naturally to him. Suddenly, life had thrown him a bunch of curves—hiding his battle with his blood sugar so he could get his contract extension being the worst—and he had to do a little extra work to overcome those challenges. Brody wasn't exactly used to having to do anything more than was necessary. He certainly didn't need a shrink to work those things out.

And he didn't need to be obsessing over her. It was time they talked.

Nate ran interference as Shay made protein shakes and doled them out to the waiting players before Thursday's practice.

"What up, Sha-nay-nay?" DeShawn was the first to make his way into the commissary. "Are you feelin' better?"

"Yeah, thanks, DeShawn. It was just a cold."

"Cold my ass! That dumb Janik obviously just doesn't know how to satisfy his woman."

As if Shay's embarrassment at DeShawn's outburst weren't enough, one of the big offensive linemen lumbered over to add his own two cents. "Yeah, Shay, but we're working on him. You just need to give him another chance, that's all."

"Seriously, Shay," Jamal Hollis joined his teammates as Shay began to pray the floor would open up and swallow her. "We need you two to make up. Obviously, he plays better when he's . . . well . . . he's—"

"Gettin' regular lovin'!" DeShawn finished for him. He took a step closer, pulling a dog-eared catalog out of the pocket of his hoodie. "Maybe something from in here will help. Brody had this on him when we went to Cleveland last month. The dude must have known he was going to need a little help in the bedroom."

Mortification gripped Shay. It was the sex toy catalog she'd given to Brody to catch the snitch. DeShawn tried to hand it to her, but the pages practically singed her fingertips.

"Just pick something out that might interest you and we'll take care of getting it to Brody," DeShawn was saying, but Shay barely heard him, her head had begun to spin. Up until now, she'd thought it impossible that a person could actually die from embarrassment. But the way she was feeling right now, she wasn't so sure. Shucking her hairnet, she hightailed it out of the commissary and back to the relative safety of Bridgett's hotel room.

She rescheduled Emma's weekly tutoring session to take place at the Richardson home rather than the practice facility. Shay didn't think she could endure another run in with DeShawn and his posse.

"So you're good with quantum numbers? You understand it for the quiz?"

Emma nodded, her blue eyes earnest as she shuffled the papers on the big farmhouse table in the middle of the keeping room off the kitchen. A fire blazed in the giant hearth, its crackles comforting against the chilly drizzle that seemed to linger over the mid-Atlantic area for the past few days. Shay was feasting on tea and homemade butterscotch cookies prepared for her by Penny, the Richardson's housekeeper.

"Daddy's still angry at Brody," Emma said. "He said if he doesn't start catching the ball he won't get his contract renewed next year."

"Brody's just in a slump right now. I'm sure he'll be fine this week." At least that's what Shay hoped because the strain of Brody's poor performance was beginning to take a toll on her as well.

"I don't know. My mom used to be a couples' therapist and she thinks maybe you and Brody need to talk things out. I mean, you guys are still a couple and all, right?"

Shay was a little chagrined that she and Brody were being discussed around the dinner table at the Richardson house, but then again it seemed all of Baltimore had an interest in Brody's love life.

"Nothing has changed in our relationship," she hedged, hoping the teenager would buy it.

But Emma eyed her skeptically. "Daddy said Brody is a lovesick puppy. Maybe you should just, I don't know, let him have his way or something. At least during the season, you know? My dad gets really grumpy when the team loses, so you'd be doing me a favor, too."

Great. As if it weren't bad enough that Brody's teammates were practically throwing sex toys at her; now she was getting relationship advice from a teenager.

"There's really nothing to let Brody *have his way* about, Emma." This was a bald-faced lie. There was *something* she could let Brody have his way on, but he'd already blown that chance. She wasn't sure she had the strength for a round two.

"I don't mean about anything big. Just maybe let him pick the restaurant or what to watch on TV. That kind of stuff." The fifteen-year-old's innocence might have made Shay laugh if she hadn't felt so on edge from her day.

"I'll do my best, Em, but I really think Brody just had two bad games, that's all."

Penny came into the kitchen. "Emma, hon, you need to get changed for dance class. Carpool will be here in ten minutes to pick you up."

Apparently reassured that all would be right with Brody and the Blaze, Emma bounded up the back stairs to change. Shay gathered up her book bag and headed for the back door.

"This is for you," Penny said, handing her a check. Then, she quickly scanned the kitchen before handing Shay a small white shopping bag with red tissue paper sticking out on top. "This, too, hon."

Shay eyed the bag cautiously.

"It's just a little something I thought you might like so you can, you know, spice things up a bit with Brody. I'm sure with a man like that it's hard to keep things . . . interesting. If he's happy in the bedroom, maybe he'll perform better on the field."

Did everyone associated with the team think it was her fault Brody wasn't performing well? On or off the field? She was afraid to look in the bag, but Penny looked so excited, Shay was forced to poke a finger in, pulling out a lacy red thong with the Blaze emblem adorning the scrap of fabric holding the strings together.

Hell's bells!

"There's a black pair in there, too."

Shay was too stunned to speak. Politeness apparently took over because she didn't realize she'd said thank you until Penny responded.

"Oh no, Shay, thank *you*. A happy Brody Janik is a productive Brody Janik and Blaze fans everywhere are grateful to you."

   Somehow Shay made it out to her car with the shopping
bag dangling off her finger. The blood was roaring through
her ears. Brody's lackluster performance on the field—and
in the bedroom—was *not* her fault. Revving her car's engine,
she decided it was time he face the music.

Nineteen

The rain was coming down at a steady clip again.
Brody had swung by Shannon's apartment, but she was still
AWOL. Even Maddox and Jackie were out. The whole
situation was getting ridiculous. She'd been in the practice
facility earlier, but she'd dashed out before he could talk to
her. His next step was to track her down at Bridgett's hotel,
but first he needed to change out of his practice clothes and
eat his prepared dinner on schedule.

Pulling his Range Rover around back of his house and
into the garage, he spied a car on the parking pad. Unfortunately, it wasn't the one he was hoping for: It was Connelly's.
Brody wasn't in the mood for another lecture on his
performance tonight. He'd had enough from his coaches to
last a lifetime.

Stomping through the mudroom, he looked around for
Will, who was likely lying in ambush. A Kenny Chesney
tune played on the sound system in the great room and
Brody walked around the high-back recliner to see his teammate stretched out in the chair, his eyes closed.

"Comfortable?" Brody rifled through his mail.

"I'd be more comfortable at home in my own bed, but Owen is teething and no one's getting any sleep at my loft."

"I'd ask how you got in, but Julianne must have given you her key."

One of the slumbering giant's eyelids lifted to half-staff. "Remind me again why my wife has a key to your house and I haven't kicked your ass for it?"

"It's only a matter of time before she gets tired of you," Brody called from the kitchen, where he checked to see if his dinner was in the fridge.

"Hell, maybe I'll just kick your ass right now."

But Connelly remained where he was, his eyes shut in repose and his body relaxed in the chair. Brody walked over to the stone hearth, his hands tucked in his pockets. He didn't have time to deal with Will Connelly right now. He needed to find Shannon.

"What do you want, Will?"

"Besides a good night's sleep?" He finally opened both eyes. "I came here to find out if you're really okay."

"Perfectly fine. Now get out."

Connelly didn't budge. "Brody, do you have a substance abuse problem? Something that needs professional attention?"

"Hell, no!"

Connelly heaved a sigh. "So is it just what the guys are saying, that you need to get laid?"

Brody flipped him off.

"Because they wanted me to pick up some pink fuzzy handcuffs for you. I'm not stepping a foot in one of those stores, but I'm sure Julianne would. For you, anyway. That would require another ass-kicking on my part, though."

"Everybody just needs to mind their own freakin' business."

"That's just it, Brody, you're part of a team. When you're hurting, we all feel it."

Brody blew out a breath in disbelief. "I'm not hurting!"

Connelly grunted. "Says you. It's not like you to get so

messed up about a woman. Maybe this one means a little more to you than the others?"

"Sorry to disappoint, Dr. Phil, but my love life has nothing to do with my game. Football is my number one priority in life."

"That's what I used to say until my whole worldview was knocked off its axis six months ago. I used to think that I could do this alone—football, my charity work, life, everything. I'll admit I was a bit slow to realize it, but it's nice to have someone to share this ride with. Thanks to a little push from you, I saw the big picture before it was too late."

Brody was getting anxious for Will to leave. He didn't want to hear his teammate's declarations of love for his wife. Connelly was way off base anyway. Brody wasn't looking for someone to share his life with. Not yet anyway. Right now, he was looking for one sassy Texan to share the night with. Once he'd done that, he could get back to the bigger issue of playing football and his contract extension.

"Well consider the favor returned. You've said your piece, now get your ass out of my chair."

The big lug remained where he was. "Come on, Brody. Something's really bugging you. Jeez, even Roscoe is worried and he's got a heart of stone."

Brody opened his mouth to tell his teammate where both he and their agent could go, but the sound of the door slamming at the front of the house distracted him. Like an angry bull charging a matador, Shannon burst into the great room, shedding her jacket as she went. Her whiskey eyes were mere slits in her face as she stormed across the room toward him.

"I am so done with this, Brody!"

"Shannon—"

She swatted him with a white shopping bag she had clutched in her hand. "Don't you dare try to use your stupid charm on me. I swear, Brody, I've had it with people thinking it's my fault that you can't . . . perform!" She put extra emphasis on the last word making it clear that she was talking about more than just football.

"Whoa," Brody said uneasily, holding up his hands. He really didn't want to have this conversation with Connelly ten feet away. "No one's blaming you, sweetheart."

She smacked his hands with the bag again. "Of course they are! Do you know what I've had to endure today? Do you?"

He started to tell her he didn't, but she wouldn't let him get a word in.

"I spent part of my day scanning the sex toys catalog with your teammates looking for anything that might *turn you on*! Do you have any idea how embarrassing that was?"

His gut clenched at the pain in her voice. Anger coursed through him at his teammates—and at himself—for putting her through this. Stepping closer, he tried to pull her into his arms, but she batted him away again.

"No! I'm not finished." Her voice was on the verge of hysteria and Brody figured it was best to listen quietly. If he had to kill Connelly to keep him from repeating any of this, so be it.

"This afternoon I got to take relationship advice from a fifteen-year-old who just wants me to let you *have your way*."

Brody cringed at the look of anguish on Shannon's face.

"Then," she waved the bag in front of his face. "This! Do you know what's in here, Brody?"

Sheepishly, he shook his head.

Pulling a scrap of red lace out, she flung the empty bag across the room. "These, Brody!"

She waved the lacy thong in front of his face and Brody was momentarily distracted, thinking about how damn good those panties would look at the apex of Shannon's long legs. He sucked in a breath.

"That's right, Brody. According to the coach's *housekeeper*, I need to wear these to add a little spice to our relationship. That way, you'll play better and Blaze fans *everywhere* will rejoice." She gulped to cover what might have been a sob, making Brody feel like shit.

He ran his palm down the back of his neck in an attempt

to ease the squeezing back there. "Shannon, I'm sorry. I don't know how to make this all stop."

"Well I do," she said as she toed off her sneakers.

The squeezing ratcheted up a notch as she yanked her sweater over her head revealing a lacy pink bra.

"Whoa, Shannon!" Clearly she was oblivious to Connelly's presence in the recliner behind her. Brody frantically looked from Shannon to his idiot teammate who had the nerve to smile smugly, clearly enjoying both Brody's dilemma and Shannon's striptease. If she knew the big oaf was sitting there leering at her, she'd be mortified.

"Shannon, stop!"

"No way, Brody. I'm taking one for the team. Right here. Right now. So you'd better be getting naked." She shoved her jeans down her long legs revealing a black lace thong with the Blaze logo emblazoned on the crotch. The breath caught in his lungs at the sight of Shannon standing proudly like an Amazon before him, her legs spread slightly and her chin belligerent. Every part of his body was alert and at attention. He forgot about Connelly and football and everything else, knowing only that he wanted her taste on his tongue and her long legs wrapped around him as he came.

"So do the panties do it for you, Brody?"

Her anger had faded to shyness and his heart ached for her. Reaching forward, he gripped the warm skin of her waist with his long fingers, pulling her in contact with his very obvious arousal.

"Oh, yeah, Shannon," he whispered hoarsely, brushing a kiss over her shoulder. "Connelly, get out of my house. And if you breathe a word of this to anyone, I swear I'll kill you."

Shannon stilled in his arms, her face going from deathly white to bright red in a matter of seconds before she shrieked. Brody quickly turned her, shielding her body with his as she gulped giant sobs that seemed to come from deep within her shuddering body.

"Shh," Brody said as he held her tightly, one hand rubbing up and down her back while the other stroked her hair.

"It's all right. He's gone. His eyes were closed the whole time. I promise," he lied.

He nuzzled her neck, letting his lips trail along the pulse point there, the sweet taste of her skin exciting him painfully. One hand moved lower on her back to caress the smooth cheek of her ass as the quaking in her body slowly relaxed.

"That's a girl, just relax," he said as his other hand brushed over her pebbled nipple.

"I think I hate you, Brody," she moaned as one of his fingers crept in between the crease in her thighs.

He didn't blame her. But he didn't want her changing her mind and locking herself in his bathroom, either.

"Give me a few hours to convince you to like me again, Shannon," he breathed beneath her ear. Her body had become pliant against his as his fingers worked on her. "Please," he whispered, hoping like hell Connelly was long gone and couldn't hear him begging. "I need you, Shannon. Please don't change your mind."

She pulled away to look at him, those whiskey eyes damp and so trusting, they made his chest ache. Her lips parted on a sigh and he nearly came right there. Then she was kissing him, her hands ripping at his clothes as her tongue plundered his mouth. Brody wanted nothing better than to take her there on the floor or in the recliner, but she wasn't ready for that yet.

"Upstairs," he murmured as he reluctantly pulled her hands out of his sweatpants.

"No, here. Now."

"Unh-uh. Connelly isn't the only one with a key to this place."

That seemed to get her attention.

"Wrap your legs around me," he demanded, gripping her bare ass and lifting her. When her body made contact with his, he nearly expired on the spot.

Shannon seemed to revel in his torture, grinding her pelvis against him.

"Unless you want to do this in full view of anyone who might walk in, I suggest you stop that," he groaned.

Smiling shyly, she leaned in to nip at his ear. "Then hurry up."

Brody hadn't run the stairs that quickly since training camp his rookie year.

Shay was lying in the middle of Brody's massive bed cocooned between the fluffy comforter he'd been too hurried to turn down and the hard warmth of his naked body. The bedside lamp served as the room's only light, illuminating their silhouettes on the wall. Almost as if she were having an out-of-body experience, she watched as his shadow crawled over hers, exploring every inch of her skin with his lips. Her body was tight as a bow and she squirmed beneath his tender kisses.

"Brody," she moaned, becoming agitated with need.

She felt his smile against her skin. "This is the fun part. You don't want me to leave anything out."

Her head thrashed against the pillows as he took her nipple in his mouth and sucked gently.

"Brody," she moaned again, her body arching into his. "Please, I want you to be able to finish."

He muttered a few choice words as he leveled his body above hers, coming up on his elbows so that his face was directly over hers. "It was *one* time," he said, his blue eyes like granite. "And those were extenuating circumstances." Balancing his weight on one forearm, he pulled her hand between them and wrapped her fingers around his erection. "I'm still locked and loaded here."

Oh my. He was hard beneath the soft velvet skin. And big. So very big. Their gazes connected as she slowly stroked her palm down the length of him. Sweat broke out on his forehead. His own hand closed more tightly over hers and her grip became firmer as she worked her hand up and down.

Brody's eyelids slid shut as she pleasured him. "God, Shannon," he breathed, his enthusiasm spurring on her confidence. Her breathing became rapid as excitement built within her own body. Without warning, Brody pulled her hand away and flipped them so he was on his back and she lay sprawled on top of him. He was breathing heavy and his face looked strained. Her hand reached between them, but he grabbed her wrist.

"Don't," he groaned. "Unless you do want it to be over before we even get started."

Then he pulled her face down for a savage kiss, her body slithering over his to gain purpose. He sucked on her tongue and kneaded her bottom and Shay felt as if she might splinter into a million pieces.

"Okay," he said as he broke the kiss. "We do it your way. But next time we get to go slow, you hear me?"

Shay wasn't sure what she was agreeing to, but she nodded anyway knowing that her body needed release soon.

"Hold on to the headboard," Brody commanded as he shifted her farther up his torso. "Now get up on your knees."

The position left her feeling exposed and a little unnerved with Brody having an excellent view of her intimate parts from his position below her.

"Brody—" she stammered.

"Hush," he ordered and then he pulled her down until she was on top of him, his mouth meeting up with the cleft between her legs. The shock was overridden by the exquisite pleasure as his tongue sucked the part of her that needed the most attention. Shay jerked up and down on her knees, matching the rhythm of his mouth. Her breath labored in her chest as she chased after what she didn't know. It snuck up on her suddenly; a crest surging through her body, seemingly controlled by the pull of his mouth.

Shay's arms and legs went limp and Brody rolled her over onto her back. Ripping open a condom, he stretched it over himself. Shay tried to reach her arms up to do it with him, but they were heavy and numb. His erection brushed up against her entrance and her whole body quivered as if it hadn't just experienced the perfect release moments before.

"I'll try to be as gentle as I can," he whispered as he pushed in slowly. It felt as if her whole body stretched to fit him. Brody swore as he slid in more deeply. "Christ,

Shannon, you feel so unbelievably good, I don't think I can take this slow."

Her body was on tenterhooks again and she didn't want it slow, either. Thrusting her hips, she took him in fully. Shay didn't remember any pain or unpleasantness, just heat and deep need. Brody's body was providing the perfect sensual haze as his mouth ate at hers in another hungry kiss. The tension built as he moved inside her and Shay's hands clung to the muscles in his back.

Seeming to sense her urgency, Brody reached between them, fingering the tender nub his mouth had given such pleasure to earlier. And just like that, she shattered as a brilliant cluster of lights gathered behind her eyelids. Shay wasn't certain how long she lay there, but when her breathing returned to normal, she dragged her eyes open. Brody watched her closely, holding himself still as he lay propped up on his forearms. The cords in his neck bulged and a sheen of perspiration glistened on his body. It was costing him to keep himself in check, but still he worried about her.

"Are you good," he asked, his voice gravely.

Shay nodded. "Better than good."

A wicked grin broke out over his face. "Excellent," he said as he thrust into her several more times before finding his own release with a heavy groan as he collapsed on top of her. Shay luxuriated under the weight and warmth of his hard body, gently trailing her fingers down his spine. Then she did something she never imagined doing in a man's bed: She fell fast asleep.

Twenty

The sixty-inch flat-screen television mounted on the wall provided ambient light to the room. Brody had the sound on low as he watched *Jimmy Fallon* from his post on the bed. Shannon lay next to him, curled up in the thick comforter fast asleep. She'd been that way for the past five hours, sated and tousled in a deep slumber, her breath steady—he'd checked it often enough. He'd slept, too, but his hunger for food had eventually won out over his hunger for her and he'd ventured down to the kitchen for something to keep his blood sugar stable.

Diving into a bowl of Greek yogurt—Shay had purged the ice cream from his freezer long ago—drowned in fresh blueberries to kill the bitter taste, Brody sat quietly beside her, his back resting against the headboard, feeling at peace for the first time in weeks. Desire for the woman dozing next to him had definitely been distracting these past few days, not that he was going to admit that to Connelly, Coach, or anyone else. He was glad to finally be able to move on in their relationship.

Whatever he expected from his encounter with Shannon,

nothing could have prepared him for what he got. While she was innocent in some ways, she was also uninhibited and exuberant in others. Not surprisingly, she was a conundrum even in bed.

A breathy sigh slipped through her lips and Brody's semi-aroused state became a bit more interested. He'd wanted her again five minutes after he'd had her the first time, but she'd relaxed into sleep so quickly—a sleep she needed from the look of her weary face—that he didn't have the heart to wake her. Not that he wasn't hoping for a second set of downs before morning.

With a muffled groan, Shannon rolled over onto her back, her eyelids fluttering open. Brody smiled down at her as wonder adorned her face before it was replaced by a flush of pink.

"Oh, gosh." Her voice was huskier than usual and Brody's skin tingled. "I fell asleep." She glanced around the room. "How long have I been lying here?"

Five hours and twelve minutes. "I don't know. I just woke up myself."

"I'm sorry, Brody. I didn't mean to."

"There's nothing to be sorry for. Great sex will do that to you. It makes you sleep like the dead." He winked at her. "I take it as a compliment that you passed out so soundly."

"Um, well, I'm sure you want to get some sleep yourself. I should be going." She eyed her clothes that Brody had brought up from the great room, now neatly piled on a chair.

"Going where?" He nearly laughed at the obvious inner battle she was having about how she would get to her clothes without parading naked in front of him. "It's the middle of the night and it's raining. Have you got another job to go to or something?"

She propped up on her elbows, the comforter slipping down to expose the tops of her breasts. His teasing had roused her completely out of her slumber. "No, Brody, I don't. It's just . . . I can't sleep here."

Brody arched an eyebrow at the comical statement. "I think we've just established that you can."

With an exasperated sigh, she flopped back down on the mattress. Brody set the bowl between them as he lay down on his side, his head resting on his hand. "Stay, Shannon," he said quietly. "That's how this usually works. We spend the night and one of us sneaks out of the other one's house the next morning. You'll miss out on that part of the ritual if you go now."

She rolled her eyes at him. Opening her mouth to likely lodge another crazy protest, she clamped a hand over her lips instead as the sound of her growling stomach filled the room.

"Well, if your excuse is that you're hungry, I happen to have plenty of food downstairs in my kitchen. I'll even share my snack if you'd like some." He dipped the spoon into the bowl of yogurt. "Open up."

She pushed up on her elbows again, this time the comforter fell lower and Brody was distracted by the peek of pink nipple he got. He held the spoon up in front of her mouth, but just as she leaned in, he dumped its contents on her breast.

"Oh, wow. What a mess. Here, let me clean that up." Brody leaned over and lapped at the yogurt, cool on her warm skin. A hiss escaped Shannon's lips as he took her nipple in his mouth and suckled. Before he knew it, he'd slathered another spoonful down her belly and beyond. Squirming beneath his tongue, she clenched her fingers in his hair as her hips rose up to meet his lips. The yogurt now forgotten, Brody crawled up her slick body to find her hot silky mouth. His fingers threaded through her hair as he devoured her lips. Shannon wrapped her long legs around his waist and he could barely hold on long enough to sheath himself with a condom.

The erotic moan she uttered when he entered her caused him to shudder. She nipped at his shoulder. "Please, Brody," she pleaded. He was only too happy to oblige, burying himself deep inside her until her body squeezed around his in climax, pulling him to his own release.

It was a few moments before both their breathing returned to normal. He pushed up on his forearms so as not to crush

her, but she kept her legs loosely draped around his hips.
Her stomach rumbled again.

"Brody," she whispered, her whiskey eyes dancing. "Can
I please have my own bowl of yogurt?"

Leaning down, he dropped a kiss on the tip of her nose.
"If you promise not to leave, you can have anything you
want."

She nodded and the tightness in Brody's chest disappeared as he left the bed in search of food for his woman.
He'd definitely gone caveman, all right.

Shay quietly slipped out of Brody's bathroom,
where she'd hurriedly washed and dressed. The sunshine
had returned and she worried the bright bedroom would
wake Brody. *Hell's bells. Too late.* He was sitting up in bed,
wide awake and naked as a jaybird.

"When I mentioned the sneaking out part, I meant sneaking out so you aren't seen by neighbors and paparazzi, not
sneaking out without saying good-bye."

"I-I was going to say good-bye," she lied, his nude mag-
nificence unnerving her.

"Uh-huh," he said, climbing out of the bed and stalking
toward her. She focused on his face so she wouldn't get weak
at the knees. His eyes told her that he didn't believe a word
she said.

"Shannon, there's nothing to be ashamed of here. This
doesn't have to be awkward." He cupped his hand against
her cheek and she unconsciously leaned into it.

"But it is awkward," she whispered. "I'm not good at this."

He chuckled softly. "I beg to differ. You're very good at
this."

Her cheeks burned as his hard body penned her in. Brody
brushed his lips across her hairline. "Okay, go home, but
walk tall. You were amazing last night."

His words made the fluttering begin in her stomach
again.

"I'll see you later, right?" he asked.

Shay nodded. "I'll be at the practice facility today. Then I have to drop off your dinner."

"Don't make me dinner tonight. Let me take you out. Some place nice. You can tell me what to order and everything."

His lips had found her juncture of her collarbone and neck and she was having trouble thinking. "I-I can't. It's Friday night and I have to work."

Brody pulled away and stared at her.

"Celtic Charm. I'm a bartender there, remember?"

He shook his head slightly as if to remind himself what they were talking about. "Call in sick."

"I can't call in sick. The money I earn pays my rent, my Internet, my cell phone bill." She didn't bother mentioning all the other things her tips helped her pay for. Brody was born with a platinum card in his hand and he'd never understand her precarious finances.

Lines appeared along his brow. "How much would you miss if you didn't go in one night?"

"A lot." A trickle of unease began to worm its way through her. "Thanks to you and my newfound celebrity, I make nearly double the tips I used to."

Brody's blue eyes narrowed and his jaw tightened. "Fine. Tell me how much that is and I'll give it to you. You shouldn't be slaving away there anyway."

The unease was now a full-blown storm rolling over her as Shay backed up against the wall. Her mouth gaped open, but for once, words failed her.

"That didn't come out right," he said, tugging his fingers through his hair as he swore.

"No, it certainly didn't," she managed to say.

He swore again. "It's just that you never seem to have any time for yourself. Let me give you that."

Shay swallowed around the massive boulder in her throat. "In exchange for sex?"

"God, no!" He paced the room, his naked body still gorgeous even in anger. "It's just . . ." His words petered out as his eyes pleaded with her to understand. But Shay already did understand. It was Brody who didn't.

"I didn't stay last night because you're a superstar athlete. I don't want to be your arm candy. And, I certainly don't want you to buy me anything or take care of me. I'm perfectly capable of taking care of myself."

"Shannon—" He took a step forward, but something in her expression must have stopped him because he halted after two paces.

"I have to go now, Brody. Please don't make this any more awkward than it has to be."

Turning on her heel, she made it through the door without him following.

Four hours into her shift at Celtic Charm, Shay poured a glass of pinot grigio for Bridgett.

"So you caved under the pressure," Brody's sister said as she sipped her wine.

"I guess I wasn't prepared for the all-out assault by everyone associated with the Blaze," Shay said, wiping the condensation off the bar. "It was a relief to have things back to normal in the commissary today, though."

She'd been a little nervous when she arrived at the practice facility that morning, wondering what sort of ambush awaited her, but the players had, thankfully, all kept their distance. It was almost as if the day before hadn't happened. *Almost*. DeShawn gave her a knowing wink when he'd grabbed his protein shake, making Shay wonder what had been said in the locker room earlier. Had Brody bragged of his conquest? Her breath still caught at the thought. Or had Will Connelly talked, recounting for his teammates her embarrassing outburst in Brody's great room the evening before? Fortunately, no one had mentioned anything in the commissary, instead the players had gone about the business of readying themselves for their nationally televised game against their rivals, the Pittsburgh Steelers, on *Monday Night Football*.

Shay had also avoided any embarrassing run-ins with Will Connelly. She wasn't sure she could ever face the man again. Brody was a different story, however. As angry as she was about his heavy-handedness in his bedroom early that morning, she knew he'd meant well. Shay just wasn't used to dealing with the opposite sex—and with men like Brody, in particular. But he, too, had bypassed the cafeteria on the way to the practice field, leaving Shay to wonder where they stood.

"So, does this make you an official couple?" Even sitting and relaxing at a bar, Bridgett couldn't resist asking the probing questions.

Shay thought of how she'd left him early that morning, angry and naked in his bedroom. But she'd been angry, too. Most of all, she'd been hurt. "Brody's got a lot of growing up to do before he's ready for an official relationship."

Bridgett saluted her with her glass of wine. "I'll say it again, you've got my undying admiration. I didn't think I'd meet a woman who was unsusceptible to my brother's charms."

Shay's face grew warm. "I didn't say I was unsusceptible to all of his charms."

"Ick!" Bridgett held up her hands. "I seriously don't want to know the specifics of my brother's charms—especially the ones he employs in the bedroom. Just knowing that you're using him the way he uses women is enough for me. I can't wait until he finds out he's your fling before your sojourn in the big house."

Grabbing two bottles of beer out of the cooler, Shay wasn't sure how she felt about Bridgett's description of her. She was pretty sure she and Brody had both used one another last night, but her emotional commitment might be a little deeper than his sister suspected. He wanted her to come back to his place after her shift tonight, and she was sorely tempted. But Shay was a rookie at all aspects of a relationship. Was she capable of having just a fling with Brody like his sister said? After enjoying last night, though, could she just walk away?

Bridgett waved a twenty-dollar bill in her face, getting Shay's attention. "I didn't realize how late it was. I really need to go."

"You barely touched your wine." Shay followed Bridgett's eyes down the bar where several of the Blaze management congregated. Donovan Carter was talking about the blogger with the only man within the Blaze organization who rivaled Brody in magazine cover appearances: the owner's godson and heir, Jay McManus. Rich, politically motivated, and obscenely gorgeous, McManus seemed to pull everyone in the bar's attention to him. Everyone but Bridgett, who couldn't seem to get away fast enough.

"Keep the change, Shay." Bridgett was out the door faster than her brother ran the forty-yard dash. Even more interesting to Shay was the way Jay McManus's eyes followed Brody's sister's progress out of the bar.

In the end, there wasn't any question where Shay would spend the night. Brody's Range Rover dwarfed her aging Corolla in the parking lot of Celtic Charm when her shift ended at two A.M. He was waiting inside, Muse blasting over the satellite radio while he played Candy Crush on his iPad.

"What are you doing here, Brody?" It was a stupid question, but she asked it anyway. His only answer was that wicked smile—the one that never failed to make her stomach drop. At that moment she hated him for his arrogant self-confidence that she wouldn't refuse him. But she hated herself more for the way that smile made her insides quiver in anticipation.

"It's late. I just want to make sure you get home okay."

"Whose home?" she asked belligerently.

His smile faded and his blue eyes blazed with hunger and something else she couldn't quite identify. "Whichever one you want." The sheer desire in his tone was her undoing.

Driving through the quiet night, Shay imagined that, in his SUV behind her, Brody's smile was smug as she passed her exit. As tired and frustrated at him as she was, however, she still wanted him. Shay wanted whatever Brody would give, and her overworked mind didn't care about the consequences.

They'd barely made it through the door before he began kissing her. His mouth was warm against her lips, chilled from the late October night. His tongue slid over hers and he tasted of coffee and cinnamon. Tugging at the buttons of her wool peacoat, Brody reached a hand inside to caress her breast, his firm touch making her hips jerk toward his.

"Mmmm," he murmured as he left her mouth to trace his lips along her jaw line. "You taste like beer. My kind of woman."

"Gross. I should have gone home and rinsed off the *eau de bar* from my skin before I came over," she breathed.

"Good thing for you I happen to have a shower here." Brody placed an openmouthed kiss on her neck and Shay moaned in both pain and pleasure as his five o'clock shadow abraded her sensitive skin.

Smiling his cat-ate-the-canary grin, he pulled her up the stairs toward his bedroom. She tried again to work up a little anger at his arrogant self-confidence, but she couldn't; not while her body was thrumming with anticipation of what was to come. Brody stopped at one of the guest bathrooms along the hall and pulled out a fuzzy white robe.

"Bridgett won't mind sharing," he said leading her into the cavernous master bathroom. The travertine tile and polished chrome fixtures glowed under the soft lights in the tray ceiling. The moon shining through the wide skylight cast an ethereal glow on the area. A giant whirlpool tub took up one end of the room while a glass-enclosed shower large enough to house a family of five stood at the other end. Between the two were a double vanity and a door that led to the commode room.

Using a panel on the wall, Brody flicked on the lights in the shower. He pushed another series of buttons and a soft spray began to cascade from the waterfall-like fixture mounted to the shower wall. James Morrison's latest CD began to play from the speakers hidden in the ceiling. Most surprising of all to Shay was the minibar disguised as a cabinet, where he pulled out a bottle of water.

His blue eyes danced at her arched eyebrow. "Don't worry. I'm not hoarding sodas or ice cream up here."

That didn't mean she wasn't going to check it the moment he left.

Brody pulled an oversized bath towel from the linen closet and piled it and the bottled water on the counter. He strolled over to where she hovered in the doorway. "Help yourself to whatever else you need," he said, before kissing her on the forehead and leaving the bathroom.

Shay's knees nearly gave way when he walked out. As sensual as showering with Brody might be, she wasn't as comfortable parading around in the buff as he was. It was a relief to know she could rinse herself off and don Bridgett's robe without having to face his scrutiny of her body under the glaring lights of the bathroom.

Ten minutes later, her body had become so relaxed within the warm steam of Brody's incredible shower that Shay could barely move her limbs. The opening of the glass door quickly roused her, however, and she turned to see Brody striding toward her, naked but for the wicked grin on his face. He was so secure in his own body, it was unnerving. There was no place for her to hide in the vast shower.

"Don't," he commanded as she reached for the only thing available—a tiny washcloth—in a futile attempt to cover herself. Stopping within inches of her, his eyes never left hers as he gently traced a finger from the curve of her shoulder and down her arm. "I don't know who convinced you that you're not beautiful, but they were wrong, Shannon. You are an incredibly desirable woman."

His other hand joined the first, tracing from her hips over her belly to her breasts, while their gazes remained locked. "You're beautiful here—" His hand moved to her back and lower. "—and here." Long fingers brushed against her sensitive nipples before tracing her cheek and her jaw. "Here, too." He slipped a finger inside her and she gasped, grabbing onto his biceps to keep from melting on the tile floor. "Oh, yeah. You're very beautiful here." She tried to keep her eyes focused on his face, but her lids were sliding closed as his finger stroked her.

"God, Shannon, just watching you gets me so fired up. Feel what you do to me." He pried one of her hands off his bicep and wrapped her fingers around his arousal. Her moan came from deep in her belly as his finger pleasured her and she gently massaged him. Both their hips began to buck, their wet skin sliding against one another as each moved closer to release. Her fingers dug into his shoulder and Brody pulled her in for a deep drugging kiss. Her body was highly sensitized from his touch and she whimpered in aggravation.

"Go for it, Shannon," he murmured as his mouth left hers in search of her hard nipple. "Come for me." He swirled his tongue around it first, before taking the pebble in his mouth and sucking. The pleasure was so great it was nearly painful. Shay's body clenched around his finger and with a deep wail, she fell over the edge of bliss.

Brody's arms supported her as he sat her sated body onto the bench built into the tile. "Don't move." Cold air swirled in as he left the shower, making Shay shiver, but she was too languid to move back beneath the warm spray. He returned a moment later, moisture glistening on his hard body and a condom sheathing his rampant erection.

"Turn around," he demanded, but Shay was having a little trouble getting her body to move and in the end he had to lift up and turn her to face the wall. He placed her palms flat on the tile bench, bending her at the waist. "Hold on," he murmured and then he was sliding into her from behind. She gasped at the sharp fullness and Brody instantly stopped leaning his body over hers. His breathing was heavy on the back of her neck as he held himself in check.

"It'll be okay, Shannon." His voice was hoarse and the sound resonated through her. "I promise I'll make it good for you, too. Please," he murmured.

Shay relaxed at his plea, lifting her hips to take him in more deeply and Brody groaned. Their slick bodies quickly found a rhythm and another rising tide of desire swarmed within her as he thrust. As if sensing her need, he reached around between her thighs and rubbed his thumb against her sensitive nub. She let out a small cry as her stomach dropped in climax. Brody's hands supported her hips as he found his own release on a strangled groan a moment later.

She wasn't sure how she got to the bed. Vaguely, she recalled Brody gently, but briskly, toweling her off and wrapping her in the fluffy robe. But she was nude now beneath the cool sheets. Her lids were heavy and she wanted to sleep, but she couldn't seem to settle without Brody next to her. Finally, he slipped into the bed behind her, his warm body curling around hers intimately.

"I'm going to fall asleep again, Brody." Tears stung her eyes. He must think she was the most boring lover on earth.

She felt his lips curve into a smile against the skin on her shoulder. "Mmmm. Me, too." He reached a hand around and palmed a breast, the gesture more comforting than erotic and Shay drifted into a deep sleep.

Twenty-one

"So whose ass do I get to kick for making you so insecure about your body?"

Shay quickly glanced around the small restaurant in Little Italy, but the other diners—most of whom had earlier been mesmerized by the arrival of the Blaze superstar and his notorious girlfriend—seemed to be finally paying attention to their own food. She and Brody were seated in a back corner, where it was difficult for prying ears to overhear anything, but where they were sure not to go unnoticed.

"Was it your twin?" he asked. "Because if it was, I have no problem putting her in her place."

While his demeanor was all playful boyish charm, Shay felt the intensity behind his words. If she let herself, she could almost believe this man would be willing to fight for her. No way she was letting him anywhere near her sister, though.

"Teryn isn't like that," she answered, spearing shrimp and some pasta on her fork. "She didn't need to put me down. Her place on the pedestal was secure at birth."

The dinner in front of him temporarily forgotten, he leaned across the table toward her. "Who then? Was it some guy?" His jaw tensed and the charm faded from his eyes. "Shannon, tell me his name and he's a dead man."

She laughed at his idle threat before he reached for her hand and squeezed. There was no mistaking the look in his eyes now and she could feel the warmth of pleasure begin deep in her belly. Shay let herself revel in the joy that a man actually cared enough to be concerned about her, but only for a moment. This was Brody Janik, after all.

"It wasn't any one person." The fact that her Meemaw headed the list was probably best left out of the conversation, Shay decided. "It's just the way things were. Mama was a Texas beauty queen. She had twin girls. One of them was beautiful just like her and the other was the smart one. Neither one of us asked to be perceived that way. Both of us tried to fight the stereotype at one point in our lives, but we lived in a small town. Eventually, it was just easier to accept fate and go with the flow."

Brody's face was incredulous. "But surely your parents objected? All parents are supposed to think their kids are perfect."

Shay shrugged. "Mama never played favorites. Daddy and I weren't close, though. He believed girls should act pretty and proper—like Teryn. I'm not sure he knew what to do with a tomboy like me. I guess you could say I was a conundrum to him as well."

"You never talk about your family. Is your father still alive?"

"Sort of." She grimaced at the questioning look on his face. "He was a professional rodeo rider for nearly eighteen years. A pretty famous one, too. Daddy was a two-time world all-around champion." It was hard to keep the pride from her voice even knowing the secret life her daddy had led. "I doubt he remembers any of that part of his life, though. Fourteen years ago, a stallion kicked him in the head. He suffered a traumatic brain injury. Today, he just sits in a wheelchair and stares at the television screen. It's hard to tell what he knows and doesn't know."

The pad of his thumb rubbed the palm of her hand as he

held it. "I'm sorry," he said quietly. "No wonder you work so hard to help out your mom. His medical expenses have got to be through the roof. Is he in a nursing home?"

"No, he doesn't need any real day-to-day medical care. His mother, my meemaw, lives with him and Mama. She takes care of him while Mama runs her business."

Brody shook his head. "If your mom is anything like mine, I can't imagine having her mother-in-law living with her goes too well."

Shay smiled. His words couldn't have been truer. "She didn't have much of a choice. Someone needed to take care of Teryn and me—and Daddy. Daddy wasn't very good about saving the prize money he earned. After the accident, finances became pretty tight."

"But at least she doesn't have to take care of you and your sister any longer. If he's not in a nursing home it doesn't make any sense why you have to take that job in the prison." His eyes narrowed as if it pained him to say the word *prison*.

"Except Teryn and I aren't the only children Daddy is responsible for."

She waited for recognition to dawn on his face. His thumb paused in its stroking of her palm. "I think I know where this is headed." Brody's jaw clenched and she could have kissed him for the indignant anger that flashed in his blue eyes.

"I have a half brother out there that I've never met. One who legally gets four thousand dollars a month in child support according to a settlement Daddy signed with his mother just before he was injured, back when his endorsement money was flush. Apparently they'd been together for nearly four years. She lived with him while he was on the road."

"And your mother never knew?"

She shrugged again. "I'm pretty sure she never knew about Aaron—that's his name—but I have no idea whether or not she suspected anything about Nora, the . . . mom." Brody squeezed her hand again. His support buoyed her to continue. "In this economy, it's been hard to keep paying the full amount each month and Mama's gotten behind on her salon mortgage. Nora is threatening to take the salon from her. The bank president is a friend and he's given Mama until January to set up a payment plan to pay both the bank and Nora. My income will be guaranteed by the government so it goes a long way in securing Mama's mortgage. Without it, not even the bank president's fondness for Mama can save her."

Brody heaved a sigh. "Jeez, Shannon. That's a pretty heavy load for you to carry."

A lump formed in her throat at the pity she saw in his eyes. "I'd do anything to protect Mama. Daddy let her down, but I won't. And now we're even."

He raised an eyebrow in question.

"Aaron's existence is a well-kept family secret. Now you have something on me."

Brody pulled her hand up to his mouth and gently nuzzled her knuckles. Shay heard the telltale beep of a cell phone camera from somewhere behind them, but he seemed oblivious, drawing the moment out as another photo was snapped. Unease began to trill through her. Pulling her hand back, she retrieved her fork and attempted to finish a dinner.

"I told you already, Shannon. I trust you." His smile was sincere, but something was off in his eyes.

They shared some tiramisu for dessert, Brody seeming to pose as more cameras beeped behind them. He pasted on the fake smile he used for fans as he steered her out of the restaurant, his hand possessive on her lower back. As if sensing her growing agitation, he let his hand slip lower, caressing her butt as he helped her into her coat. She turned to glare at him and he gave her a quick shake of his head.

"Wait until we're in the car," he murmured.

The valet had already brought the Range Rover around and she quickly climbed in, but not before several other onlookers with cell phone cameras snapped their photo. She stared stonily ahead as Brody tipped the valet and took his place behind the steering wheel. A flash went off as they turned a corner, winding their way to the on-ramp of the Baltimore beltway.

"What was that back there?" she demanded once he'd put the cruise control on.

"That, Shannon, was a typical night in the life of a celebrity." A passing streetlight illuminated his tense jaw as he kept his eyes focused on the highway in front of him. "My life is not my own when I'm out in public," he said tersely.

"But did you have to play up to them? Those pictures are probably all over the Internet. I'm sure someone snapped a shot of you grabbing my butt." Anger—and hurt—was welling inside her now. "It felt like the whole dinner was practically a . . . photo op." She had to choke the last two words out around her tight throat.

Brody white-knuckled the wheel. "Damn it, Shannon, it wasn't. But when people started pulling out their cell phones, I figured we should take advantage of the situation."

"*We?* There was no *we* in that decision. And what were *we* taking advantage of?"

He shot her a blistering look before turning his eyes back to the road. "If you must know, I took it as an opportunity to refute that damn blogger's information. I was letting the world know that we are a couple and we're perfectly fine. Maybe now she'll leave us the hell alone!" he yelled.

Shay sat in stunned silence as he drove the remaining ten minutes to his house. Her brain had chosen to replay his words about them being a couple on a continuous loop. His frequent use of the word *us* was also getting a lot of airtime in her mind. She argued with her inner self not to believe him. This was just semantics. But a fluttering had begun in her chest and the rest of her body ignored her head.

He pulled the SUV into the garage, killing its engine as the double door slid closed behind them. Brody leaned his head back against the headrest and closed his eyes.

"I'm used to the paparazzi, Shannon. Hell, I know practically everyone I meet is going to sell me out sometime. But you shouldn't have to suffer for it. I don't want that blogger spewing lies about you. Making you feel like you're not worthy, as if being with me was some kind of special honor. I want her to stop. To leave us—you—alone."

Shay felt her face grow warm. "Well, I did feel pretty honored this morning. And last night," she whispered shyly.

"And I'm not going to sell you out, Brody. I thought you trusted me."

He turned his head to face her. "God, I do trust you, Shannon. But I feel like I'm selling you out every time she prints something in her stupid blog. You're right; I even did it tonight. You didn't ask for this. Any of it."

"I'm tougher than I look."

Brody's eyes got that now familiar hungry look in them. "Tough enough to climb on over here and have some makeup sex?"

Shay bit her lip as her sex began to throb. "I have something else I'd like to try."

"Oh really?" His husky voice made her ache more.

Reaching over the console, she unbuckled his belt and slowly drew the zipper down on his pants. Apparently he was as aroused as she was because his erection sprang free immediately. She eased her palm up over the head as she leaned over.

"Um, Shannon . . ." But his voice trailed off in a groan as she closed her lips around the head of his penis. She circled her tongue, tasting the tangy saltiness, and she thought she heard Brody swear. Ignoring him, she moved up and down, sucking and licking as she took him more fully into her mouth, her own body becoming more and more excited. His hand fisted in her hair guiding the rise and fall of her head until he climaxed with a silent scream.

Grabbing some Kleenex from the consol, she cleaned Brody off before gently zipping his pants again.

"Christ, Shannon, where'd you learn to do that?" He lay slack-jawed against the headrest, his eyes closed.

She didn't bother to hide a sly grin. "I read it in a book somewhere."

He grunted a laugh, opening one eye. "You have five minutes to get upstairs and get naked, woman, before I come up to return the favor."

"Only five minutes?" she teased.

"Go!" he roared and she laughed as she hurried from the car.

True to his word, Brody returned the favor and more as he leisurely made love to her. Afterward, with their bodies tangled together in his giant bed, they whispered stories about their childhoods. It felt good to share part of her family's burden with someone, her earlier unease long gone. She knew he had his reasons for wanting the blogger to leave him alone, but she was touched at his protectiveness toward her.

"My plan was all wrong," she said.

"Which one?"

She elbowed him in the ribs. "The one to catch the snitch. My data analysis doesn't support it being one person on each team."

Brody propped himself up on his forearm and studied her face. She tried not to get miffed at the look of humor in his sparking blue eyes. "You've done data analysis?" He had difficulty keeping a straight face and she elbowed him again.

"Yes, Brody, I have. It's a perfectly useful way to solve a problem." Exasperated at his unsuccessful attempt to conceal his laughter, she pulled the comforter against her body and crossed her arms over her chest. Brody snaked his hand beneath the sheet and began tracing his finger along her hip bone.

"And what does this data analysis consist of?"

His finger slid to the inside of her thigh and she was having difficulty focusing her thoughts. "It's-it's a spreadsheet of all the events she's reported this year and all the possible scenarios of how she could have obtained the information."

Brody's finger stilled near her belly button. "All?"

She nodded.

"Jeez, Shannon. You've put as much time into this as you have your dissertation."

She arched an eyebrow at him. "Up until a week ago, I had pretty good reason to want the snitch selling Blaze stuff to her found. Now I just want her burned at the stake."

He laughed and his finger eased lower.

Shay bit her lip. "Maybe if I just look at it again and think about it differently—ahh." She gasped as his sneaky finger slid inside of her.

"That's your problem, you think too much," he murmured as he nipped at her ear.

"An hour ago, you liked my studious mind," she reminded him.

"Mmm," he said rolling over on top of her. "I still do. Let me show you how much."

The football got lost in the lights, but only for a moment. Ignoring the defender ready to take him out at the knees, Brody leaped up and snagged the ball, clutching it to his chest with his gloved fingers. The cold turf was hard against his back, nearly stealing his breath, but the roar of the crowd told him everything he needed to know: touchdown. It was Brody's sixth catch of the game and his second one for a score. One of the offensive lineman yanked him up, and Devlin was pounding him on the shoulder pads as other players slapped him on the helmet.

"Nice to have you back, Janik," Coach said as he cuffed Brody on the back.

Connelly gave up his spot on the bench for him. "Great catch," the linebacker called before trotting over to huddle up with his defense.

It was the fourth quarter and the Blaze were up by seventeen. If the defense held here, the team would finally put another one back in the win column.

"Relax," Devlin said as he chugged a sports drink. "You played awesome tonight, Brody. This game's in the bag."

Brody hoped so. He was starting to feel a little lightheaded. It was the team's first night game since their home opener and, despite Shannon's modified schedule, his sugar was bordering on low at halftime. He needed to get back to the locker room and get some food in him soon. Not to mention that the sooner the game ended, the sooner he'd see Shannon again.

Since he hadn't had to report to the team hotel until Sunday afternoon, they'd spent Sunday morning napping and talking. Brody was surprised at how comfortable he felt with her, how relaxed. He didn't have to hold anything back and it stunned him to realize how much he'd been holding back from people and relationships these past few years. It was a relief to know he could be himself with her.

And the sex wasn't bad, either. Sure, he'd been with women a hell of a lot more experienced than Shannon, but none more enticing. Or studious. His body grew hard just thinking about what she might have looked up today.

"Ah, hell! Wipe that silly smirk off your face, Brody," Devlin complained as he picked up his helmet. "Connelly let the running back out of bounds and now the clock is stopped. Looks like I'm going to have to go out there and take a knee. Try not to let anyone sneak around you and *accidently* tackle me, will ya?"

Brody swore as he followed his quarterback onto the field. "It happened one time, Devlin, and it really was an accident. The dumbass slipped on his shoelace!"

In the locker room after the victory, Brody's light-headedness had abated thanks to a protein bar and an orange Shannon had tucked into his bag.

"She keeps you prepared, doesn't she?" His personal trainer, Erik, didn't bother to hide his displeasure with Shannon. As best as he could tell, the trainer didn't like the fact Brody was relying on Shannon to prepare his menu and not Erik or someone of his choosing.

"Yeah, she's thorough," he responded quietly, careful that no one in their vicinity could overhear.

"But not a professional."

"Is that what's bothering you?" Brody zipped up his bag and hefted it over his shoulder. "She's very nearly a professional and her plan is working, Erik, so I don't see what your concern is."

Erik shrugged one shoulder. "Maybe I think it's a bad idea, you mixing business with pleasure."

Brody glared at his friend of the past seven years. Erik was highly regarded among players in the league and Brody knew he was lucky to be among the handful of athletes the trainer individually coached. He also knew he paid the man an obscene salary to keep him at his athletic peak, but that salary didn't allow him to malign Shannon.

"You're over the line here, Erik."

"So you trust her?"

"Unequivocally." Brody didn't bother to keep the displeasure for this line of discussion from his voice. "Shannon is completely vested in helping me manage my condition."

"Until she isn't."

Brody froze on his way to the exit where the bus that would take them back to the practice facility waited. Erik's ominous words burned in his gut.

"Face it, Brody. When you break her heart, and you will, you know, she'll sell you out in a heartbeat. They all do."

He faced down the trainer, checking the nod he nearly gave acknowledging the partial truth of Erik's statement. But that had been in the past.

"This is different." Defiantly turning on his heel, he headed for the bus determined that, indeed, this time would be different.

Twenty-two

"Ah, man, I love Milk Duds." Brody shook the tiny box and the balls of chocolate-covered caramel bounced around inside.

"You can have 'em," Maddox said around the wad of bubble gum in his mouth.

"No, Maddox, he may not. And that's enough candy for you, too." Shay shoved the mountain of Halloween candy back into the plastic bag.

"Dang, Brody," Maddox said. "How come she never lets you have any candy?"

Maddox and Brody were sprawled on a sofa in the Blaze entrance area. Kids of all ages—children of players and staff, as well as some from local organizations the Blaze sponsored—roamed about dressed in Halloween costumes and trading candy. Maddox's plastic X-Men mask was pushed back upon his head, his feet dangling over the side of the sofa.

"Because she's a mean ol' sheriff, Maddox, and she likes to punish me." Brody's fingers brushed the back of her thigh just below her skirt and Shay blushed at both his double entendre and the burn his touch brought to her skin. She'd dressed as a cowgirl, wearing her boots, her Stetson, a chamois shirt, and khaki skirt. A sheriff's star and holster she'd bought at the dollar store rounded out her costume. There'd been a few snickers about handcuffs from some of the players, but Brody's glare had taken care of them instantly.

As expected, Brody had no trouble getting into the spirit of Halloween, dressing as Iron Man. A big kid himself, he led a parade of children trick-or-treating throughout the facility. The return of his game meant the return of the happy-go-lucky Brody everyone knew. Shay took some of the credit in the improvement of his on-field performance, but only in so far as she was no longer a distraction to him. He'd move on soon enough—his kind always did—but in the meantime, she was determined to get the most out of their relationship. There wasn't another man like Brody in her future.

"Come on, Maddox. Grab your stuff. Tomorrow is a school day and we need to get you home," Shay said, gathering up the posters and mini footballs the boy had managed to collect throughout the evening.

"I gotta say good-bye to Troy first." Before she could stop him, Maddox was jogging across the room to find the other ball boys.

Brody's long fingers manacled her wrist and he pulled her down practically in his lap. "Tonight, I want you to wear that hat. The holster, too," he murmured. "And nothing else."

Shay could feel her face burning as stroked the skin on her calf beneath her boot. "Brody!" she whispered, looking around to see if anyone was paying attention to them.

"Okay, maybe these sexy boots, too, but that's all," he said, seemingly not caring a lick who heard him.

He stared at the boots as if fixated on them, a slow smile spreading over his face, never doubting that she wouldn't refuse him. And she wouldn't. Try as she might, she couldn't. She dug her fingers into his bicep to capture his attention.

"I thought you didn't need toys," she challenged.

His nostrils flared and his grin turned wicked as he stood them both up, palming her bottom on the way to his feet.

"Giddy up, sheriff. Let's drop off the X-Man and then"—he

breathed into her ear—"I'm going to take you for a ride you won't forget."

It was a good thing he had hold of her arm, because the heat of the words on the bare skin of her neck nearly brought her to her knees.

Two hours later, she lay spent on top of Brody's broad chest, his heart still pounding beneath her cheek. His hand was tracing figures on her hip again, almost as if he were diagramming plays. Her fingers stroked his jaw, the stubble of his five o'clock shadow rough beneath her caress. Brody turned his head slightly to kiss the tender skin on her fingers.

"You were right, you know," she said.

"Mmmm. I told you it would be the ride of your life."

"Not that." She halfheartedly swiped at his chest and he quirked an eyebrow at her. "Although it was amazing," she said, the blush stinging her face. "But I was talking about the blogger. She's totally left you alone after those pictures were posted of us in Little Italy."

"Correction. She's left *us* alone." He snuggled her more closely against his body. "And while I may not be as smart as the great Dr. Shannon Everett, I do know how to manage the paparazzi."

"I'm not a doctor yet. I still have six more weeks."

His hand stilled on her hip. "Six more weeks? That's all?"

"After four years, six weeks doesn't sound like a lot, but I can't wait for it to be over."

Brody was so quiet for the next few moments that Shay thought he'd gone to sleep. She rolled over on top of his chest to peek at his face. His eyes were wide open as he contemplated the ceiling. "Brody?"

"And then you'll be working in a prison." That invisible spot on the ceiling still held him transfixed. "You actually sound excited."

Shay sighed, resting her chin on her hand over Brody's heart. "I wouldn't call it excited as much as relieved. It's a really good-paying job and it will save Mama. For once in my adult life, I'll be working normal hours and only one job. So, yeah, for those reasons I'm excited."

"But it's in a damn prison!"

"*At* a prison, Brody. I'll have an office on the grounds, but I won't be walking the cell blocks."

"You're awfully cavalier about this, Shannon." Brody's body had become tense beneath hers. "You could do so much more. Be so much more."

"I know I can and I will. But right now I have to do this to help Mama. I realized a long time ago that my life wasn't going to be a fairy tale, Brody, and I'm good with it. Not everyone gets to have *your* life."

She realized the unfairness of her words as soon as she said them. Brody's jaw firmed and it seemed as if his whole body bristled. Shay knew he wrestled with his celebrity and the ease with which he achieved it. But she also knew he'd never had to make the tough choices, so it was difficult for him to comprehend her path in life—one that had been chosen for her as a child much as his had been.

Trying to lighten up the mood, she leaned down and flicked her tongue over his nipple. "But this has definitely been a great way to finish out four years of studious drudgery."

With a growl, Brody flipped them over so he was on top, his nose touching hers and his hips pinning hers in place. "But you don't start until January, right." He made the question into a statement of fact. "So it's really eight weeks."

She didn't bother arguing with his logic she was too busy enjoying what his finger was doing between her legs. "Yes," she sighed.

"Good," he said, before his mouth found her nipple.

It wasn't until hours later that Shay realized he managed to charmingly negotiate their fling—or whatever it was they were doing—to last through the end of the season.

Brody quietly shrugged off his jacket at the back of the church and slid into the pew next to Sister Agnes. She eyed him speculatively, but didn't speak. The monsignor began the seven A.M. service before a sparsely populated sanctuary. It was a relief for Brody to finally get back to his game-day routine after a month when the Blaze had only played once at home on a Sunday. Since that Monday night game at the end of October, they'd won all four outings, with Brody and his teammates handling the toughest part of their schedule relatively easily. But he was a creature of habit and he liked his life to be predictable.

Of course, the most changeable element in his life now was Shannon and he could no sooner control her then he could the wind swirling around inside the stadium. She wasn't needy or clingy like the women he'd been in relationships with in the past and that should have made him happy. *Except it didn't.* Her independence and dogged determination irked him. It's not that he wanted her undivided attention all the time, but maybe more than just when they were in bed.

Brody was aware that he wasn't being fair; Shannon worked harder than anyone he'd ever known. She'd spent the last month pounding out her dissertation while still teaching water aerobics, tutoring Emma, working in the commissary, and tending that stupid bar. Most important, she'd kept scheduling and preparing meals for him and he'd never felt better. Thanks to her attentiveness in the kitchen—and in the bedroom—he was at the top of his game again. Sure, she was hanging around to pad the data in her research, but he hoped she was doing it for other reasons as well.

His trainer Erik's concerns about Brody breaking Shannon's heart and her unleashing his secret on the media were laughable because Brody was fairly certain her heart wasn't engaged. When the season was over, they could part ways as friends; Shannon with her doctorate and Brody with his contract extension. He just had to keep reminding himself how that was a good thing.

Sister Agnes rapped his thigh with her rosary beads and Brody folded his long legs onto the kneeler and bowed his head.

"You'd better be paying better attention when Devlin throws you the ball today." Sister Agnes whispered sternly. "Houston's secondary isn't as forgiving as the Lord is."

He mumbled an apology, realizing that he'd daydreamed

through the first half of the mass. As they took their seats
again, his cell phone vibrated in his pocket. Discreetly, he
checked the screen. A picture of Shannon appeared and
Brody squirmed in his seat. Last night, he'd tried his best
to get her to play along with some phone sex, only to end
up with her dissolving into peals of laughter on the other
end of the call. He'd gone to sleep frustrated and horny,
picturing her blushing enchantingly as she laughed her way
through their unsuccessful attempt. It was a bit easier to see
the humor this morning and, smiling, he eased his body to
a more relaxed position.

Sister Agnes elbowed him in the ribs and Brody slid his
phone back into his pocket like a chastised schoolboy, mumbling another apology.

The nun broke out into a huge grin. "She's a lovely girl,"
she whispered. "It's nice to see you in love, Brody."

His head cocked to the right abruptly. "I'm not in love."
He'd forgotten to whisper and a few of the early morning
parishioners craned their necks to listen. *Hell.* Just when
he'd thrown the blogger off his scent.

"Pffft," Sister Agnes whispered. "Oh, Brody. I'm old and
wise and I have connections." She pointed to the rafters high
above. "You're in love."

Sister Agnes rose to take communion and Brody followed
her mutely. He wasn't in love with Shannon. Sure, he loved
the way she'd taught him how to tame his illness and manage
it while he played. And, yeah, he loved the way she made
him feel: relaxed and grounded. Not to mention the way she
felt when she was wrapped around him. But that didn't mean
he was in love with her.

Brody wiped the sweat off his brow as he made his way
back to the pew where Sister Agnes sat deep in reflection,
a smug smile on her face. His phone vibrated a second time
and he scanned the text message.

"Holy . . ."

Sister Agnes rapped him with her beads again.

Shoving the phone back in his pocket, he grabbed his
jacket. Sister Agnes eyed him with concern.

"Devlin's wife just had her baby," he whispered.

"Sweet mercy," she said. "Kickoff's at one." With that she leaned over her beads and began praying in earnest.

There was a nervous buzz in the air when Brody got back to the hotel. Usually Sunday mornings before kickoff, the players were reflective and quiet, getting their game faces on. Even the coaches and staff kept it low-key until they would arrive at the stadium. But today, players were anxiously swarming the lobby, openly wondering whether the team's leader would be playing.

"When that crazy television guy shot at Carly, and Troy got knocked out, Devlin walked out on the game and went to the hospital," DeShawn was saying to the crowd of assembled receivers and rushers.

Brody stepped in among them. "That was a preseason game and Troy had a head injury. Carly and their daughter are fine. He'll be here." At least he hoped so. When he'd spoken to Shannon on the walk back to the hotel, she'd said everything had gone as planned during the delivery, according to Julianne, and the quarterback had every intention of playing.

"You better hope so, dude, because if I remember right, our backup, Mr. Potato Head over there, threw multiple pick-sixes that night." DeShawn pointed toward the lobby door, where Jake Larson, the Blaze second-string quarterback trudged to the bus, the position coach peppering him with information as they walked.

"Yeah, well he was a rookie then," Brody said, trying to add some confidence to his voice. The fact of the matter was, Jake took ten reps a week in practice, the rest of the time leading the practice squad against the Blaze defense. Brody had no freaking idea if the guy was ready.

"Shit," Brody swore as he grabbed his bag and headed for the bus behind Larson. Maybe he could sit next to the guy on the ride over and try to calm his nerves. But when he boarded the bus, he spied Will Connelly sitting quietly in one of the front seats, a pained look on his face. He looked from his friend to the second-string quarterback at the rear of the bus.

Double damn!

Brody was one of only a few people who knew the truth about Will and Julianne's early relationship. The linebacker had been devastated when he found out he had a son he hadn't known existed. Worse, Julianne never intended to let him know about the baby until Owen's near brush with death. Devlin becoming a father earlier this morning likely reminded his friend of all that he'd missed.

Sensing his hesitation, Connelly waved Brody off.

"You good?" Brody asked, not wanting to leave the cerebral linebacker to his troubled thoughts, but needing to work on calming Larson's nerves.

"Yeah, Brody, I'm good."

Brody squeezed his shoulder. "You'll get your chance, dude."

"Oh, believe me, I'm working on it." Connelly gave Brody a short-lived smile; one that held a lot of hope in it.

Moving down the aisle of the charter bus, Brody tried to come up with some words of encouragement for the team's backup, but as he slid into a seat, a cheer went up at the front. Shane Devlin had arrived, looking jubilant and ready for battle.

Brody let out a relieved sigh, sending up a silent prayer to both God and Sister Agnes.

Twenty-three

"You've been awfully scarce this month, Bridgett." Shay slid the sweet potato casserole into the oven.

Thanksgiving had turned into an impromptu celebration of young Veronica Marie Devlin's early arrival. Brody and Shay had been invited to dinner at the quarterback's house along with Will and Julianne, and Will's mother and her husband, Blaze GM Hank Osbourne. Naturally, Carly's sister, Lisa, and her husband, Coach Richardson, and their children were dining with them also. It was a happy, fun afternoon—especially since the Blaze had won their game on Sunday.

Brody's family usually spent the holiday in Baltimore, but a forecasted nor'easter kept them home in Boston. Bridgett tried to plead that she had too much work, insisting she'd have dinner in her hotel, but Brody would have none of it. She'd relented under her younger brother's badgering, but only after dramatically stating for the record that her attendance at Thanksgiving dinner was under protest.

"I've been really busy with the trial," Bridgett said as she sipped her whiskey sour. "Besides, I figure you two need your privacy. I wouldn't want to walk in on something that would gross me out."

Shay tossed the oven mitts on the counter, shooting Brody's sister a disgusted look. "For your information, I've been busy finalizing my dissertation, so the only thing you'd walk in on would be me swimming in a pile of spreadsheets and my advisor's comments." Which wasn't entirely true. Brody had managed to distract her multiple times this week, including a mind-blowing encounter in the shower earlier that morning.

"Your blush says otherwise." Bridgett snickered. "When is the big day defending your thesis, anyway?"

"One week from today. It's basically perfunctory at this point. I've had to endure some rigorous reviews along the way and my work is pretty solid. The information I gathered this fall was secondary to my overall research, but it was helpful in driving home my theory."

Bridgett gave a delicate snort. "Don't tell Brody he was secondary. He's used to being first in everything."

Shay glanced across the breakfast bar into the family room, where the object of their discussion sat rolling a ball across the floor to a delighted Owen, who had just learned to sit up on his own. It was hard to tell who was enjoying their game more, the baby or the man-child. Brody had mastered getting everything he wanted at a young age and Bridgett and her sisters were partly to blame for that. But there was a difference between being competitive and being spoiled and Shay was the only one who recognized how Brody struggled with that concept. He wanted people to expect more from him, but he hadn't been given the skills to know how to earn that respect. And that frightened him. That was a side of Brody he kept well-hidden from his family.

"And then it's off to prison." Bridgett's tone was joking, but her eyes told Shay the lawyer was fishing, trying to figure out how serious her relationship with Brody really was.

Shay didn't bother laughing at the reminder. She'd been a fool to give in to Brody and agree to stay a few more weeks, but she knew he needed her help keeping his blood sugar in check. And she knew she'd be a bigger fool to give up whatever time she had with him. When she headed home at the end of the season, he'd have his contract renewal and he could disclose his condition to the team without worrying about getting cut. Meanwhile, Mama would finally be safe from financial ruin, but Shay would be sleeping alone at night with only the memories of Brody's hard body to keep her warm.

The future was fact for Shay so she didn't bother commenting, instead giving Bridgett a shrug.

"Interesting," Bridgett said taking another sip of her drink.

"What's interesting?" Brody walked into the kitchen carrying a slobbering Owen like a football, the baby's legs kicking gleefully.

Bridgett opened her mouth to comment, before closing it quickly, her face suddenly paling. "Nothing," she said softly, standing and grabbing her glass. "Nothing at all." With a nod she wandered over toward the fireplace.

"What's up with her?" Brody's eyes followed his sister while he held Owen on the counter. The baby chortled as he tried to stand on his tiptoes.

"I have no idea. Maybe it's just the trial. Is she always like this during a big case?"

"Not usually." Brody didn't bother to hide the concern in his voice. "She's always prickly, but lately she's been a bit more isolated than usual."

"Maybe you should talk to her. See what's going on." Shay reached over and tickled Owen's tummy.

"My sisters have already tried. She'll tell me when she's ready. She always does."

A whistle sounded from the area of the television.

"Wow, Shay! Can I meet your sister the next time we play Dallas?" C.J. Richardson, the coach's teenage son called from the other room. A picture of her sister, Teryn, smiling for the camera, filled the sixty-inch television screen. Since the initial blogs, Teryn had received a lot more camera time during Cowboys games and she was no doubt loving the extra notoriety.

Coach cuffed his son on the back of his head. "Stick to girls your own age."

"Jeez, Dad. I just want to meet her. Not marry her."

Owen tugged on a piece of Shay's hair and Brody stepped in closer, shielding her from the debate between father and son. "Both you and your sister aren't home for Thanksgiving. What will your mom do today?"

She pried the baby's fingers loose and wrapped his hand around her own finger, holding him so he could bounce on his toes. "Meemaw will complain about cooking a big dinner with no one to eat it, so Mama will just go to one of the hairdressers' homes. It's actually a pretty quiet day for her. She can relax before the busy holiday season. Teryn and I haven't been home for years, so she's kind of used to it."

"My mother would whine for weeks if one of her children wasn't at her dinner table. That's why they always come here, so I don't have to listen to it."

Shay laughed. "That's probably why Bridgett is so testy. She knows she's going to hear it from your mama. But Mama knows I'll be home in a few weeks. Teryn and I are always in Texas for Christmas."

Brody's mouth grew tight and his eyes clouded. "Christmas is still a month away."

"Only three weeks, actually." Owen reached his hand up for Shay and she lifted him into her arms. She watched as Brody absorbed the information, a brief panic flashed in his eyes. She stepped closer so as not to be overheard. "It's going to be fine, Brody. I'll just be a phone call away and I'll leave you with enough menus that you'll manage."

Something else flickered quickly over his face, but it was gone before Shay could interpret it. "Yeah, sure," was all he said. The moment stretched as the baby gripped both of their shirts, pulling them closer. Brody's eyes never left hers and it seemed as if he wanted to say something more, but they were interrupted by a brewing disagreement between Julianne and Shane, both of whom were trying to baste the turkey.

"I've been cooking turkey for ten years, Julianne, I think I know what I'm doing," the quarterback said.

"Hmmpf," Julianne wrinkled her nose at her best friend's husband. "Just because you're opening a restaurant doesn't make you the superior cook."

Brody grabbed Owen from Shay's arms. "No, but in his kitchen, he's the boss," he said handing Julianne the baby while winking at Devlin over the top of her head.

"Suck up," Julianne mumbled, snuggling her son to her chest. "I'm going to find my husband and tell him to beat you both up."

"By the way, Shay, thanks for pitching in and coming to Denver with the team this weekend," Hank said as he brought the appetizer plates to the kitchen. "We've gone through our share of tragedies in catering this season and I don't know what we would have done without you."

"Trust me, the guys will appreciate you being there helping Nate. He's the best there is at his job, but his personality can grate on you," Coach called from across the room. "You'll be a welcome relief."

Shay wasn't too thrilled about the cross-country trip this weekend. Not only was she going to miss a paying shift at Celtic Charm—the team was leaving early Saturday morning to accommodate the time change—but she wouldn't have much downtime to prepare for her thesis review. Not to mention that Nate had returned to his narcissistic self once she and Brody had become involved for real. Emma insisted it was because the trainer had a secret crush on Shay, but she didn't think Nate's attitude could be explained away by a high school scenario.

"I'm happy to do it," she replied as Brody winked at her.

Dinner was a casual buffet in deference to the new mother and baby, but mostly because there was football on television and all of the men in the room were enjoying watching the game from the sofa rather than the sidelines. With delicious food and lots of laughter, even Bridgett finally relaxed. Brody was more relaxed, too, after their conversation in the kitchen. Whatever he'd been about to say was forgotten as he spent the rest of the evening at Shay's side, his arm around her shoulders or his warm body making contact with hers every time he got the opportunity.

"Any luck on the search for that blogger?" Coach asked Hank during dessert.

"No luck at all. Whoever it is, they're well and truly hidden," Hank said.

"I'm just glad she's got her claws into a few other teams right now. It's such a disruption to the locker room, all that gossip."

"It's the price of fame," Bridgett said nonchalantly over the rim of her teacup. The adults in the room were quiet for a moment as they processed her statement. All of them had been kicked by the media before at some point in their lives.

"Hey!" C.J. cried, shattering the silent reflection. "Troy just took the last piece of pumpkin pie." The subject was dropped and everyone's attention turned back to the game as more pie was retrieved from the kitchen.

Brody's overattentiveness continued into the bedroom later that night. As they made love in his big bed, he took his time, allowing his hands and mouth to trace over every inch of her body, now feverish after his slow deliberate exploration.

"Brody," she gasped as he blew on her sensitive nipple.

"Hmmm," he mumbled, kissing his way between her breasts.

"I need . . ."

"What do you need?" His breath fanned over the other aroused nipple and she bucked against him.

That seemed to spur him along, but then his lips lingered at her collarbone, gently nibbling at the skin there.

"Oh, please, Brody."

Unable to take it any longer, she threaded her fingers in his hair and yanked his mouth up toward hers. He chuckled low in his belly and she felt it in her own. Grabbing her hands, he laced his fingers with hers and pinned her to the mattress with his hard body. He brought his forehead down to meet hers.

"Please what, Brody?" he teased. "What is it you want,

Shannon? This?" He pumped his hips so his erection rubbed between her legs and she moaned.

"Is that all you need? All you want?" he demanded.

She couldn't make out his eyes in the shadowy room, but his voice was anxious, almost belligerent.

"You're sure you don't want anything more?" he asked hoarsely.

Shay shook her head in exasperation, unsure what he was getting at but wishing whatever it was, he'd get there quickly.

He took her bottom lip between his and sucked gently. Her hips arched again making contact with the part of him she desperately wanted inside of her.

"You sure you don't want me?" His voice was strained as he touched the tip of his nose to hers.

Shay's breath hitched in her throat. *How did he know?* Over the past few weeks, she'd been holding back. Reserving a small part of her heart and her sanity for that day when he'd no longer need her. *Want her.* But typical of Brody, he not only knew, but he insisted on charming it out of her. Conquering her with the caress of his hands and his mouth so that he could then steal that last piece of her and take it for his own. Her body overwrought with desire, Shay was tired of holding out. It was no use. When this ended a few weeks from now, her heart would be in pieces anyway.

"Yes," she cried. "I want all of you, Brody. All of you!" She lifted her head up to kiss him more fully and he responded with a growl. His mouth ate at hers as he thrust deeply inside her, their hands still clasped on either side of her head. Brody was relentless, pushing her to release, and then, with a throaty moan, finding his own.

Brody stretched out his hip on a foam roller on the floor of his hotel room. A hit two weeks ago still left the joint stiff and the cold Denver air carrying the threat of snow didn't help any. Kickoff wasn't for another six hours—six thirty Mountain time. The team had already had breakfast and an early morning meeting and now the players had two hours of downtime. Had the weather not been so ominous, he might have sweet-talked Shannon into going for a walk to stretch out his hip.

Shannon likely had her nose buried deeply in her note cards by now anyway, so Brody settled for a session with his personal trainer, Erik, who was in Denver working with one of the Broncos this weekend. Going to Nate and the team training staff would only alert management to a potential injury, and Brody was playing tonight no matter what.

He got up to answer the knock at the door and was pleasantly surprised to find not Erik, but Shannon standing in the hallway. Wearing her puffy jacket, formfitting jeans, and her cowboy boots, she looked bright-eyed and fresh leaning against the doorjamb with her ever-present book bag over her shoulder. Her hair was windblown and her cheeks red; she'd obviously just come in from outdoors. He cursed himself for not going with his original plan.

"Hey there," she said softly.

Brody quickly scanned the hallway before yanking her inside and slamming the door.

"Hey yourself," he said before covering her mouth with his. Her hands were chilly as they slid beneath his T-shirt to roam over his bare skin, but he didn't object. He liked this new Shannon; the one he'd discovered in his bed Thanksgiving night. As her sexual experience grew, so had her confidence, but the raw passion was new. Whatever had been tethering Shannon was gone and Brody craved this version of her even more than he wanted to admit to himself. He unzipped her jacket eager to get his own hands on her skin.

"Where's Jamal?" she breathed, bringing Brody back from his baser self. He'd forgotten about his roommate and Erik who would be here any minute.

"Shit." He put a few inches between them. "He's with the chaplain at the service. But my trainer is on his way here."

She pulled out of his arms. "Your personal trainer? Is everything okay?"

"Yeah, yeah. I'm fine. My hip hurts and Erik is going to stretch me out, that's all."

Shannon walked over to the bed and Little Brody jumped with joy.

"Your trainer flew to Denver just for that?" She pulled off her jacket. "You couldn't get Nate to do that for you? From what I hear, he's the best at injury rehab."

"Yeah, but Nate talks too much and I don't want the coaching staff to know."

Shannon rolled her eyes as he stalked toward her. "You and your ego."

Ignoring her dig, he wrapped his hands around her narrow waist. "And Erik was already here in Denver. He trains one of the Broncos." A piece of her long hair was stuck to her lips and Brody reached a hand up to wipe it away, caressing her cheek in the process.

"Isn't that a conflict of interest?" She leaned into his hand, giving his lips access to her smooth neck.

"No. He works for the athletes, not the teams. His only allegiance is to the big check we each pay him every month. Erik has only ten clients, but he probably banks half a million a year." Brody kissed the cool skin beneath her ear.

"And he trains clients for many different teams?" Her hands lay flat on his pecs.

"Yeah. Here in Denver, Detroit, Miami, Minnesota. Lots of places." Brody didn't want to talk about Erik anymore. He wanted to call the guy and tell him not to bother, his hip was fine. Or it would be once he got Shannon naked beneath him.

She pushed him away. "Hell's bells! I've been looking at this all wrong." Rummaging through her book bag, she pulled out a spreadsheet he recognized. "All this time, I've been looking for people with access to each team, but not one person with access to a lot of teams. Don't you see, Brody? Instead of there being a bunch of snitches, there very well could be just one snitch."

Brody scrubbed his hands down his face. "Not this again. Shannon, forget about the snitch. You don't have to prove anything to me, okay." He took the spreadsheet from her hands and tossed it on the bed. "I'm more interested in why you're wearing a freaking Broncos T-shirt."

She looked genuinely flustered as she ran a hand along the horse on her chest. "It was all they had at the hotel gift shop. Brody, forget about my T-shirt and listen—"

"No! I don't want to hear about your theories on the damn snitch. Hell, I can't listen to a word you say when you're wearing the other team's colors." His frustration grew as she reached for her jacket.

"For pity's sake, Brody, you are such a baby sometimes." She shoved her arms into her jacket. "There's a blizzard coming and Mr. Osbourne said we'd likely be stuck here for the night. I didn't pack for more than overnight and this was the only thing in my size. Grow up and deal with it." She yanked the zipper up to her throat before turning on her heel and heading for the door.

Brody swore, reaching out and snaring her by the belt loop of her jeans, pulling her back up against him. "I'm sorry," he whispered against the back of her head as he wrapped his arms around her. "But it's called being competitive, not a baby. I don't like it when my best girl is wearing the other guy's logo."

She blew out a breath. "This isn't high school, Brody. And besides, maybe I'm wearing something else with the Blaze logo."

Little Brody sprang back to life, snug up against her round ass. He groaned as he pictured her parading around in that Blaze thong in his great room that night. "Let me see." When he reached his fingers into the waistband of her jeans she wriggled against him and he nearly died on the spot.

"Shannon, come in the bathroom. We'll—"

His cell phone beeped on the nightstand and Brody let out a string of obscenities. Shannon pulled out of his embrace.

"That'll be your trainer," she said as she hefted her book bag onto her shoulder.

"I'll tell him I'm fine. Stay." Brody desperately wanted a look at her in those panties—and out of them.

"No, Brody. I have to go study. And you need to save your energy. It's a night game, with bad weather at a mile-high altitude. Even with normal blood sugar that's not easy on a body. Make sure you eat at the intervals on your schedule. I'll see you before the game."

She made her way out the door without so much as a kiss good-bye.

The dire predictions about the weather turned out to be true. The snow started falling about four in the afternoon and by halftime, there was nearly a half foot of white powder on the ground with what seemed like another half foot swirling in the air. The Broncos were up by seven, and with the weather conditions deteriorating and DeShawn's hamstring cramping in the cold, the Blaze's chances were looking as bleak as the weather.

Making matters worse, Brody's head was a little fuzzy; a result of his blood sugar taking a nosedive in the first half. But Shannon was prepared, meeting him in one of the deserted training rooms with a bottle of orange juice.

"That should do the trick." She glanced at the reading on his OneTouch. "You're not that low, but you might want to take another bottle to the sidelines with you just in case you start to feel woozy."

Brody only had a minute before he'd be missed in the locker room. He nuzzled her cool cheek. "I'm only woozy when I think about you wearing that thong."

Laughing, she pulled out of his embrace. "You have a one-track mind, Brody. Try to get it back into the game, will you?"

"When I catch the winning touchdown, I'm coming to your room tonight to celebrate."

"I wouldn't try it. Nate's probably got my door booby-trapped." She handed him his OneTouch just as Nate stormed the room.

Brody slid the tester behind his back, as the three stood in charged silence.

"I thought you had more professionalism, Shannon," the trainer said in disgust.

Brody stepped between Shannon and her boss. "Hey, lay off, Nate. I asked her down here to do me a favor."

Nate held up a hand. "I don't want to hear what kind of *favor* she was doing for you. I need the room. Now."

The insinuation that something sexual was going on in the training room made Brody bristle. This guy controlled Shannon's future and he didn't need him thinking badly of her. It was all he could do to keep from ripping the trainer's head off, but he had the blood sugar monitor in his hand and he didn't dare let Nate see it. Still, he used his body to intimidate the pipsqueak.

"Watch what you say about her," Brody warned as he slid out the door, Shannon close behind him. As they entered the hallway, she made a fast break for the elevator to the visitor's skybox. "Hey!" he called after her. But she marched on, her boots clicking on the concrete floor and her head bowed. Brody swore as he entered the locker room, worried now about more than just how his team was going to pull off a win in the deteriorating weather.

The game ended with the score unchanged and the Blaze going down in defeat. The mood among the players the following morning was as heavy as the blanket of snow holding them captive in the hotel. Brody had been texting Shannon since the game ended, but she'd only responded once, a cryptic message saying she was sorry and they'd talk the next day. As far as he was concerned, Nate was the one who needed to apologize. But Shannon was still skittish about certain things and the trainer's accusations had obviously embarrassed her. He needed to reassure her. A few minutes in one of the stairwells should suffice; as long as he could hold her. But first he needed to find her.

The ballroom where the team was eating breakfast was less subdued than Brody expected. The frantic whispering died down as he crossed the threshold, however. He didn't have time to worry about what was eating his teammates. His first priority was to make peace with Shannon. A text from his agent buzzed across the screen of his cell phone, but Brody ignored the summons to call him immediately, instead stalking into the kitchen looking for a particular hairnet.

But Shannon wasn't there. His cell buzzed again. Bridgett demanded that he call her. She'd have to wait along with Roscoe. A sharp tightness settled into his chest when he couldn't find her. Something wasn't right. He turned to find Nate bearing down on him.

"Where is she?" Brody growled.

"Don't you know? Hank called her up to his suite." The trainer looked at Brody with disgust. "I tried to warn her about guys like you, but she wouldn't listen."

Brody had the muscled trainer pinned up against the wall in an instant. He should have known Nate would find a way to get Shannon in trouble. She'd said he had it in for her from the start.

"What did you do to her?" he demanded, his forearm pressed to the trainer's neck, making it impossible for him to answer.

"Brody!" Connelly pulled him off Nate, but not before Brody got a well-placed punch in.

"Hey! Brody, stop!" The linebacker held both his arms.

"I didn't do anything to her, Janik!" Nate swiped at the cut on his lip. "*You* did this!"

Brody tried to deck him again, but Will had his arms pinned behind him. Devlin stepped between him and the trainer. "Brody you need to see this." He shoved his iPad in front of Brody. *The Girlfriends' Guide to the NFL* blog was open on the screen. A roaring began in his ears as he read.

No!

THE GIRLFRIENDS' GUIDE TO THE NFL

Well here's something sweet for you to nibble on ladies: It seems that everyone's favorite tight end has been keeping a few secrets. Very dangerous secrets, if you ask me. According to a *very* close acquaintance with number eighty, the Blaze star has been hiding the fact that he suffers from diabetes, the same disease his mother has. This would of course explain his current "love interest," the not-so-interesting Shannon Everett, who also happens to be a PhD candidate in nutrition science. It seems this is one of those "you scratch my back, I'll scratch yours" arrangements, but does anyone believe our blue-eyed beauty would be caught dead scratching the back of a homely scientist? More important, this explains our Brody's sudden lack of interest in Candi.

Obviously, number eighty would love to keep this secret under wraps until his contract extension has been finalized, but we girlfriends believe in safety first. So consider this a public service announcement, Brody. Either get yourself seen by a real doctor or play doctor with someone a little easier on the eyes.

Twenty-four

The room swam before her and Shay was having difficulty concentrating on what Hank Osbourne was saying. They were seated in the large suite the general manager ran the team's road operations out of; she in one of the over-stuffed armchairs and he on the elegant chintz sofa. A cherry coffee table complete with a silver tea service separated them. As he had before, the Blaze security chief, Donovan Carter, sat above her, this time on the arm of the sofa. The scene was civilized and polite, yet Shay had the chills.

"Tell me again how you, not a medical doctor and not yet a PhD, were overseeing Brody's health?" Mr. Osbourne asked.

"I-I really think you should be talking to Brody about this." Shay was having trouble making the words pass through her trembling lips. This was it. The secret was out. Brody would be devastated, but he'd survive on his charm, his talent, and this celebrity. She, on the other hand, stood to lose everything.

"Oh, you can bet I will be talking to Brody about this, just as soon as I can wrangle his sorry ass up here." Mr. Osbourne

slid his wire-framed glasses to the top of his nose, pausing
seemingly in an effort to rein in his temper. "Right now,
we're talking about you. An unpaid intern of all things. How
did someone whose job it was to make protein shakes
become responsible for the daily nutrition of a multimillion-
dollar commodity in this organization?" His attempt to curb
his anger failed as the last part of the question came out in
a shout, making Shay cringe in her chair.

"I blackmailed her."

Shay's shoulders sagged with relief at the sound of Brody's voice behind her. She wanted to leap into his arms, but
when he slumped into the chair next to her, his face was
stony and his eyes focused everywhere but on her. A hol-
lowness was forming deep inside her belly at his lack of
reassurance.

Mr. Osbourne pinched his nose again before blowing out
an exaggerated breath. "Please don't add felonies to your
offenses here, Brody. I have very little patience for your
flippancy right now. I take it you're not going to deny the
blogger's report, either."

Brody slouched lower in the chair. His demeanor belligerent. "It's the truth."

Both the GM and Mr. Donovan turned their gazes on
Shay. "Is this true, Miss Everett? Was he blackmailing you
to help him conceal his ailment from the team?" Mr.
Osbourne asked.

She opened her mouth to answer, but the words wouldn't
come out. Did it really matter now if they knew she'd been
in the locker room looking for something to sell to the blogger? All that stood between her and her PhD was a performance review from the team. Without it, she wouldn't get her
degree this month and she wouldn't get her federal job. *And
Mama would lose everything.*

"What exactly were you blackmailing her with, Brody?"
Mr. Carter asked.

"Sex."

Shay's cheeks burned and her stomach rolled. She snuck
at look at Brody, who was trying to appear nonchalant in

the chair, but his jaw was tight and his fingers were white-knuckled where they gripped the arms. He was afraid, too. Afraid of what this would do to his contract extension and his beloved career. But she knew he was more fearful of facing what was after that career and he'd do anything to push that reality far back. So, like any little boy who was scared, he was striking back. While she appreciated his attempt to protect her secret, she wasn't sure she appreciated his assassinating her character.

"I'm told I'm worth it," he said smugly. "Even by those less-experienced studious types."

Shay felt as though he'd punched her in the gut.

"Hey!" Coach Richardson yelled from behind her.

Brody leaped out of the chair and began pacing the room, now cloaked in uncomfortable silence. Shay's eyes grew heavy with unshed tears. He walked to the window, staring out at the white snow before turning to face the occupants of the room again. Their gazes connected for the first time since he'd entered the suite. His blue eyes were a mix of anguish and fear, with hurt shining in them, too. But they turned stony with anger when he glanced at her.

He crossed his arms over his chest and rested his hip against the window ledge. "I told her I'd scuttle her performance review so she wouldn't get the last internship credits she needs to get her degree. She has a job waiting and if she doesn't have her doctorate this semester, they'll give it to someone else."

"Jesus," Coach muttered behind her.

"Do you have anything to add, Miss Everett?" Mr. Osbourne asked.

Shay clamped her lips shut, afraid that if she opened her mouth she'd wail. She shook her head.

"Well that brings us to the blogger, then," Mr. Carter said. "Brody, how many people knew about your . . . condition?"

Brody's jaw was clenched so tightly, she almost thought he wouldn't answer. "Four."

Mr. Carter arched a brow, waiting for him to elaborate.

"My agent, my personal physician, my personal trainer,

and . . ." He didn't bother saying her name, instead jerking his chin in her direction.

The anger rolling off him hit her like a shotgun blast. He didn't trust her after all. *Had he ever?* Shay slipped her trembling hands beneath her thighs as she tried to tamp down on the sob that threatened to escape.

The silence in the room was overwhelming as each man refused to make eye contact with her. Everyone except Brody, whose gaze bored into her. Unable to stand it any longer, she sprung from her chair.

"It wasn't me!" The tears threatened to fall, but Shay's pride was stronger. She pleaded her case with Mr. Osbourne. "I've been analyzing the blog for possible suspects for months—"

"Here we go with the damn spreadsheet again," Brody muttered.

The breath seized in her lungs. He really didn't trust her. It had all been a lie to get what he wanted. All so he could continue playing a game and never have to grow up to face the real world. Swallowing around the lump in her throat, she stomped over to Brody, but he held up a hand before she could speak.

"Save yourself the embarrassment. You're the only one of those four people who needs the money. I don't need a spreadsheet to know that." The scorn in his voice made her nauseous, but she was Shannon Everett from Lake Hamilton, Texas, and she wasn't going to let him have the last word.

"Yes, Brody. But I needed that money three months ago just as much as I do today." She turned on her heel to face the others. "If you're not going to arrest me, I'd like to go back to my room, please."

"No one's getting arrested here, Shay." Coach Richardson went to wrap a protective arm over her shoulders, but Shay stepped out of his reach. He turned to Mr. Osbourne. "Hank?"

Mr. Osbourne looked at Mr. Carter, who gave a slight shake of his head. The GM cleared his throat before answering. "You can ride back on the charter with us, Miss Everett, but once we reach Baltimore, consider your internship terminated."

She gave a terse nod, needing to get out of the suite before the tears erupted. "May I go now?" she managed to choke out.

Mr. Osbourne nodded and Shay bolted for the door.

"Not you, Brody," she heard him say as she reached the hallway. "We've got a lot more to talk about."

Shay was grateful for that. Because the last person she wanted to see was Brody Janik.

It was no surprise that the entire team knew about the blog, but Shay was unprepared for the media lined up outside the hotel as they boarded the charter buses. They peppered her with questions, but Coach Richardson's tall body shielded her from the cameras. He'd appointed himself her new knight in the face of Brody's sudden defection.

"You don't have to do this," Shay told him as he shoved a guy with a cell phone camera aimed at her off to the side.

"No, I don't have to. I want to." He gave her shoulder a gentle squeeze. "Nothing about this makes sense, except that you're not one who sells out someone she cares about."

Shay climbed the steps up into the bus, her throat tight again. It was nice to have someone in her corner. She took the first seat, directly behind the bus driver. The tinted windows allowed her to stare at the paparazzi, trudging through the snow to get a shot of her or Brody. They would be out of luck on that score. According to Coach Richardson, Brody had been escorted back to Baltimore on the owner's private plane.

Even after all that had transpired this morning, her heart ached for him. His fears about his future had to be magnified tenfold, but he'd hide behind his charm and bravado so no one knew. Not even his family. For a man who had so much, he bore his apprehension in solitude. Shay knew he'd survive this crisis just fine, however. His condition was easily manageable and the Blaze would do anything to keep their star player on board. Too bad Brody didn't realize that.

The rest of the team filed on the bus, all of them ignoring

her presence. DeShawn glared at her as he passed by, obviously believing she'd been the one to rat him out to the blogger, costing him a huge endorsement contract. The man made millions of dollars for appearing in magazines with his shirt off and he was upset because he was caught using one toothpaste instead of the one he was paid more millions to endorse. The irony was almost laughable.

Unable to stand the freeze-out from the players any longer, Shay turned back to the window. A body slid into the seat next to her. She hoped it wasn't Coach Richardson because she wasn't sure she could hold off the tears if he said something nice again.

"Here." It was Nate.

Shay turned and took the envelope he held out for her, raising an eyebrow in question.

"It's your performance review. I e-mailed a copy to your advisor this morning, but this is the hard copy for you to keep."

She ran a finger over the glossy envelope, her heart in her throat. Mama and Teryn had been calling all morning. Both professed to be worried about her, but she knew their bigger fear was whether or not she'd get the necessary requirements fulfilled to get her degree in time.

"It's the review I wrote up last week," Nate said. "Nothing has changed. You worked hard and you fulfilled the basic requirements of the internship. I know it wasn't exactly what you expected, but then, you got added research with Brody, didn't you?"

Shay tried not to cringe at his tone. "Thank you."

Nate waved a hand in the air. "If in fact Brody has diabetes, you did a great job helping him control it without insulin. You're going to be a successful nutritionist. That's all I care about."

"I'm pretty sure it's just reactive hypoglycemia," Shay said, her spirits buoyed a bit by Nate's compliment.

"Is that how you went about preparing a plan for him?"

Shay nodded.

"Impressive. I'll need whatever you've got. His meal

plans, schedule, etcetera. I don't want to shake up things too much."

Nate was going to handle Brody's diet? Brody was going to have a fit.

"E-mail me everything as soon as we get back, okay?" It wasn't so much a question as it was a demand. Grateful for the performance review, she had no choice but to agree.

"Sure. Thank you, Nate. For believing in me."

Nate eyed her curiously. "Oh, hey. I don't care if you sold Brody out to that blogger or not. The point is, he's just like every other professional athlete, trying to bend the rules. They all get their own personal trainers and nutritionists just so they can hide things from management. It's not right. It's my job to take care of the members of this team and keep the GM and the coaching staff apprised of their status. Brody and his teammates just want to take that decision out of my hands. He was using you, Shay, and he got what he deserved."

Shay wasn't so sure about that. She'd been using him, too, for a lot more than just research.

"You take care of yourself, Shay," Nate said as he stood.

Apparently, even he didn't want to be seen sitting with her. Shay carefully placed the envelope into her book bag, pulling out her note cards. All that was left was the pro forma defense of her dissertation, but she wasn't taking any chances. Mama was depending on her. And the sooner she got home to Texas, the better.

The media hadn't expected Brody to arrive in Baltimore two hours before the team, so he was able to slip into his house unobserved. Unfortunately, his kitchen wasn't unoccupied.

"Ohmigod, Brody!"

Bridgett nearly hurdled a barstool, spilling her tea in the process, to get to him. His normally uneffusive sister wrapped her arms around him in a bear hug.

"Are you okay?" she mumbled against his chest.

Chagrined by her concern, he draped his own arms around her and returned the hug.

His parents and sisters had been texting and calling him all day. It was a miracle that the entire Janik clan wasn't assembled in his kitchen right now, but he'd told his parents he needed rest. The team was insisting on a complete physical first thing in the morning. He'd see his family after the team's verdict. Whatever it was.

"I'm fine, Bridge. Perfectly fine." He patted her back for good measure.

"Good," she said, pulling out of the embrace and punching him, hard as she could.

"Ow!" Brody rubbed his shoulder. "What was that for?"

"For being an idiot and keeping something as serious as diabetes from your family! What were you thinking?"

Brody's stomach growled and he headed for the fridge. His schedule was pretty jacked up with the time change. Shannon would have allowed for that, prescribing exactly what he should eat—protein or fiber and carbohydrates—and how much. But Shannon wasn't here anymore. She'd sold him out. And of all the things that pained him today, that one hurt the most.

He knew their relationship was just temporary; they were both using each other to achieve their goals. They'd been honest about that from the start. Somewhere along the line, however, it had become something more. And just like everyone else he'd shared his real self with, she'd turned his secrets into profit.

"Should you be eating that?" Bridgett asked.

Brody was piling some turkey on the nasty sawdust bread Shannon made him eat. "If you're gonna nag me, Bridgett, you can go back to your hotel. I've been doing this for a few months now. I can handle it."

"I knew there was more to your and Shay's relationship than what you wanted us to see. She was teaching you how to manage your diet, wasn't she?"

He snagged a barstool with his foot and pulled it up to

the breakfast bar, sitting down to eat his snack. If his mouth was full, he couldn't answer his sister's questions.

Bridgett poured him a glass of skim milk. "Poor Shay. She must be mortified by the way that blogger portrayed her. How is she?"

Brody shrugged, taking another bite of his sandwich.

"What's that supposed to mean, Brody?"

Bridgett was using her courtroom voice and it was starting to irk him. He ignored her.

She snapped the dishtowel she'd been using to wipe up her spilled tea. "Brody, she's your girlfriend. She's been hurt by this, too."

"Damn it, she's not my girlfriend!" he shouted, tossing the sandwich on the plate and escaping to the great room.

He'd stunned his sister into silence. But her mind was quick and she'd figure it out even without him having to connect the dots. It's one of the things he appreciated about Bridgett. *And Shannon.*

"Brody, please don't tell me she was the one who gave this information to the blogger," she asked quietly, following him from the kitchen.

Gripping the mantel with his fingers, he bowed his head, staring into the empty fireplace. "Okay, I won't tell you."

He heard her sink into the leather recliner behind him. "Oh, Brody. I don't believe it. What would motivate her to do such a thing?"

"You're a lawyer." He laughed at her honest confusion, but it sounded empty in the big room. "What motivates most people to do things they shouldn't? Money. Notoriety. Women will tell my secrets for just about anything."

"Oh, Brody."

"Don't feel sorry for me, Bridgett. It comes with the territory. I've come to expect it."

"But it hurts even more when you love that person."

He whipped his head around to face his sister, ready to deny that he ever loved Shannon, because he damn well didn't. But the pain on his sister's face stopped him.

"Trust me," she whispered more to herself than to him. "I know how it feels."

"Bridgett?" He kneeled down on the floor next to her. She wiped a tear from her eye and he wondered if he'd ever seen her cry before. "Hey? Has someone upset you? Tell me who it is. I'll kick his ass."

She patted him on the shoulder. "It's okay. It's over and done with and I survived. You will, too."

He watched her carefully, wondering how many secrets she had hidden from their family. His sister was more like him than he thought.

"I just can't believe Shay would do this. She loved you, too. Only you both were too stupid to know it."

Brody groaned as he got to his feet. He opened his mouth to refute her statement, but she held up a hand.

"And another thing, she had a job lined up, what did she need the money for?"

He stalked back into the kitchen to retrieve his half-eaten sandwich, Bridgett on his heels.

"Hell, Bridgett, I don't know. Maybe she decided she didn't want to work in a prison after all."

"Yeah, but that brings up another question. How much money would your story bring? Enough to pay off her debts? And if so, who was bankrolling it? And for what purpose?"

"Jeez, Bridgett. You sound like Shannon. She had a whole freakin' spreadsheet she was analyzing to find the blogger."

Bridgett poured more hot water from the kettle. "Which just proves that she wasn't the the informant. If she was, she'd already know who the blogger was."

"Or," Brody said around a mouthful of sandwich, "she's a brilliant gold digger who was covering her tracks."

His sister shook her head vehemently. "No. Something here doesn't make sense. Where's the money? Stories about who's cheating or who uses which toothpaste are pretty easy to get for pay. But your story and the supposed gay player in Minnesota, those are big-dollar bribes to get. It just

doesn't make sense that she's paying money for them."
Bridgett tapped her finger on the counter. "No, if I were
investigating this, I'd flip it around. The blogger might not
be paying for information as much as she's extorting information. Maybe she has something on someone who knows
a lot of football players."

One person with access to a lot of teams.

Brody nearly choked on his sandwich as Shannon's voice
reverberated through his head.

He grabbed for his duffel bag, rifling through its contents
to pull out the spreadsheet she'd left in his hotel room.

"What is that?" Bridgett came to stand and peer over his
shoulder as he scanned through the pages.

"Shannon's spreadsheet." The answer was staring him
right in the face. He had been betrayed, all right. But not by
the woman he thought.

"Shit."

Twenty-five

The locker room was empty at eight the next morning, just as Brody had anticipated it would be. The only witness he needed for this meeting was Donovan Carter, who stood quietly off in the shadows. Brody had been twitchy since the night before when he realized he had been wrong about the snitch. This time, instead of a lover selling him out, it was someone he had trusted his entire career. While it was a relief to know his faith in Shannon hadn't been misguided, Brody was still raw from the defection of a supposed friend.

The door opened and, without conscious thought, Brody lunged at the man who entered.

"You son of a bitch!"

His trainer, Erik, was gasping as Brody's grip tightened around his throat.

"Brody!" Donovan Carter yelled, pulling Brody off the trainer. "Don't kill him until we find out who the damn blogger is."

"Nobody is killing anyone in my locker room," Hank roared as he and Roscoe entered, joining in the fray.

Donovan held the trainer's arms, but Erik wasn't putting up much of a struggle. Brody sucked in a few deep breaths to combat the rush of adrenalin he'd felt at the sight of his so-called friend. He wanted to pummel the trainer for his betrayal, but Erik seemed resigned—almost relieved, in fact—by Brody's discovery. Erik's demeanor sickened Brody more and he took a step toward the trainer, only to have Roscoe yank him back.

"Calm down," his agent barked.

Donovan eased Erik into one of the folding chairs, the man's eyes now red as tears threatened.

"I'm sorry, Brody," Erik said.

Disgust clogged Brody's throat and he was barely able to get the question out. "Why?"

Erik shook his head. "I had no choice. I'm being black-mailed."

Brody's gut clenched. It seemed that all roads led back to blackmail with this blogger.

"Blackmailed by whom?" Donovan demanded.

The trainer shook his head again. "I have no idea. It all started with an anonymous text message. At first, they were satisfied with the small innocuous stuff, but as time went on, it was the sensational gossip they demanded. They were relentless and I didn't know how to make it stop without . . ." Erik's voice trailed off. Clearly, he was more interested in protecting himself from the blogger than his friends and clients.

"I want that number." Donovan's tone brokered no argument.

"It won't do you any good," Erik said. "It changes constantly."

"What does this person have on you?" Hank asked.

Erik swallowed and, for a moment, it seemed he wouldn't answer. He looked at Roscoe. "I don't suppose you'd be interested in representing me?" he asked the lawyer-agent.

"Not a chance in hell." Roscoe's loyalty buoyed Brody.

"Just spit it out," Brody said through clenched teeth.

Heaving a sigh, Erik wiped both his eyes. "Human growth hormone," he whispered.

Brody's chest constricted as three heads whirled on him. "He is definitely not talking about me," he shouted, pulling himself away from the wall and charging toward Erik. "I have never taken a needle or anything so much as a crumb from this man. And if you insinuate I did in any way, Erik, I will kill you!"

Roscoe wrapped an arm around Brody, holding him back.

"Not Brody," Erik said. "A baseball player."

There was a palpable sigh of relief in the locker room—except for Brody who was still chafing against Roscoe's hold. "You sold me and others out to protect one client?" he accused.

Erik shot from his chair before Donovan could grab him. "I was protecting myself! One mistake and I could lose everything, while you athletes get paid millions. You have no idea what it is to struggle financially, Brody. To be desperate to secure your livelihood!"

He was wrong; Brody did know. He'd been watching Shannon scrape by and fight to stay afloat these past few months. And the snitch in front of him had not only damaged her reputation but possibly her job chances. Brody was furious. "But you didn't care who you took down along with me, did you? To hell with the innocent people who might be hurt by this."

Donovan stepped between them as Erik scoffed at Brody. "After all the women who've sold you out, Brody, you're worried about your little nutritionist?"

"You made it look like she was the one who leaked the story!"

"I didn't have to. Like I said, there's a long list of women who preceded her to the tabloids. People just saw what they wanted to see. It was what I was counting on."

Brody strained against Roscoe's arm as he tried to reach the trainer. "Well they were wrong!"

"Maybe," Erik taunted. "But who says she wouldn't have sold you out in the future?"

"Enough!" Hank yelled over the roaring in Brody's ears. "Brody, we'll deal with the slander issues later."

Erik slouched back down on the chair, his bluster seemingly forgotten as the consequence of Hank's words hit him. "I didn't slander anyone. This is all the blogger's fault."

"That remains to be seen," Hank said. "Right now, I want to get everything on record. How were you contacted and how were you paid?"

"I told you, everything was done via texting. I never got paid. As long as I kept feeding whoever it was the information, they kept my secret."

Roscoe stepped out from behind Brody. "But that doesn't make sense. The blogger never asked for any money to keep the story of the HGH quiet?"

Erik shook his head. "I don't get the impression that the blogger is in it for the money."

Donovan swore. "Great. We're probably dealing with some scorned woman who wants to get back at jocks everywhere. Which means tracking her down is still next to impossible."

"We're not giving up." Hank's voice was determined. "The commissioner is on his way with the league's investigators. Let's move this to the conference room so that Erik can answer the questions before we address the media."

"I want Shannon completely exonerated from this mess," Brody demanded.

The GM shot a measuring glance Brody's way before giving a slight nod. "As she should be. In the meantime, you've got an appointment with the team physician. Don't be late."

"You're not going to involve the police, are you?" Erik whined as Donovan led him out of the locker room, Hank on their heels.

"That's up to the commissioner." Hank's voice trailed down the hall.

Brody sank down into one of the leather sofas in the center of the room, resting his head in his hands. The confrontation with Erik left him deflated. His story was out and the snitch was caught, but Brody still felt unbalanced.

"You need to get to the hospital for those tests," Roscoe reminded him. "I'll hang back here and make sure the media get the entire story. Shay will be heralded as your girlfriend again by the noon news cycle."

"No." Brody dragged his fingers through his hair. "I want her totally removed from this mess. Release a statement saying that she was working as my nutritionist. We were only posing as a couple to throw off Blaze management. It's the truth."

Roscoe snorted. "It didn't look like you two were pretending."

Brody sprung from the sofa. "I blackmailed her! Don't you see? I'm just as bad as that damn blogger. Not only that, but I told her I trusted her to get her to sleep with me. Then I turned on her the first opportunity I got. Believe me, Shannon has no interest in continuing a relationship with a hypocrite. Besides, her dissertation is complete; she doesn't need any more data."

"Huh," was all Roscoe said.

"Huh, what?" Brody snapped at him. "Aren't you always telling me not to get tied up with women during the season? You say they're too distracting or some bullshit like that. Well, I'm following your advice. There are four weeks left and then the playoffs. And that's if they even let me play!"

"You picked a fine time to start following my advice." Roscoe walked toward the door. "Too bad, because I liked this girl. But you're right. Football comes first. Especially right now. Go to your physical, Brody. I'll make sure Shay isn't muddied by this mess any longer."

Brody stood in the quiet locker room a moment longer, the tightness in his throat making it difficult to swallow. *It's better this way.* He'd only need to repeat that phrase another thousand times to believe it.

"Shay, what's *die beet ease*?" Maddox asked around a mouthful of Cap'n Crunch.

Jackie had worked the overnight shift and her son was home from school with pinkeye. Shay had volunteered to watch him for the morning while Mrs. Elder took care of baby Anya.

"Diabetes," she said pouring him a glass of orange juice. "It's a condition where your body produces too much sugar and it makes you sick."

The local news had been covering the story of Brody's health all week. Cameras had followed him into Johns Hopkins Hospital on Tuesday, where it was reported he'd gone through a barrage of tests. A team of endocrinologists was assembled to assess his condition and deem him fit to play in the NFL. Shay doubted they'd find anything to keep him off the field. The blood sugar readings she'd compiled were all consistent with reactive hypoglycemia, but as Mr. Osbourne had pointed out, she wasn't a medical doctor.

"So if Brody eats candy, he could die?"

Maddox's face was anxious, his eyes round and damp.

"No, sweetie. Only if he eats a lot of candy," she reassured him.

"Oh, that's good. Cuz once I gave Brody some M&M's and I don't want him to die."

Shay kissed the top of the young boy's head. "Nothing you do is going to make Brody die."

"Is he ever going to come see us again?" Maddox's voice was small and Shay's heart squeezed.

"I'm sure he'll come see you soon, Maddox. It's just been a crazy week for him, that's all."

"But he said on TV that you're not his girlfriend anymore. That you never were. You were just helping him with his *die beet ease.*"

The squeezing spread throughout her body now. The commissioner of the NFL had held a press conference the day before saying the source of the blogger's information had been identified. It was Erik Hjelmstad, Brody's trainer. She and everyone else had been stunned to learn the trainer was being blackmailed by the blogger. The details of the blackmail weren't given, but Julianne had stopped by last night to reveal that Erik had apparently given a client HGH and that the blogger had the proof. While the identity and purpose of the blogger were still a mystery, the snitch had finally been publically outed. And it wasn't her.

Brody's agent, Mr. Mathis, had followed the commissioner with a brief statement exonerating Shay. He told the media that the relationship between her and Brody was a professional one only. Their supposed romance was only a cover to keep his team from questioning him. Shay nearly lost her lunch when she heard that sound bite. Sadly, it rang true. Mr. Mathis also praised her abilities as a nutritionist saying it was her skills that had Brody in such fine condition.

It was likely the only apology she'd ever see from Brody. It was also the cleanest breakup she'd ever heard of.

"We're friends, Maddox. And I was helping him with diabetes. He's your friend, too. You'll see him again." She made a mental note to ask Julianne if she'd bring Maddox to a game in the future.

"I hope so."

Pathetically, Shay hoped to see Brody again, too. But she wasn't getting her hopes up.

"Come on, little buddy. It's my last day of studying forever. Why don't we make some brownies to help us get through it?"

"Yay!" Maddox cheered.

If Shay decided to write another dissertation, it would be about the healing powers of chocolate.

At two o'clock the following afternoon, Shay walked out of Johns Hopkins University with the piece of paper she'd worked four long years to get. Her dissertation defense had lasted nearly two hours. The room had been packed with her advisors, the faculty committee members, and her colleagues in the department, many of whom she'd taught undergraduates with. Thankfully, the department chair had banned all cell phones and cameras before the meeting began. Given her notoriety and the subject of her defense, it was understandable that a member of the media might sneak in.

"And to think, not a single person mentioned the fact that you'd achieved this honor at the ripe old age of twenty-four," her advisor chuckled as they walked down the corridor to the entrance of the building. "I'm proud of you, Shay. You're going to do great things. When you're financially able, you call my friend at the Olympic Training Center in Colorado Springs. They'd love to have you."

"That's my dream job, Dr. Brahm. Hopefully, I'll be there soon."

"If you change your mind about graduation, you let me know. You can always walk through next spring." He held the door for her and the December wind whipped at her skirt.

"My family doesn't travel much with my father's illness, so I doubt it. But thank you for everything, sir. I really appreciate it."

He gave her a fatherly hug. "Well done, my dear. Now go out and be brilliant."

She couldn't help but smile as she walked briskly to her car. Finally, it was over.

"Yay! Is that the great Dr. Everett I see?"

Julianne's voice startled Shay. Her friend was leaning up against the trunk of her car. Her mother-in-law, Annabeth, waved from the driver's seat of her Lexus, parked behind Shay.

"What are you doing here?"

"I'm kidnapping you!" Julianne clapped her hands in delight. "You've just accomplished a major feat. It's time to celebrate."

"But—"

"No buts. Your family is far away, so you have to celebrate with your Blaze family instead."

The mention of the Blaze made her knees nearly buckle. "I couldn't."

"Yes, you can. It'll be easy," Julianne said as she steered Shay around to open the car door. "I'll ride with you, and

Annabeth will follow in my car. All you have to do is relax and enjoy yourself."

Shay slid into the driver's seat as Julianne sat on the passenger side of her little Corolla. "Where are we going?"

"To the practice facility," Julianne said, her tone matter-of-fact.

"No! I can't!" Shay's hands started to shake on the steering wheel.

Julianne covered one with one of her own. "Yes you can, sweetie. Emma has been planning this for weeks. She's even gotten little Maddox involved. Please let us do this for you. Brody hasn't been cleared to practice with the team yet, so he won't be there. If he were, I would be tempted to poke his eyes out. Come, Shay. It'll be fun."

Shay hated that her and Brody's disastrous relationship had come between him and Julianne. But a part of her was secretly glad the woman was still her friend. And she didn't want to let Emma down.

"Okay," she said finally and Julianne blew the horn to alert Annabeth to move on.

Roscoe was meeting with the team management and physicians at four. The fact that Brody had been excluded from the meeting could only mean one thing: He was on the IR—or injured reserve—list. His agent had insisted he stay away from the meeting, but there was no way in hell he was going to let them decide his future without him. Taking the steps two at a time, he charged up the stairs of the training facility toward Hank Osbourne's office.

"Brody!"

Maddox's squeal stopped him in his tracks. Glancing around, he realized he'd walked into the middle of a party of some sort. Silence fell over the room that was filled with his teammates, their wives, even his own sister. *And Shannon.* Standing regally among the well-wishers with a mortarboard trimmed out in Blaze colors propped jauntily on her head, she looked stunning in her fitted black suit and high-heeled boots.

Bridgett eyed him warily from across the room, but Julianne didn't bother to hide her displeasure. Marching through the crowd, she hissed at him. "Go away!"

Maddox had a death grip on his leg. "No! Brody don't leave. Shay is a doctor now. We were going to take her to dinner to celebrate. Remember?" The boy looked up at him with his puddle-brown eyes and a familiar squeezing began in Brody's chest.

Shit, shit, shit! Today was the day Shannon was defending her dissertation. By the looks of everyone, it had gone well. He felt an enormous swell of pride for her. All her hard work had paid off. He'd never had any doubt that it would.

Maddox was telling the truth, he had planned to take her to a celebration dinner followed by a night of pampering at the Ritz-Carlton. But that was before. When they were still . . . whatever it was that they had been.

"It's okay, Julianne." Shannon's mama would be proud of her perfect Southern manners.

Julianne gave him the evil eye she'd perfected fending off men in Italy before moving away. The rest of the guests began their chatter again, giving him and Shannon a modicum of privacy.

"Congratulations." Brody awkwardly moved forward to shake her hand or kiss her, he wasn't sure which, but her slight recoil had him jerking back.

Her whiskey eyes were anxious and Brody figured it was best to make his way out of there as quickly as possible. *Best for both of us.* "So, you're still planning on heading to the job in Texas."

"Yes, Brody, I am." There was no resignation in her voice. Just determination. She had a plan, a mission, and she was sticking to it.

His mantra of the last few days slid out of his mouth, but his chest ached as he said the words. "It's better this way." Except he finally believed it was better this way; better that their relationship end here and now because he wouldn't trust again. Ever.

She smiled as if she'd heard and understood his unspoken words. But then, she always had understood him.

"So we're good?" It was a stupid question for him to ask. Her eyes and her posture told him she might splinter into a million pieces at any moment. Not that he was much better.

"Yes," she whispered. "We're good."

He heaved a sigh at her dismissal, patting Maddox on the head. "Little dude, I'm going to have to take a rain check. I have a meeting I've got to go to."

The boy pulled away, his face crestfallen. "But Brody, this is Shay's special day! We have to do it today."

Brody hated himself for what he was doing to the boy. And to Shannon. But he had no choice. It was just too much work to forge a relationship with anyone when he didn't trust a soul.

"Maddox," Shannon said, gently pulling the boy underneath her arm. "Grown-ups don't always get to do what they want. Sometimes they have to make tough choices that aren't always fair."

Brody would have felt that sucker punch even if he were wearing a cup. She'd said the words to Maddox, but they were clearly meant for him. But she didn't understand. She knew who she was and where her life was going—even after her pit stop as a prison matron. Shannon had made it all work. He had no idea about his future and even less control.

"Why don't you go get a piece of cake?" She caressed the boy's cheek gently and Brody's whole body went hard.

Maddox narrowed his eyes at Brody. "Sure. But it's got sugar in it so Brody can't have none." The boy stomped off toward his mother.

"You don't want to miss your meeting." It was costing her to remain calm; her short staccato breaths gave her away.

He stood there drinking her in with his eyes. The conundrum that wasn't his anymore. "Good luck, Shannon."

She gave him a brief nod, but it took him a moment before he could turn and leave the room.

"Brody," she said softly. "You're gonna find who the grown-up Brody is, I promise. And he's going to be awesome." Not giving him a chance to respond, she quickly turned on her heel and slipped back into the crowd of well-wishers.

Brody strode from the building, figuring it was probably better to let Roscoe handle things with management after all.

Shay called the manager of Celtic Charm and told him she wouldn't be working there any longer. It was a crummy thing to do to him on a Friday morning, but she knew there were more than enough bartenders who'd want her shift and she just didn't have the energy to smile and make nice to strangers all night. Besides, she didn't need rent money next month; she'd be back in her old bedroom at Mama's soon enough.

Sorting through her meager belongings, she packed her books into a box to ship home.

"That's gonna cost a fortune you know," Julianne said from her seat on the kitchen floor, where she was stacking Shay's few dishes into a box for Goodwill.

"Probably, but I might need them for something in the future." Shay pulled the packing tape over the box. "Besides, they're kind of like a badge of honor. I can always line my bookshelves with them to intimidate people."

Julianne laughed. "Oh, Shay, you don't need to intimidate anyone. But you could clunk a prisoner over the head with one of those massive tomes if he gets out of line."

It was Shay's turn to laugh. "How many times do I have to tell y'all, I'm not going to have any direct interaction with the prisoners. I'll be doing the dietary planning and other things from an office on site, but that's as close as I'll come."

"I know, but it makes you sound tougher my way."

Shay laughed again. Her friendships with Julianne and Bridgett had turned out to be one of the fringe benefits of her relationship with Brody. She figured the friendships would peter out in the months ahead—although both women claimed they were going to visit Shay in Texas—but she was glad for their company now.

Julianne's cell phone buzzed. "Oh my," she said as she scanned the screen.

"Everything okay with Owen?" Shay asked, concerned by the anxious look on her friend's face.

"Actually, this is from Will. It's about Brody."

Shay's breath seized in her lungs and she felt a little light-headed. Surely, he'd been monitoring his blood sugar and watching his diet? Had he been injured? But he wasn't cleared to practice yet. "Is he all right?" she asked.

Julianne looked up from her phone. Her amber eyes softening as she took in Shay's anxiety. "Of course he is. He's Brody." She laughed in amazement. "The team has cleared him to play. Apparently, he is still in the prediabetes stage and may stay that way for the rest of his life. Will says he just has to watch when he exerts himself because he gets something called—"

"Reactive hypoglycemia."

"Yes, that. But, of course, you already knew that." Julianne nodded at the box of books, a wide grin on her face. "Because you're so smart."

Shay slid into a chair. "That's wonderful. I'm so happy for him." And she was. They'd both gotten what they wanted. Their crazy pact had been successful. Yet, her heart was still heavy, weighed down by a sadness she'd never felt the likes of before. All those weeks of holding back her feelings had been for nothing. Because Brody had made her fall in love with him and then he'd walked away.

Julianne snorted, rousting Shay from her musing. "It just puts off the inevitable."

"I don't know," Shay said. "I think he's ready to grow up. He just doesn't know how to take that leap. But he will."

Her friend eyed her shrewdly. "Brody doesn't like doing things that require too much effort."

Shay's lips curved into a smile of agreement. "No, but one day he'll find something that will make him put forth a little effort and take that leap of faith."

"Huh," Julianne said. "I have a feeling that day has already come and gone."

Before Shay had the opportunity to question her friend's cryptic statement, a knock sounded at the door.

"That's probably Mr. Metz with more boxes." Shay stood to get the door.

But it wasn't her neighbor standing at the threshold.

"Teryn!" Shay gasped.

It was her sister.

Twenty-six

"Mama didn't want you driving all the way back to Texas alone." Teryn picked the croutons out of her salad, neatly piling them to the side.

Five hours later, Shay was still getting over the shock of seeing her twin standing in her doorway. Julianne had departed shortly after Teryn arrived, saying she needed to get back to Owen. The two sisters finished the small amount of packing relatively quickly. Shay's belongings fit into five small boxes. Everything else she was leaving to Goodwill.

"Don't you have to cheer this weekend?" Shay asked.

"It's an away game." Teryn peeled the pepperoni off her slice of pizza.

"But what about work?"

Teryn dabbled in modeling and she made some appearance money as a Dallas Cowboys cheerleader, but not enough to support her. To make ends meet, she worked as a receptionist for a celebrity dentist in Dallas while she was putting herself through hygienist school.

"Lordy, Shay, what's with the twenty questions? I do get vacation days, you know." She poured herself a Diet Coke.

"It's just that I thought you'd rather spend your vacation doing something other than a three-day road trip with me."

"I've never been on a road trip with you. It might be fun."

Shay doubted three days in her cramped Corolla with her sister would be fun. The two girls had seen each other rarely these past seven years. After graduating high school early at seventeen, Shay had taken her swim scholarship and finished undergraduate school and earning her master's degree in four years. During that time, Teryn had been homecoming queen, prom queen, and fifth runner-up for Miss Texas. While Shay was slaving away in graduate school, trying to help Mama, Teryn had been parading around in short-shorts and pom-poms enjoying the good life.

Now, she'd suddenly shown up here in Baltimore in an act of supposed sisterly love. Shay wasn't buying a word of it.

"Who paid for your plane ticket?"

Teryn jumped up from the small card table, tossing her half-eaten dinner into the trash.

"Jesus, Shay! Am I so incapable that I can't even afford a plane ticket? Or do you think I batted my eyelashes and shook my girls in front of some sugar daddy and he gave me the plane fare?"

"That's not what I meant." Except it was and a twinge of guilt began to unfurl in Shay's belly.

"I don't know why I bother. You're just as bad as Meemaw."

Those were fighting words. "What did you just say?"

"You heard me." Teryn marched over to the door, where her overnight bag was. "All my life, do you know what I've had to listen to? *Why can't you be as smart as your sister? God gave your sister all the common sense and you the boobs. You're not going to amount to anything other than a rich man's trophy wife, while your sister is going to be the CEO of a company someday.* No one ever gives me credit for having a single thought in my head that's my own because of your big egghead!" She jabbed a toothbrush at Shay. "Thanks to you, I'm just a dumb, washed-up beauty queen. At twenty-four! While you're a PhD. You open your mouth to speak and people actually listen instead of staring at your boobs!"

Astonished, Shay contemplated what her sister said as Teryn charged into the bathroom and vigorously brushed her teeth. Apparently, their Meemaw hadn't discriminated in her narcissism. But that wasn't Shay's fault.

"Hey," she yelled at her sister over the electric toothbrush. "Don't you dare blame me for the things she said to you! She was doing the exact same thing to me, you know. *God gave your sister all the beauty, and when he got to you, there was nothing left but ugly. It's a good thing you have a brain, because otherwise we'd have to put a bag over your big head.*"

Tears were streaming down her face now. Teryn spit into the sink before turning to pull Shay into her arms, the two of them gulping in sobs.

"I hated when everybody made a fuss over me and they ignored you. I swear it. I did," Teryn cried. "But I was young and felt so inferior to you, that I . . . I didn't know how to stop it."

They slid down the wall to the floor where they sat holding each other.

"Do you think Mama knew how she treated us?" Teryn asked when their sobs had subsided somewhat.

"I think Mama was in a fog for so long. She was all alone after Daddy's accident and betrayal. There were medical bills and legal bills, not to mention child support. And she had no one to help her. What choice did she have but to leave us in Meemaw's care? She had to make a success of the salon."

"She should have divorced Daddy."

Shay looked at her sister in stunned silence. Teryn had always been Daddy's girl.

"I know," Teryn said. "She can't divorce him while he's incapacitated. But still, I hate what he did to our family. And we have a brother out there who's living large, while our Mama works her fingers to the bone. I swear I'm never going to give a man that kind of power over me."

"What do you mean by that?"

Teryn shrugged her shoulders. "You can't get hurt if you don't ever give a man your heart."

Shay's own heart clenched. She knew all too well what

kind of trauma a woman could suffer when she gave a man her heart. Something must have shown in her eyes because Teryn pulled her in close again.

"Oh, baby, you fell in love with him, didn't you?"

She didn't bother denying it, instead letting the tears fall on her twin's shoulder.

"When I saw pictures of the two of you, he looked at you as if he felt the same way. And that was most definitely not pretending. Hell's bells, in most of the pictures he looked at you as if he were going to gobble you up. But not in the same way men look at me. It was almost . . . almost as if he couldn't believe how lucky he was to have you."

Shay sobbed harder as her sister stroked her hair.

"And that idiot was lucky to have you," Teryn went on to say. "Because you are smart and beautiful." She pushed back to an arm's length. "Well, not at the moment. Right now you look horrible. But we're gonna fix that in a jiffy. When I get through with you, we're going to parade you around Baltimore and make that boy sorry he pretended anything."

Shay pushed to her feet, stabbing at the tears on her face. "We're leaving, remember. I have to get home and get ready for my new job."

Teryn got to her feet behind her. "That's another thing. How come you get to play martyr and rescue Mama? No one asked me to help."

She turned to see Teryn with her hands on her hips, genuinely angry.

Baffled, Shay tried to make her words not sound harsh. "You're still establishing your career. How can you help?"

"I've been offered a quarter of a million dollars to pose for *Playboy*," Teryn said swiftly, looking everywhere in the room but at Shay.

"Teryn!" Shay hissed. "You can't do that!"

"Who says? Apparently that's all I'm good for. I'll get kicked off the squad for sure, but I'm pretty much aging out anyway. Thanks to that blogger, I have a little notoriety. Why shouldn't I make a little money to help Mama?"

"Because you don't want to, that's why," Shay argued.

"Do you want to work in a prison?"

The room was quiet for a moment as they both stared at one another, the enormity of the decision weighing on them. There was no way Shay was going to let her sister pose for *Playboy*. Mama would be humiliated. But Teryn very much wanted to be a part of the solution and Shay didn't want to shatter the fragile bond they were reforming.

"Remember how we used to decide who got the last Popsicle in the box or the last cookie?" Shay asked.

"You wanna flip a coin?" Teryn's face was incredulous.

Shay smiled as she thought of those days gone by. "Yeah. We'll flip for it. It's the fairest way."

Teryn sighed as she reached for her purse. "I guess so. But one flip. Winner gets to be the martyr."

"Deal. But not here. We'll do it under the magnolia tree behind the house, just like always."

"You wanna wait until we get home?" Teryn asked.

"Yep. That way we can enjoy the road trip."

Her sister broke out into a wide grin. "I'm in."

They dug in to the pints of Ben & Jerry's ice cream they'd bought earlier at Santoni's as they caught up on their lives. Teryn had a vast circle of friends in Dallas and she was excited to have Shay be a part of it. Thanks to her time with Brody—and Julianne's tutoring—Shay didn't feel apprehensive at all about joining in. Perhaps going home to Texas wouldn't be so bad after all. Later that night as the twins crawled into bed, their hands automatically linked together as they had for so many years when they'd slept together as girls, and Shay finally believed she'd survive life after Brody.

Brody's house had been infested. By his own family. His mother had insisted on monitoring his condition and nothing short of a nuclear holocaust was going to stop her. Gwen and Ashley had descended upon him with the intent of decorating his house for the holidays.

"Really, nobody sees this place but me," he told them over breakfast—a meal his mother was closely supervising. "Why do you have to go to all this trouble of putting up this junk?"

"So you'll have some Christmas spirit, Mr. Grinch," Gwen said as she hung a heavily scented wreath on the mantel.

"I don't need any Christmas spirit. I just need my house back," Brody grumbled. Secretly, however, he was relieved to have other people around distracting him. Bridgett had gone back to Boston, her pretrial work complete. His home was quiet without her popping in unexpectedly all the time. *And without Shannon.*

There was nothing left of her in his house any longer. Her smell was gone from his pillow. Her spreadsheets no longer littered his kitchen table. There weren't any containers with Post-it Notes in the fridge any longer. It was almost as if she'd never been there. Until he went to bed at night; then the memories crowded into the room with him so that he couldn't sleep.

"Try not to get carried away, ladies," he warned. "You are all quick to fly down here to put this crap up, but I always get stuck with taking it down."

"Go to practice, Brody, and leave us to our fun," his mother said. "And make sure you keep an eye on your sugar."

Brody didn't need to keep an eye on his damn sugar levels because everyone else in the world was too busy doing it for him. He barely got through an hour of practice before someone—Nate, the team physician, one of the coaching staff—was checking his readings. Hell, even Jay McManus, the Blaze owner's godson, was having him monitored.

"It'll all blow over after a few games, Brody," Roscoe told him as they walked from the practice field to the training center. "Just let them reassure themselves that you're not going to keel over on the field. It'll make the contract extension talks go more smoothly if they feel like they have some control over the situation."

"Control over the situation or control over me?"

Roscoe chuckled ominously. "Right now, the two are one in the same. If you want to play football, you'll deal with it."

Nate didn't let up the entire road trip to Miami, following

Brody around like a mad scientist collecting his urine and drops of blood. Not for the first time, Brody cursed his former trainer for his big mouth. The other night, when Bridgett had forced him to finally put the pieces together, Brody had been numb. He'd spent twelve hours thinking he was betrayed by another lover, only to find out it was his friend. And Erik hadn't even sold him out for money. It was just another reason why Brody couldn't trust anyone with his secrets. His future looked lonely, but it beat the alternative.

Fortunately, the weather in Florida was a lot more hospitable than it had been in Denver. Brody snagged two touchdowns and DeShawn ran for over a hundred yards to carry the Blaze past the Dolphins. The flight back to Baltimore was festive with Christmas carols and talk of the playoffs.

Devlin took the seat beside Brody, a groan escaping his lips as he eased into the seat.

"You gonna make it through the season, old man?" Brody teased. The quarterback had taken a few punishing licks today when one of the offensive lineman had gone down.

"Yeah, I'll be just fine if you can remember to block when you're told to."

Brody shot his teammate his killer grin. "Dude, I caught what you threw to me—even the wobbly ones—and I didn't miss a single block." It was true. His game had been on fire this afternoon.

"None of my passes were wobbly, dumbass. Anything that came into your hands less than perfect was tipped at the line."

"Whatever you say, old man." Brody had enormous respect for Shane Devlin and he'd be truly sorry to see the quarterback hang up his spikes. But he knew that day was coming and he couldn't resist teasing his friend when he could.

"Hey, that little boy, Maddox. Do you have his address?" Devlin asked.

"Sure. Why?"

"I promised him an autographed jersey. He wanted it to send to his father for Christmas. I totally forgot about it with the baby coming early. I want to get it to him so his mom can send it out. Hopefully, it will get there in time."

Brody felt a little miffed that Maddox hadn't asked him for a jersey. He'd already sent balls and Blaze caps to the boy's father's unit. But Devlin had been the Super Bowl MVP. If anything, Brody should feel a little guilty about how he treated the boy the night of Shannon's party.

"Just give it to me. I'll take it to him," he heard himself saying.

Devlin stared him down, but Brody wasn't some rookie receiver.

"Dude, you don't trust me to take a kid a stinking jersey?"

"It's not the kid or the jersey I'm worried about. It's whether or not I trust you to do it without messing with his neighbor again."

Brody blew out a breath. "Shannon and I are fine."

It was Devlin who blew out the breath now. "Look, Brody, don't make my mistake—"

"Jeez, Devlin, I didn't know you made mistakes," Brody said trying to fend off another lecture.

"Stop being a wiseass and listen to what I have to tell you. I was so caught up in thinking about my football career that I nearly lost Carly—twice; the second time to some joker's bullet. If there's something there between you and Shay, don't throw it away because of a damn game. Or, worse, your stupid pride."

"Like I've told you and everyone else, there's nothing between Shannon and me." His teeth nearly ground to dust in his head as he said it. "Now, do you want me to take Maddox the jersey or not?"

Devlin shook his head with a disgusted sigh. "Sure, Brody. Take the jersey. Just don't trip and fall with those thick blinders on." He clicked on his iPad and focused his eyes on the screen.

It was Monday afternoon before Brody made it to Shannon's apartment complex. A hodgepodge of Christmas lights decorated the railings outside the various apartments, already lit up as dusk fell. He knocked on the door of Maddox's apartment and the boy pulled the door open.

"What have I told you about opening the door to strangers?" Brody chastised the boy. It was a familiar refrain between the two, but today, instead of cheering in excitement at the sight of him, the boy's eyes were wary.

"Brody!" Jackie's greeting was more cheerful as she came out of the small kitchenette, wiping her hands on a dishtowel. "What are you doing here?"

He lifted the two shopping bags. "Christmas gifts. Although one was a special request to be sent to Afghanistan, so I hope it's not too late. Devlin got a little wrapped up in his new baby and he's behind in getting it to you."

Maddox inched toward the bag and peered in. "Whoa! Is that the jersey?"

"Signed by the MVP himself."

"Oh, Brody. That's so sweet. Tony will be thrilled. But Maddox will be able to give it to him in person." Jackie's face lit up in delight. "He's coming home on Christmas Eve."

"Hey, that's terrific. I bet you're excited to see your dad again, huh, Maddox."

"Yep. And we're moving to Texas. So we're going to see Shay." The boy's chin went up a notch as if to say "up yours." Brody would have laughed at the kid's bravado if he wasn't feeling a touch of jealousy. Crouching down on his knees, he looked Maddox in the eye and smiled. "I'm glad, little dude. Because that will make her happy. And it will make me happy knowing you'll be there taking care of her."

The boy's chest puffed out. "Whatcha got in the other bag?"

"Oh, that. It's just something I thought you'd like."

The boy looked from the bag to his mother. Jackie nodded and Maddox ripped into the gift. Brody had stopped at the Hess gas station earlier and picked up the holiday toy truck. It was loud with flashing lights and a detachable helicopter, everything a seven-year-old could want.

"Cool!" Maddox shouted, ripping at the box.

"What do you say, Maddox?" his mother prompted.

"Thank you, Brody." He looked over at the adjoining door to Shannon's apartment with longing.

It was devious using a kid like he was, but Brody found himself wanting just one more opportunity to be around Shannon. "I'll bet Shannon would love to see that. Why don't you go show her?"

Maddox's chin went to his chest. "I can't."

"Oh, Brody," Jackie admonished him.

When he glanced up at Maddox's mother, her eyes held both pity and disgust. Brody got to his feet.

"She's already gone," she said.

Brody ran his hand through his hair, confused. "She was going to stay until Christmas, next week."

Jackie shook her head looking at Brody as if he were an idiot. "She changed her mind. After all, it's not like there was anything keeping her here anymore."

Twenty-seven

Brody sat in the back of the church listening but not really hearing the mass. Usually Advent was his favorite of the church seasons, but he wasn't feeling it this year. He wasn't feeling much of anything. The city itself was decked out for the holidays and snow was in the air. The Blaze had secured a spot in the playoffs and the team was firing on all cylinders. Even better, his health was under control and his contract extension had been finalized. But that feeling of wanting something, but not knowing what, still nagged at Brody.

Sister Agnes patted his hand with hers, much like his grandmother used to do. When he glanced over at her, there was a ghost of a sad smile on her face. He raised an eyebrow in question, but she just shook her head, her hand remaining atop his on his thigh.

"What?" he mouthed to her. Maybe the nun had had a stroke and she couldn't talk. His heart leaped into his throat. "Are you all right?" he whispered reaching into his jacket pocket for his cell phone.

"I'm fine," she whispered. "It's you who are troubled."

Brody slouched back in the pew. "I was fine until you nearly gave me a heart attack," he mumbled.

She patted his hand again and he released a tight breath.

"I'm thinking about the game," he lied. "Chicago has a tough defense."

Sister Agnes shook her head again. "Tsk-tsk, Brody. Stop hiding behind football."

He yanked his hand out from under hers. "I'm not!"

She gave him that pitying grin again. "Yes, you are. You miss the girl. Just tell her you love her and get it over with. It won't hurt. I promise."

Brody stared at her, dumbfounded. Had the nun been smoking the incense before mass? "I don't miss her." Except he did. "And I'm definitely not in love with her."

Sister Agnes tsked at him again.

"No," he whispered hoarsely. "Loving someone means trusting them and I'm through with that. Forever."

"And how's that working out for you, Brody?" she asked.

A roaring began in his ears. He wanted to rail at the nun. "Is that all you've got?" He kneed the Bible tucked into the holder on back of the pew in front of them. "A whole book of scripture and you give me that?"

Her smile had gone from pitying to smug.

"Everyone I get involved with sells me out, Sister. It's only a matter of time before you do, too."

She pulled in a sharp breath but her gaze didn't waver. Brody saw disappointment in her eyes and it made his stomach crawl. He dragged his fingers through his hair again as his temples began to throb. "I'm sorry, but I'm feeling pretty raw in that area right now."

"I have a question," she said gently. "The girl, did she sell you out?"

Brody swallowed around the boulder in his throat before shaking his head.

"There," she said, patting his thigh again. "Deceit isn't in you either, Brody. You were lying to everyone about your involvement with the girl. But you were lying to yourself, too. Your heart was involved. It still is. Don't waste this opportunity, Brody." With another pat to his thigh, she pulled out the kneeler and knelt for prayer.

Chicago's defense punished the Blaze, but their own defense was just as ruthless. DeShawn managed to punch in the winning touchdown with twenty-nine seconds left on the clock and the crowd left the stadium jubilant and primed for Christmas on Wednesday. Coach presented DeShawn with the game ball amid a chorus of cheers.

"Thanks to a helluva block from Brody," DeShawn shouted and the team cheered again.

"Great game, men. We'll have training staff at the practice facility tomorrow, so make sure everyone gets their aches and pains looked at. Tuesday and Wednesday are off days, but I want everyone back ready to practice bright and early Thursday. We've got a short week. Don't make me regret giving you an extra day off," Coach barked. "Merry Christmas, fellas!"

Brody dressed quickly, wanting to get home, where he could clear his head. Sister Agnes's words were still bouncing around annoyingly. He passed through the training room to give Nate his drop of blood when Devlin called him from the big whirlpool tub he was soaking his hip in.

"That was a pretty wicked block, Brody," the quarterback said. "We wouldn't have won without it. Well played."

"Thanks." Brody wasn't in the mood for conversation and he made his way toward the door.

"Something eating you, Brody?" Devlin asked, sounding like he actually cared.

"Nah, I just want to get home."

"You going to Boston for Christmas?" Devlin was turning into a real Chatty Cathy tonight.

"Tomorrow night."

The quarterback took a pull from a bottle of water. "You're lucky to have a big family to spend it with. I can remember spending lots of holidays alone." He smiled one of his rare grins. "It's nice to finally have one of my own."

Brody thought about being smothered by his sisters and their families. It was chaotic and boisterous, but when it came right down to it, he was still alone in the crowd.

"Yeah," he said. "Enjoy your daughter's first Christmas, Devlin." He made his way out of the stadium to his car. Still mulling over Sister Agnes's comments and now Devlin's, Brody went home and ate a solitary dinner Nate had had some dietician prepare. Restless, he climbed back into his Range Rover and drove to the Hampden area of Baltimore to see the famous Christmas lights. An entire block of Thirty-Fourth Street was lit up as neighbors in the row houses strung lights across the streets and on their houses. Inflatable snow globes, musical trains, and blinking angels illuminated the area. It was so over-the-top, Brody was pretty sure the city block was visible from space. He walked, unrecognized, among the throngs of families enjoying the spectacle. The feeling of loneliness swelled.

Driving back through the city, he made his way to Federal Hill, pulling his car in front of Will and Julianne's loft apartment. Julianne was the wisest woman he knew, aside from Shannon. But Shannon wasn't here and he was pretty sure she was at the center of his melancholy anyhow. Will answered the door, his normally impeccable appearance rumpled in flannel sleep pants and a dark T-shirt adorned with spit-up on the shoulder. Owen wailed from the vicinity of the kitchen.

"At least you knocked first," his teammate said as he led the way to the kitchen, where Owen sat in his bouncy seat crying and gnawing on his fist at the same time.

"I surrendered my key a long time ago. Where's your wife?"

That got the linebacker's attention. He eyed Brody menacingly while he flung the baby over his shoulder, gently bouncing him up and down. "She's taking a bath. She needed a break."

"Not much of a break if the kid is wailing. Are you sticking pins in that baby again?"

"He's got a cold and he's fussy. It happens." Will moved

the baby to his other shoulder, Owen's wails started to calm as his eyes drifted shut.

"Is she gonna be long? This is important." Brody glanced into the small living room where the lights of the Christmas tree flickered against the backdrop of the Inner Harbor. A small stuffed elf wearing a "Baby's First Christmas" hat was lying on the back of the sofa. Brody picked it up and wondered if Devlin had one of these for his daughter. Hell, it wouldn't be long before his childhood friend Robbie-Rob had one for his inevitable kid. Brody's stomach rolled.

"You look like hell." Will's voice had gotten quieter to accommodate his son who was slumbering finally.

"You wouldn't win any contests yourself." Brody gestured to the spit-up on his teammate's shirt as Will laid the baby into a small crib in the living room.

Will chuckled. "My, how the mighty have fallen."

"Can you just get your wife, please?"

"In a minute," Will crossed his arms over his chest as he leaned his big body against the island separating the kitchen from the rest of the loft. "Right now, I'm enjoying seeing the great lady-killer Brody Janik being laid low by a woman."

"That's not what this is."

"Take it from one who's been where you are—in this very room with you as my tour guide—you're always the last to know."

Brody thought back six months to when his friend's new marriage nearly didn't get off the ground because of a serious lack of trust on both their parts. Yet they'd made it work. They were both happy. The squeezing sensation was back in Brody's chest. He leaned over the crib and gently put the elf in the corner.

"Your kid's got the hands of a receiver."

Will scoffed. "He's too smart for that. He's gonna be a linebacker all the way."

"Nonsense," Julianne said as she climbed down the stairs wrapped in a flowing robe and silk pajamas. "Owen is going to be an artist."

Both men choked on that as they followed her to the kitchen, where she pulled coffee mugs out of the cabinet.

"What do you want, Brody?"

Julianne, still obviously on Team Shannon, gave him the cold shoulder. This was the hard part, trying to convey to his friends what he wanted when he wasn't entirely sure himself.

"Brody, it's nine thirty. We'll be lucky to get six hours of sleep before he wakes up again. What. Do. You. Want?" Will demanded.

"I want what you have!" he growled, suddenly realizing what he wanted. *All of it.*

Will took an angry step forward before Julianne placed a hand in the center of his chest giving him a soothing caress. "Down, boy. I'm fairly certain he means our lives and not me."

She stretched up on her bare toes and bussed Brody on the cheek. "Sit," she said, pushing him onto one of the barstools. "I'll make some cappuccino." She filled the coffee machine. "Brody, you always told me you were looking for the woman who gets you. And when that one extraordinary woman came along—the one who totally gets you—you sent her away. Why?"

Brody raked his fingers through his hair. "Because she's a good person," he whispered. "The best I've ever met. I want to always hold that image of her in my heart: the warm, trustworthy woman who she is. If I let her in—all the way in—I'll give her the opportunity to sell me out."

Will sucked in a breath.

"Oh, Brody." The pity in Julianne's voice made Brody cringe. "That's no way to live your life. You can't go around believing the worst in people. Especially someone who you already admit is a wonderful person. When you find someone like that—like Shay—you need to hold on to them. Not push them away."

"You're telling me it's too late? That I screwed up?"

"I didn't say that." She pulled a carton of cream out of the fridge. "Although you did screw up."

Will nodded behind his wife.

"But you can fix it. You just have to be willing to put yourself out there, Brody. To trust."

There was that damn T-word again. Brody pushed through a few hard breaths. Life without Shannon had become nearly unbearable. He was just going through the motions. Brody wanted more and that meant he had to do whatever it took.

"Okay," he agreed. "Tell me what I need to do."

Will laughed. "A good place to start would be groveling."

Brody ignored his smart-ass teammate, instead looking to his wife for advice.

"Sorry, Brody, but I agree with Will. This is going to call for some serious groveling," she said with a mischievous grin as Brody dropped his head into his hands.

The Platinum Palace was nothing like Brody expected. Instead of being housed in a strip mall or, worse, Shannon's mother's garage, the salon was located in a three-thousand-square-foot craftsman-style building, dwarfed by two towering river oak trees. Despite the fact that it was mid-day on Christmas Eve, the sprawling parking lot was filled. Not only that, but the spaces were occupied by Beemers, Mercedes, and Ford F-150 pickups.

There was lots of blond hair, too. All shades and sizes. Brody was nearly blinded by it; that and the futuristic platinum Christmas tree blinking in the foyer. The mood inside the salon was festive. Clients dressed in black capes, some wearing tinfoil in their hair, milled around sipping something that looked like eggnog and smelled a lot like bourbon.

Brody stood in the empty foyer scanning the room for Shannon, but she was nowhere in sight. He'd already tried her mother's address, only to be told by her grandmother that both girls were working at the salon today. Hanging over the reception desk was a poster-sized photo of Teryn all decked out in her Dallas Cowboys cheerleader outfit. On a shelf next to it was a photo of both sisters dressed in identical white dresses. In the picture, Shannon's hair was wild and her smile impish.

"That's my favorite picture of my girls," a voice said beside him.

Brody didn't realize he'd picked up the frame until it was being taken from his hands. He glanced up at the attractive woman beside him. June Everett was pleasingly plump but with the face of a goddess and a head full of the hair that gave the place its name. It was easy to see where her girls got their beauty.

"They were ten. It was a chore getting them both to stay clean while the photographer fiddled with his equipment. Lordy, but that feels like a lifetime ago." Her voice was wistful as she replaced the picture on the shelf. Turning to Brody, she got right to the point. "Shay's in the back. I keep a loaded gun back there, too, and she knows how to use it, so you best mind your manners."

Brody nearly laughed at the woman's bravado until he realized she was serious. Pushing his Ray-Bans on top of his head, he followed where she'd pointed toward the back of the salon. As he made his way past the chairs of women, a silence descended like a bow wave until the only sound in the cavernous room was Blake Shelton belting out "Jingle Bell Rock" over the stereo system.

Inside the large storage room a washer spun while Shannon stood at the dryer pulling out towels and folding them on a table beside it. A fluffy white cat sat beside the pile, swishing its tail as Shannon sang along to the Christmas song, her jeans-clad hips swaying nicely to the beat. The sight was so enticing, Brody let out a load groan. Shannon froze in mid-fold, taking a moment before turning toward him, her face a mask.

"Oh, for the love of Christ, Shannon! What are you wearing?" Not what he'd planned to say, but seeing her in the flesh again was doing crazy things to his body.

She looked down at her gray T-shirt, Redskins embla-zoned across her fine chest. Lifting her chin again she arched an eyebrow at him. "Seriously? That's what you're gonna lead with, Brody?"

His brain was telling him to shut the hell up and stick to the script, but that same brain had scrambled once he'd caught sight of those whiskey eyes again. "You have plenty of Blaze T-shirts you stole from me. Why are you wearing that?"

"To goad my sister and all the Dallas fans in the salon."

"Well it goads me!" He wanted to touch her, but he knew he was already screwing everything up. Badly. "At least tell me you're wearing your Blaze panties," he asked.

No reaction. Not even her telltale blush.

"You didn't come all this way to discuss my panties, Brody."

He'd come all this way to get her *out* of her panties, but he figured now was not the time to bring that up. He reached a hand behind his neck to rub at the muscles that were squeezing so hard they were cutting off his circulation and common sense.

"No, I came here to bring you your Christmas present."

She arched a delicate eyebrow at him. "I wasn't aware we were exchanging Christmas presents, Brody."

He pulled an envelope out of his pocket. "Not exchanging. I'm just giving." He handed it to her.

Shannon was careful not to touch him, taking the envelope between her fingers as if it had cooties. Carefully, she pulled out the contents and unfolded the papers inside and scanned them.

"You paid off Mama's mortgage?!?" Her angry tone and wild eyes were definitely not what he expected.

A gasp at his back alerted him that they had visitors. *Damn you, Jerry Maguire, for making this look so easy.* Shannon swatted him with the paperwork that freed up the rest of her life.

"Hell's bells, Brody! What in the Sam Hill did you do that for?"

"So you wouldn't have to work in a prison!" He seriously thought she might be more grateful.

"Oh, Brody. I don't even know if I am going to work in a prison, Teryn and I haven't flipped the coin yet."

"What? Flipped what coin?" He was having a little trouble keeping up.

She shook her head at him. "Never mind. It doesn't matter because you've done *this*." She waved the papers again. "I told you that I'm not one of your girlfriends who you can just pay off when you're through with her!"

"I'm not trying to pay you off, because I'm not through with you!" he yelled. There was another gasp behind him. He grabbed the paperwork out of Shannon's hands and went to the door where her mother and her sister, Teryn, stood and he shoved the papers at them. "Here. Merry freakin' Christmas." Then, he slammed the door in their faces, drowning out Teryn's laughter.

When he turned to face Shannon again, there was a definite softening of her attitude.

"Now, can we get to the real reason you're here, Brody."

He rubbed a hand through his hair.

"I'm an ass," he said quietly.

"Tell me something I don't know."

He muttered softly to himself. Hooking a stool on wheels with his foot, he pulled it directly in front of Shannon and sat down. This would be a lot easier if she wasn't slaying him with those eyes. Reaching up to span her hips with his hands, he leaned his forehead against her belly. The familiar scent of her filled his nostrils giving him the strength to go on. He could feel her heartbeat against his head, its steady rhythm calming him. Her hands stayed fisted by her side, but this was his big move and Brody figured she was going to make him work for it.

"This is hard and you know I don't do hard," he said.

"Mmmm. You're going to have to grow up sometime, Brody."

Yep, he definitely had to work for it. But since she was still allowing him to hold her, he figured he was safe to go all in.

"All this time, I kept thinking there was something more I'm supposed to be in life, something more I'm supposed to be doing," he began, relieved that her hands had unclenched and found his shoulders. "But I've been chasing something that doesn't exist. What I should have been looking for is something I'm supposed to *have*. Well not a thing exactly. It's you. What's been missing in my life is you, Shannon."

He looked up into those eyes he loved, now damp with unshed tears, and he made the greatest leap he'd had to make in his life. "If I'm going to grow up, I want to do it with you. Alongside you."

Straddling his legs, she crawled into his lap, so her face was level with his. She draped her arms around his neck. "But do you trust me, Brody?"

He leaned his forehead against hers. "I must. Because I love you madly."

She was silent for a long moment and Brody's breathing stopped.

"By all means, keep me hanging here, Shannon."

Her whiskey eyes danced as she wrapped her legs around his waist. "I've never had a man tell me he loved me before. I'm just savoring the moment."

"Damn it, Shannon," he growled. "You'd better not have any other man tell you he loves you."

"It wouldn't matter if they did. Because the only man I'll ever love is you, Brody Janik."

And then she kissed him. The feel of her sweet mouth was like coming home. At last, he'd unraveled the conundrum and found what he'd been looking for.

Epilogue

THE GIRLFRIENDS' GUIDE TO THE NFL

Well, girlfriends, it's official. Everyone's favorite tight end tied the knot today. Looking sexy in a Versace tux, number eighty's blue eyes were focused solely on his brainy scientist bride. It turns out the homely PhD cleans up quite nicely. Of course, she had a little help from bridal gown designer Julianne Connelly, who decked her out in a stunning sleeveless sheath gown that transformed the gawky nutritionist into an elegant woman worthy to be seen on sinfully sexy Brody Janik's arm.

Until she pulled on a pair of cowboy boots for the reception. Can you say tacky? Several of the guests, including the bride's twin, former Dallas Cowboys cheerleader Teryn Everett, and the groom's sister, high-profile environmental lawyer Bridgett Janik, as well as an elderly nun, took to wearing boots for the dancing. Not that the rest of the guests weren't pretty raucous during the after-party as well. Lots of two-stepping and twelve ounce curls by the Blaze players and their WAGs.

The only dateless member of the organization was the team's hot, young new owner, Jay McManus, which just goes to show you, girlfriends, women aren't attracted to cold-blooded reptiles.

Brody was deliciously naked. Again. He carefully stepped over Shay's discarded wedding gown that was pooled on the floor where he'd peeled it off of her an hour earlier. Smiling his wicked grin, he prowled toward the bed carrying a flute of champagne in each hand. Shay shivered with anticipation as she snuggled deeper among the silk sheets. Darkness had fallen over Dallas and the lights of the skyline framed his tall body as he paused in front of the windows of the honeymoon suite at the Ritz-Carlton.

"You do realize you don't have to get me drunk to have your way with me," she teased.

Brody chuckled as he handed her a glass before sliding beneath the sheets and leaning his broad shoulders against the headboard. "You are delightfully easy, doc. It's one of the many things I love about you." He draped an arm over her shoulder, pulling her in close to him. "But I wanted to make a toast. A private one."

A warm glow settled over Shay as she peered into her husband's blue eyes, now reverent and serious as he held her gaze. Brody brushed his lips along her hairline, lingering a moment before he spoke softly.

"From this day forth, you are all that matters to me. You are the most important thing in my life. Whatever happens after football, I'll face it because all I ever need to make my life complete is you. Whatever makes you happy makes me happy. Wherever you are I want to be. You're my everything, Mrs. Dr. Janik."

Tears stung Shay's eyes as Brody clinked his glass against hers. "So, I've gone from Shannon to Mrs. Dr. Janik. Are you always going to be so formal with me? Will you ever call me Shay?" she whispered.

Brody shook his head. She watched as he swallowed

deeply. "Everybody calls you Shay. And I don't ever want to be lumped in with everybody."

"I don't think that could ever happen to you, Brody Janik," she laughed through her tears. "Because you're definitely one of a kind. And you're *my* everything."

And with those words, she proceeded to show her husband how lucky they both were.

AUTHOR'S NOTE

Back in the days when local television news actually dedicated a portion of its program to sports, I was privileged to grow up watching a guy named Glenn Brenner. A pitcher in baseball's minor leagues and briefly with the Philadelphia Phillies, Brenner left baseball when his arm gave out and went on to earn fame as a sportscaster for WUSA-TV, the CBS affiliate in Washington, D.C. For fifteen years he made his viewers—and anyone sitting alongside him at the broadcast desk—laugh as he delivered his sportscast with a style and wit that rivaled a late night comic. Often times, he was cracking up right along with everyone else. He never took himself or his subject matter too seriously, making him a rarity in the ego-filled world of professional sports.

Brenner was often described as a big kid and viewers loved his contagious smile, his irreverent style and his shtick that included the Weenie of the Week, Encore Wednesdays and the Mystery Prognosticator. When I was plotting this book, I couldn't help but base a character—Sister Agnes—on one of Brenner's more famous mystery prognosticators: Sister Marie Louise, a myopic, elderly nun who was prolific at picking the winners of that week's NFL match-ups. Brody's line to Sister Agnes about cheering against the Cardinal's echoes a quip Glenn Brenner used with Sister Marie Louise. (Several of Sister Agnes' lines come from another man I respect tremendously, Pastor Rick Barger, President of Trinity Lutheran Seminary.)

At the height of his popularity in 1992, Glenn Brenner died prematurely from an inoperable brain tumor. He was forty-four years old. His death saddened us all and left a huge void in local sports reporting. Members of Congress paid tribute to his life in speeches on the House floor. Then President George H. W. Bush also honored Brenner with an official tribute. The Washington Redskins, who were in the midst of a dominating Super Bowl run at the time of Brenner's death, dedicated their NFC Championship win over the Detroit Lions to him. Veteran sports columnist for the *Washington Post*, Leonard Shapiro, reported that Sister Marie Louise was one of Brenner's final visitors. Brenner was said to have lifted up his head to wink at her, which would be so typical of the Glenn Brenner we all loved.

Read on for a special preview
of Tracy Solheim's all-new

SECOND CHANCE SERIES

Coming soon from Berkley Sensation

Like a recovering addict counting the days of sobriety, Ginger Walsh calculated the amount of time remaining until her triumphant return to financial independence: eighty-four days. If she were more like the woman she'd been before being cast as an evil teenager on a television soap opera, she'd optimistically mark the time as *only* twelve weeks or *just* three short months. But Ginger was much more jaded than her alter ego. Real life had toughened her up. It was eighty-four days any way she looked at it.

Every morning, she gave herself a pep talk to mark the passing of another day. She blamed the economy, the industry, and her own stupid decisions for her current situation. But, she always told herself she'd find her way out. Her way back. If that didn't work, she blasted Kelly Clarkson on her iPod and went for a run.

Presently, Ginger's road to career redemption passed through a greasy diner in Chances Inlet, North Carolina; a small, historic coastal town situated at the junction of the Cape Fear River and the Atlantic Ocean. It might as well have been a million miles from Broadway.

"Is it possible to get turkey bacon on my BLT?" Ginger asked, her fingertips sticking to the laminated menu. She tried to infuse just the right amount of deference to her tone while pasting a gracious smile on her face. The tactic never failed her when requesting special orders.

Until now.

The waitress glanced up from her pad, a pained expression on her face. "Sweetheart, you're in North Carolina. This is swine country." Her tone implied Ginger was either an idiot or traitor for requesting anything else.

"Oh." Ginger regarded the woman, willing her to offer up a more nutritious option. When none was forthcoming, she let out an anguished sigh. "Well, is the mayonnaise at least fat free—owwh!"

Diesel Gold, her companion at the small, window table, kicked her in the shin. *Hard*. He raised his tattooed arms along with his eyebrows in either impatience or contempt, she wasn't exactly sure. Clearly, his blood sugar had dropped substantially because he was normally pretty laid back.

The waitress shifted from one sneaker clad foot to the other. Next to them, the table filled with gaffers and grips, boom operators, and the camera men who completed their production crew sat in silence, their faces shifting expectantly between the waitress and Ginger. Apparently their order wouldn't be filled until she had Ginger's.

"Just bring me wheat toast and put the mayo, the bacon, the lettuce, and tomato on the side." She handed over her menu in defeat.

"Do you want fries with that?"

"Ughh!" Diesel dropped his head in his hands.

Ginger shot him a withering look before pasting a polite smile on her face for the waitress. "No, thank you." It was always best to be kind to the wait staff, her mother taught her. Being nice ensured excellent service. In this case, Ginger figured it might ensure the woman didn't spit into her food. "You can give him my fries." She gestured at Diesel. The crew nearly broke out in applause as the waitress headed for the kitchen.

"I liked you better when you weren't such a food weenie," Diesel said.

"For your information, I've been a food weenie all my life. It's the cornerstone of a dancer's existence. And, I liked *you* better when you were Elliot Goldman and not some tattooed, spike-haired, wannabe, music video producer who took his name from a Chippendale dancer."

"Shh!" Diesel quickly glanced around to see if any of the crew were listening, but the opposite table had gone back to discussing the logistics of their go-carting expedition planned for the evening.

"Oh please." Ginger carefully inspected a lemon slice before squeezing it into her water glass. "They all know your dad owns the network. You're twenty-six-years-old. You look like the lead singer for Maroon Five—aside from your glasses, of course—and suddenly you're the producer of a network home improvement show when your only experience is creating a small indie film that never made it off *YouTube*. Face it, you've got nepotism written all over you. Maybe you should get it in a tattoo."

Her friend of nearly a decade wasn't amused. The two had met as teenagers when both were freshmen at Julliard. He was the awkward, but musically gifted son of a television mogul, and she was the scholarship dance phenom living out her mother's dream. Partnered up on a literature project—Plato's *Allegory of a Cave*—they'd been best friends ever since. Their friendship survived not only the class, but the destruction of each of their dreams.

"This isn't funny, Ginger." Diesel leaned across the table, his gravelly voice a near whisper. "The crew has to respect me. I need this gig. My dad won't give me another chance if I screw it up." He gestured to the table next to them. "So far these guys have been pretty tolerant letting me call the shots, but we still have a few months to go."

Eighty-four days to be precise, Ginger thought. She contemplated Diesel, taking in the stress lines bracketing his mouth and the weariness of his eyes. Marvin Goldman, Diesel's narcissistic jerk of a father, took great pleasure in bending his son to fit his own ideal. He was dangling a carrot on a string and would likely yank it away before giving it to his son. It was a frequent pattern between the two. But Diesel continued to hold out hope his father would reward his hard work by allowing him to produce the network's new music reality show. Ginger wanted to tell her friend not to count on his father, but it was difficult not to hope along with him. Because if Diesel got the job, he'd promised her the position of choreographer.

"Hey." Reaching for his hand, she gave it a squeeze. "It's gonna work out. These guys are really good at what they do. They won't let you down."

"You've been here one day and you already know the crew is made up of Emmy winners?" At least his face had begun to relax.

"What can I say? I know my way around a television production."

"It must be those seven months you spent on the soap opera set. I guess you noticed a lot during the ten weeks your character was in a coma."

"Very funny." She sat back as the waitress plunked down a bowl filled with what looked like fried egg rolls. Ginger picked one up between her thumb and forefinger and looked at it quizzically.

"They're called hushpuppies and, no, I'm not going to tell you what's in them. Just eat one and enjoy." He popped two of them in his mouth.

Ginger pulled out her iPhone and searched for hush puppies. She really hoped the bowl didn't contain diced up shoes.

"Fried batter, yuck!" She placed it on the paper placemat, wiping her hands on her napkin.

"Food weenie," Diesel mumbled with a shake of his head. He was right, of course, although Ginger preferred to think of herself as someone more evolved in her nutritional standards. Years of her mother micro managing her diet had left her with a few food hang-ups, but she was working on that. *Sort of.* For the millionth time in her life, Ginger marveled at the unjustness of her body's metabolism as Diesel devoured the bowl of deep fried calories.

"So, what exactly are my responsibilities here?" she asked. "I've done most of the research on the Dresden House and it's fascinating. Imagine if those walls could talk. What sorts of stories could they tell about the last two hundred years the building has been standing? And, the woman it was originally built for never lived to see it; such a tragic love story." Ginger looked over at Diesel who had a finger to his head as he feigned shooting himself. "Okay, clearly, you don't see the romance in the project at all. So let's talk about me. What else besides research do I do as your production assistant?"

"Anything I ask you to do." He gave her a wolfish wink just as the waitress set a plate of barbeque in front of him.

"We've already been there and we both know it wasn't a success." She carefully assembled her BLT with mostly lettuce, tomato, one slice of bacon, and a small smear of mayonnaise.

"Okay, if you're not willing to sleep with me, my second choice is for you to handle makeup."

Ginger nearly choked on her sandwich. "Excuse me? Did you say makeup? I thought this was a show about restoring an eighteenth century mansion. What do you need makeup for?"

"The hot contractor doing the renovations. And, lest you think I play for the other team, *hot* is the network's term, not mine."

Ginger rolled her eyes. "Why is it men always have to reinforce their masculinity?"

"Testosterone," he said between bites of his sandwich. "Anyway, the suits in L.A. are hoping the *hottie* contractor will be a hit with the ladies and increase network viewership. Apparently, he was once *Cosmo*'s Bachelor of the Month, back in his days as a New York architect."

"But doesn't the network have a staff of makeup people?"

"Yes, but the one assigned to the show is having a problem with her pregnancy and just when I was about to hire another one," he pointed a fry at her, "you called and said you were down to your last five hundred bucks. Now, you have a job—with all your expenses paid for the next three months, I might add."

"But you said I was your assistant!"

"You are my assistant, Ginger. But you're also gonna have to be the makeup artist. I can't afford both. It'll look good to my dad if I come in under budget, so before you ask, I'm not paying you both salaries. I've already earmarked that money for a couple of other upgrades to the show."

"I don't want both salaries, Diesel. And I'm very grateful for the job, but what makes you think I'm qualified to be a makeup artist?"

Diesel swallowed another bite of his sandwich. "You took two years of stage production at Julliard. And, you did your own makeup all those years when you were in your mom's ballet company. I've seen your work. It's magical."

Magical, yeah, if they were filming Beauty and the Beast, she thought to herself. Somehow, Ginger didn't think that was what the network had in mind. She stared at Diesel. His enthusiasm—like his confidence—was so fragile right now. She didn't dare let him down. Not when she owed him so much. She forced a tight smile meant to reassure him. At the same time, her mind whirled with fear. And possibilities. Her dad often said she was like a cat, graceful and fluid and always landing on her feet. Which, in a way, was true, Ginger Walsh did always land on her feet. Of course, at the rate she was going, she'd blow through the nine lives before she hit thirty.

"Okay." She pushed her half eaten sandwich to the side. "The B&B has Internet access, right?"

"Sure." Diesel dragged a fry through some ketchup before putting it in his mouth.

"Great." She was still friends with several of the makeup artists from the soap. If she was lucky, she could Skype with one or two of them later that night to pick up some pointers. "I'm going to head back then." Ginger hoisted her messenger bag off the floor and stood up from the table.

"Give me a minute to finish my lunch and I'll drive you," Diesel said. "It's clear across town."

He was right, the inn was clear across town. But since Chance Inlet boasted only one stop light, *clear across town* barely equaled three New York City blocks. Obviously, Diesel had gone soft in the six weeks he'd been in North Carolina for the show's pre-production.

"I think I can manage. Besides, it's a beautiful day for a walk." It was mid-March and while slush still lingered on the ground in Manhattan, a warm breeze blew along the Carolina coast, with trees and flowers blooming in the bright spring sunshine. "I'll see you back there later." Ginger gave him a cheeky grin as she headed for the door.

"Don't forget we have a full production meeting at the B&B this afternoon during tea time. They serve these awesome cupcakes with their tea." Diesel's voice took on a reverential tone as he mentioned the cupcakes.

Great, now I have to battle cupcakes. The man hadn't even finished his 'heart attack on a plate' sandwich and he was thinking about dessert. Life was seriously unfair, she thought as she set a brisk pace toward the B&B.

"I don't think it's the plumbing. I think it's the dang dishwasher that's gone all catawampus on ya."

Gavin McAlister propped his hip against the large granite island anchoring the kitchen of the Tide Me Over Inn, staring at a pair of ancient work boots stretching out from under the sink.

"I told ya when we put the second dishwasher in, the lines were solid. It's not my plumbin'." The voice underneath the sink was a bit defensive, but Gavin was used to the old man's blustering. Morgan Balch had been working for McAlister construction since Gavin was in kindergarten and he was the same cantankerous character today he'd been 25 years ago. Gavin put up with the old coot because Morgan was the best plumber south of Wilmington and because he knew that behind all the complaining, the man was loyal and honest as the day was long.

"Are you saying I need a new dishwasher?" Patricia

McAlister, Gavin's mother, passed through the kitchen on her way to the inn's industrial laundry room, her arms filled with used towels. In her late fifties, his mom still looked ready to take on the world. Her shoulder-length red hair had faded to a champagne color years ago. Gavin was surprised it wasn't gray after raising five children, three of them boys born barely four years apart. Soft laugh lines fanned out beside her hazel eyes and a few more wrinkles showed up each passing year, but she still turned heads wherever she went, even dressed in a pair of worn jeans and a gray cashmere cardigan.

"I'll call in the morning," Gavin said reaching down to help Morgan to his feet. "It's still under warranty."

"No, *I'll* call." Patricia dumped the towels in the laundry room and returned to the kitchen. "It's my inn. I've been running it alone for over two years. I certainly know how to call a repairman." She stopped in front of Gavin, waiting for him to disagree, but she was right. She had been running the B&B on her own since it opened, and quite successfully, too. In fact, the Tide Me Over Inn had received a four diamond rating each year it had been in operation.

"Okay." Gavin leaned down to kiss her on the forehead. "You win. But don't let them try to sell you a new one. This one's not even six months old."

His mother patted him on the chest; she hadn't been able to reach the top of his head since he was fourteen. "I may not have all the advanced degrees my children have, but give me a little credit for having street sense."

"Don't know why you need two dishwashers, anyhow," Morgan mumbled.

"Because," Patricia said patiently, as if it was the first time she and Morgan had had this discussion. "On days when the inn is full and we have a large crowd for tea, we need the extra machine. With two dishwashers, I don't have to stand at the sink all night hand washing. I have other things to do with my time."

Morgan let out an indignant snort. He'd been a close friend of Donald McAlister, Gavin's late father, and he wasn't afraid to voice his disapproval of Patricia's active social life, especially since it included dating. Gavin's older brother, Miles, was pretty vocal in that area as well. But his mother had been a widow for over two years. She was young, attractive, and vibrant and Gavin didn't begrudge her a little happiness.

"You've only got the couple of crew from the Historical Restorations show staying here tonight." Gavin cut off Morgan's mumblings before Patricia could take offense. "With the rest of them staying in the chain hotel in town where they can smoke, you shouldn't need both dishwashers."

Patricia eyed Morgan as he loaded up his toolbox before turning to her son. "Yes, but the whole crew usually comes for tea. And the little soap opera star they brought along apparently has food issues. She asked if she could prepare her own meals here while the show is in production."

"Soap opera star?" Gavin grabbed a bottle of water out of the two-door Subzero fridge.

Patricia began arranging cookies on platter. "Destiny Upchurch, from *Saints and Sinners*."

"You're lettin' that gal stay here?" Morgan asked.

"Why is there a soap opera actress here?" Gavin asked at the same time.

"She's just the actress who played Destiny, Morgan. I'm sure she's nothing like the little witch she played on the show. Except for being a bit of a diva about her food, of course."

Morgan snatched a cookie from the plate. "I didn't like that girl when she was on the show."

"Nobody did." Patricia covered the platter in plastic wrap so Morgan couldn't pilfer the rest of them. "She was a nasty teenager, always pretending to be sweet and innocent. Then, wham, she was causing trouble for Savannah Rich."

"Ahh," Morgan said wistfully. "Now, that Savannah is one sweet gal. Pretty, too."

"Hey!" Gavin raised his voice in an attempt to regain control of the conversation. "Enough about the soap opera, already." Morgan and his mother were talking about these people as if they really knew them. He turned to the plumber.

"I can't believe you actually watch that crap. And you, Mom . . ."

"What? I fold a lot of laundry each afternoon, not that I should have to explain myself to my son." Patricia snapped a dishtowel at her son. "I like something mindless on the TV while I work and, really, since Bob Barker left, *The Price Is Right* just isn't the same."

"Yeah, I don't care for that Drew Carey fella, either," Morgan added.

Gavin rubbed the back of his neck, trying in vain to rein in his annoyance. "Can we fast forward to the actress here at the inn?"

"She's a teenager," Morgan said. "Too young for the likes of you. Anyway, everyone in town knows you've got some little chippy up in Wilmington."

Gavin groaned. Nothing was sacred in a small town, his dating life in particular, which seemed to be the focus of everyone living in Chances Inlet.

Patricia laughed. "I'm pretty sure she's older than her character on TV." Still smiling at Gavin, she filled the two kettles. "She's probably mid-twenties. Kind of cute, if you like girls who are leggy, waif-like, and all angles around the face. She probably got that way by analyzing every morsel she's ever eaten."

"Mom . . ." Everyone in the family—and in town, for that matter—said Gavin was the McAlister with the most patience, but it began to fray as his mother continued to evade his question.

"She does have pretty eyes." Patricia turned from the sink. "They're very unique."

"But. What. Is. She. Doing. Here?" Gavin demanded.

His mother had a habit of taking in strays; mostly women who needed a safe place to land. Occasionally, these women came with a crazy husband/boyfriend/father in pursuit. He didn't want the soap opera diva to be another one of those women. Gavin wouldn't interfere in his mother's efforts to run the inn or her social life, but he'd damn sure protect her from herself when necessary.

"Oh, well, her name is Ginger and she's working with Diesel."

As if that said it all.

It was Morgan's turn to groan at the mention of the heavily tattooed, managing producer of Historical Restorations. "That guy looks like a little punk."

"Don't judge, Morgan." Not surprising, Patricia stuck up for the producer. "I get the sense there's a lot more to Diesel than he wants us to see. Maybe even more than he knows. I don't think he had a very loving upbringing."

Which was his mom's way of saying Diesel was another one of her strays. Gavin's mother was all about the power of family. She bought into the whole story of the founding of Chances Inlet. As the lore had it, it was the town of second chances and Patricia McAlister believed everyone who wandered into town deserved a second chance.

Morgan let out another snort before waving his way out the back door.

"It's like I always say: God puts these people in front of us for a reason. We need to help them," Patricia said softly.

Gavin glanced out of the large box bay window above the sink. Out in the yard, Lori Hunt, the current maid/kitchen helper at the B&B, who was another of his mother's strays, played with a pair of dogs.

Patricia followed his gaze. "She may tell me her story one day. But for now, she needs a safe place to stay. And you have to admit, she makes a wonderful cupcake."

"I just don't want to see anyone get hurt. Especially you, Mom."

"She won't hurt me."

No, but what kind of trouble would she bring to his mother's doorstep, he wondered.

"Are you excited about the project?" his mother asked, deftly changing the subject. "You've been fascinated with Dresden house since you were a little boy. Daddy always said it was the reason you became an architect."

Gavin took a drink of water as his mother pulled out china tea cups, placing them on a silver serving dish. She was right; he'd loved that old house. But what once was a place to play pirates or, later, study classic architecture, now held the key to his escape from this small town. But his mother didn't need to know that.

"It's a great opportunity, but it isn't going to be easy. I'm glad McAlister Construction is doing the renovation, but I'm not looking forward to being followed around by a television crew."

"Well, you couldn't afford to do the renovation without those TV cameras and Marvin Goldman footing the bill. And the women will be beating down your door after the first episode."

Gavin leaned against the island again and rubbed his hand over the back of his neck. "That's hardly the purpose of doing the show." He had enough notoriety in his home town. He still hadn't lived down his Bachelor of the Month in *Cosmo* and that was years ago. Then, there was the whole mess with Amanda. He didn't want any more attention from women trying to fix his love life. It was one of the reasons he couldn't wait to leave again.

But first, he had to get out from beneath the mountain of debt his father had left the firm buried under. Thankfully, his younger brother, Ryan, played for the major league baseball team owned by America Cable. A few select words by their star second baseman in the appropriate ears, and McAlister Construction had a reality TV show. It felt a little like Gavin had pimped himself out, but the ends justified the means.

Patricia nudged Gavin's hip so he'd slide away from the utensil drawer. Humming happily, she pulled out spoons and set them on the silver tray. His mother could easily relate to his obsession with restoring Dresden house. She'd been equally as obsessed about renovating and operating the inn. And his father had, against all odds, made it happen for his wife. Gavin just couldn't let his mother know what it had cost Donald McAlister.

He bent to kiss her on the head. "I'm out of here. Call me tomorrow and let me know what the repairman says."

"Don't you want to stay for tea? It's Sunday. Or, have you

got something better planned? Maybe in Wilmington?" she teased.

"I stay out of your personal life, Mom. You stay out of mine."

"Words your brother Miles should live by," his mother called as he walked out the screen door onto the large veranda that wrapped around three sides of the inn.

Gavin put on his Ray-Bans and headed for his Jeep. "Midas!" He whistled for his dog as he punched the unlock button on his key fob.

The big golden retriever bounded around the corner of the inn just as a woman entered the driveway. She was too far off for Gavin to make out her face, but she strode purposefully toward the B and B as if she belonged there. It had to be the soap star. Dressed in black yoga pants that accentuated a pair of long, shapely legs and a hot pink, zippered hoodie that hid everything else, she didn't exactly fit his mother's description of 'waiflike'. He couldn't make out her eyes—his mother said something about them being unique—because they were hidden behind a pair of aviator sunglasses. Her hair was pulled up in a messy knot that was probably meant to look artless, but it had likely taken her an hour to complete.

Midas skidded to a halt, eyeing both the open Jeep door and the woman obliviously walking up to the veranda. Gavin tensed as he realized the potential for disaster.

"Come!" he commanded. He was calculating the distance to the dog just as Midas bolted for the unsuspecting woman. "Ah, shit!" He raced after his dog.

From *New York Times* Bestselling Author
JACI BURTON

Melting *the* Ice

Everything's coming together for budding fashion designer Carolina Preston. Only months away from having her own line, she could use some publicity. That's when her brother suggests his best friend as a model—hockey player Drew Hogan.

Carolina and Drew already have a history—a hot one, back in college. Unforgettable for Carolina, but for Drew, just another slap shot. This time, though, she could use him.

Drew is all for it. Plus, it would give him a chance to prove to Carolina that he's changed. If only he could thaw her emotions enough to convince her to let down her guard—and let him in just one more time...

"Hot enough to melt the ice off the hockey rink."
—*Romance Novel News*

jaciburton.com
facebook.com/AuthorJaciBurton
facebook.com/LoveAlwaysBooks
penguin.com

M1387T1013